THE
SILK
CODE

A TOM DOHERTY ASSOCIATES BOOK

NEW YORK

THE
SILK
CODE

PAUL
LEVINSON

THE SILK CODE

An earlier version of "The Mendelian Lamp" was published as "The Mendelian Lamp Case" in *Analog,* April 1997.

Book design by Victoria Kuskowski

Edited by David G. Hartwell

A Tor Book
Published by Tom Doherty Associates LLC
175 Fifth Avenue
New York, NY 10010

www.tor.com

Tor® is a registered trademark of
Tom Doherty Associates LLC

Library of Congress Cataloging-in-Publication Data

Levinson, Paul.
        The silk code / Paul Levinson.—1st ed.
            p.   cm.
        "A Tom Doherty Associates book."
        ISBN 0-312-86823-5
        I. Title.
    PS3562.E92165S5   1999
    813'.54—dc21   99–33992
                                                    CIP

First Edition: October 1999

Printed in the United States of America

0   9   8   7   6   5   4   3   2   1

TO HY AND IDA VOZICK

CONTENTS

THE

SILK

CODE

PART ONE

THE

MENDELIAN

LAMP

ONE

Most people think of California or the Midwest when they think of farm country. I'll take Pennsylvania, and the deep greens on its red earth, any time. Small patches of tomatoes and corn, clothes snapping brightly on a line, and a farmhouse always attached to some corner. The scale is human. . . .

Jenna was in England for a conference, my weekend calendar was clear, so I took Mo up on a visit to Lancaster. Over the GW Bridge, coughing down the Turnpike, over another bridge, down yet another highway stained and pitted, then off on a side road where I can roll down my windows and breathe.

Mo and his wife and two girls were good people. He was a rarity for a forensic scientist. Maybe it was the pace of criminal science in this part of the country—lots of the people around here were Amish, and Amish are nonviolent—or maybe it was his steady diet of those deep greens that quieted his soul. But Mo had none of the grit, none of the cynicism, that comes to most of us who traverse the territory of the dead and the maimed. No, Mo had an innocence, a delight, in the lights of science and people and their possibilities.

"Phil." He clapped me on the back with one hand and took my bag with another.

"Phil, how are you?" his wife, Corinne, yoo-hooed from inside.

"Hi, Phil!" his elder daughter, Laurie, probably sixteen already, chimed in from the window, a quick splash of strawberry blond in a crystal frame.

"Hi—," I started to say, but Mo put my bag on the porch and ushered me toward his car.

"You got here early, good," he said, in that schoolboy conspiratorial whisper I'd heard him go into every time he came across some inviting new avenue of science. ESP, UFOs, Mayan ruins in unexpected places—these were all catnip to Mo. But the power of quiet nature, the hidden wisdom of the farmer, this was his special domain. "A little present I want to pick up for Laurie," he whispered even more, though she was well out of earshot. "And something I want to show you. You too tired for a quick drive?"

"Ah, no, I'm Ok—"

"Great; let's go then," he said. "I came across some Amish techniques—well, you'll see for yourself; you're gonna love it."

STRASBURG IS FIFTEEN minutes down Route 30 from Lancaster. All Dairy Queens and 7-Elevens till you get there, but when you turn off and travel a half a mile in any direction you're back a hundred years or more in time. The air itself says it all—high mixture of pollen and horse manure that smells so surprisingly good, so real, it makes your eyes tear with pleasure. You don't even mind the few flies flitting around.

We turned down Northstar Road. "Joseph Stoltzfus's farm is down there on the right," Mo said.

I nodded. "Beautiful." The sun looked about five minutes to setting. The sky was the color of a robin's belly against the browns and greens of the farm. "He won't mind that we're coming here by, uh—"

"By car? Nah, of course not," Mo said. "The Amish have no problem with non-Amish driving. And Joseph, as you'll see, is more open-minded than most."

I thought I could see him now, off to the right at the end of the road that had turned to dirt, gray-white head of hair and beard bending over the gnarled bark of a fruit tree. He wore plain black overalls and a deep purple shirt.

"That Joseph?" I asked.

"I think so," Mo replied. "I'm not sure."

We pulled the car over near the tree and got out. A soft autumn rain suddenly started falling.

"You have business here?" The man by the tree turned to address us. His tone was far from friendly.

"Uh, yes," Mo said, clearly taken aback. "I'm sorry to intrude. Joseph, Joseph Stoltzfus, said it would be OK if we came by—"

"You had business with Joseph?" the man demanded again. His eyes looked red and watery—though that could have been from the rain.

"Well, yes," Mo said. "But if this isn't a good time—"

"My brother is dead," the man said. "My name is Isaac. This is a bad time for our family."

"Dead?" Mo nearly shouted. "I mean . . . what happened? I just saw your brother yesterday."

"We're not sure," Isaac said. "Heart attack, maybe. I think you should leave now. Family are coming soon."

"Yes, yes, of course," Mo said. He looked beyond Isaac at a barn that I noticed for the first time. Its doors were slightly open, and weak light flickered inside.

Mo took a step in the direction of the barn. Isaac put up a restraining arm. "Please," he said. "It's better if you go."

"Yes, of course," Mo said again and I led him to the car.

"You all right?" I asked when we were both in the car and Mo had started the engine.

He shook his head. "Couldn't be a heart attack. Not at a time like this."

"Heart attacks don't usually ask for appointments," I said.

Mo was still shaking his head, turning back onto Northstar Road. "I think someone killed him."

NOW FORENSIC SCIENTISTS are prone to see murder in a ninety-year-old-woman dying peacefully in her sleep, but this was unusual from Mo.

"Tell me about it," I said reluctantly. Just what I needed—death turning my visit into a busman's holiday.

"Never mind," he muttered. "I babbled too much already."

"Babbled? You haven't told me a thing."

Mo drove on in brooding silence. He looked like a different person, wearing a mask that used to be his face.

"You're trying to protect me from something, is that it?" I ventured. "You know better than that."

Mo said nothing.

"What's the point?" I prodded. "We'll be back with Corinne and the girls in five minutes. They'll take one look at you and know something happened. What are you going to tell *them?*"

Mo swerved suddenly onto a side road, bringing my kidney into sticking contact with the inside door handle. "Well, I guess you're right about that," he said. He punched in a code in his car phone—I hadn't noticed it before.

"Hello?" Corinne answered.

"Bad news, honey," Mo said matter-of-factly, though it sounded put on to me. No doubt his wife would see through it, too. "Something came up in the project, and we're going to have to go to Philadelphia tonight."

"You and Phil? Everything OK?"

"Yeah, the two of us," Mo replied. "Not to worry. I'll call you again when we get there."

"I love you," Corinne said.

"Me, too," Mo said. "Kiss the girls good night for me." He hung up and turned to me.

"Philadelphia?" I asked.

"Better that I don't give them too many details," he said. "I never do on my cases. Only would worry them."

"She's worried anyway," I told him. "Sure sign she's worried when she didn't even scream at you for missing dinner. Now that you bring it up, I'm a little worried now, too. What's going on?"

Mo said nothing. Then he turned the car again—mercifully

more gently this time—onto a road with a sign that advised that the Pennsylvania Turnpike was up ahead.

I rolled up the window as our speed increased. The night had suddenly gone damp and cold.

"You going to give me a clue as to where we're going or just kidnap me to Philadelphia?" I asked.

"I'll let you off at the 30th Street Station," Mo said. "You can get a bite to eat on the train and be back in New York in an hour."

"You left my bag on your porch, remember?" I said. "Not to mention my car."

"All right, I'll drive you back to my place—we can turn around at the next exit."

"I'd just as soon come along for the ride, and then we can both go back to your place. Would that be OK?"

Mo just scowled and drove on.

"I wonder if Amos knows?" he said more to himself than me a few moments later.

"Amos is a friend of Joseph's?" I asked.

"His son," Mo said.

"Well, I guess you can't very well call him on your car phone," I remarked.

Mo shook his head, frowned. "Most people misunderstand the Amish—think they're some sort of Luddites, against all technology. But that's not really it at all. They struggle with technology, agonize over whether to reject or accept it and, if they accept it, in what ways, so as not to compromise their independence and self-sufficiency. They're not completely against phones, just against phones in their homes, because the phone intrudes on everything you're doing."

I snorted. "Yeah, many's the time a call from the captain pulled me out of the sack. Telephonus interruptus."

Mo flashed his smile, for the first time since we'd left Joseph Stoltzfus's farm. It was good to see.

"So where do Amish keep their phones?" I might as well

press my advantage with the chance that it would get Mo to talk.

"Well, that's another misconception," Mo said. "There's not one monolithic Amish viewpoint. There are many Amish groups. They have different ways of dealing with technology. Some allow phone shacks on the edges of their property, so they can make calls when they want to but not be disturbed in the sanctity of their homes."

"Does Amos have a phone shack?" I asked.

"Dunno," Mo said, like he was beginning to think about something else.

"But you said his family was more open than most," I persisted.

Mo swiveled his head to stare at me for a second, then turned his eyes back on the road. "Open-minded, yes. But not really about communications."

"About what, then?"

"Medicine," Mo said.

"Medicine?" I asked.

"What do you know about allergies?"

My nose itched—maybe it was the remnants of the sweet pollen near Strasburg.

"I have hay fever," I said. "Cantaloupe sometimes makes my mouth burn. I've seen a few strange deaths in my time due to allergic reactions. You think Joseph Stoltzfus died from something like that?"

"No," Mo replied. "I think he was killed because he was trying to prevent people from dying from things like that."

"OK," I said. "Last time you said that and I asked you to explain you said never mind. Should I ask again or let it slide?"

Mo sighed. "You know, genetic engineering goes back well before the double helix."

"Come again?"

"Breeding plants to make new combinations probably dates almost to the origins of our species," Mo said. "Darwin understood that—he called it artificial selection. Mendel doped out the first laws of genetics breeding peas. Luther Burbank developed way many more new varieties of fruit and vegetables than have yet to come out of our gene-splicing labs.''

"And the connection to the Amish is what—they breed new vegetables now, too?'' I asked.

"More than that,'' Mo said. "They have whole insides of houses lit by special kinds of fireflies, altruistic manure permeated by slugs that seek out the roots of plants to die there and give them nourishment—all deliberately bred to be that way—and the public knows nothing about it. It's biotechnology of the highest order, without the technology.''

"And your friend Joseph was working on this?''

Mo nodded. "Techno-allergists—our conventional researchers —have recently been investigating how some foods act as catalysts to other allergies. Cantaloupe tingles in your mouth in hay fever season, right? Because it's really exacerbating the hay fever allergy. Watermelon does the same, and so does the pollen of mums. Joseph and his people have known this for at least fifty years—and they've gone much further. They're trying to breed a new kind of food, some kind of tomato thing, that would act as an anticatalyst for allergies, would reduce their histamine effect to nothing.''

"Like an organic Hismanol?'' I asked.

"Better than that,'' Mo said. "This would trump any pharmaceutical.''

"You OK?'' I noticed Mo's face was bearing big beads of sweat.

"Sure,'' he said, and cleared his throat. He pulled out a hankie and mopped his brow. "I don't know. Joseph—'' He started coughing in hacking waves.

I reached over to steady him and straighten the steering wheel. His shirt was soaked with sweat, and he was breathing in angry rasps.

"Mo, hold on,'' I said, keeping one hand on Mo and the wheel, fumbling with the other in my inside coat pocket. I finally got my fingers on the epinephrine pen I always kept there, and angled it out. Mo was limp and wet and barely conscious over the wheel. I pushed him over as gently as I could and went with my foot for the brake. Cars were speeding by us, screaming at me in the mirror with their lights. Thankfully Mo had been driving on the right, so I only had one stream of lights to blind me. My sole finally made contact with the brake, and I pressed down as gradually as possible. Miraculously, the car came to a reasonably slow halt on the shoulder of the road. We both seemed in one piece.

I looked at Mo. I yanked up his shirt and plunged the pen into his arm. I wasn't sure how long he'd not been breathing, but it wasn't good.

I dialed 911 on the car phone. "Get someone over here fast!" I yelled. "I'm on the Turnpike, eastbound, just before the Philadelphia turnoff. I'm Dr. Phil D'Amato, NYPD Forensics. This is a medical emergency."

I wasn't positive that anaphylactic shock was what was wrong with him, but the adrenaline pen couldn't do much harm. I leaned over his chest and felt no heartbeat. Jeez, please.

I gave Mo mouth-to-mouth, pounded his chest, pleading for life. "Hang on, damn you!" But I knew already. I could tell. After a while you get this sort of sickening sixth sense about these things. Some kind of allergic reaction from hell had just killed my friend. Right in my arms. Just like that.

EMS got to us eight minutes later. Better than some of the New York City times I'd been seeing lately. But it didn't matter. Mo was gone.

I looked at the car phone as they worked on him, cursing and trying to jolt him back into life. I'd have to call Corinne and tell her this now. But all I could see in the plastic phone display was Laurie's strawberry blond hair.

"You OK, Dr. D'Amato?" one of the orderlies called.

"Yeah," I said. I guess I was shaking.

"These allergic reactions can be lethal all right," he stated, looking over at Mo.

Right; tell me about it.

"You'll call the family?" the orderly asked. They'd be taking Mo to a local hospital, DOA.

"Yeah," I said, brushing a burning tear from my eye. I felt like I was suffocating. I had to slow down, stay in control, separate the psychological from the physical so I could begin to understand what was going on here. I breathed out and in. Again. OK. I was all right. I wasn't really suffocating.

The ambulance sped off, carrying Mo. He *had* been suffocating, and it killed him. What had he been starting to tell me?

I looked again at the phone. The right thing for me to do was drive back to Mo's home, be there for Corinne when I told her—calling her on the phone with news like this was monstrous. But I had to find out what had happened to Mo—and that would likely not be from Corinne. Mo didn't want to worry her, didn't confide in her. No, the best chance of finding out what Mo had been up to seemed to be in Philadelphia, in the place Mo had been going. But where in Philadelphia?

I focused on the phone display—pressed a couple of keys and got a directory up on the little screen. The only 215 area code number listed there was for a Sarah Fischer, with an address that I knew to be near Temple University.

I pressed the code next to the number, then the Send command.

Crackle, crackle, then a distant tinny cellular ring.

"Hello?" a female voice answered, sounding closer than I'd expected.

"Hi. Is this Sarah Fischer?"

"Yes," she said. "Do I know you?"

"Well, I'm a friend of Mo Buhler's, and I think we, he, may have been on his way to see you tonight—"

"Who are you? Is Mo OK?"

"Well . . . ," I started.

"Look, who the hell are you? I'm going to hang up if you don't give me a straight answer," she said.

"I'm Dr. Phil D'Amato. I'm a forensic scientist—with the New York City Police Department."

She was quiet for a moment. "Your name sounds familiar for some reason," she said.

"Well, I've written a few articles—"

"Hold on." I heard her put the phone down, rustle through some papers. "You had an article in *Discover,* about antibiotic-resistant bacteria, right?" she asked about half a minute later.

"Yes, I did," I said. In other circumstances, my ego would have jumped at finding such an observant reader.

"OK, what date was it published?" she asked.

Jeez. "Uh, late last year," I said.

"I see there's a pen-and-ink sketch of you. What do you look like?"

"Straight dark hair—not enough of it," I said. Who could remember what that lame sketch actually looked like?

"Go on," she urged.

"And a mustache, reasonably thick, and steel-rimmed glasses." I'd grown the mustache at Jenna's behest and had on my specs for the sketch.

A few beats of silence, then a sigh. "OK," she said. "So now you get to tell me why you're calling . . . and what happened to Mo."

SARAH'S APARTMENT WAS less than half an hour away. I'd filled her in on the phone. She'd seemed more saddened than surprised, and asked me to come over.

I'd spoken to Corinne and told her as best I could. Mo had been a cop before he'd become a forensic scientist, and I guess wives of police are supposed to be ready for this sort of thing, but how can a person ever really be ready for it after twenty years of good marriage? She'd cried; I'd cried; the kids cried in the background. I'd said I was coming over—and I know I should have—but I was hoping she'd say, "No, I'm OK, Phil. Really. You'll want to find out why this happened to Mo" . . . And that's exactly what she did say. They don't make people like Corinne Rodriguez Buhler anymore.

There was a parking spot right across the street from Sarah's building—in New York this would have been a gift from on high. I tucked in my shirt, tightened my belt, and composed myself as best I could before ringing her bell.

She buzzed me in and was standing inside her apartment, second-floor walk-up, door open, to greet me as I sprinted and puffed up the flight of stairs. She had flaxen blond hair, a distracted look in her eyes, but an easy, open smile that I didn't expect after the grilling she'd given me on the phone. She looked about thirty.

The apartment had soft, recessed lighting—like a Paris-by-gaslight exhibit I'd once seen—and smelled faintly of lavender. My nose crinkled. "I use it to help me sleep," Sarah said, and directed me to an old, overstuffed Morris chair. "I was getting ready to go to sleep when you called."

"I'm sorry—"

"No, I'm the one who's sorry," she said. "About giving you a hard time, about what happened to Mo." Her voice caught on his name. She asked, "Can I get you something? You must be hungry." She turned around and walked toward another room, which I assumed was the kitchen.

Her pants were white, and the light showed the contours of her body to good advantage as she walked away.

"Here, try some of these to start." She returned with a bowl of grapes. Concord grapes. One of my favorites. Put one in your mouth, puncture the purple skin, jiggle the flesh around on your tongue—it's the taste of Fall. But I didn't move.

"I know," she said. "You're leery of touching any strange food after what happened to Mo. I don't blame you. But these are OK. Here, let me show you," and she reached and took a dusty grape and put it in her mouth. "Mmm." She smacked her lips, took out the pits with her finger. "Look—why don't *you* pick a grape and give it to me. OK?"

My stomach was growling and I was feeling light-headed already, and I realized I would have to make a decision. Either leave right now, if I didn't trust this woman, and go somewhere to get something to eat—or eat what she gave me. I was too hungry to sit here and talk to her and resist her food right now.

"All right, up to you," she said. "I have some Black Forest ham and can make you a sandwich, if you like, or just coffee or tea."

"All three," I decided. "I mean, I'd love the sandwich, and some tea please, and I'll try the grapes." I put one in my mouth. I'd learned a long time ago that paranoia can be almost as debilitating as the dangers it supposes.

She was back a few minutes later with the sandwich and the tea. I'd squished at least three more grapes in my mouth and felt fine.

"There's a war going on," she said, and put the food tray on the end table next to me. The sandwich was made with some sort of black bread and smelled wonderful.

"War?" I asked and bit into the sandwich. "You think what happened to Mo is the work of some terrorist?"

"Not exactly." Sarah sat down on a chair next to me, a cup of tea in her hand. "This war's been going on a very long time. It's a biowar—much deeper rooted, literally, than anything we currently regard as terrorism."

"I don't get it," I said, and swallowed what I'd been chewing of my sandwich. It felt good going down and in my stomach.

"No, you wouldn't," Sarah replied. "Few people do. You think epidemics, sudden widespread allergic reactions, diseases that wipe out crops or livestock or people just happen. Sometimes they do. Sometimes it's more than that." She sipped her cup of tea. Something about the lighting, her hair, her face, maybe the taste of the food, made me feel like I was a kid back in the sixties. I half-expected to smell incense burning.

"Who are you?" I asked. "I mean, what was your connection to Mo?"

"I'm working on my doctorate over at Temple," she said. "My area's ethno/botanical pharmacology—Mo was one of my resources. He was a very nice man." I thought I saw a tear glisten in the corner of her eye.

"Yes, he was," I agreed. "And he was helping you with your dissertation about what—the germ warfare you were talking about?"

"Not quite that," Sarah said. "I mean, you know the academic world; no one would ever let me do a thesis on something that outrageous—it'd never get by the proposal committee. So you have to finesse it, do it on something more innocuous, get the good stuff in under the table, you know, smuggle it in. So, yeah, the *subtext* of my work was what we—I—call the biowars, which are actually more than just germ warfare, and yeah, Mo was one of the people who were helping me research that."

Sounded like Mo, all right. "And the Amish have something to do with this?"

"Yes and no," Sarah said. "The Amish aren't a single, unified group; they actually have quite a range of styles and values—"

"I know," I said. "And some of them—maybe one of the splinter groups—are involved in this biowar?"

"The main biowar group isn't really Amish—though one of their clusters is situated near Lancaster, been there for at least 150 years. But they're not Amish. They pretend to be Amish—gives them good cover—but they're much older. People think they're Amish, though, since they live close to the land, in a low-tech mode. But they're not Amish. Real Amish are nonviolent. But some of the Amish know what's going on."

"You know a lot about the Amish," I said.

She blushed slightly. "I'm former Amish. I pursued my interests as far as a woman could in my Church. I pleaded with my bishop to let me go to college—he knew what the stakes were, the importance of what I was studying—but he said no. He said a woman's place was in the home. I guess he was trying to protect me, but I couldn't stay."

"You know Joseph Stoltzfus?" I asked.

Sarah nodded, lips tight. "He was my uncle," she finally said, "my mother's brother."

"I'm sorry," I said. I could see that she knew he was dead. "Who told you?" I asked softly.

"Amos—my cousin—Joseph's son. He has a phone shack," she said.

"I see," I said. What an evening. "I think Mo thought that those people—those others, like the Amish, but not Amish—somehow killed Joseph."

Sarah's face shuddered, seemed to unravel into sobs and tears. "They did," she managed to say. "Mo was right. And they killed Mo, too."

I put down my plate and reached over to comfort her. It wasn't enough. I got up and walked to her and put my arm around her. She got up shakily off her chair, then collapsed in my arms, heaving, crying. I felt her body, her heartbeat, through her crinoline shirt.

"It's OK," I said. "Don't worry. I deal with bastards like that all the time in my business. We'll get these people; I promise you."

She shook her head against my chest. "Not like these," she said.

"We'll get them," I said again.

She held onto me, then pulled away. "I'm sorry," she said. "I didn't mean to fall apart like that." She looked over at my empty teacup. "How about a glass of wine?"

I looked at my watch. It was 9:45 already, and I was exhausted. But there was more I needed to learn. "OK," I said. "Sure. But just one glass."

She offered a tremulous smile and went back into the kitchen. She returned with two glasses of a deep red wine.

I sat down and sipped. The wine tasted good—slightly Portuguese, perhaps, with just a hint of some fruit and a nice woody undertone.

"Local," she said. "You like it?"

"Yes, I do," I replied.

She took a sip, then closed her eyes and tilted her head back. The bottoms of her blue eyes glinted like semiprecious gems out of half-closed lids.

I needed to focus on the problem at hand. "How exactly do these biowar people kill—what'd they do to Joseph and Mo?" I asked.

Her eyes stayed closed a moment longer than I'd expected—like she'd been daydreaming or drifting off to sleep. Then she opened them and looked at me and shook her head slowly. "They've got all sorts of ways. The latest is some kind of catalyst—in food; we think it's a special kind of Crenshaw melon—that vastly magnifies the effect of any of a number of allergies." She picked up her wine with a trembling hand and drained the glass and got up. "I'm going to have another glass—sure you don't want some more?"

"I'm sure, thanks," I said, and looked at my wine as she walked back into the kitchen. For all I knew, a catalyst from that damn melon was in this very glass—

I heard a glass or something crash in the kitchen.

I rushed in.

Sarah was standing over what looked like a little hurricane lamp, glowing white but not burning on the inside, broken on the floor. A few little bugs of some sort took wing and flew away.

"I'm sorry," she said. She was crying again. "I knocked it over. I'm really not myself tonight."

"No one would be, in your situation," I told her.

She put her arms around me again, pressing close. I instinctively kissed her cheek, just barely—in what I instantly hoped, after the fact, was a brotherly gesture.

"Stay with me tonight," she whispered. "I mean, the couch out there opens up for you, and you'll have your privacy. I'll sleep in the bedroom. I'm afraid. . . ."

I was afraid, too, because a part of me suddenly wanted to

pick her up and carry her over to her bedroom, the couch, anywhere, and lay her down, softly unwrap her clothes, run my fingers through her sweet-smelling hair, and—

But I also cared very much for Jenna. And though we'd made
no formal lifetime commitments to each other—

"I don't feel very good," Sarah said, and pulled away slightly.
"I guess I had some wine before you came and—" Her head
lolled and her body suddenly sagged and her eyes rolled back in
her skull.

"Sarah!" I first tried to buoy her up, then picked her up
entirely and carried her into her bedroom. I put her down on the
bed, soft silken sheets, gently as I could, then felt the pulse in her
wrist. It may have been a bit rapid but seemed basically all right.
I peeled back her eyelid—she was semiconscious, but her pupil
wasn't dilated. She was likely drunk, not drugged. I put my ear to
her chest. Her heartbeat was fine—nothing like Mo's allergic reaction.

"You're OK," I said. "Just a little shock and exhaustion."

She moaned softly, then reached out and took my hand. I
held it for a long time, till its grip weakened and she was definitely
asleep, and then I walked quietly into the other room.

I was too tired myself to go anywhere, too tired to even figure
out how to open her couch, so I just managed to take off my
shoes and stretch out on it before I fell soundly asleep. My last
thoughts were that I needed to have another look at the Stoltzfus
farm, the lamp on her floor was beautiful, so was Sarah on those
sheets, and I hoped I wasn't drugged or anything, but it was too
late to do anything about it if I was. . . .

I AWOKE WITH a start the next morning, propped my head up
on a shaky arm, and leaned over just in time to see Sarah's sleek
wet backside receding into her bedroom. Likely from her shower.
I could think of worse things to wake up to.

"I think I'm gonna head back to Joseph's farm," I told her

over breakfast of whole wheat toast, poached eggs, and Darjeeling tea that tasted like a fine liqueur.

"Why?"

"Closest thing we have to a crime scene," I replied.

"I'll come with you," Sarah said.

"You were pretty upset last night—" I started to object.

"Right, so were you, but I'm OK now," Sarah said. "Besides, you'll need me to decode the Amish for you, to tell you what you're looking for."

She had a point. "All right," I agreed.

"Good," she said. "By the way, what *are* you looking for there?"

"I don't really know," I admitted. "Mo was eager to show me something at Joseph's."

Sarah considered, frowned. "Joseph was working on an organic antidote to the allergen catalyst, but all that stuff is very slow-acting—the catalyst takes years to build up to dangerous levels in the human body—so I don't see what Joseph could've shown you on a quick drive-by visit."

If she had told me that last night, I would have enjoyed the grapes and ham sandwich even more. "Well, we've got nowhere else to look at this point," I said, and speared the last of my egg.

But what did that mean about what had killed Mo? Someone had been giving him a slow-acting poison, too, which had been building up inside both of them for x number of years, with the result that both of them died on the same day?

Not very likely. There seemed to be more than one catalyst at work here. I wondered if Mo had told Joseph anything about me and my visit. I certainly hoped not—the last thing I wanted was that decisive second catalyst to in some way have been me.

WE WERE ON the Turnpike heading west an hour later. The sun was strong, and the breeze was fresh—a splendid day to be out for a ride, except that we were going to investigate the death of one of the nicest damn people I had known. I'd called Corinne to make sure she and the girls were all right. I'd told her I'd come by in the afternoon. I should have gone there first—given Corinne and the girls the hugs they needed, plus their car. . . . But I had to get back to the Stoltzfus farm as soon as possible. Sometimes even a few minutes could make the difference between an important piece of evidence clinging to the scene or going missing. . . .

"So tell me more about your doctoral work," I asked Sarah. "I mean your real work, not the cover for your advisors."

"You know, too many people equate science with its high-tech trappings—if it doesn't come in computers, God-knows-what-power microscopes, the latest DNA dyes, it must be magic, superstition, old-wives'-tale nonsense. But science is at core a method, a rational mode of investigating the world, and the gadgetry is secondary. Sure, the equipment is great—it opens up more of the world to our cognitive digestion, makes it amenable to our analysis—but if aspects of the world are already amenable to analysis and experiment with just our naked eyes and hands, then the equipment isn't all that necessary, is it?"

"And your point is that agriculture, plant and animal breeding, that kind of manipulation of nature has been practiced by humans for millennia with no sophisticated equipment," I said.

"Right," Sarah answered. "But that's hardly controversial, or reason to kill someone. What I'm saying is that some people have been doing this for purposes other than to grow better food—have been doing this right under everyone's noses for a very long time—and they use this to make money, maintain their power, eliminate anyone who gets in their way."

"Sort of organized biological crime," I mused. The *Godfather* theme crept into my head. But instead of Marlon Brando behind that desk, there was an old farmer with coveralls. Far-fetched, to say the least. . . .

"Yeah, you could put it that way," Sarah said.

"And you have any examples—any evidence—other than your allergen theory?" I asked.

"It's fact, not a theory, I assure you," Sarah responded. "But here's an example: ever wonder why people got so rude to each other, here in the U.S., after World War II?"

"I'm not following you," I said.

"Well, it's been written about in lots of the sociological literature," Sarah continued. "There was a civility, a courtesy, in interpersonal relations—the way people dealt with one another in public, in business, in friendship—through at least the first half of the twentieth century in the U.S. And then it started disintegrating. Everyone recognizes this. Some people blame it on the pressures of the atomic age, on the replacement of the classroom by the television screen—which you can fall asleep or walk out on—as the prime source of education for kids. There are lots of possible culprits. But I have my own ideas."

"Which are?"

"Everyone was in the atomic age after World War II," Sarah said. "England and the Western world had television, cars, all the usual stimuli. What was different about America was its vast farmland—room to quietly grow a crop of something that most people have a low-level allergy to. I think the cause of the widespread irritation, the loss of courtesy, was quite literally something that got under everyone's skin—an allergen designed for just that purpose."

Jeez, I could see why this woman would have trouble with her doctoral committee. But I might as well play along—I'd learned the hard way that crazy ideas like this were pooh-poohed at one's peril. "Well, the Japanese did have some plans in mind for balloons carrying biological agents—deadly diseases—over here near the end of the war."

Sarah nodded. "The Japanese are one of the most advanced peoples on Earth in terms of expertise in agriculture. I don't know if they were involved in this, but—"

The phone rang.

McLuhan had once pointed out that the car was the only place you could be, in this technological world of ours, away from the demanding ring of the phone. But that of course was before car phones.

"Hello," I answered.

"Hello?" a voice said back to me. It sounded male—odd accent, youngish but deep.

"Yes?" I said.

"Mr. Buhler, is that you?" the voice said.

"Ahm, no, it isn't; can I take a message for him?" I asked.

Silence. Then, "I don't understand. Isn't this the number for the phone in Mr. Buhler's car?"

"That's right," I said, "but—"

"Where's Mo Buhler?" the voice insisted.

"Well, he's—" I started.

I heard a strange clicking, then a dial tone.

"Is there a call-back feature on this?" I asked Sarah and myself. I pressed *69, as I would on regular phones, and then pressed Send. "Welcome to AT&T Wireless Services," a different deep voice said. "The cellular customer you have called is unavailable, or has travelled outside the coverage area—"

"That was Amos," Sarah said.

"The kid on the phone?" I asked, stupidly.

Sarah nodded.

"Must still be in shock over his father," I said.

"I think he killed his father," Sarah said.

WE DROVE DEEP into Pennsylvania, the blacks and grays and unreal colors of the billboards gradually supplanted by the greens and browns and earth tones I'd communed with just yesterday. But the natural colors held no joy for me now. I realized that's the way nature always had been—we romanticize its beauty, and that's real, but it's also the source of drought, famine, earthquake, disease, and death in many guises. . . . The question was whether Sarah could possibly be right in her theory about how some people were helping this dark side of nature along.

She filled me in on Amos. He was sixteen, had only a formal

primary school education, in a one-room schoolhouse, like other Amish—but also like some splinter groups of the Amish, unknown to outsiders, he was self-educated in the science and art of biological alchemy. He had been apprentice to his father.

"So why would he kill him?" I asked.

She hesitated. "Some of this is personal, between Amos and his father," she said. "I'm not sure Joseph would have approved my telling . . . a stranger. . . ."

"I understand," I said. "But two people have died here, and you're telling me it's some kind of murder. I'm all for respecting people's privacy, but not when it costs other people their lives."

"Amos is not only a budding scientist, Amish-style; he's also a typically headstrong Amish kid," she finally said. "Lots of wild oats to sow. He got drunk, drove cars, along with the best of them, in the Amish gangs."

"Is that all?"

"That's a lot, if you're Amish," Sarah said.

"The Amish have gangs?"

"Oh, yeah," Sarah said. "The Groffies, the Ammies, and the Trailers—those are the three main ones. Hostetler writes about them in his books. But there are others, smaller ones. Joseph didn't like his son being involved in them. They argued about that constantly."

"And you think that led to Amos killing his father?" I asked, still incredulous.

"Well, Joseph's dead, isn't he? And I'm pretty sure that one of the gangs Amos belongs to has connections to the biowar Mafia people I've been telling you about—the ones that killed Mo, too."

We drove the rest of the way in silence. I wasn't sure what to think about this woman and her ideas.

We finally reached Northstar Road and the path that led to the Stoltzfus farm. "It's probably better that we park the car here and you walk the path yourself," Sarah said. "Cars and strange women are more likely to arouse Amish attention than a single man on foot—even if he is English. I mean, that's what they call—"

"I know," I said. "I've seen *Witness*. But Mo told me that Joseph didn't mind cars—"

"Joseph's dead now," Sarah interrupted. "What he liked and what his family like may be two very different things."

I recalled the hostility of Joseph's brother, another of Sarah's uncles, yesterday. "All right," I said. "I guess you know what you're talking about. I should be back in thirty to forty minutes."

"OK." Sarah squeezed my hand and smiled.

I TRUDGED DOWN the dirt road, not really knowing what I hoped to find at the other end.

Certainly not what I did find.

I smelled the smoke, the burnt quality in the air, before I came upon the house and the barn. Both had been burned to the ground. God, I hoped no one had been in there when these wooden structures went.

"Hello?" I shouted.

My voice echoed across an empty field. I looked around and listened. No animals, no cattle. Even a dog's rasping bark would have been welcome.

I walked over to the barn's remains and poked at some charred wood with my foot. An ember or two winked into life, then back out. It was close to noon. My guess was this had happened—and quickly—about six hours earlier. But I was no arson expert.

I brushed away the stinking smoke fumes with my hand. I pulled out my flashlight, a powerful little halogen daylight simulation thing Jenna had given me, and looked around the inside of the barn. Whatever had been going on here, there wasn't much left of it now. . . .

Something green caught my eye—greener than grass. It was the front cover, partially burned, of an old book. All that was left was this piece of the cover—the pages in the book, the back cover, were totally gone. I could see some letters, embossed in gold, in the old way. I touched it with the tip of my finger. It was warm, but not too hot. I picked it up and examined it.

"of Nat," one line said, and the next line said "bank."

Bank, I thought, *Nat Bank.* What was this, some kind of Amish bankbook, for some local First Yokel's National Bank?

No, it didn't look like a bankbook cover. And the *b* in this *bank* was a small letter, not a capital. Bank, bank, hmm . . . wait; hadn't Mo said something to me about a bank yesterday? A bank . . . Yes, a Burbank. Darwin and Burbank! Luther Burbank!

Partner of Nature, by Luther Burbank—that was the book whose charred remains I held in my hand. I'd taken out a copy of it years ago from the Allerton Library and loved it.

Well, Mo and Sarah were right about at least one thing: the reading level of at least some Amish was a lot higher than grade school—

"You again!"

I nearly jumped out of my skin.

I turned around. "Oh, Mr.—" It was the man we'd seen here yesterday—Joseph's brother.

"Isaac Stoltzfus," he said. "What are you doing here?"

His tone was so unsettling, his eyes so angry, that I thought for a second he believed I was responsible for the fire. "Isaac. Mr. Stoltzfus," I began. "I just got here. I'm sorry for your loss. What happened?"

"My brother's family, thank the Deity, left to stay with some relatives in Ohio very early this morning, well before dawn. So no one was hurt. I went with them to the train station in Lancaster. When I returned here, a few hours later, I found this." He gestured hopelessly, but with an odd air of resignation, to the ruined house and barn.

"May I ask you if you know what your brother was doing here?" I hazarded a question.

Isaac either didn't hear or pretended not to. He just continued on his earlier theme. "Material things, even animals and plants, we can always afford to lose. People are what are truly of value in this world."

"Yes," I said, "but getting back to what—"

"You should check on your family, too—to make sure they are not in danger."

"My family?" I asked.

Isaac nodded. "I've work to do here." He pointed out to the field. "My brother had four fine horses, and I can find no sign of them. I think it best that you go now." And he turned and walked away.

"Wait . . . ," I started, but I could see it was no use.

I looked at the front cover of Burbank's book. This farm, Sarah's bizarre theories, the book—there still wasn't really enough to any of them to make much sense of this.

But what the hell did Isaac mean about my family?

Jenna was overseas and not really family—yet. My folks lived in Teaneck, my sister was married to an Israeli guy in Brookline . . . what connection did they have to what was going on here?

Jeez—none! Isaac hadn't been referring to them at all. I was slow on the uptake today. He'd likely mistaken me for Mo—Isaac had seen both of us for the first time here yesterday.

He was talking about Mo's family—Corinne and the kids!

I raced back to the car, the smoky air cutting my throat with a different jagged edge each time my foot hit the ground.

"WHAT'S GOING ON?" Sarah asked.

I waved her off, jumped in the car, and put a call through to Corinne. *Ring, ring, ring.* No answer.

"What's the matter?" Sarah asked again.

I quickly told her. "Let's get over there," I said, and turned the car, screeching, back onto Northstar.

"All right, take it easy," Sarah said. "It's Saturday—Corinne could just be out shopping with the kids."

"Right, the day after their father died—in my arms," I retorted.

"All right," she said again, "but you still don't want to get into an accident now. We'll be there in ten minutes."

I nodded, tried Corinne's number again, same *ring, ring, ringing.*

"Fireflies likely caused the fire," Sarah said.

"What?"

"Fireflies—a few of the Amish use them for interior lighting," Sarah said.

"Yah, Mo mentioned that," I said. "But fireflies give cool light—bioluminescence—no heat."

"Not the ones I've seen around here," Sarah said. "They're infected with certain heat-producing bacteria—symbionts, really, not an infection—and the result gives both light and heat. At least, that's the species some of these people use around here when winter starts setting in. I had a little Mendelian lamp myself—that's what they're called—you know, the one that broke on the floor in my place last night."

"So you think one of those . . . lamps went out of control and started the fire?" I asked. Suddenly I had a vision of burning up as I slept on her couch.

Sarah chewed her lip. "Maybe worse—maybe someone set it to go out of control. Or bred it that way—a bioluminescent, biothermic time bomb."

"Your biomob covers a lot of territory," I said. "Allergens that cause low-level irritation in millions of people, catalysts that amplify other allergens to kill at least two people, anticatalytic tomato sauce, and now pyrotechnic fireflies."

"Not that much distance at all when you're dealing with coevolution and symbiosis," Sarah said. "Hell, we've got acidophilous bacteria living in us right now that help us digest our food. Lots more difference between them and us than between thermal bacteria and fireflies."

I put my foot on the gas pedal and prayed we wouldn't get stopped by some eager-beaver Pennsylvania trooper.

"That's the problem," Sarah continued. "Coevolution, bio-mixing-and-matching, is a blessing and a curse. When everything's organic and you cross-breed, you can get marvelous things. But you can also get flies that burn down buildings."

We finally got to Mo's house.

"Damn." At least it was still standing, but there was no car in the driveway. And the door was half-open. I didn't like it.

"You wait in the car," I said to Sarah.

She started to protest.

"Look," I told her. "We may be dealing with killers here—you've been saying that yourself. You'll only make it harder for me if you come along and I have to worry about protecting you."

"OK." She nodded.

I got out of the car.

Unfortunately, I didn't have my gun—truth is, I never used it anyway. I don't like guns. The Department issued one to me when I first came to work for them, and I promptly put it away in my closet. Not the most brilliant move I'd ever made, given what was going on here now.

I walked into the house, as quietly as I could. I thought it better that I not announce myself—if Corinne and the kids were home and I offended or frightened them by just barging in, there'd be time to apologize later.

I walked through the foyer and then the dining room that I'd never made it into to taste Corinne's great cooking yesterday. Then the kitchen and a hallway, and—

I saw a head, strawberry blond, on the floor, poking out of a bedroom.

Someone was on top of her.

"Laurie!" I shouted and dived into the room, shoving off the boy who was astride her.

"Wha—," he started to say, and I picked him up, bodily, and threw him across the room. I didn't know whether to turn to Laurie or him—but I figured I couldn't do anything for Laurie with this kid at my back. I grabbed a sheet off the bed, rolled it tight, and went over to tie him up.

"Mister, I—" He sounded groggy, I guess from hitting the wall.

"Shut up," I said, "and be glad I don't shoot you."

"But I—"

"I said shut up." I tied him as tightly as I could. Then I dragged him over to the same side of the room as Laurie, so I could keep an eye on him while I tended to her.

"Laurie," I said softly and touched her face with my hand. She gave no response. She was out cold on something—I peeled back her eyelid and saw a light blue eye floating, dilated, drugged out on who knew what.

"What the hell did you do to her? Where's her mother and sister?" I bellowed.

"I don't know—I mean, I don't know where they are," the kid said. "I didn't do anything to her. But I can help her."

"Sure you can," I told him. "You'll excuse me if I go call an ambulance."

"No, please, mister, don't do that!" the kid said. His voice sounded familiar. Amos Stoltzfus! "She'll die before she gets to the hospital," he said. "But I have something here that can save her."

"Like you saved your father?" I asked.

There were tears in the kid's eyes. "I got there too late for my father. How did you know my—oh, I see; you're the friend of Mo Buhler's I was talking to this morning."

I ignored him and started walking out of the room.

"Please. I care about Laurie, too. We're . . . we've been seeing each other—"

I turned around and picked him up off the floor. "Yeah? That so? And how do I know you didn't somehow do this to her?"

"There's a medicine in my pocket. It's a tomato variant. Please—I'll drink half of it down to show you it's OK; then you give the rest to Laurie. We don't have much time."

I considered for a moment. I looked at Laurie. I guess I didn't have anything to lose having the kid drink half of whatever he was talking about. "OK," I said. "Which pocket?"

He gestured to his left front jeans pocket.

I pulled out a small vial—likely contained only five or six ounces.

"You sure you want to do this?" I asked. I suddenly had a queasy feeling—I didn't want to be the vehicle of some sick patricidal kid's suicide.

"I don't care whether you give it to me or not," Amos said. "Just give some to Laurie already! Please!"

I have to make gut decisions all the time in my line of work. Only usually not about families I deeply care about. I thought for another second and decided.

I bypassed his taking the sample and went over to Laurie. I hated to give her any liquid when she was still unconscious—

"It's absorbed on the back of the tongue," Amos said. "It works quick."

God, I hoped this kid was right—I'd kill him with my bare hands if this wasn't right for Laurie. I put an ounce or two on her tongue. A few seconds went by. More. Maybe thirty seconds, forty . . . "Goddamnit, exactly how long does this—"

She moaned, as if on cue. "Laurie?" I asked, and patted her face.

"Mmm . . ." She opened her eyes. And smiled! "Phil?"

"Yeah, honey, everything's OK," I said.

"Laurie!" Amos called out from across the room.

Laurie got up. "Amos? What are you doing here? Why are you tied up like that?"

She looked at him and then me like we were both crazy.

"Long story, never mind," I said, and went over to untie Amos. I found myself grinning at him. "Good for you; you were right, kid."

He smiled back.

"Where are your mom and Emma?" I asked Laurie.

"Oh." Laurie suddenly looked sadder than I'd ever seen her. "They went over to the funeral home this morning—that's where

Dad is—to make arrangements. They took your car; Mom found the keys for it in your bag." And she started crying.

Amos put his arms around her, comforting her.

"You have any idea what happened to you? I mean, after your mom and sister left?" I asked gently.

"Well," she said, "some nice lady was coming around selling stuff—you know, soaps, perfumes, and little household things, like Avon, but some company I never heard of. And she asked me if I wanted to smell some new perfume—and it smelled wonderful, like a combination of lilacs and the ocean, and then . . . I don't know, I guess you were calling me, and I saw Amos tied up and . . . what happened? Did I pass out?"

"Well—," I started.

"Uhm, mister, Phil—," Amos interrupted.

"It's Dr. D'Amato, but my friends call me Phil, and you've earned that right," I said.

"OK, thanks, Dr. D'Amato—sorry, I mean Phil—but I don't think we should hang around here. These people—"

"What do you mean?" I asked.

"I'm saying I don't like what the light looks like in this house. They killed my father; they tried to poison Laurie; who knows what they might have planted—"

"OK, I see your point," I said, and saw again the Stoltzfus farm—Amos's farm—ashes in the dirt.

I looked at Laurie. "I'm fine," she said. "But why do we have to leave?"

"Let's just go," I said, and Amos and I ushered her out.

The first thing I noticed when we were out of the house was that Sarah and my car—Mo's car—were gone.

The second thing I noticed was a searing heat on the back of my neck. I rushed Laurie and Amos across the street and turned back to squint at the house.

Intense blue-white flames were sticking their scorching tongues out of every window, licking the roof and the walls and now the garden with colors I'd never seen before.

Laurie cried out in horror. Amos held her close. "Fireflies," he muttered.

The house burned to the ground in minutes.

WE STOOD MUTE, in hot/cold shivering shock, for what felt like a long, long time.

I finally realized I was breathing hard. I thought about allergic reactions. I thought about Sarah.

"They must've taken Sarah," I said.

"Sarah?" Amos asked, holding Laurie tight in a clearly loving way. She was sobbing.

"Sarah Fischer," I said.

Laurie and Amos both nodded.

"She was a friend of my father's," Laurie said.

"She's my sister," Amos added.

"What?" I turned to Amos. Laurie pulled away and looked at him, too. He had a peculiar, almost tortured sneer on his face, a mixture of hatred and heartbreak.

"She left our home more than ten years ago," Amos said. "I was still just a little boy. She said she could no longer be bound by the ways of our *Ordnung*—she said it was like agreeing to be mentally retarded for the rest of your life. So she left to go to some school. And I think she's been working with those people— those people who killed my father and burned Laurie's house."

I suddenly tasted the grapes in my mouth from last night, sweet taste with choking smoke, and I felt sick to my stomach. I swallowed, took a deliberate deep breath.

"Look," I said. "I'm still not clear what's really going on here. I find Laurie unconscious—you, someone, could've put a drug in her orange juice for all I know. The house just burned down—could've been arson with rags and lighter fluid, just like we have back in New York, New York." Though I knew I'd never seen a fire quite like that.

Laurie stared at me like I was nuts.

"They were fireflies, Mr. D'A—Phil," Amos said. "Fireflies caused the fire."

"How could they do that so quickly?"

"They can be bred that way," Amos answered. "So that an hour or a day or week after they start flying around, they suddenly heat up to cause the fire. It's what you *scientists*," he said with ill-concealed derision, "call setting a genetical switch. Mendelian lamps set to go off like clockwork and burn—Mendel bombs."

"Mendel bombs?"

"Wasn't he a genetical scientist? Worked with peas? Insects are simple like that, too—easy to breed."

"Yeah, Gregor Mendel," I said. "You're saying Sarah—your sister—was involved in this?"

He nodded.

I thought again about the lamp on Sarah's floor.

"Look, Amos; I'm sorry about before—I don't really think you did anything to Laurie. It's just—can you show me any actual *evidence* of this stuff? I mean, like the fireflies *before* they burn down a house?"

Amos considered. "Yeah, I can take you to a barn—it's about five miles from here."

I looked at Laurie.

"The Lapp farm?" she asked.

Amos nodded.

"It's OK," she said to me. "It's safe. I've been there."

"All right, then," I agreed. But Mo's car and my car were still gone. "How are we going to get there?"

"I parked my buggy at my friend's—about a quarter of a mile from here," Amos said.

CLOP, CLOP, CLOP, looking at a horse's behind, feeling like one—based on what I was able to make sense of in this case. Horses, flames, mysterious deaths—all the ingredients of a Jack Finney novel set in the nineteenth century. Except this was the dawn of the twenty-first. And so far all I'd done was manage to get dragged along to every awful event. Well, at least I'd managed to save Laurie—or let Amos save her. But I had to do more—I had to stop just witnessing and reacting and instead get on top of things. I represented cutting-edge science, for crissake. OK, it wasn't perfect; it wasn't all-powerful. But surely it had taught me enough to enable me to do *something* to counter these fly-bombs and allergens, these . . . Mendelian things.

I'd also managed to get through to Corinne at the funeral home from a pay phone on a corner before we'd gotten into Amos's buggy. Time for me to get a pocket cell phone already. I'd half-expected Amos's horse and buggy to come with a car phone—a horse phone?—that was how crazy this "genetical" stuff was getting me. On the other hand, I guess the Amish could have rigged up a buggy with a cell phone running on a battery at that. . . . Well, at least I was learning. . . .

"We should be there in a few minutes." Amos leaned back from the driver's seat, where he held the reins and clucked the lone horse along. He—Amos had told me the horse was a he— was a beautiful dark brown animal, at least to my innocent city eyes. The whole scene, riding along in a horse and buggy on a bright, crisp autumn day, was astonishing—because it wasn't a buggy ride for a tourist's five-dollar bill; it was real life.

"You know, I ate some of your sister's food," I blurted out the qualm that occurred to me again. "You don't think, I mean, that maybe it had a slow-acting allergen—"

"We'll give you a swig of an antidote—it's pretty universal— when we get to John Lapp's; don't worry," Amos leaned back and assured me.

"Sarah—your sister—was telling me something about some low-grade allergen let loose on our population after World War II. Didn't kill anyone, but made most people more irritable than they'd been before. Come to think of it, I suppose it indeed could have been responsible for lots of deaths, when you take into account the manslaughters that result from people on edge, arguments gone out of control."

"You're talking the way Poppa used to," Laurie said.

"Your dad talked about those allergens?" I asked.

"No," Laurie said. "I mean he was always going on about *manslaughter* and how it had just one or two little differences in spelling from *man's laughter* and how those differences made all the difference."

"Yeah, that was Mo all right," I said. Life to him was one big anagram. Like maybe life to some of these Amish was rearranging the codes of life. . . .

"That's John Lapp's farm up ahead," Amos said.

THE MEADOW WAS green, still lush in this autumn. It was bounded by fences that looked both old and, implausibly, in very good condition. Like we'd been literally travelling back in time.

The barn, a big barn, was no different on the outside from hundreds of other barns in the countrysides of Pennsylvania and Ohio.

But how many had what this one had inside?

Variations of Sarah's words played in my ears. Why *do* we expect science to always come in high-tech packages? Darwin was a great scientist—wasn't he?—and just the plain outside world was his laboratory. Mendel came upon the workings of genetics by cultivating purple and white flowering peas in his garden. Was a garden so different from a barn? If anything, it was even lower-tech.

A soft, pervasive light engaged us as we walked inside—keener than fluorescent, more diffuse than incandescent, a cross between sepiatone and starlight maybe, but impossible to describe with any real precision if you hadn't actually seen it, felt its photons slide through your pupils like pieces of a breeze.

"Fireflight," Amos whispered, though I had realized that already. I'd seen fireflies before, loved them as a boy, pored over Audubon guides to insects with pictures of their light, but never anything like this.

"We have lots of uses for insects, more than just light," Amos said, and he guided me over, Laurie on his arm, to a series of wooden contraptions all entwined with nets. I looked closer and saw swarms of insects—bees, butterflies, moths, larvae—each in its own gauzed compartment. There were several sections with spiders, too.

"These are our nets, Phil," Amos said. "The nets and webs of *our* information highway. Our insects are of course far slower and smaller in numbers than your electrons, but far more intelligent and motivated than those nonliving things that convey information on yours. True, our communicators can't possibly match the pace and reach of the broadcast towers, the telephone lines, the computers all over your world. But we don't want that. We don't need the speed, the high blood pressure, the invasion of privacy, that your electrons breed. We don't want the numbers, the repetition, all the clutter. Our carriers get it right, for the jobs that we think are important, the first time."

"Well, they certainly get it just as deadly," I replied, "at least when it comes to burning down houses. Nature rides again." And I marveled again at this boy's and his people's wisdom—which, though I disagreed about the advantages of bug-tech over electricity, bespoken a grasp of information theory that would do any telecom specialist proud—

"Nature was never really gone, Dr. D'Amato," a deep voice that sounded familiar said.

I turned around. "Isaac. . . ."

"I apologize for the deception, but my name is John Lapp. I pretended to be Joseph's brother at his farm because I couldn't be sure that you weren't videotaping me with some kind of concealed camera. Joseph and I are roughly the same height and weight, so I took the chance. You'll forgive me, but we have great distrust for your instruments." His face and voice were "Isaac Stoltzfus" all right, but his delivery was more commanding, and urbane.

I noticed in the corner of my eye that Laurie's were wide with awe. "Mr. Lapp," she stammered, "I'm very honored to meet you. I mean, I've been here before with Amos." She squeezed his hand. "But I never expected to actually meet you—"

"Well, I'm honored, too, young lady," Lapp said, "and I'm very, very sorry about your father. I met him only once—when I was first pretending to be Isaac the other day—but I know from Joseph that your father was a good man."

"Thank you," Laurie said, softly.

"I have something for you, Laurie Buhler." Lapp reached into his long, dark coat and pulled out what looked like a lady's handbag, constructed of a very attractive moss green woven cloth. "Joseph Stoltzfus designed this. We call it a lamp case. It's a weave of special plant fibers and silk dyed in an extract from the glow-worm, with certain chemicals from luminescent mushrooms mixed into the dye to give the light its endurance. It glows in the dark. It should last for several months, as long as the weather doesn't get too hot. Then you can get a new one. From now on, if you're out shopping after the sun sets, you'll be able to see what you have in your case, how much money you have left, wherever you are. From what I know of young ladies' purses—I have three teenage daughters—this can be very helpful. Some of you seem to be lugging half the world around with you in there!"

Laurie took the case and beamed. "Thank you so much," she said. She looked at me. "This is what Poppa was going to get for me the other night. He thought I didn't know—he wanted to pick this purse up, at Joseph Stoltzfus's farm, and surprise me for my birthday tomorrow. But I knew." And her voice cracked and tears welled in her eyes.

Amos put his arms around her again, and I patted her hair.

"Mo would've wanted to get to the bottom of this," I said to Lapp. "What can you tell me about who killed him—and Amos's father?"

Lapp regarded me without much emotion. "The world is changing before your very eyes, Dr. D'Amato. Twelve-hundred-pound moose walk down the main street in Brattleboro, Vermont.

People shoot four-hundred-pound bears in the suburbs of New Hampshire—"

"New Hampshire is hardly a suburb, and Mo wasn't killed by a bear—he died right next to me in my car," I said.

"Same difference, Doctor. Animals are getting brazen; bacteria are going wild; allergies are rampant—it's all part of the same picture. It's no accident."

"Your people are doing this, deliberately?" I asked.

"My people? . . . No, I assure you, we don't believe in aggression. These things you see here"—he waved his hand around the barn, at all sort of plants and small animals and insects I wanted to get a closer look at—"are only to make our lives better, in quiet ways. Like Laurie's handbag."

"Like the fireflies that burn down buildings?" I asked.

"Ah, we come full circle—this is where I came in. Alas, we unfortunately are not the only people on this Earth who understand more of the power of nature than is admitted by your technological world. You have plastics used for good. You also have plastic used for evil—you have semtex, which blew up your airplane over Scotland. We have bred fireflies for good purposes, for light and moderate heat, as you see right here." He pointed to a corner of the barn, near where we were standing. A fountain of the sepiatone and starlight seemed to emanate from it. I looked more carefully and saw the fountain was really a myriad of tiny fireflies—a large Mendelian lamp. "We mix slightly different species in the swarm," Lapp continued, "carefully chosen so that their flashings overlap to give a continuous, long-lasting light. The mesh is so smooth that you can't see the insects themselves, unless you examine the light very closely. But there are those who have furthered this breeding for bad purposes, as you found out in both the Stoltzfus and Buhler homes."

"Well, if you know who these people are, tell me, and I'll see to it that they're put out of business," I said.

For the first time, I noticed a smear of contempt on John Lapp's face. "Your police will put them out of business? How? In the same way you've put your own criminals out of business? In the same way you've stopped the drug trade from South America? In the same way your United Nations, your NATO, all of your wonderful political organizations have ended wars in the Middle East, in Europe, in Asia all of these years? No thank you, Doctor. These people who misuse the power of nature are *our* problem—they're not our people any longer, they're not anyone's people, though once they were everyone's—but we have a long history together, and we'll handle them in our own way."

"But two people are dead—" I protested.

"You perhaps will be, too," Amos said. He proffered a bottle with some kind of reddish, tomatoey-looking liquid. "Here, drink this, just in case my sister gave you some slow-acting prison."

"A brother and a sister," I mused. "Each tells me the other's the bad guy. Classic dilemma—for all I know this is the poison."

Lapp shook his head. "Sarah Stoltzfus Fischer once was good," he said solemnly. "I once thought I saw something that could be rekindled in her, but now . . . Joseph told Mo Buhler about her—"

"Her name was on Mo's car phone list," I said.

"Yes, as someone Mo was likely investigating," Lapp said. "I told Joseph he was wrong to tell Mo so much. But Joseph was stubborn—and he was an optimist. A dangerous combination." He looked at Laurie with hurt eyes. "I'm sorry to say this, but Mo Buhler may have brought this upon Joseph and himself because of his contacts with Sarah."

"If Poppa believed in her, then that's because he still saw some good in her," Laurie insisted.

John Lapp shook his head sadly.

"And I guess I made things worse by contacting her, spending the night with her—" I started saying.

All three gave me a look.

"—*alone,* on the couch," I finished.

"Yes, perhaps you did make things worse," Lapp said. "Your style of investigation, Mo Buhler's, can't do any good here. These people will have you running around chasing your own tail. They'll taunt you with vague suggestions of possibilities of what they're up to, what they've been doing. They'll give you just enough taste of truth to keep you interested. But when you look for proof, you'll find you won't know which end is up."

Which was a pretty good capsule summary of what I'd been feeling like. The truth was, events had cascaded so quickly in the less than twenty-four hours that I'd been in Pennsylvania, I hadn't had a chance to launch any kind of normal investigation, Mo's style, my style, or otherwise—

"They introduced long-term allergen catalysts into our bloodstreams, our biosphere, years ago," Lapp went on. "Everyone in this area has it. And once you do, you're a sitting duck. When they want to kill you, they give you another catalyst, short-term, any one of a number of handy biological agents, and you're dead within hours of a massive allergic reaction to some innocent thing in your environment. So the two catalysts work together to kill you. Of course, neither one on its own is dangerous, shows up as suspicious on your blood tests, so that's how they get away with it. And no one even notices the final innocent insult—no one is ordinarily allergic to an autumn leaf from a particular type of tree against your skin or a certain kind of beetle on your finger. That's why we developed the antidote to the first catalyst—it's the only way we know of breaking the allergic cycle."

"Please, Phil, drink this." Amos pushed the bottle on me again.

"Any side effects I should know about? Like I'll be dead of an allergic attack in a few hours?"

"You'll probably feel a little more irritable than usual for the next week," Lapp said.

I sighed. "What else is new?"

Decisions. . . . Even if I had the first catalyst, I could live the rest of my life without ever encountering the second. But no, I couldn't go on being so vulnerable like that. I liked autumn leaves. But how did I know for sure that what Amos was offering me was the antidote and not the second catalyst? I didn't—not for sure—but wouldn't Amos have tried to leave me in Mo's house to burn if he'd wanted me dead? Decisions. . . .

I drank it down and looked around the barn. Incredible scene of high Victorian science, like a nineteenth-century trade card for an apothecary I'd once seen. Fluttering butterflies and dragonflies, iridescent in the light. . . . Enough to make my head spin. Then I realized it *was* spinning—was this some sort of re-action to the antidote? Jeez, or was the antidote the poison after all? No, the room wasn't so much spinning as the light, the firef-light, was flickering . . . in an oddly familiar way—

Lapp was suddenly talking, fast, to Amos. "—see if you can stop that . . . ," Lapp said.

The flickering grew more powerful. Each burst of light felt like it was pressing against my stomach—

A burly man approached, with a woman he was half escorting, half pulling along.

"We found her lurking around outside—," he began.

Sarah!

"There's a Mendel bomb here!" she shouted. "Please. You all have to leave."

Lapp looked desperately around the room, back at Sarah, and finally nodded. "She's right, there's no time," he said and caught my eye. "We have to leave now."

He put his arm protectively around Laurie and beckoned me to follow. The burly man started toward the door, with Sarah in tow. Everyone else was scurrying around, grabbing what netted cages they could.

"No," I said. "Wait." An insight was just nibbling its way into my mind.

"Doctor, please," Lapp said. "We have to leave. Right now."

"No. You don't," I said. "I know how to stop the bomb."

Lapp shook his head firmly. "I assure you, we know of no remedy to stop it at this stage. We have perhaps seven, maybe eight minutes at most. We can rebuild the barn. Human lives we cannot rebuild."

"No," I insisted. "You can't just keep running like this from your enemies, letting them burn you out. You have incredible work going on here. I can stop the bomb."

Lapp stared at me.

"OK, how's this?" I said. "You clear out of here with your friends. No problem. I'll take care of this with *my* science and then we'll talk about it, all right? But let me get on with it already."

Lapp signaled the last of his people to leave. He squinted at the flickering fireflies. They were much more distinct now, as if the metamorphosis into bomb mode had coarsened the nature of the mesh.

He turned to me. "I'll stay here with you. I'll give you two minutes and then I'm yanking you out of here. What does your science have to offer?"

"Nothing all that advanced," I said, and pulled my little halogen flashlight out of my pocket. "Those are fireflies, right? If they've retained anything of the characteristics of the family *Lampyridae* I know about, then they make their light only in the absence of daylight, when the day has waned—they're nocturnal. During the day, bathed in daylight, they're just like any other damn beetle. Well, this should make the necessary adjustment." I turned up the flashlight to its fullest daylight setting and shone it straight at the center of the swirling starlight fountain, which now had a much harsher tone, like an ugly light over an autopsy table. I focused my halogen on the souped-up fireflies for a minute and longer. Nothing happened. The swirling continued. The harsh part of their light got stronger.

"Doctor, we can't stay here any longer," Lapp said.

I sighed, closed my eyes, and opened them. The halogen flashlight should have worked—it should have put out the light of least some of the fireflies, then more, disrupting their syncopated overlapping pattern of flashing. I stared hard at the fountain. My eyes were tired. I couldn't see the flies as clearly as I could a few moments ago. . . .

No . . . of course!

I couldn't see as clearly because the light was getting dimmer!

There was no doubt about it now. The whole barn seemed to be flickering in and out, the continuous light effect had broken down, and each time the light came back, it did so a little more weakly. . . . I kept my halogen trained on the fireflies. It was soon the only light in the barn.

Lapp's hand was on my shoulder. "We're in your debt, Doctor. I almost made the fool's mistake of closing my mind to a source of knowledge I didn't understand—a fool's mistake, as I say, because if I don't understand it, then how can I know it's not valuable?"

"Plato's Meno Paradox," I said.

"What?"

"You need some knowledge to recognize knowledge, so where does the first knowledge come from?" I smiled. "Wisdom from an old Western-style philosopher—I frequently consult him—though actually he probably had more in common with you."

Lapp nodded. "Thank you for giving us this knowledge of the firefly that we knew all along ourselves but didn't realize. The Mendel bombs won't be such a threat to us now—once we notice their special flicker, all we'll need to do is flood the area with daylight. Plain daylight. Sometimes we won't even need your flashlight to do it—daylight is, after all, just out there, naturally, for the asking, a good deal of the time."

"And in the evenings, you can see the flashlight—it's battery-operated, no strings attached to central electric companies," I said. "See? I've picked up a few things about your culture after all."

Lapp smiled. "I believe you have, Doctor."

———

BUT I KNEW there was a lot more I needed to learn—about John Lapp and Amos Stoltzfus, about their enemies, who would no doubt come up with other diabolical breedings of weapons. No one ever gets complete victory in these things. But at least the scourge of Mendel bombs would be reduced. I'd given Lapp a kind of laser defense for these pyro-flies—imperfect, no doubt, but certainly a lot better than nothing.

As for Sarah Fischer, who could tell? She'd come back to the barn to warn us, she'd said. She couldn't take the killing anymore. She said she had nothing directly to do with Mo's or Joseph's— her father's—deaths, that she could no longer be any part of a community that did such things. She had started telling me about the allergens—the irritation ones—because she wanted the world to know. I wanted to believe her. But for all I knew, she had planted that Mendel bomb in Lapp's barn herself and was just thinking quickly on her feet after she got caught.

I'd thought of calling the Pennsylvania police, having them take her into custody, but what was the point? I had no evidence on her whatsoever. Even if she had set the Mendel bomb in John Lapp's barn, what could I do about that anyway? Have her arrested for setting a bomb made of incendiary flies I'd been able to defuse by shining my flashlight—a bomb that Lapp's people were unwilling in any way to even acknowledge to the outside world, let alone testify about in court? No thank you—I'd been laughed out of court enough times already.

And Lapp said his people had some sort of humane program for people like Sarah—to help her find her own people and roots again. She was a woman without community now. Shunned by all parties. The worst thing that could happen to someone of Sarah's upbringing. It was good that John Lapp and Amos Stoltzfus were willing to give her a second chance—offer her a lamp of hope, maybe the real meaning of the Mendelian lamp, as Lapp had aptly put it.

I rolled my window down to pay the George Washington Bridge toll. It felt good to finally be back in my own beat-up car again, I had to admit. Corinne was off with the girls to resettle in California. I'd said a few words about Mo at his funeral, and now his little family was safely on a plane out west. I couldn't say I'd brought his murderers to justice, but at least I'd put a little crimp in their operation. Laurie had kissed Amos good-bye and promised she'd come back and see him, certainly for Christmas. . . .

"Thanks, Chief." I took the receipt and the change. I felt so good to be back I almost told him to keep the change. I left the window rolled down. The air had its customary musky aroma— the belches of industry, the exhaust fumes of even EPA-clean cars, still leaving their olfactory mark. Damn, and didn't it feel good to breathe it in. Better than the sweet air of Pennsylvania and all the hidden allergens and catalysts it might be carrying. It had killed both Joseph and Mo. They'd been primed with the slow-acting catalyst years ago. Then the second catalyst had been introduced, and whoosh . . . some inconsequential something in their surroundings had lit the last short fuse. Just as likely a stray firefly of a certain type that had buzzed at their ankles or landed on their arm as anything else. Joseph's barn had been lit by them. The lamp was likely the other thing Mo had wanted to show me. There were likely one or two fireflies that had gotten into our car on the farm and danced unseen around our feet as we drove to Philadelphia that evening . . . a beetle for me, an assassin for Mo. . . .

I smashed a small brown moth against the inside of my windshield.

The virtue of New York, some pundit on the police force once said, is that you can usually see your killers coming. Give me the soot and pollution, the crush of too many people and cars in a hurry, even the mugger on the street. I'll take my chances.

I unconsciously slipped my wallet out of my pocket. This thinking about muggers must have made me nervous about my money. It was a fine wallet—made from that same special plant and silk weave as Laurie's handbag. John Lapp had given it to me as a little present—to remember Joseph's work by. For a few months, at least, I'd be able to better see how much money I was spending.

Well, it was good to have a bit more light in the world—even if it, like the contents it illuminated, was ever-fleeting. . . .

PART
TWO

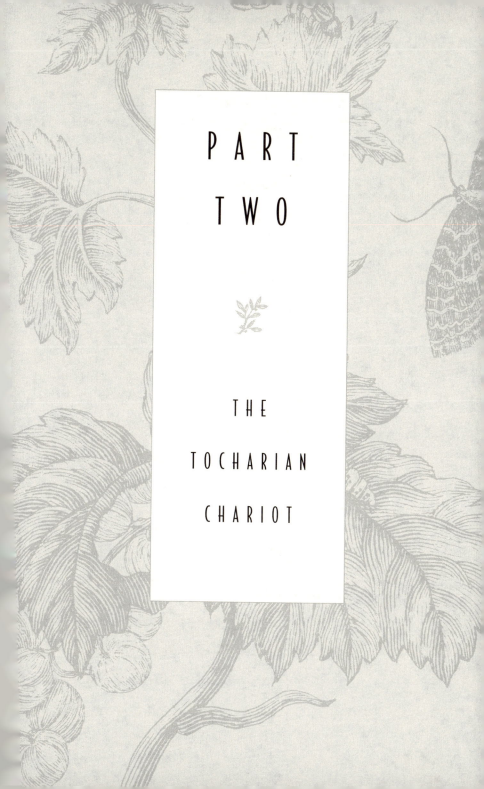

THE
TOCHARIAN
CHARIOT

TWO

A man of forty and a man of fourteen sat on a hill overlooking a river that some called the Tarim, near a settle-
ment that would someday be called Aksu, in a province
known as Xinjiang.

"So the Tangs no longer have their secret," the fourteen-
year-old said. "Soon the whole world will know how to make their
precious silk."

The older man, who was the younger's father, frowned. "Secrets come and go. All that really matters are the realities they
contain."

"You take no pleasure that we have finally broken the Eastern
hold?"

"They never had that hold in the first place. There are things
about silk—"

A third man, age sixteen, came running up to them. "Father,
Gwellyn, there's a dead singer down by the river."

The three walked quickly, without words. All knew there was
no point talking about the singer until they actually saw the body.

The older man gasped when he saw it. Skin, parched with
age, over thickset bones. Eyes mossy green, framed by brows that
protruded like cliffs, and the withered remnants of half-closed
lids. . . . "Yes. He was a singer."

"How long has he been dead?" Gwellyn, the fourteen-year-
old, asked.

"A very long time," the father answered.

"Was he a maker, too?" Allyn, the sixteen-year-old, asked.

"Impossible to tell just by looking at his corpse."

"What should we do with him?" Gwellyn asked.

"Burn him. Then grind up his bones and spread the dust to the wind, as the laws prescribe," the father answered.

"Should we tell anyone about this, or—," Allyn persisted.

"No. Just do as I instructed."

Gwellyn rankled. "It doesn't seem right just to destroy all trace of him, without even telling anyone, as if he never existed."

"That's the very reason we must do this," the father replied.

GWELLYN LOOKED AT his face in the river, muddy red first blush of beard on ancient silt of a similar color. His blue deep-set eyes were lighter than the water, but heavier now with the burden they carried. He could still see the singer, first stretched out by the water here, as he had been found, then burned, charred, ground into dust, as Gwellyn's father had commanded.

"Legend says the singers looked like us, before they died." Allyn had joined Gwellyn at the river and had guessed what was still very much on his mind. Likely because it was still on Allyn's.

"And the sorcerer of death gave them their brutish appearance?" Gwellyn asked.

"Father says sorcerers are for children," Allyn replied. "He says men of reason look for explanations in the natural world. I suppose he got this idea from the Philosopher."

"From Aristotle? From the Byzantine teachings?"

"Yes," Allyn replied. "You know the texts—Father keeps them next to his favorite spices."

Gwellyn nodded. "He wants me to continue with the lessons—so I can read those teachings for myself." Gwellyn sighed. "Comes from being a shaman's son. You've read those teachings already. Do they speak of singers and their changes after death?"

"No," Allyn said. "The Byzantine writings speak of the need to find explanations in natural causes, in the world at hand."

"Ah, I see," Gwellyn said. "So what does Father think are

the natural causes for the singers and the way they look in death?''

"Father says it's an illness," Allyn replied. "Except it is deeper than just an illness, and it's very old, and it will still be alive long after we are gone."

Gwellyn's brows furrowed. "I never thought of an illness as alive."

"Well, they are in some way tied to life," Allyn said. "Our livestock get sick, fruit trees get sick, we get sick, but rocks and tents do not."

"Are we sick with this . . . this illness now?"

"No one knows," Allyn said. "Perhaps we are. There's an idea—very ancient, Father told me—that everyone has illness. And the difference between those who get sick and those who do not is that the healthy ones have also an illness of illness that preys upon the illness, renders the illness lifeless so it can do us no harm."

"This second illness is our friend," Gwellyn mused, "like a dog who stops a wilder animal from attacking us in the night."

"Yes."

"But how do we know which is which?" Gwellyn asked. "How can we try to keep out one and welcome the other? Where do we find illness when it isn't already within us?"

"The legends say everywhere. In the food we eat, the air we breathe, the women we love."

"Women?" For the first time Gwellyn smiled, because making love was still a thrill to him that far outweighed any thought of illness, even one that might cause death. His smile deepened as he attached a specific face and body, one that he had seen just last week, to the general prospect of making love.

"Yes," Allyn replied, smiling a bit, too. "And we them. The legends say we are all brothers and sisters in illness."

Gwellyn nodded, but he was thinking more of Daralyn's face and body than his sisters'. . . .

Allyn continued anyway. "Some of the legends say that our

seed can do more than one thing, that sometimes it can leave evil inscriptions in the souls of women it may come to know.''

DARALYN WAS A woman Gwellyn had very much enjoyed coming to know and, in fact, was still enjoying.

Despite her name, Daralyn was not entirely of Gwellyn's people. Though she had muddy red hair, her eyes were almond and their color had an iridescent edge closer to brown than blue. Her maternal grandfather and perhaps others in her line had come from the Land of Silk. She had high intelligence, noble bearing— altogether fit, Gwellyn's father had concluded, to educate his son, five years younger than she, in some of the world's ways.

They lay in each other's arms, her legs still wrapped yet relaxed around his waist, after a third round of lovemaking.

"There are really only three kinds of people in this world," Daralyn said, picking up a thread of conversation from their last brief interval of rest. "Our people; the people from the Far East, of whom I'm also a part; and the people from the hot, humid southern land."

"The singers look like none of those," Gwellyn said.

"Maybe that's because they're dead."

Daralyn meant that as a joke and Gwellyn laughed, but he still took it seriously. "Has anyone ever seen one of them alive?"

"I don't think so," Daralyn said.

"Then why do we call them singers?" Gwellyn asked. "Surely they don't sing when they are dead?" He thought again about how he had helped destroy the corpse they had found, how they had committed those smoky green eyes, that neck like a tree trunk, to the flames. . . . Would he have felt even worse about destroying it if there was some chance that that neck could sing? Or was there a way of singing without words, without the impact of vocal cords upon the air, an impact that a corpse could have on the world without actually singing?

"I'm not sure," Daralyn said. "Whenever I've heard them called by a name, it's always been 'the singers.' I think someone once told me that the way they talk is by singing—that they have no words to speak, just melodies and harmonies to sing.''

"But that sounds like someone must have seen them alive," Gwellyn said.

"Melodies sound like life, yes." Daralyn smiled. "I like that. But you're right—no one has seen them alive."

"But how can that be?" Gwellyn asked.

"I don't know," Daralyn replied. "Maybe they were alive a long time ago, before any one of us or our people, but other people saw them then and passed word down to us about what the singers were like when they were alive."

"But they don't look like they have been dead that long . . ." Gwellyn didn't want to, but he blurted out to Daralyn what he and his brother had done with the corpse. He felt better after his confession in his lover's arms.

"True, they don't look like they have been dead that long," Daralyn said soothingly, stretching out her legs over Gwellyn's. "But if no one alive has seen them alive, what other possibility could there be?"

Gwellyn considered. "How long can a corpse stay a corpse?"

"Not very long," Daralyn said. "Usually they're picked clean. But I've heard stories of people found in the ice almost good enough to kiss, though they were dead for fifty years."

"I wonder," Gwellyn mused, "if there are some illnesses that work like the ice, but from the inside." And he was struck again by the thought that maybe he and his brother had ground into dust something—someone—that was somehow still alive.

HE TOOK IN the deep cerise of the setting sky.

"Looks good enough to drink," Jakob said, and joined in the contemplation.

"Yes," Gwellyn replied, "like the wine of your Passover. But the only trace we soon will have of this sky will be in our minds."

"Many of the beautiful things are like that—perhaps that's why they are beautiful." Jakob was a merchant from Antioch. He had travelled the Silk Road many times in his long life, the hostile northern route as well as kinder southerly. He had strode upon the Indian Grand Road, too, and traversed the Spice Route by water in pursuit of trade with the Byzantines, the Persians, the Mohammetans.

Gwellyn regarded Jakob as a master of judgment in things beautiful. Yet . . . "I could write a description of it anyway," Gwellyn said. "I could try to capture that color in my words, so that others could know of it."

The older man scoffed. "Impossible. Your very words would change the color they were attempting to describe—like trying to fathom the texture of a snowflake between your fingers."

Gwellyn looked back up at the sky.

"Writing is wonderful," Jakob continued, "but it is not for everything. The Philosopher's mentor's mentor—Socrates—had no use for it. He said reliance on it would cause our memories to dissolve."

Gwellyn smiled, because he knew enough to know that he had just gotten the better of Jakob at least in this tiny round. "And how do we know this?" Gwellyn inquired.

The smile was returned. "Yes, fortunately—or unfortunately— for Socrates, Plato troubled to record in writing the objections of Socrates to writing. Otherwise, we would never know of those objections. I'll grant you that. Just as Julius Caesar himself wrote somewhere that he admired the Druids, because they refrained from writing. And we would not know of Julius Caesar's admiration for lack of writing had *he* not troubled to record that admiration in writing. But that still does not mean that writing is advisable in all circumstances."

"When is it not advisable?"

"Writing is a chariot to the future," Jakob said. "It usually conveys the voice of someone no longer present. If I say something now that confuses you, you can ask me to explain. If I write something that confuses you and you read it after I am gone,

whom do you ask for clarification? I myself am not in the chariot—just my words."

"But aren't your words—in writing—better than no words at
all?"

Jakob stroked his gray-white beard. "Yes. But that is not the
choice. We will always have words. The question is whether we
prefer them to be spoken or written. For the keeping of records
of commerce, I agree that writing is best. For communication of
confusing things—like philosophy—I would rather pass my words
on to someone else by speech, so he can question me, and understand my meaning, and then pass his words on to someone
else again, who can question him."

"I still think writing is more dependable," Gwellyn said.
"What if someone makes a mistake as the words are being passed
along from speaker to speaker?"

Jakob shrugged. "That could happen, yes. But words in writing are in their own way not very dependable, either. The Library
at Alexandria has been burning on and off for centuries!" Jakob
lowered his voice to a conspiratorial whisper, louder actually than
his normal speech. "They blame it on the Mohammetans. But my
friends tell me it's the Christian bishops, too—they're afraid of
the learning!"

Gwellyn took no offense, being a believer in neither Mohammet nor Christ. He believed in the sun and the stars and the
moon and the trees—true to the Druid lines that still ran through
the mixed weave of his people. But unlike the Druids, he believed
in writing.

And so he was horrified by the burnings in Alexandria. Just
as he had been horrified by burning the corpse by the river.

"We found a singer by the river last month," he said.

Jakob put an urgent bony finger to his lips. "It's better not
to talk about such things!"

Gwellyn laughed in exasperation. "I see. The singer is not only
someone I can't write about, but someone I can't talk about!"

Jakob held up a quieting hand again and whispered even more intensely than about the burnings in Alexandria. "You want to learn more about the singers?"

Gwellyn nodded.

Jakob sized up his young friend, so passionate for wisdom. "All right," he said. "I'll tell you where you can go to find out more about them. It will require a long trip, by sea. And years, perhaps, of your life."

GWELLYN JOINED HIS father and Allyn at the entrance to an underground canal. He joined them on his hands and knees, sifting the soil, assessing its moisture.

His father was not happy. "The mountain springs have been stingy this year," he said. "Melons all along the road are in jeopardy."

"Can we widen the canals?" Allyn asked. "That would bring more water here."

The shaman shook his head no. "We haven't the knowledge—the Sogdians built the canals more than a hundred years ago, but they have surrendered to Islam."

"But their Prophet values knowledge," Allyn said. "He said, 'Seek for learning, though it be far away.' "

The shaman smiled. "Yes, I think he did say something like that—I see your education has not been wasted. But when one people takes over another—when one belief replaces another— something is always lost. And the Sogdians, however much they may value knowledge in their new beliefs, are different now from the people who built the canals. . . ."

The shaman stood up, as did his sons. He looked toward the long, dry horizon in the west. ". . . as we ourselves are changing into a people different from what we once were," he continued. "The whole world is changing. Our ancestors understood things that we can only vaguely see, or maybe not at all. Loss is inevitable; loss is life itself."

"Why not gain?" Gwellyn objected. "Why can't the change be an improvement?"

"You live; you grow old; you die," the shaman said. "If you are lucky—as I have been—sometime before that second event your seed blossoms into new human beings." He looked at his sons and kissed the brightly colored silk scarf he had around his neck, for luck, for thanks. "You try to pass on all you have learned—but how can you? Something is always lost. And more is lost with each generation. That is what I mean."

"But couldn't that process itself be changed?" Gwellyn insisted.

"How?" Allyn asked.

"I don't know," Gwellyn said, "perhaps create a more intelligent seed? A seed whose fruit is not as forgetful?"

"We have control over the accuracy of our ideas," Allyn answered, "not of our seed."

"Why not?" Gwellyn countered. "The melons that Father was talking about have been improved by breeding. So have the grapes and, I've heard, even the willows. And the horses and camels and yaks—the seeds of all have been improved over the aeons, have they not?"

"We are not yaks," Allyn replied.

"It's too dangerous," the shaman observed. "Our traditions warn us about such attempts to improve our own seed. If we go wrong with a camel—if it winds up with too many humps, or no humps at all—where's the damage? But if a man winds up with two cocks, well, I suppose some women—and men—might enjoy that, but . . ."

Allyn joined his father in hearty laughter.

Gwellyn only smiled, then asked, "Are the singers the result of such tampering with our seed?"

The shaman stopped laughing. "A better question might be: are we the result of their tampering with ours? . . ."

———

"I'M GLAD YOU'RE coming with me to Hotan," Gwellyn said, later, to Daralyn.

"Your father wants me to keep an eye on you," she responded. "I may come with you farther than that."

"Mmm. . . ." Gwellyn said, running his hand along the fine hair below her stomach. "My father thinks about just about everything. I'm surprised he hasn't opposed my going on this journey."

"You're the younger son," Daralyn said. "There could be tension between you and Allyn as you grow older and he gets first helpings. And you're smart—too smart. You ask questions. You write too many things down. I think your father feels that everyone benefits with you off on a journey of discovery to the West."

"I still want to write things down," Gwellyn said. "I want to write what I've learned, what I think I already know, about the singers. But how can I?"

Daralyn nodded. "Your father will seek out and destroy any writing about the singers that you leave behind. There's no point."

"But it's wrong!" Gwellyn was starting to get angry again. "What value is there in ignorance when we could have knowledge?"

"Perhaps you will find the answer to that on your journey," Daralyn said.

"Perhaps," Gwellyn replied. "And someday I will return to this place, and I will tell my father and brother and any who will listen what I have learned, and I will write it all down and hide it somewhere if necessary, so that others in the future, our descendants, may learn and understand."

THREE

BARBARICON, NEAR THE INDUS RIVER,
CIRCA A.D. 751

Gwellyn stood at the foot of a vast sea, near the mottled mouth of a muddy river.

"They're calling it the Arabian sea now," Jakob said, still strong, still encyclopedic in his knowledge, a merchant who had been plying the dunes, the waves, and the mountain passes for better than half a century.

Gwellyn turned from the sea to his staff, his companion for the past half year. "The color of your sash goes well with the distant waters," Gwellyn observed.

"This?" Jakob fingered his silken garment, and made a deprecating noise. "Some call it 'Phoenician royal purple,' because once upon a time only kings could afford it, and anyone found wearing it who wasn't royalty could be put to death. Now," he shrugged, "the silk worm's in Hotan and Constantinople, the Phoenician formula for purple is known worldwide, and a poor merchant like me can dress like an emperor!"

"And what is the Phoenician formula?"

"Shellfish!" Jakob smiled in contemplation of a forbidden pleasure. "Freshly killed shellfish, that's how the Phoenicians made the dye. My people are not supposed to eat shellfish—it comes from the sea and it has no backbone. But I've had it more than once, and it's delicious. Rules are meant to be broken—what else is living for!"

"I've never eaten shellfish," Gwellyn said.

"Spend enough time near the sea, and you will," Jakob said.

"Spend enough time *alive*—live long enough—and you definitely will!" He lowered his voice to his conspiratorial whisper that was loud enough for anyone in shouting distance to hear. "It gives you—you know, more excitement when you make love. That's important for someone my age." Jakob winked at Gwellyn.

Gwellyn smiled. "So the Phoenicians were experts at making love in rainbow colors."

"At more things than that," Jakob said. "They were a great seafaring people. They mined tin from the northern edge of the world; they found precious stones on the Nubian continent. And to keep good records of all of these transactions, to make quick notes as they milked the ports for all they were worth, they invented the system of writing that you are so fond of—the Greek alphabet."

"Then why is it called the *Greek* alphabet?"

"Ah, the Greeks adopted much, invented little, renamed everything," Jakob said. "They took the Phoenician writing system, added what we now call the vowels, and it all became known by the names of the first two letters in Greek—*alpha* and *beta*—the alphabet."

Gwellyn nodded. "The Greeks traveled far, Alexander to the banks of this very river. And they carried much along with them. . . . And we are the detritus of it all, of the Greeks as well as the Indus!"

"There are sediments at work here far older than your people *and* my people combined," Jakob said. "Come. The flute awaits us."

"BARBARICON IS NOT the city it once was," the tall Nestorian said to the two men he guided, one even taller than he, the other considerably shorter, but with a voice that boomed even in sotto voce. "When Parthia—Persia—charged too high a toll for the roads to the West, the Romans prized this city for the silk it conveyed to them by sea. As did the Byzantines, for the same reason."

"And now Islam conquers the world, and the roads through

Persia are once more closing," the loud whisper advised. "Perhaps this city by the Indus will rise again!"

"Yes, the followers of Mohammet are changing many things," the Nestorian agreed. "Their armies are contesting with those of the Land of Silk, near the Talas River, even as we speak."

Jakob shuddered. "That would not be a good thing, were the Land of Silk to fall."

The Nestorian nodded. "Their emperors have been very kind to my people. But change is everywhere these days, and not necessarily for the better."

As if on cue, a narrow alleyway opened before them.

Gwellyn, still accustomed to the open spaces and whistling winds of his homeland by the Tarim, cringed involuntarily at the sight and the smell.

"There is a sweet music in the dwelling." The Nestorian pointed to what looked like a piling of stones in the faint moonlight at the end of the alley. "So at least one of your senses will be gratified this evening."

The air inside the dwelling was even worse, and Gwellyn took shallow breaths, so as to ingest as little as possible. But there was a sad bright sweet music in the room indeed, barely discernible at first, that seemed to brush against his toes and move up his legs and chest and underneath his arms, where it tickled him, until it presented itself, shy and beckoning, to his ears. . . .

Gwellyn's eyes adjusted slowly to the light, even less in supply here than it had been outside, soft and flickering and almost starlike. Eventually he saw the source—a small smokeless lamp glowing whitely in a corner—and then the source of the diatonic scales that rose and fell like rain in reverse, from earth to the sky. It was a man, not much older than he, with sallow skin, hollow cheeks, and eyes that clearly could not see.

"Captivating," Jakob whispered, though Gwellyn could barely hear him for the music. "May we talk to him?" Jakob inquired of the Nestorian.

"For the proper amount of money, one can do anything with anyone in these parts," the Nestorian replied.

Jacob produced some coins from an inner pocket. He gave them to the Nestorian, who pressed four of them against the flautist's bare soles and kept one for himself. The music stopped.

"He of course will not understand Tocharian," the Nestorian said. "I will do my best to translate."

Jakob nodded and asked where the instrument had originally come from.

"He says it was given to him by his father, who was given it by his father, but originally it was made from the bone of a bear, by a very ancient people."

Gwellyn's eyes gleamed with excitement. "Ask him if we might examine this marvelous instrument."

"I'm sure the answer will be yes," the Nestorian said, "for a price."

Jakob grunted and produced another five coins, four of which again made their way to the base of the flautist's foot.

The Nestorian carefully handed the flute to Gwellyn.

"It's much harder than bone," Gwellyn said. "I wonder if that accounts for the depth of its sound."

Jakob ran his fingers over the instrument. "It appears to be some mixture of stone and bone. Perhaps these ancient people knew some secret of how to mix the two substances—this is not the first time I have seen such mixtures, sometimes in the human remains themselves."

Gwellyn recalled the bones of the singer he and his brother had pulverized. They were just bone, no stone.

"A kind of embalming, perhaps?" the Nestorian asked.

"Perhaps," Jakob replied. "Or maybe, God forbid, some illness that half turns bones into stone. Health—if you have it, you have wealth!"

"Ask him if he knows where these people are now," Gwellyn said, "the ancient people who made this stone-bone flute."

The Nestorian conveyed the question in the language of

clicks and grunts he was speaking to the flautist. He listened for the answer.

"He says almost all are bones themselves now, but some still live."

"Yes, but where?" Gwellyn pressed.

"He says, 'Everywhere. In all of us.'"

"That's no answer," Gwellyn said. "Ask him, where most on this Earth? In what land?"

"He says, 'They live most in a land beyond the land.'"

"Riddles," Gwellyn said. "I don't want riddles. Ask him the name of the closer land."

"He says, 'The Land of Silk. The Land of the T'angs,'" the Nestorian translated.

"And where is this farther land in relation to the Land of Silk," Gwellyn asked. "Up in the clouds, beyond some desert?"

"He'll tell you it's beyond a vast sea," Jakob interjected.

"I know," Gwellyn said. "I want to hear it from him."

"He says, 'The farther land is beyond a vast sea,'" the Nestorian supplied.

"See? I told you so!" Jakob reinforced his point with a bony finger.

Gwellyn nodded.

"These stone-bone flute players always give the same answer," Jakob said.

"Precisely your Socratic complaint about the *written* word," Gwellyn said. "It gives but one unvarying answer, as if written in stone. . . ."

The two proceeded with yet another rendition of their debate about writing and its benefits and drawbacks, and then progressed to seas, and how to get to them, and where they might lead. . . .

The Nestorian stood quietly, taking it all in. Eventually he returned the flute to its owner, who resumed his diatonic melodies.

Still later, the three left the dwelling.

The music was still in Gwellyn's ears as he left the alleyway, and as he left the precincts of Barbaricon completely for the small camp he and Jakob and others from their party kept on its outskirts.

The music stayed in Gwellyn's ears that evening, and the next morning and evening, too, a living embodiment of Xeno's paradox of a half of a half never diminishing to zero, a thread of asymptotically thinning honey that connected him to the man with the flute and the sallow skin and the sad bright sweet music. . . .

He came to realize it would never leave him.

"ALEXANDER CONQUERED HALF the world already when he was my age! What are you so worried about?"

"Not quite," Daralyn said. "Alexander was twenty when he succeeded his father and twenty-two when he started his campaign east. And Aristotle was his teacher. And that was a thousand years ago anyway—times have changed."

Gwellyn slapped her backside and kept his hand there. "Yes, they have at that. And we know much more now than they did in Alexander's day—much more about travelling long distances by land and sea."

"Do we?" Daralyn removed the hand but gave it an affectionate squeeze.

"Of course! Merchants like Jakob travel everywhere now— from Rome to Antioch to the Land of Silk. In Alexander's day, it was considered a miracle that he even got as far as the Indus."

"Yes, but even that is a far cry from setting out in a ship to who knows where. At least Alexander always had his feet on the ground. Every people he encountered would tell him something about the people who lived a little farther east. In many cases, they had actually seen that land with their own eyes. You would be sailing on nothing but wild rumors," Daralyn said.

Gwellyn said nothing.

"Your father doesn't want this," Daralyn said, quietly.

"Ah, somehow I knew it would come to that," Gwellyn replied.

"He loves you."

"He knew when I left that I would travel as far as need be to find the singers. My continuing the search should come as no surprise to him."

"I think he was hoping you would get it out of your system in Barbaricon," Daralyn said.

"I'll get it out of my system when I find the singers."

"I don't know how much farther I can accompany you," Daralyn said.

"Then I'll miss you," Gwellyn replied.

"DARALYN'S NOT WRONG about our sailing on rumors," Gwellyn said.

"If we knew more about the singers, then I suspect you would not find their pursuit so tantalizing," Jakob replied. "Still, there's the singing pottery. . . ."

Gwellyn sighed. "The Nestorian's going to bankrupt us before our voyage even begins." He frowned. "OK, I'll have a look—a listen—at it."

They found the potter outside a series of lean-tos, near the river.

"He speaks no Tocharian," the Nestorian advised.

"No, of course not," Gwellyn said.

"Do you understand what you'll be hearing, how it came to be?"

Gwellyn nodded.

"Let me make sure I understand," Jakob said. This encounter had cost them twenty coins, and he wanted to make sure they were getting their money's worth. "There is a kind of pottery that captures the sounds that are made all around it, as it is being created. Like a painting of sound."

"Yes," the Nestorian answered.

"And the sounds make lines upon the pottery, such that

when you run a comb or stylus of the right composition over the
lines, the sounds come back to life."

"Yes," the Nestorian said. "This potter has a collection of
them, thousands, from all over the world and through the ages."

The potter looked up and smiled at them.

"Perhaps he understands Tocharian after all," Gwellyn observed.

"He is just a happy man," the Nestorian said, and went on
to explain to the potter, in the clicking and grunting language
he had used with the stone-bone flautist, what kinds of selections
his clients were most interested in hearing.

Gwellyn and Jakob listened to many selections that day. The
process of listening was very personal—only one person could
listen at a time, because the point of the pottery from which the
sounds emerged could accommodate only one ear. The sounds,
at first, seemed faint and indistinct. But by the third or fourth
listening, Gwellyn's ear had adjusted, and each time the potter
ran his comb across a different piece of pottery, Gwellyn found
himself transported to a new world. He heard women having or-
gasms that made Daralyn's sound like whimpers . . . old men
groaning and dying . . . children laughing . . . birds singing,
snakes hissing . . . winds rustling, things fluttering, through trees
. . . and music, all kinds of music. . . .

"Those potters knew how to live," Jakob said.

They continued to listen, taking turns.

"Extraordinary," Gwellyn said, at last. "I think we're ready
to hear what we came for."

The Nestorian conveyed that in clicks and grunts to the
potter.

"He says rub your hands on this, for good luck." The Nestorian took a bolt of silk from the potter, who had taken it from
a large oval vase he had retrieved from a lean-to nearly hidden
by the others. The pottery was a fleshy ocher, with lines so deep
in some places that Gwellyn was surprised they didn't crack the
vase.

He lent his ear to the ocher as the potter caressed it with the comb.

He heard a sad bright sweet music again, the music that had never left him, though this time it was outside as well as inside his ears, in his face as well as his memory.

He heard a murmuring, a dog barking, and then the most compelling voice he had ever known. It was something between a plea and a prayer, a song of incredible gentleness, comprised of pieces less than words but more than sounds, a wispiness, a sigh, more vibrant than a scream. . . .

And he knew at once and forever more why these brutish people from the dawn of humanity were called singers.

"SO YOU HEARD their voices, so you know they existed," Daralyn said. "You already knew that."

"Yes, I knew that when my brother and I burned the singer's body and ground his bones into dust."

"But you still don't know they exist today—and if so, where."

"True," Gwellyn replied.

"But you're determined to sail out onto the sea to try to find them, anyway."

"True."

Daralyn turned away, in exasperation.

"The boat will be small," Gwellyn offered. "The crew will be few. I'm entitled to risk my own life for what I believe in. So are the others."

"Small? You intend to sail out in the vast sea with a small boat?"

"Jakob knows someone who comes from a distant island, where they make small boats, very seaworthy, called *curraghs*. The name itself appeals to me—it sounds like it has some connection to my people. One is under construction right now."

Daralyn started to speak but was interrupted by a rustle in front of the tent.

"Come in," Gwellyn said.

It was Li-Hsien, the Buddhist who served as Gwellyn's father's liaison to the people of the Jade Gate, at Yumen.

"Forgive my intrusion. . . ." Li-Hsien began.

Gwellyn waved off the apology and offered Li a pouch of fermented mare's milk, which he accepted and guzzled down.

"More?" Gwellyn asked.

Li hesitated, then nodded yes.

"So you have news from my father," Gwellyn said, as Li drank down the second pouch. "Let me guess—he sends his commandment that I not proceed on this voyage of discovery."

Gwellyn turned to Daralyn. "What did you do? Send him a message of warning by moonlight? Even a bird could not get from here to there so fast!"

Li started to speak, stammered, cleared his throat, said nothing.

"It's OK," Gwellyn said. "You can give me the message from my father. I don't believe in killing the messenger."

"The message is not from your father," Li finally told him.

Gwellyn looked confused.

"The message is *about* your father," Li said. "His spirit has moved on to another plane. And Allyn is nowhere to be found."

"What?"

"Your father is no longer on this Earth," Li said.

"Who did it?" Gwellyn demanded. "The followers of Mohammet?"

"No, it was an illness. Some are saying they should burn your father's corpse and pulverize his bones."

Daralyn took his hand. Her warm fingers felt comforting against the ice that had settled into the center of his palm. But he was still shivering.

She looked into his eyes, with an expression that said, *surely you will return now, to be shaman for your people. I will accompany you. I will support you.*

But if there had been even the slightest doubt in Gwellyn's mind that he should undertake this insane journey, that doubt vanished now, more quickly than ice in the sun.

FOUR

Unreliable winds had blown their small ship far off course. They made landfall on a large island that their guide said was about 250 miles off the mainland, the southern continent, which he called Ifrica. Their guide was a Mohammetan, Ibrim al-Hibris. Gwellyn wasn't completely sure at first that he could trust him. But Ibrim had been willing to guide them, at no cost other than his share of the treasures they might find. And as Jakob had said, "We're all beggars when it comes to the sea and its ways, so we can't be choosers." Gwellyn also felt that, considering the huge unknowns that awaited them, the differences based on their pasts were meaningless. . . .

"Some people call this place Monkey's Island," Ibrim mentioned, as he sat with Gwellyn and Jakob around their first fire on the shore. Paschos, an Aristotelian zoologist from Constantinople with a bounty on his head for some misconduct with animals, was the fourth member of their expedition, and he was asleep. Jakob had vouched for him.

"It looked big enough to be a continent," Gwellyn said.

"Take my word for it," Ibrim said. "If the winds had pushed our ship much farther west, we would have found ourselves between Ifrica, a true continent, and this little paradise for monkeys, which some of its inhabitants believe is itself a ship upon the sea."

"I've also heard this island referred to as the Malagasy," Jakob said, "assuming it's the same place. Lots of different kinds of monkeys are supposed to live here—they say as many as there are different kinds of people in the world. That should make you happy." He looked in Gwellyn's direction.

"Why would that be?" Gwellyn responded. "Why should I care a fig about monkeys?"

"Because monkeys are related to people," Jacob replied. "They bear more than a passing resemblance to us. Haven't you noticed?"

"Who could deny it?" Ibrim said.

"And perhaps they will provide some insights into the singers," Jakob said.

"That I couldn't say," Ibrim said.

"Enough about monkeys," Gwellyn said. "What kind of people live here?" He warmed his hands over the fire. Maybe it was the warmth, or being on land for the first time in months and months, that made him especially miss Daralyn this evening. Not a night went by that he hadn't regretted leaving her in Barbaricon—and it was almost a year already—but there was no way he could take a woman like her, any woman, on a voyage like this. If she hadn't refused to come along, he would have been obliged to leave her anyway.

"Islam has yet to reach here in any force," Ibrim was saying, "but it will come. In the meantime, from what I've heard from fellow travellers who have come this far, there seem to be two kinds of people on this island—black Ifricans from just across the channel, and people from the ocean worlds, from far off in the East."

"Ocean worlds?" Gwellyn asked.

"Oh, yes," Ibrim said. "There are many islands to the south and east of the Land of Silk. Some even farther than that."

"That was where we were supposed to be going," Jakob added, ruefully, "to a huge land, separated from the Land of Silk by a huge water, in the far distant East."

"I know," Ibrim commiserated. "But we have no control over the winds—we are completely at their mercy in a boat such as ours. That is why the Silk Road is preferable to the Spice Route, except when the road is closed."

"Perhaps we can talk to some of these ocean people," Gwellyn said. "Perhaps they know about singers on those far islands."

Ibrim smiled. "We'll have to find them first. And then hope we understand their language. But Paschos is a man of many talents."

As it turned out when they finally made contact nearly five weeks later, everyone except Gwellyn understood something of their language, and even Gwellyn understood a little, for the ocean people on this island spoke a language that seemed cousin to more than one of the languages spoken in Barbaricon.

"They have the aspect of those who inhabit some of the archipelagos in the northeast section of the Spice Route, near where our voyage originated," Paschos said to Gwellyn as the two surveyed the small group of ocean people engaged in conversation with Jakob and Ibrim. The discussion had to do with how to get fresh food and whom to pay for it—their most pressing need, after security had been established. And that had been established easily. These islanders seemed innocent of weaponry.

"I've never been to those islands, so I don't know what those people look like," Gwellyn said. "But I have seen some people like these in Barbaricon. Not dressed like these, though—those vegetable fibers are quite appealing." He was thinking especially of the two women, both about his age, he guessed, and both wearing skirts, parched grass in color, from waist to ankle. One also wore a large square garment draped over the upper part of her body, like a Roman toga. The other had nothing on at all above her skirt. Gwellyn couldn't take his eyes off her breasts, beautiful, like suns peeking up just above a horizon.

"They wear no animal skin for clothing," Paschos said. "They say skin should be connected to a beating heart."

"I can see the logic in that," Gwellyn agreed, his gaze on the woman and where he envisioned her beating heart, below, to be.

"And once the heart stops, the skin should be shown the respect the spirit within deserves, and not flaunted as clothing," Paschos continued.

Gwellyn saw skin as it rose and fell in a tender rhythm of breath. "I hope her heart beats a very long time," he said quietly.

Jakob and Ibrim concluded their business.

"They say we are welcome to their food," Jakob explained to Gwellyn and Paschos in Greek, the only language that the four seafarers could easily understand. One of the islanders, a man about twenty with a loincloth and a toga and presumably no understanding of Greek, stood beside Jakob. Ibrim was walking in the other direction with the islanders.

"He's going off with them to dig up some roots for us," Jakob said. "The inhabitants say these roots are sweet and nourishing and last a long time out of the ground."

Gwellyn nodded, still focusing on the woman with just the skirt.

"They say they're also willing to be our guides to anywhere on this island," Jakob said.

"And what is their price for this?" Paschos asked.

"That we take one of them along with us on our ship when we leave the island. They say as an ocean people their heritage requires it."

"Is there room on our boat?" Gwellyn asked, now paying more attention.

"Only if one of us stays behind," Paschos said.

Jakob nodded. "That's right."

"And what response did you give to that?" Gwellyn asked.

"The standard one, in these circumstances," Jakob replied. "I told them we could not guarantee that. I told them one of us would stay behind only if we made that choice of our own free will."

"And their response?"

Jakob smiled. "They said that would be fine—that they were

sure there would be no shortage of volunteers to stay on this island."

Gwellyn looked at the islander, who smiled now, too.

"And there's something else." Jakob reverted to his loud whisper, even though he was still talking in Greek. "He's willing to guide us right now to a pit of bones in the forest, which he says may have something to do with the singers."

"You told him about the singers?"

"Yes," Jakob replied. "They asked why we came here, and I told them. I described for them the singers and their bones."

Gwellyn looked back in the direction of Ibrim and the departing islanders. "Does Ibrim know where we're going?"

"He was part of the conversation, yes," Jakob said.

"How long will it take us to get to the pit of bones?" Gwellyn asked.

"The whole trip forth and back should take no more than a week," Jakob said. "Ibrim should have a good store of supplies by then."

Gwellyn could barely see the individuals in the receding group. For a moment he imagined that the woman in just the skirt turned around and rewarded him with the sweetest fleeting smile he had ever seen. Or maybe it wasn't his imagination. . . .

"Let's go to the forest, then," Gwellyn said.

ZANA, THEIR GUIDE, motioned for silence and pointed to a clearing beyond the ferns.

Gwellyn dropped to his hands and knees as quietly as he could and extended his head toward the clearing. A ribbon of deep mauve moths left a shrub in a hurry and ascended to the dusky sky—like a sash of Phoenician silk, Gwellyn thought. A small animal with a long bushy tail nosed its way out of the shrub.

"Aye-aye," Zana said, in a low, mellifluous voice.

Paschos chuckled softly. "Means 'always' in Greek—purely coincidental, I'm sure. It's the islanders' name for that little monkey."

"Monkey? It looks more like a cat," Gwellyn whispered.

"Look again then," Paschos said. "Look at its face."

Gwellyn looked, and caught his breath. There was real intelligence in those eyes, closer to human intelligence in some ways than a cat's.

"So you still think that monkeys have no connection to people?" Jakob whispered, more sonorously than anyone had spoken.

Zana made a face.

"But how can it be that a creature as small as a cat can have more in common with people than cats?" Gwellyn asked.

They made camp for the evening in the clearing.

It was warm enough that they didn't need a fire for heat.

It was light enough in the fullness of the moon that they didn't need a fire for vision.

The aye-aye, after first retreating when the people entered the clearing, returned with its mate a few minutes later and eagerly accepted the pieces of bamboo with caterpillars that first Zana and then the others extended, in between the human consumption of the succulent roots that Zana had unearthed near a riverbed that afternoon. Eventually the moon went behind the trees, and the starlight reflected in the four huge eyes of the aye-ayes were the brightest spots in the clearing.

"You see," Paschos said, "we look at life in this world and most of the time contemplate the differences. Aristotle teaches that the good naturalist must also pay attention to the similarities—to the formal causes, as he put it."

"Ah, yes," Jakob agreed, recalling a philosophy he, too, had once studied intensely, in his youth. "The Philosopher says that four kinds of causes move the world. Efficient causes are the immediate things that make other things happen—like my biting into this root gives me the taste of sweetness, or water makes me wet. Material causes are the composition of things—that's the cause that makes things look different, sand from water from roots. Final causes are where things are going—the goal that every being, living and nonliving, has. The root grows into a tree. And

Formal causes, those are the underlying patterns that shape things, that give things their forms. Some say a root looks like a penis, a melon like a breast. Like Plato's ideal forms, except with Aristotle, the forms are somehow inside us, inside the beings already. Am I right?''

Paschos nodded in appreciation. "Should I ever get my name cleared and return to Constantinople, I'll make a point of inviting you to the Academy!''

Jakob laughed. "A merchant picks up a thing or two in the way of knowledge as he travels the world.''

"So you're saying that those little monkeys and we have similar causes—similar forms, on the inside—even though we don't look exactly alike on the outside?'' Gwellyn asked. He took one last root from Zana and smiled his thanks. "But we can recognize that inner form when we look into the face of these monkeys?''

"Yes, and more than that,'' Paschos said. "If we follow Aristotle to his logical conclusion—a conclusion that the Philosopher himself may not have reached, though that is very hotly debated—then we see a deep kinship in all living things, an underlying similarity of form not only in monkeys and people, but in those caterpillars Zana is feeding to the monkeys as well. In fact, in the bamboo, too.''

"I'm not sure I understand what you're saying,'' Gwellyn said.

"I'm saying that on the form level—the shapes on the inside that shape us on the outside, that make our material not so much look but *act* a certain way—I'm saying that if we could capture the forms of us, and of those monkeys, and of the caterpillars, and the bamboo, there might be more similarities than differences among them. On the deepest level, those forms might be *interchangeable.*''

"But Aristotle knew that different kinds of animals could not interbreed,'' Jakob said.

"Yes,'' Paschos replied, "but that's because our *material* differences get in the way.'' He lowered his voice, smiled at Zana, and asked if he minded the rest of the group conversing in a language Zana could not understand. Zana said he did not mind but would appreciate a summary from time to time. Paschos responded with as accurate a summary as he could manage in the islanders' language, and the less than complete command he had of it.

Paschos then turned to Gwellyn and Jakob and spoke in Greek. "Consider this," he said. "I cannot have sexual relations with the female of that monkey because, well, she is too small for my flesh to fit. That's *material* causes getting in the way. But let's say there was some way I could get my seed into her nonetheless— let's say there was a way that our *forms* could meet. Do you see where this hypothetical reasoning leads?"

Gwellyn thought he did—and also that perhaps the reasoning had not always been completely hypothetical for Paschos, and perhaps that's what had gotten him in trouble for the animal misconduct in Constantinople. . . .

THEY REACHED THE pit of bones late the next day. It was located on the edge of a barren plateau that rose above the forest.

Looking up, they could see a jagged mountain peak rising in the southwest.

"*Tsi-afa-javona*," Zana said.

"That which the mists cannot climb," Paschos translated.

Looking down, they saw a depression in the plateau, as deep as it was wide, as if rained on by torrents for a thousand years. Bones of all sorts and sizes glinted in the sunlight.

They worked over the bones for two full days. Paschos made careful notes with a reed on the several rolls of papyrus he had brought along. The others called out discoveries, in some cases bringing over bones and bits they had found. Except for Zana, who seemed more interested in the writing process than what it was Paschos was writing about.

They sat around the fire in the evening and discussed their discoveries. "Most of these bones look like they could have come from those little monkeys," Paschos said, "though they all have stone in them. The biggest bones seem to be of a tremendous tortoise—the skeleton is almost complete."

"What about the bones of that impossibly big bird?" Jakob asked.

"Yes," Paschos said. "I suppose that bird could have been bigger than the tortoise."

"But the point he's making," Gwellyn said to Jakob, "is that however big those bones may be, none seem to be anything like those of a man." He knew they had certainly found nothing in the pit that looked like the bones of a singer—he knew what those bones looked like from personal, pulverizing experience. He could still smell their charred dust in his brain.

All three looked at Zana. "So let me ask him," Jakob said. "And see why he thinks this Noah's Ark graveyard has something to do with the singers."

Zana listened to the question, smiled, then hummed a melody.

"It's hard to tell the difference between his speech and his music," Gwellyn said.

"That was just music," Paschos said.

Gwellyn sighed.

They resumed their poking and prying—and Paschos his cataloging—the next day.

"Ibrim will be worried that we haven't returned," Jakob said, as they pulled loose a large jaw.

"He'll understand," Gwellyn assured Jakob, then helped him clean some of the dirt from the jaw. "Paschos says we should be careful not to break any of these bones as we free them from the earth—the less broken they are, the easier to identify."

"Makes sense." Jakob stepped back and examined the jaw in its entirety. "Looks like a crocodile—I'm glad we were not here when this jaw was alive!"

"A crocodile couldn't live here now—it's too dry up here," Gwellyn said. He had seen crocodiles in Barbaricon, and shared Jakob's gladness about not seeing them again in motion.

Paschos joined them. "There must have been a river up here at some point in history," he said. "Once you find the premise of a bone, you can proceed to a conclusion about what kind of world its owner lived in."

Gwellyn nodded.

"Come," Paschos said. "I have something to show you."

They walked about two hundred feet to the spot where Paschos had been working—digging and cleaning and writing. "What do you think of that?" He pointed to a bone, about as wide as a human hip, and perhaps half as long. But it wasn't human—even Gwellyn knew that.

"An ox of some sort?" Jakob asked. "Perhaps a piece from a more slender part of its leg?"

"Yes, that seems like a good guess," Paschos said. "And what do you think those holes are?"

Gwellyn looked more closely at the bone, and ran his hand over it. There were indeed a series of holes in it, obscured at first by the light color of the sediment immediately beneath the bone, but clear as day now. . . .

No, *clear as a whistle* would be a better way of putting it, Gwellyn realized, if there was such an expression.

Zana was smiling, humming his melody again.

And Gwellyn knew what he was looking at.

"It's a piece of a flute," he said. "Like the flute player's in Barbaricon!"

THEY RETURNED TO their base camp on the northeast shore five days later. This was a full week beyond their expected return date, and in the interim Ibrim had departed for a two-day journey southward down the shore "to teach the people writing," one of Zana's friends told them.

"Good to see Ibrim was so concerned about us," Jakob observed, sourly.

Paschos translated to Zana and his friend.

"No need to do that—," Jakob began.

Paschos interrupted, pointing toward Zana's friend, who was half-speaking, half-gesturing some kind of story.

"What is he saying?" Gwellyn asked.

"He's saying Ibrim was not concerned about our absence," Paschos translated, "because Zana had communicated our situation, our safety, to a flock of birds, who brought the message back here to Zana's friend."

Gwellyn looked at Zana. "I don't recall his doing that. Can birds be trained to do that?"

"Actually, the word he used means 'moths,' not 'birds,' " Paschos said, "but even I thought that too preposterous to translate."

Jakob rolled his eyes. "Let's eat—I'm starving."

Some of the islanders joined them for dinner around the fire. Gwellyn was disappointed that the woman with the sweetest smile he had ever seen wasn't among them, but he controlled himself from asking where she was and consoled himself by focusing on the piece of flute.

"Would be nice to hear the music this made," he finally said.

"With half a flute you can't make music," Jakob said.

"Depends what kind of half you have, doesn't it?" Paschos observed, and bit into a very colorful, fragrant fruit. "A flute cut off horizontally, in the middle, might still make you music. But, yes, a flute cracked down its vertical pole like this can only be looked at."

"You know not only your Aristotle but your Pythagoras and your Euclid," Jakob said.

Paschos smiled. "Byzantium's a very rich culture, a marriage of many ancient parts."

"The two of you with your talk of half-flutes and marriage remind me of Jakob's famous saying, 'With one behind, you can't dance at two weddings,' " Gwellyn said.

"Are you implying we're all asses?" Jakob retorted, and the three burst out laughing.

Zana asked for a translation.

"His humming recalls the music of the flute we heard in

Barbaricon, would you agree?'' Gwellyn asked Jakob.

"Difficult to say," Jakob considered. "I can hear a similarity, yes. But for me, all music that is not civilized sounds much the same."

"Maybe this music is *more* civilized," Gwellyn said.

"What makes you say that?" Jakob asked.

"I don't know," Gwellyn said. "It's soothing in a way that no other music is."

They had asked Zana, right after they had discovered the piece of flute, and many times on the trip back, what had made him bring them to that pit of bones. Did he know the flute was there? Did he know some connection between it and the singers? It seemed too much to be coincidence, but Gwellyn could not get a clear answer from Zana. All the islander did when questioned about the flute was hum his inchoate, haunting melody.

Gwellyn asked Paschos to ask Zana again.

They were treated to the same reply.

"Perhaps he's not unwilling but unable to tell us," Jakob said. "Perhaps he's just a guide—and a hummer—and someone else among these islanders can provide the explanations. . . .''

Gwellyn had already turned his attention to another islander, but not for the explanations to which Jakob was referring. . . .

The woman with the sweet attributes had entered the camp. She sat down on the far side of the fire and made eye contact for a shy split second with Gwellyn.

She was fully, opaquely clothed now, but Gwellyn could see right through the garment.

There would be no further discussion of flutes and singers by Gwellyn this night. Jakob could see that, and smiled with a surrogate fatherly satisfaction.

IBRIM RETURNED THE day after next.

"I've been told where to find the other half of the flute," he said.

Paschos looked up from his writing. "Let's tell the others."

Jakob was summoned from his work on the ship, Gwellyn from a dip in a nearby lagoon with Lilee.

"I still can't conceive how a flock of moths could have given you such detailed information," Gwellyn said. The hot sun felt especially good upon his wet skin.

"I can't explain it, either," Ibrim said, "but obviously I received the information."

"I can see how it could be possible," Paschos said. "I write squiggles on a piece of parchment, and they speak words from voices not here, describe events that happened yesterday, may happen tomorrow, may not happen at all. That a group of moths could also signify such meanings—each two or ten or twenty of them arranged in such a way to represent a spoken utterance, like our letters of the alphabet—is not so strange to consider. All you would need are moths of two different colors. A moth of one color is Alpha, a moth the other color is Beta, two Alpha moths are Gamma, two Beta moths are Delta, an Alpha moth and a Beta moth are Epsilon, three Alpha moths are Zeta, three Beta moths are Eta . . ."

"Like an abacus with beads of two colors from the Land of Silk," Jakob said.

Paschos nodded.

"Fascinating," Gwellyn remarked. "Tell us more about the other half of the flute," he said to Ibrim. "How many days from here?"

Ibrim smiled, shook his head. "Not days. Months. Maybe years."

Jakob raised his eyebrows.

"Here, let me show you." Ibrim took a stick to the dirt. "They drew a map for me, and I have a good memory for those things." He sketched a small oval. "This is the island we are upon." He sketched a much larger landmass to its left, much wider at the top than the bottom. "This is the continent across the channel—Ifrica."

The three other men nodded.

"Now," Ibrim continued, "we are at this place, right here." He pointed to the upper right-hand side of the oval. "To find the other half of the flute, we must take our ship and travel like *this*." He drew a line down the right-hand side of the small oval, then over to the right-hand side of Ifrica, then south for a small distance, then around the tip of Ifrica, then up its left-hand coast, up, up, all the way . . .

"That's where the flutes come from!" Ibrim jabbed the dirt at an unsketched place somewhere above the continent. "The islanders say the flute people once visited their island, in the early morning of their history—"

"How long ago was that?" Gwellyn asked.

"I don't know," Ibrim replied. "I still don't understand completely the way they keep track of time here."

Gwellyn looked at the mark in the dirt above the continent. "Where exactly is that? Does it have a name?"

"Near Rome, Gaul?" Jakob asked.

Ibrim nodded. "Yes, that's the general area. Islam has already gone farther west than that, on the northern edge of Ifrica, across the narrow straits, to a land by an ocean where the Romans once were but they are no more. I will give you a letter—informing my brothers of your good intentions. So when you arrive there, you'll be treated well."

Gwellyn laughed, thinking Ibrim had made a joke. "You'll be taking a vow of silence?"

"No," Ibrim said. "I'd prefer not to continue on our voyage—I'll be the one to stay behind."

"Impossible! You're the navigator!" Now Gwellyn wasn't laughing.

"Zana can be trained," Ibrim said. "Just about any of these people can. They know a lot more about the sea and its ways than we think. They live here by choice—not obligation—and I cannot say that I blame them."

Nor could any of the other three, as they pondered their futures.

"I was thinking of staying here somewhat longer myself," Paschos said, "to make a more complete catalog of those bones. We only scratched the surface up there."

"I'm an old man already," Jakob said. "The winters here will be kind. And the women . . ."

Yes, the women, Gwellyn agreed. *One woman in particular. . . .*

"You're thinking about Lilee," Jakob said.

"She's like no woman I've ever had before," Gwellyn replied.

"Forgive me," Jakob said. "But you've only had a total of one woman before—Daralyn—am I right?"

Gwellyn's cheeks flamed with embarrassment and anger.

Paschos mumbled a hasty leave-taking and joined Ibrim, who had already gone to talk to some of the islanders by the shore. Paschos knew better than to intrude upon, even be witness to, the kind of discussion Jakob and Gwellyn were about to have.

"I'm only saying this because you're young, you'll find other women, and you of all people should continue on this voyage," Jakob said.

"I didn't say I wouldn't continue," Gwellyn replied. "Only you, Ibrim, and Paschos said that."

"OK," Jakob said. "But you were thinking about it. As we all are. And that's understandable. But you must continue—without you, there would be no voyage. We'll never find out more about the singers."

"I never realized you were so interested," Gwellyn said.

"Why do you think I've come along with you this far? My people are an ancient people—we go back more than four thousand years on our continuous calendar. We've been persecuted by Egyptians, Babylonians, Greeks, Romans, and yet we have survived. I've travelled the world, spent my life, in pursuit of money, true, but that doesn't mean I'm not also interested in knowledge. The two are not mutually exclusive."

"You sound like Paschos," Gwellyn said.

"He is a very wise man. As is Ibrim. As are you. And if we can find out what happened to the singers—were they persecuted,

like my people, except they did not survive, or maybe they did—
then we must continue our voyage."

"Except . . . I love her," Gwellyn said. "I feel like I want to
stay with her, always—like I never want to leave here."

"How long have you felt this way?" Jakob asked.

"I don't know," Gwellyn said. "Maybe not until just now."

IN THE END, all four of them went on the ship anyway, in addition
to Zana. There was no room on the original ship for five, but his
people constructed a larger boat, with room enough for six. "My
people travelled in boats like this on the open sea for far greater
distances than we will be travelling," Ibrim translated for Zana.
"That's how we got to this island from the far, far east in the first
place."

"Don't accept the limits of a problem," Paschos said. "Re-
define the limits; extend them through *techne*—technology. I like
that." He made a copy of his notes about the bones and left them
with the islanders for safekeeping. "Perhaps I'll return to this
island in the future," he said. "In the meantime, I'll bring my
notes, what I know about the bones, to the rest of civilization."

Ibrim nodded. "I've taught them the rudiments of Arabic
writing. They learned quickly. They'll be ready for Islam when it
arrives. They'll take good care of your notes—they know the value
of writing. Zana told me it's the only way of preserving the truth
about where they came from, who they are. He said stories told
only in speech are like mist in the sun."

Zana smiled. "*Tsi-afa-javona.*"

Gwellyn informed them he was taking Lilee on the ship.

Jakob took him aside.

"They built the ship for six," Gwellyn said. "There's room
for her."

"That's not the point," Jakob argued. "You can't take a
woman along on a ship that small with five men for a voyage that
might take five, ten months—who knows? Maybe more than a
year."

"Paschos doesn't seem to be very interested in women," Gwellyn said, "at least, not human women."

"OK," Jakob replied. "You can't take a woman like that, so young and so beautiful, on a ship that small with *four* men. You understood that with Daralyn."

"Lilee's not Daralyn."

"In regard to this problem, they are one and the same," Jakob said. "Your loving Lilee doesn't change that."

"I'm taking her," Gwellyn insisted.

But he made love to her that night, his soul pouring into hers, her spirit into his, and he wondered if this love, strong as it was, was a match for Jakob's logic. As Gwellyn looked at Lilee, so warm in his arms, and thought of Zana, Ibrim, any other man with her, he could see that taking her on the boat with them was a path to madness. He tried to put it out of his mind, but it reappeared with increasing ferocity. He would kill them all with his bare hands if they touched her. . . .

"I came here once by the sea; I can come here again," he told her. "And I will. I promise you, my love."

And though she understood no word other than *love* and *I* in the Tocharian that Gwellyn spoke, she understood the tears in his eyes, the timbre of his voice, all too plainly. . . .

She held him close, sobbed softly, and promised him and herself that she would wait for him, forever. . . .

So there was no joy in Gwellyn's heart when their ship left the shore at last. *Room on the ship for six,* was all he could say to himself, *yet we bring only five. . . .*

And yet, within a month of their new voyage, as they approached the southern tip of the continent, Gwellyn had reason to be glad he had not taken Lilee along.

Each of the four men said a prayer, in their own language, as they consigned Zana's body to the sea.

Ibrim shook his head sadly. "His people sailed the seas at great lengths," he said. "The stories of his people are filled with these events. That he should die of some illness from the sea after so short a voyage is very strange."

"We don't know the illness came from the sea," Paschos said. "For all we know, it came from one of us or someplace he visited, maybe the pit of bones."

"But none of us has illness," Gwellyn said.

"Sometimes a person can have an illness inside and not get sick but give it to other people," Jakob said.

Gwellyn sighed. "I wonder if it was the same illness as my father's. I wonder if it has anything to do with the singers and their bones. I wonder if all of us—the whole world—is cursed with this!" And inside he thought, *I could not bear to see Lilee die. I'm glad, at least for that reason, she did not come on the ship.*

Later, Gwellyn asked Jakob a question.

"Do you think it at all strange that we came upon the island by accident—that we were pursuing the singers in a completely different direction—yet we found a flute of the singers on the island anyway?"

"What are you saying, that you think Ibrim may have steered us to the island deliberately?" Jakob replied. "Why? To lay the groundwork for another conquest for Islam? But that still would not explain why we found the flute."

"No, it would not," Gwellyn agreed. "Only Ibrim—and maybe Islam—having some connection to the singers, to the flute, could explain that."

Jakob considered. "There's a better explanation."

Gwellyn looked out at the water. "Yes?"

"It's that the singers were in many more places in the world than at first we realized."

FIVE

The boat constructed by Zana's people was not as sea-worthy as they had claimed . . . or the seas on the far side of Ifrica were more obstinate than the islanders had re-alized or remembered . . . or perhaps Ibrim wasn't as good a nav-igator of Zana's boat as Zana would have been. . . .

The boat foundered at last on the north shore of the conti-nent, having been blown far off course to the east as they clutched the coastline for protection from the storms. Ibrim had urged that they travel yet farther east until they found a spot suitable for repair of their vessel and restocking of their energy. Now they needed to travel a sizable distance back over the western Medi-terranean, retracing the last stretch of their voyage, just to reclaim their position on the way to the place the islanders had marked on their map.

Except they had no boat—it turned out to be quite beyond repair.

"Can we know that their map is any more reliable than their boat?" Gwellyn asked.

"We cannot," Jakob replied. "But it makes no sense to give up, having come this far." The fifteen months of their voyage, its innumerable stops and starts at ports friendly and otherwise, had taken more of a toll on him than the younger men. Jakob had nearly died at one point; only Paschos's bizarre medicine—"you fight the living death of illness with other living things"—had saved him. But Gwellyn was pleased to see that Jakob's spirit still burned strong—like the lamps of light of his people celebrating the victory of Judas Maccabaeus over the Greeks. "Those Greeks," Jakob often joked, "you can't live with them; you can't live without them."

The boat's final foundering was not far from Carthage, once seat of the great maritime empire founded by Phoenicia, of alphabetic and purple-dyed fame. Carthage had long ago been absorbed by Rome—"*Carthago delenda est*," Jakob had muttered—and later was capital city of the Vandals. More recently, Belisarius had reclaimed Carthage for the Second Rome of Byzantium, but now Islam had leveled most of it and was firmly in charge. "Which is why I say it's good fortune for us to have landed near here," Jakob concluded his historical summary for Gwellyn. "Ibrim will find many friends to help us on the last leg of our voyage."

"This voyage has had too many last legs already," Gwellyn grumbled. "We're like a millipede."

"Don't let discouragement crush us, then," Jakob replied.

Paschos approached them on a hilltop the inhabitants called Byrsa. "Ibrim's making arrangements," he said, and joined the two in their viewing of the ruins and the harbor. "These people stood at the edge of another world, didn't they? They had the sea in the palms of their hands."

"What went wrong?" Gwellyn asked.

"Something. This thing, that thing, another thing. Something always goes wrong. We know that now. It's the way of civilizations. Something always undoes them. It's almost not important what that thing is. Alexander dies too young. Rome gets lazy. Byzantium and Islam are in the ascendancy now. But that will pass, too. Only humanity endures."

"Do we?" Gwellyn asked.

"Well, we're here talking about that now, aren't we?" Paschos replied. "Humanity is the one thing common to Carthage, Alexander, Rome, Byzantium, and Islam—no reason to suppose we won't still be around when newer glories arise."

"I wonder if the singers thought that, too," Gwellyn said.

"Perhaps you'll have a chance to ask them," Paschos told him. "One of Ibrim's friends says he knows the place where the brutes still live."

"THIS IS GOOD news," Ibrim said to Gwellyn, Jakob, and Paschos as the four sipped wine on a quiet stone embankment by the partially ruined artificial lagoon that had once served as the mighty harbor of Carthage. "It confirms what the islanders told us."

"Would have been better news if the singers had been seen right here." Gwellyn gestured to the ruins of the Temple of Saturn Balcaranesis, the crown of the mountain chain on the horizon. "I'm tired of travelling."

"You expect too much of Carthage," Jakob said. "Look around you—it's amazing anyone lives here at all now."

"Carthage may rise again someday," Paschos said. "It has come back before. But you'd be unlikely to find the singers near a place like this in any case—relics of the distant past tend to persist best in places least trodden."

"Carthage is irrelevant now," Ibrim agreed. "And when it wasn't so, the Romans were right to destroy it, as was Hasan ibn en-Noman. But let me show you what my friend told me." He produced a palm leaf with a map upon it. "You see where we are now?"

Gwellyn nodded.

Ibrim traced a route back to the west, beyond the Mediterranean, and then northward and to the east. "Here." He made his own mark over the one already on the map. "My friend says they speak a language there like no other. They mine iron and live off the sea. They've been isolated from the rest of world for aeons by these mountains." He drew a long straggly line under the two marks and jabbed them with his brush. "Here are your singers!"

"Ah, Strabo's Vascones," Paschos said.

"The Roman Cantabria?" Jakob asked.

"I think that's a bit to the west," Ibrim replied, "though they could be the same."

"Either way, that's a big leap from speaking an unknown language to being the singers," Gwellyn said. "The singers are not supposed to speak any language."

"Still," Paschos persisted, "that spot coincides pretty well with the general area indicated by the islanders on their map—it would be odd if that was *just* coincidence. And the Cantabrian access to the sea could explain how that flute might have ended up on the other side of Ifrica."

"Then it would have to be a lot easier to travel north to south than south to north," Gwellyn said, "or the singers would have to have been much better at shipcraft than the islanders."

Jakob stroked his beard. "Both could be true, for all we know. Same about the singers speaking a language as well as singing. The point is we don't actually know enough about them to rule any of this out."

Paschos nodded. "Aristotle wrote a treatise about the peoples and languages of the world, and I believe he told of a people who lived by the sea beyond the sea in the west, with the mountains to their back, and they spoke an unknown language that had no words for abstract concepts. They could be the Vascones described later by Strabo."

"Really?" Gwellyn asked. "I never heard of such a treatise—and I was well educated by my father in the Philosopher's writings."

Paschos sighed. "Not surprising. The catalog of Alexandria 220 years before the birth of Jesus Christos listed 186 different treatises by Aristotle—fewer than 80 are known today."

"I heard less than 60," Ibrim said. "But what do I know?"

Paschos smiled. "Byzantium yet has some secrets."

"Here is something that is no secret," Jakob said. "Our funds are very low. How much will it cost us to get to this place between the sea and the mountains?"

Ibrim quoted the figure he had negotiated for a ship and a

proper crew to take them there. "Believe me, it's the best we can do," he said.

Gwellyn scowled. He fingered the purse with the jewels he had purchased in Barbaricon with most of the money his father had given Jakob and him, a purse he kept close to his body at almost all times. "That will leave us paupers—with no means of return."

THEY MOVED PAST the Pillars of Hercules again some eight weeks later. The sky was crystal azure this time—the storms that had obscured their entrance now long gone—and they could see the massive square castle on the Rock as clear as Ibrim's beaming face when their ship passed by. "Jebel Tarik," Ibrim said with pride, and Gwellyn thought he saw Paschos flinch in the periphery of his vision. What really occupied Gwellyn's sight, though, were the group of singers standing on the edge of the Rock. . . . He saw their bones, charred and pulverized, rise from the ground and regain first their form and then their flesh and composure. And now they softened the ship's passage with their flutes. . . . "Europa," Jakob said. And the sound of his voice caused the concert of flutes to vanish. . . .

The Islamic ship Ibrim had chartered with a crew of six— plus his friend Aziz, who seemed to know so much about the singers—was far sturdier than the craft the islanders had given them. It made the short but difficult distance to Cantabria without incident.

It turned immediately around after the four of them and Aziz had disembarked, Gwellyn's gems having been sufficient for purchase of just a one-way trip. Aziz assured them that means would be at hand in the coastal settlements for the makings of a return trip. "If you want to go back," he said. "Among those few who come here, most want to stay." Gwellyn wondered if that was due to the persuasion of Cantabria or the dissuasion of the sea.

They made shore on the inside of a rocky peninsula, nestled against two mountain ranges, near a village that Aziz called Portus

Victoriae. "To commemorate the victory of Marcus Agrippa and the Romans over the native Cantabrians," Aziz advised. "If Allah allows, perhaps we'll live to see the village with an Islamic name."

There were all kinds of people in the village—spearheads of Islam, Christians fleeing the Islamic conquests from the east, Visigoths, children with faces of Rome, even descendants of the original Cantabrian inhabitants who had long ago held off the Romans with ten years of disorganized but effective warfare, as Aziz explained. But none were the people with the strange language.

"Truthfully, their strongholds are farther west," Aziz said.

"So why did we land here?" Gwellyn asked.

"Because this was the farthest west that we could be assured of a safe port," Aziz said. "These Vascones, as Paschos calls them, are not always friendly to outsiders, especially followers of Islam who come in a ship."

"Will they be friendlier to people who approach them on foot?" Jakob asked.

"My concern exactly," Aziz said. "I know a place, about two days by horse up the coastline, where these people have a small village. Ibrim and I can get horses from our friends and be back here with word about the Vascones by the end of the week."

"A good plan," Gwellyn agreed. "Except I'll make the trip with you instead of Ibrim."

"I don't think that's a good idea—" Aziz began.

"I don't care what you think," Gwellyn snapped. "My gems paid for this voyage; my thoughts are the ones that count."

"Of course," Aziz said patiently, "but let me explain. This whole area is still very unstable—Islam doesn't quite control it all as yet. There are lots of little skirmishes going on all over the place. Let's say something happened to me up the coast. You might well be at risk—forgive me, a Tocharian, with no connections to anyone from anyplace around here."

"At risk from whom?" Gwellyn demanded. "You mean from some zealot follower of Islam who thought I was the enemy?"

Jakob put his hand on Gwellyn's shoulder. "He's right," he said quietly. "You could easily be mistaken for a remnant of Vandal or Visigoth. But you're right, too. You're both right in your own ways. So I'll go instead of you. I know how to talk to Mohammetans." He smiled serenely.

Aziz exhaled derisively and shook his head. "Please, you're too old to ride hard two full days and then back again."

"Is that so?" Jakob flushed. "I could ride *you* into the ground any day—"

"I'll go," Paschos said. "I'll go with Aziz. We Greeks have had plenty of experience communicating with zealous followers of all kinds. Is that acceptable?"

Aziz looked at Ibrim. "Yes," he finally said.

"Yes," Jakob relented.

"No," Gwellyn insisted. Everyone stared at him. He grunted his assent at last.

"Look at the bright side," Ibrim said. "We can sample the hospitality of this village while Aziz and Paschos are gone."

Which they did. Jakob's coins, of which they still had a few, bought them fine fruity wines and delicious fish and herbs. Gwellyn's charm, of which he seemed to have more than ever as he approached his eighteenth birthday, brought him a woman with fiery dark eyes and pitch-black hair.

He enjoyed himself immensely with her. But he still saw Lilee when he closed his eyes. . . .

Paschos returned four days later.

He didn't have to say a word.

He showed them the flute.

"THEY CALL THEMSELVES *Euskaldunak*," Paschos said to Gwellyn as the two rode horses on the shore with Ibrim and Jakob. They proceeded at an easy pace.

Ibrim had somehow come up with the four mounts. It was clear now to Gwellyn—and he assumed Jakob and Paschos as well—that Islam would do anything it could to strengthen its hold on this area, including gaining whatever possible knowledge of some of the strange people who inhabited various valleys between the mountains and the sea. Gwellyn shrugged inside: If that helped his search for the singers, then so be it, as Jakob might say. The success or failure of Islam in this area was no concern of his.

"*Euskaldunak*," Gwellyn replied. "Doesn't seem too far a stretch from *Vascones—Euska, Vasco*— so perhaps your Strabo was talking about the same people."

Paschos smiled. "You have the makings not only of a good zoologist but of a linguist as well. The real question, of course, is not whether these are the people Strabo talks about, but the people Aristotle describes."

"In that lost manuscript?"

The smile deepened. "Yes. We should be there soon. Unfortunately, there was no one in the village really knowledgeable enough in . . . in their *pictures* to tell us what we wanted to know. But they promised to have such a man available to talk to us, upon our return."

"What do you suppose they mean by *pictures*?"

"I don't know," Paschos mused. "Recall what Aristotle says about them—if these are the same people—they have no words for abstractions. By that he must mean no words for that which is not physically present—"

"No words for the past or future?"

"Yes, and no words for generalities like truth and beauty," Paschos said. "So to describe them, these people would need something more than words. Perhaps that's what they mean by *pictures* . . . something deeper than what we mean—"

"How did you understand what they were saying—if their language is unique?" Gwellyn asked.

"Aziz speaks a bit of their language—"

Gwellyn frowned.

"—but some of them speak some peculiar variant of Latin as well. Peculiar, but I can make most of it out. Likely you will, too."

"Good." They rode on a bit farther. "You think the pictures are a codex of some sort?" Gwellyn asked.

"Perhaps," Paschos said. "All I know is that these people place some very special importance on them and the pictures have some connection to the flute."

GWELLYN KNEW THAT the Vascones were not themselves the singers. Paschos had made it clear that the Vascones were physically not much different from people like Paschos and Gwellyn, and conversed in speech, not song. But Gwellyn still held some secret hope that somehow Paschos was wrong and the Vascones would, in fact, look like the man whose bones he and his brother had crushed and burned by that river in their homeland so long ago.

When Gwellyn finally saw the Vascones in the flesh, five days later, he sighed. Paschos of course had not been wrong. Gwellyn would have to settle for second-best: perhaps these strange people had some firsthand knowledge of the singers and their whereabouts.

The Vascones were almost as good as their word: a guide took Gwellyn and his party to the "man" who knew about the "pictures" right after dinner. Except the man's name was Mitxeleta, a woman with gray hair and keen eyes the same color who looked to be about forty. Aziz dropped the smile he had been sporting since his reunion with Gwellyn and the others.

"I thought you said he was a man," Aziz said testily to the guide in the dialect of Latin that some of the Vascones spoke.

The guide shrugged.

"Something was no doubt lost in the translation," Paschos said, clearly enjoying Aziz's discomfort at seeking profound counsel from a woman.

"Don't be so rigid," Ibrim whispered to Aziz in Arabic. "Different places require different rules."

"No," Aziz replied in the same tongue. "Not when *we* are participating in the places. In that case, Islam requires the different places to operate by *Islamic* rules; otherwise Islam means nothing!''

Ibrim shook his head slowly.

The others looked as if they did not comprehend the conversation, though only the Vascones were not pretending.

Paschos began talking to the woman in her Latin.

Aziz grunted. "I guess for now we can proceed with this," he said to Ibrim in Arabic, "wrong as it is. I don't expect to reform the world with a single stroke."

"... the flute and the pictures go together," Mitxeleta was saying.

"Can you tell us how?" Paschos asked.

"They speak to us," she replied.

"How?" Paschos pressed.

"Not with words," she replied. "The flute tells us whether the story should be happy or sad. The pictures tell us the story."

"Could we see the pictures?" Paschos asked. "Tomorrow morning perhaps? Or are they better seen in the evening?"

"It does not matter when they are seen. We bring the light. What matters is someone who knows how to prepare the light. And someone who can play the flute."

"Can you prepare the light?" Paschos asked.

"Yes."

"Can you play the flute?"

Her face reddened. "It is forbidden—"

"I'm sorry," Paschos said. "I didn't know."

Mitxeleta continued. "It is forbidden for a woman to play the flute."

"Rules," Ibrim said again quietly in Arabic. "The whole world is bound by rules—"

"Forgive me." Paschos spoke again to Mitxeleta. "Who could play the flute then?"

Mitxeleta pointed to the guide. "He can. If you ask him nicely." She smiled.

The guide smiled in return and nodded to Paschos and the

others. "Certainly," he said. "I would be honored to play it."

"Could I just ask one question?" Gwellyn asked.

"Of course," Paschos said.

Gwellyn addressed Mitxeleta. "Could you tell me what connection these pictures have to the people we call the singers?"

"We call them by a different name, but they are no doubt the same people, based on what I have been told of your descriptions," she said.

"Yes?" Gwellyn urged. "And their relation to the pictures—did the singers make the pictures?"

"No," Mitxeleta replied. "The singers *are* the pictures—the pictures are their story. And, in a way, our story as well."

"I'm not sure I understand—" Gwellyn began.

"When could we see these wondrous pictures?" Paschos interjected.

"Right now," Mitxeleta replied. "They are less than an hour's walk from here. And I have the makings of the light already prepared."

THE GROUP TRUDGED along an upward path in full moonlight. Mitxeleta carried three small lamps, each of which gave off a slightly different flickering light. The guide carried the flute.

"I wonder why she doesn't wait until we get to the pictures to light the lamps," Gwellyn mused.

"She says the lamps come on of their own accord," Paschos replied, "every evening as the sun sets. They are lit by insects."

"Ah, yes," Jakob said. "I've seen them fly with their pinpoints of fire in many a twilight."

"Yet she said she prepared the light," Gwellyn said. "How can light be controlled with insects?"

"I don't know," Paschos said. "I heard that the flickering has to be in just the right pattern for the pictures to emerge."

"Amazing that these people are willing to go to such trouble for us when they hardly know us," Gwellyn muttered.

"Perhaps it's no trouble for them—maybe to them it's a pleasure," Jakob said.

"I took care of all the arrangements before you arrived," Aziz stated testily. "They have been well compensated."

Mitxeleta signaled a halt by a patch of low, leafy shrubs. She pushed them aside, bent over, and disappeared inside them.

The guide gestured everyone else to follow and did the same.

Gwellyn was the last. He had to get down on his hands and knees to proceed through the bushes, but when he got to the other side he was able to recover most of his height.

He glanced around and saw he and the others were apparently on the inside of an ugly, splotchy-looking cave. The lamps seemed to be flickering more keenly now, or maybe it was just that they had the dark to themselves, with no competition from moonlight.

"Come." Mitxeleta pointed to a corner of the cave, which looked like it had an opening into something else. Her gray eyes gleamed in the lamplight.

As they approached the opening, a flock of moths suddenly roused themselves and flew out of the first entrance.

"Perhaps they are sending someone a message," Paschos said, only half-joking.

The opening led to a second cave, which was much like the first, except Gwellyn noticed the dried excrement of some kind of animal.

This, in turn, led to a third cave, with a similar opening.

The fourth cave, which they all had to crawl into but in which they were able to stand totally erect once inside, was the prize.

"My God," Jakob gasped.

The walls and ceiling of the cavern were alive with three-dimensional overlapping paintings of bison, horses, reindeer, and other animals Gwellyn could not identify. They came in and out of vision in the flickering lamplight, in orange, yellow, red, blue-black . . .

"Like Heron's wheels of life," Paschos murmured. "I saw

them once, in what was left of Alexandria. . . . Individual pictures presented so quickly that they trick the eye into believing the images within are in motion. . . ."

Gwellyn became aware of someone, Mitxeleta, pulling at his sleeve. "Sit there," she said, and pointed to a spot on the far side of the cave. "From there the story becomes clear."

Gwellyn and the others moved to that spot. Mitxeleta urged them again to sit. They did. Gwellyn noticed that Aziz did so very uncomfortably.

Mitxeleta did something to her lamps.

The guide sat motionless, flute in hand, near the front of the cave.

The flickering seemed to change—was somehow faster and slower at the same time. Its intensity seemed to fluctuate, too, throbbing whiter, softer, brighter, lower, in a pattern that meshed in some way with the alternating speeds. . . .

"Now look," Mitxeleta said. "First there, then there, then there." She pointed to a far wall, then the ceiling, then a wall closer to them.

The animals seemed to move slowly on the far wall. They looked like bison. Now they moved more quickly, running over one another, starting to stampede over a cliff. . . .

Some thing, some form, was chasing them. . . .

A flute was playing . . . an unfamiliar melody, spare, deep, powerful. . . .

Gwellyn's breath caught in his throat.

The form chasing the bison was a singer . . . a single singer. . . . Gwellyn could recognize the eyes in that head anywhere. . . .

The singer carried a flute in one hand. He seemed to look at them. He put the flute to his lips, and more unfamiliar melody emerged. He walked in flickers to the ceiling. . . .

There he joined others of his kind, some clearly women and some children, as they sat by a blue-black river. . . . They ate meat. . . . Horses grazed in the back . . . reindeer poked in and out of a forest . . . and now in a stab of pulsing light the reindeer bolted away, across the river . . . the horses ran . . . some new form emerged from the forest . . .

Gwellyn realized with a start that the melody coming from the flute had changed. . . . He stole a quick look at Jakob, who was staring at the ceiling, transfixed. . . . The melody was the one they had heard in Barbaricon. . . .

The new form from the forest was human, a man such as Gwellyn, Paschos, Ibrim, the Vascones, except differently clothed. He carried a knife in his hand. . . . The singer's people smiled at the man, who repaid the smile by thrusting his knife into one of their children. . . . The other singers wailed—or perhaps it was the flute. One of them—not the first singer—jumped on the man and his knife. Both bled orange-red on the ceiling and died there. The other singers walked slowly, sadly, on to the nearest wall. . . .

Now images of brightly colored butterflies, some orange, some blue, suddenly appeared and flew off the near wall. The singers caught some of them in their bare, gentle hands—

Mitxeleta made a sharp noise, which sounded sacred and anguished to Gwellyn's ears. . . .

The flute continued its Barbaricon melody. . . .

And now every reindeer, every horse, every other shape on the near wall—except the few singers—changed into men with knives. They approached the singers, each of whom stood up, with just a flute in one hand, a butterfly in the other. They put the flutes and butterflies into their mouths as the men with the knives slashed at them. . . .

And the wall dissolved into a wash of orange-red . . . and the images grew fainter . . . until just one clear image remained. . . .

The original singer, now at the very edge of the closest wall, who looked out at Gwellyn with an intensity he had never seen coming out of anyone's eyes. . . . Gwellyn couldn't tell if the emotion was hate or love. . . .

The flute screeched.

Another sharp sound emerged—this one from Ibrim or Aziz.

The lights went out.

The cave was dark and silent, for a moment.

Then the flickering lamplight came on again, in a different pattern.

"Would you like to see again?" Mitxeleta asked.

Gwellyn was about to say, "Yes, please," but Jakob grabbed his arm and pointed to Aziz.

His neck and arms were coated in blood.

Aziz stood up, fell over, hands clutching at his throat for air. He was dead before anyone could utter another word.

JAKOB CAME TO Paschos very early the next morning.

Paschos put down his writing implement.

"We should talk now about last night," Jakob said.

"Yes." Paschos motioned Jakob to sit. "Can I get you some refreshment? Have you eaten?"

"Yes, I had a wonderful bread before," Jakob said, and cleared his throat. He leaned over and spoke in his loud, rasping whisper, even though no one else was in the dwelling. "I know my history—I know why you might have hatred for Aziz and Ibrim."

Paschos looked at Jakob, said nothing.

"Carthage was destroyed completely by Hasan in 698," Jakob continued. "Many died at Islamic hands, and brutally. They were not Carthaginians, Phoenicians, or Romans, those who died— they were *your* people, from Byzantium. Ioannes the patrician was defending the city when it was besieged by Hasan."

"So?"

"So? I saw how you wince every time Aziz and Ibrim chortle about Islamic conquests. I know my history. Was someone in your family killed when Hasan took the city? Is that it? It would give you ample reason to want to kill them!"

Paschos shook his head.

"Look," Jakob whispered more insistently. "I don't blame you. I'm sure I would feel the same, in your circumstances. But there's more at stake here than your historical or personal grievances. . . . Already the Vascones are refusing to show us anything more. They're talking of making sure no one ever sets loose those murderous demons in the caves again—"

"You really know nothing about me and what I'm capable of, old man." Paschos was white with anger. He calmed himself. "I apologize," he said, sincerely. "Your age has nothing to do with your error."

"Forget about apologies," Jakob responded. "None are needed, not to me. But tell me about my error regarding you—I want to learn."

"Yes, I hate many things about Islam—I hate any religion that clouds in any way the reason of men. And I had no use for that pompous Aziz. I had the pleasure of spending two uninterrupted days in his exclusive braying company our first trip out here—"

"That's what I was thinking of," Jakob said.

"But I didn't kill him, you understand? I'm a zoologist, a philosopher—I study life, however revolting. I don't kill it! I kill stupid ideas, instead. I seek out errors and try to kill *them*—not the people who make them."

"Well, then, who?" Jakob asked. "Why would the Vascones kill just one of us? As part of their ceremony? And then what, they let the rest of us go on our merry way? I don't believe that—"

Gwellyn burst into the dwelling—looking for Paschos, surprised to see Jakob.

"Come!" Gwellyn shouted. "There's fire in the hills."

THEY CAUGHT UP with Ibrim at the entrance to the cave. It looked very different in the thick gray smoke pouring out of its mouth and the daylight pouring out of the sky. A line of ten Vascone men stood between Ibrim and the cave.

Gwellyn noticed that Ibrim's eyes were tearing, presumably from the acrid smoke.

"They're destroying all the pictures within—" Ibrim began.

"I can see that," Gwellyn said. He made a move toward the Vascone men. Paschos and Ibrim restrained him.

"It's no use," Ibrim said. "This has been going on for hours—since before sunrise. It's all gone inside."

"Why?" Gwellyn demanded.

Ibrim shook his head. "These people—these Vascones—practice a very ancient religion, from what I can tell. Goes back before Mohammet, before Christ, before Moses and Abraham himself, for all I know." His eyes turned from Paschos to Jakob.

"My religion goes back a long way, too," Gwellyn said.

"I know," Ibrim said. "And these people are very protective of their religion, as I'm sure your people are. Most of the Vascones are already Christian. Some may soon be Islamic, if my people have their way. But these people, of this village, they're worried; they see bad omens in every event. And they see what happened last night to Aziz as a *very* bad omen—so they seek to protect themselves against that omen by destroying the vessel that brought it to them. They say their lamps knew it and erupted on their own to destroy the vessel—the sacred cave—that Aziz's death had profaned."

"Just what *you* were trying to prevent, wasn't it?" Paschos said.

Ibrim looked at Paschos, then nodded.

"What do you mean?" Gwellyn asked Ibrim. "You *knew* that the Vascones planned to sacrifice Aziz to their . . . their singer gods—you knew that they would then seek to destroy the realm of that sacrifice, to cleanse the place of that murder, and you tried to prevent it? How could you know that?"

Ibrim said nothing.

"No," Paschos said. "I don't think that's how it happened."

"How then?" Gwellyn turned to face Paschos, as did Jakob. Ibrim turned away.

Finally, Ibrim spoke. "Not all followers of the Prophet are alike," he said slowly. "Some see our most profound teachings and our most casual inclinations as one and the same—they think all must be followed with equal severity, with no room for change."

"Aziz was like that," Jakob said.

"Aziz believed, as all of us who follow the Prophet do, that pictures of the Prophet are a sacrilege. Aziz also believed, as some of us do, that pictures of anything profound are a sacrilege. He found the pictures last night very profound—"

"Islam destroys what it believes to be sacrilege," Paschos said.

"Most religions do that," Jakob said.

"He told me last night," Ibrim continued, "while we watched the singers butchered on the walls—come to life again and then butchered—he told me no one should ever see this or anything like it again. Imagine, as I watched this on the walls, watched what probably no one from my people had ever seen before, watched what we have travelled years now to learn more about—imagine that as I see that, I hear as accompaniment Aziz hissing in my ear about how all of this must be *erased,* and as soon as possible. How he would torch this and every cave like this he could track down in these hills. How once Islam had converted this area, had made it see the light of Allah, how he, Aziz, would make it his personal mission to destroy every trace of this moving picture obscenity, this light that mimicked life, this outrage . . ."

More smoke billowed out of the cave. More people arrived. More butterflies flew to the skies. . . .

"So I *killed* him," Ibrim said. "I killed him, to protect this—I slashed his stupid throat, my brother's throat, may Allah forgive me, with my knife. To *protect* all of this." He waved his hand at the cave, the smoke. "But now look at this—look what I've done. . . ."

No one said a thing.

"Perhaps there are other caves like this, with other stories of the singers," Gwellyn said.

"Perhaps," Ibrim replied. "But we'll never find them—the Vascones killed our guide, the man with the flute, this morning.

They said his flute had called forth the killers from the walls and into our world—"

"Called forth the killers of the singers," Gwellyn said. And he saw again that one singer, the first singer on the walls, the one who survived, and that look in his eyes. . . .

"We might yet find another cave with pictures," Jakob said.

"How? Where?" Gwellyn asked.

"I know where Mitxeleta is. She's still alive."

S I X

The hills reeked of smoke for a long time.

Just looking at them, even from afar, made Gwellyn's eyes smart.

"They're burning out every cave they know that has pictures, aren't they," Gwellyn lamented.

"They say: 'Our lamps are purifying the chambers,' " Jakob intoned.

Gwellyn scoffed.

"It's the way of humanity," Jakob said. "Burn, purify, what you don't understand. It's the same thing. Better that than you keep it, even though it disturbs you, so that, God forbid, you might learn something from it someday."

"You're getting cynical in your old age," Ibrim said.

"They're burning the moving pictures of the singers, just like we burned their bones—my brother Allyn and I," Gwellyn said.

Paschos approached the three men. "She's ready," he informed them. "But she's stubborn. Only the two of you"—he pointed to Gwellyn and Jakob—"can accompany her. Ibrim and I must stay back here."

Jakob nodded. "She doesn't trust Ibrim after what happened to Aziz—the Vascone with the flute saw it all. He confessed what he witnessed, before he died. And she doesn't trust Ibrim left alone with her people. That's why Paschos must stay."

"I was trying to safeguard those pictures," Ibrim said ruefully.

"I know," Jakob said.

"Perhaps my brothers are right after all that nothing good ever comes of pictures that mimic life—"

"We'll be fine back here," Paschos said. "I would have liked to get another look at those pictures, though—Mitxeleta says the ones she'll be taking you to see are the very last of that kind, with singers. Well, maybe later on, when these fires are more a memory than such a stink in the air. . . ."

"Yes, I'm sure there will be another time for you to see the pictures," Jakob lied, and Paschos knew he was lying, and the two men hugged. And then everyone hugged one another, except Paschos and Ibrim, who waved good-bye to Jakob and Gwellyn, who walked off into the hills to collect Mitxeleta.

"There's something important you'll want to know, and I did not tell you," Jakob said when Paschos and Ibrim were well out of sight. "I was afraid they might have insisted on coming with us if they knew."

"Yes? What is it?" Gwellyn asked.

"Well, I can't be sure, of course. . . ."

"Yes?"

"Mitxeleta says it's more than the last cave with pictures she's taking us to. That's why she trusts us with this—she says I'm too old to do any harm, and she likes the prism of your eyes. . . ."

"I'm pleased," Gwellyn said. "But what's this about?"

"She says in this cave, unlike any of the others, the singers come off the walls and the ceiling and join us in the climax of the ceremony. There's always this problem with language and translation, but I think she may be saying that, in this cave, the singers are actually still alive. . . ."

GWELLYN, JAKOB, AND Mitxeleta proceeded on horses—black, gentle, and surefooted—up into the mountains, east and north.

"Such lushness and coolness in one place!" Jakob said. "The air is sweet enough to sip."

"Yes, it's very different here from the Mediterranean," Gwellyn observed. "Greenness, sunshine all around, the last days of August, and we're barely sweating."

Mitxeleta smiled, though she understood not a word of the Tocharian they were speaking.

Gwellyn thought she was smiling at the beauty of the mountains and the forests and the sunlight.

"Where are the lamps?" he suddenly asked her in the variant of Latin they were both able to speak somewhat. Their leaving had been so hurried that he hadn't noticed the lamps missing until now.

"The light will be there for us when we arrive."

"Ah, like the new flute player?"

"There will be many flute players where we are going."

Gwellyn looked at her quizzically. For some reason, he had assumed that the flutes were as rare in the singers' lives as they were in their deaths. "The singers make many flutes?"

Perhaps Gwellyn had not learned enough of the Latin dialect to communicate as clearly as he wished. Or perhaps Mitxeleta was one of those people, common in every place Gwellyn had ever conducted a conversation, who seemed to answer questions with preset passages, as if the question elicited a small codex of information already wrapped up somewhere in the head. "Legend says that wolves made the first flutes," she said.

"Wolves?"

"Yes," she continued. "A dying wolf bit into a bone, desperate for food. The marrow had already been sucked dry from the bone, so it gave the wolf no sustenance, and it died. But the teeth of the hungry, dying wolf made holes in the hollow bone. A singer picked it up, blew into it, tried to measure the holes with the tips of his fingers. . . . And the singer found the flute had preserved the soul of the wolf, could recall its cry. . . ."

"Sometimes that flute music does remind me of a wolf's dying howl," Jakob said.

"It does," Gwellyn agreed. Perhaps Mitxeleta had understood his question perfectly after all.

Now she stopped by a small piece of frothy, fast-flowing stream, barely visible as it rushed from one lichen-covered promontory to another. She pointed at the stream and talked again of the singers.

"Their lives are short and fast, like that stream. Most of them live no longer than thirty of our years."

"Many of us live no longer than thirty, either," Jakob said. "I'm just a lucky exception."

"That's because we do not care for ourselves—we ignore what our bodies tell us," Mitxeleta said. "For the singers, there are far fewer exceptions. Whatever they do, their bodies give out. That is why music and memory are so important to them. They live through music and memory."

"Do they hate us?" Gwellyn asked. "We killed them whatever their age, according to those pictures. There were children on that wall."

"We didn't kill all of them," Mitxeleta said. "We can never kill all of them—that cannot be."

"Why not?" Gwellyn asked.

"You'll see."

THEY REACHED WALKING distance to the cave five days later.

"The rest is too narrow even for these wonderful animals," Mitxeleta said.

Gwellyn looked up at the path beyond and agreed. "Will the horses be here when we return?"

"If not them, others like them," Mitxeleta replied.

Gwellyn looked at Jakob, who shrugged.

"We came this far; *Adonai* will provide!" Jakob said.

"What? You're suddenly finding religion now?"

Jakob smiled. "Under the circumstances, I'll take whatever I can get."

Gwellyn shook his head. "Can he make the climb?" he asked Mitxeleta about Jakob.

"*Adonai*," she said, and laughed.

"Great, you've got a convert here," Gwellyn said to Jakob. "All right, I guess we'll just walk slowly and stop whenever you need to. At least the walk back down will be easier."

"Actually, at my age, walking up is sometimes easier than walking down," Jakob said.

Their dinner was an ibex Gwellyn had hunted in the morning and tubers Mitxeleta had unearthed in the afternoon. "A little stringy, but good," Jakob said about the ibex, which Mitxeleta had quartered and he had roasted over a small fire. All agreed that the tubers were delectable.

They began their climb at sunrise. The leaves overhead sliced the light into bright shifting packets. "If Paschos were here, he'd say those medleys of leaves were better than the stained-glass windows of Byzantium, and he'd be right," Jakob said.

They climbed for two days. Mitxeleta had extended the edibility of the ibex meat by applying salt she had long ago recovered from the sea, and the tubers tasted even sweeter than they had on the day they were unearthed. . . .

On the third afternoon, Mitxeleta stopped and looked carefully at some shrubbery.

She did that two more times.

The fourth time, she not only inspected the shrubbery but also pushed her way through it and motioned Gwellyn and Jakob to do the same.

"I have to bend again," Jakob muttered.

The other side of the shrubbery opened onto a small clearing, with grass as high as their knees.

"Looks like a grain of some kind," Gwellyn said.

But Jakob tugged on Gwellyn's arm and pointed to a rock formation, perhaps an entrance to a cave, on the far side of the clearing.

Two figures appeared in front of it.

Gwellyn squinted but couldn't make them out.

Mitxeleta saw them, too, and gestured to Gwellyn and Jakob that they should stay still. She walked quickly toward the two figures, arms outstretched. She made a high-pitched sound with her voice, oddly soothing.

"Like Christ on the cross," Jakob said in his loud whisper.

Gwellyn tried to bring the two figures into clearer focus. Were they singers? The flickering light in the cave with the moving pictures had not been strong enough for him to see precisely what they looked like. . . . Somehow this sunlight and shadow, at least at this distance, was even worse. . . .

He scrutinized the two in front of the rock formation. Mitxeleta reached them. And appeared to disrobe—

Gwellyn started to move, but Jakob restrained him.

"She's probably just showing them that she has no weapons," Jakob rasped.

Gwellyn nodded and relented a bit. "Are those singers?"

"I don't know," Jakob said.

"She said the singers would come off the cave walls—those are outside."

"So maybe she was wrong about that detail," Jakob said.

"I can't see Mitxeleta at all now," Gwellyn said. "We can't just stand here."

Jakob hesitated. "OK, let's move forward, slowly. . . . No, wait! Ah! There she is!"

Mitxeleta was visible again, fully clothed. She started walking back toward them.

Gwellyn kept his eyes on the two other figures, as if looking at them steadily would prevent them from leaving.

Mitxeleta approached. She looked intense yet calm. "You see what I just did? You walk toward them the same way—arms outstretched." She extended her arms again, palms up, horizontal to the ground.

"Do we make the same noise, too?" Gwellyn asked.

Mitxeleta glared at him. "If you're making a joke, this isn't the time. If your question is serious, then do not worry; I will see to the greeting."

"I was serious," Gwellyn said. "I just did not know your word for musical greeting."

"You will have to take your clothes off, too."

"OK," Gwellyn said. "Do we put them on again before we enter the cave?"

"We won't be entering the cave," Mitxeleta responded. "They won't allow any of us to enter their caves, after the killing and the fires below. Those two were put there to guard the cave."

"They know about Aziz?"

"Yes. The hills have eyes and wings," Mitxeleta said. "The singers have butterflies. My name means 'butterfly.' "

THE SINGERS WERE about five and one-half feet tall, shorter than Gwellyn, but just about Jakob's height. Their skin was a dark ocher—reminiscent to Gwellyn of the complexions he had once seen on some travelers who had come to the Tarim Basin from Mongolia, but not quite that shade, either. Their brows protruded, but they did not look as brutish as their skeletons suggested, assuming those were skeletons of the same race. Something about the way their skin rode upon their faces, the way their eyes, keen and musty green, moved inside their sockets when they regarded Gwellyn, made them seem serenely intelligent—the complete opposite of anything brutish or less than human.

They look like children, Gwellyn realized, and mentioned this to Jakob.

"Yes, I see what you mean," Jakob said. "There is a theory—I heard Paschos talk about it once—that human beings are more intelligent than the beasts because we maintain our childhood longer and thus extend our time to learn."

"These look like children only in their faces," Gwellyn noted as he and Jakob put their clothes back on. The singers had penises which, even in their flaccid state, were half again as long and thick as Gwellyn's and Jakob's. The only clothes the singers wore were animal skins of some sort draped partway over their shoulders.

That couldn't have been enough to keep them warm—but given the temperature, that would not have been a necessity, and Gwellyn concluded that the function of the skins was ceremonial, perhaps to identify these two singers as guardians of the cave.

"Can we talk to them?" Gwellyn asked Mitxeleta. "Can we ask them questions?"

"They have no language," she answered. "They have song."

"Then how—" Gwellyn began.

"Could you sing to them that we intend them no harm?" Jakob interrupted.

"They already know that," Mitxeleta replied. "If we were their enemy, I would not have approached them with song."

"A dangerous proposition," Gwellyn said. "What would prevent their enemies from learning their greeting song, as you have?"

"Their enemies never bother with that—they just kill them."

"Could you ask them to sing the song they have to describe people like us—people who look like us but are not their enemies?" Gwellyn smiled at the singers. Their eyes seemed to smile at him, but not their lips. But their eyes seemed to smile continuously. . . .

Mitxeleta sang a wordless song that sounded indistinguishable from the greeting, at least to Gwellyn. It sounded one-third flute, one-third bird, one-third human voice. Then he realized there would be no difference between flute and voice in this conversation—her voice *was* the flute.

As were the voices of the singers. They were the many flutes. They responded with deep fluid tones that began in unison but branched in and out of harmony, sometimes so quickly that it sounded to Gwellyn like three-way harmony, as tones lingered over others, even though only two voices were singing. . . .

Or perhaps that fleeting third line was coming from Mitxeleta, who occasionally made a low musical note in the bottom of her throat. Or perhaps from Jakob, who, Gwellyn realized, was humming an harmonic line of some sort, too, reminding Gwellyn of a Jewish prayer session he had once attended on some Jewish holiday years ago in the Tarim Basin with his father and his brother, Allyn. Gwellyn had joined in the singing prayers then . . . and realized he was singing with the singers now, too. . . .

And each time a chord was achieved, for a trembling instant or longer, it called forth some meaning, tapped on some nerve or well of understanding, already deep in Gwellyn's mind. He remembered Plato's Meno Paradox—everyone is already born with some knowledge, for how else would we know knowledge when we encountered it?—but soon the knowledge evoked by the chords was the only thing in his head. . . .

The singing-knowing continued, in part the musical equivalent of the restless light Gwellyn had noticed darting among the leaves, similar to the flickering light in the cave . . . and also the same, every tiny once in a while, as the music he had heard on the singing pottery back in Barbaricon. But there were no images here, no lines in clay that a comb in a sure hand could coax back into life. This was life itself. . . .

It seemed to go on for hours, days, but it could not have, for it was not yet dark when it ended, and Gwellyn was sure it had been late in the day already when they first had entered this clearing.

And then it was over.

And Gwellyn knew many things.

He knew that he and Jakob, not only Mitxeleta, were somehow connected to these singers, for how else could they have all been part of the same song, and how else could this song have communicated any meaning to them?

"I harmonize with birds sometimes," Jakob said, whispering softly for once in his life. "But I never learned so much from that."

Gwellyn nodded—exhausted, satiated . . . yet troubled.

For he also knew other things now, from the singing.

He knew that the harmony between the singers and human beings like Jakob and Mitxeleta and Gwellyn was only natural, because the singers were to them as pulsating caterpillars were to butterflies. Or maybe Gwellyn was the caterpillar and the singers the butterflies—he wasn't sure. But he also knew—felt, more than knew, for this was only hinted at in undertones, in the merest sketches of minor chords not fully formed—that some of the butterflies, or maybe the caterpillars, were poisonous, bent on destruction. And he also knew that the singers—and Gwellyn and Jakob and Mitxeleta, too—were losing in this . . .

"Could you ask them to sing of the conflict?" Gwellyn asked Mitxeleta.

"No, not today," she said. "None of us could survive a song like that again on such a long day. Maybe tomorrow."

GWELLYN AWOKE EARLY the next morning and saw the problem immediately: whereas Jakob was snoring a few feet away, Mitxeleta and the singers were gone.

Gwellyn roused Jakob. They walked out of the clearing, through the shrubbery, and looked upward on the narrow path, beyond the place they had stopped at yesterday. Not a footprint, not a broken twig, not a thing that could be attributed to a human being treading could be seen.

"If they went this way, they flew," Gwellyn said.

He turned to the path below, the one they had walked upon the preceding afternoon. He stretched out on his belly and examined the ground. Gwellyn was good at this. He got to his feet, cursing. "Nothing I can see here that wasn't made by two men and a woman—meaning, you, me, and Mitxeleta—yesterday. I can't be as sure of that as I am that no one travelled the upward path, but I'm pretty sure."

"They must be in the cave, then," Jakob said.

"My thought as well," Gwellyn agreed.

"Mitxeleta said they didn't want us going into the cave," Jakob said. "Suppose they just went into the cave to fetch us something for breakfast—no point in infuriating them by going in after them."

"OK," Gwellyn replied. "Let's go back to the cave and see if they bring us breakfast."

Eventually they ate the last of the ibex and some of the tubers in Jakob's sack, supplemented by the sweet black berries they found on several of the shrubs. But their disposition was anything but sweet.

"Are you satisfied that they're not bringing us breakfast now?" Gwellyn jibed.

"Yes."

"Should we see if we can find them in the cave now?" Gwellyn continued.

"I suppose so," Jakob said, with no enthusiasm.

Gwellyn thrust his head in the cave. "Mitxeleta!" he called out. "Mitxeleta!" he called out several more times, ever more loudly.

He received no reply, not even an echo in return.

They entered the cave and immediately saw that they had another problem—which was that they couldn't see more than a foot or two ahead.

"Did you notice any starfly lamps at the mouth of the cave?" Jakob whispered, still softly.

"No need for you to whisper," Gwellyn said. "There doesn't seem to be anyone here to hear us. And no, I didn't see any lamps."

"I didn't think so," Jakob said.

They pawed their way around the wall of the cave—looking for an opening to another cave or perhaps a picture or carving on the wall, anything—but did not get very far. Jakob cried out as he gashed his finger on some sharpness on the wall.

"Are you hurt?" Gwellyn asked.

"It's just a cut," Jakob replied.

"This is useless, not being able to see what we're doing," Gwellyn said. "Let's at least wait a bit, until our eyes adjust to the darkness."

Gradually, the walls and the dimensions of the cave resolved into a bit more clarity. There were no pictures on the walls near them, and the cave looked enormous—so big that the middle was jet-black, more than an hour after their eyes had made the most of whatever little light had leaked in as far as they had progressed.

"Let's go back outside and consider our choices," Gwellyn said.

They blinked in the admonishing sunlight.

"It must have rained while we were inside." Gwellyn knelt on the ground and ran his hand over wet grass. "It's too damp to make a torch out of anything we could find here. I was thinking we might make one and see a little more in the cave."

They realized they had no choices other than walking back down the hill, retrieving the horses, and riding back to the Vascone village. They began walking.

"We have learned a lot from the singers," Jakob said. "We should communicate that to the others."

"Last night was just a prelude," Gwellyn said. "I learned next to nothing—I want more."

"You're just angry now," Jakob said. "I saw your face last night—I saw what you felt. I felt it, too. We learned a lot already."

"Is that so? And what, exactly, did we learn?"

"We learned that the singers are real, are alive, and are aptly named," Jakob said.

"How can we know for sure that they were singers? How can we know for sure we were not dreaming?" Gwellyn persisted.

"Don't start that solipsistic Greek insanity again," Jakob replied. "You've gone over and over this with Paschos. How can we know anything, everything, is not a dream? How can we know this very conversation is not a dream? The answer is: we cannot. We have to start with faith in something—so it might as well be faith that the world is real. It cannot be proven logically—because that very proof could still be part of the dream; that's why it's faith."

"It cannot be proven as an absolute fact, but the more times we see it, the more confidence we can have that it's real," Gwellyn said. "That's why I need to talk—sing—again with the singers."

"If you see a million white clouds, should that give you any more confidence that the next cloud you see will be white? Maybe there's a gray or black one lurking just over the next treetop."

"You're giving me a headache with your clouds," Gwellyn replied.

"Good, let's stop talking about this, then," Jakob said.

They trudged on.

"I admit that we now know the singers are real," Gwellyn said a few minutes later. "I believe what happened yesterday was not a dream. But who else will believe us? Will Paschos and Ibrim? Why should they?"

"What would you have done? Taken the singers back as evidence they exist? Perhaps that is why they left."

Gwellyn shook his head. "We need to know more about that conflict. I need to know why my father ordered me to burn their bones! That's why I started this journey in the first place!"

"We know why your father so ordered you," Jakob replied. "It has to do with an illness that comes from the singers."

"That's no more than we knew before yesterday," Gwellyn retorted. "We have seen bits and pieces of that for years now."

"No," Jakob said. "I learned something about it in the singing yesterday—it struck something in me, some kind of memory."

Gwellyn looked at him. "I'm not sure anymore what I learned. I thought I understood some things yesterday. . . ."

Jakob closed his eyes. "Perhaps it has to do with my people—the Jewish people. In the series of events that led to the Passover—when my people were slaves in Aegypt—the Lord our God Almighty, *Adonai*, struck out at our oppressors and slew their first born. But His angels passed over all the homes with Jewish first-born sons, because our doors were marked with blood—with the blood of the Paschal Lamb. That's the story that has come down to us. But my father always believed—and I agreed with him—in a different interpretation. He thought our ancestors, fighting for their freedom from the Pharaohs, unleashed a fearsome plague upon them—a plague to which my people, the Jews, were immune."

"A plague that only took firstborn males? What kind of plague could that be?"

"Well, I didn't say there were no problems with my father's interpretation," Jakob said. "But perhaps there was a time when illnesses were more specifically attuned than they are today—when they killed not just people, but only certain kinds of people. Even today, we know of illnesses that fell just children. But I think my father was on the right track, anyway. And I saw something about a plague, an illness, in the singing yesterday."

"Then how come I did not see that?"

"Perhaps because what the singing conveys to you is based on what is already in your mind," Jakob replied. "Or perhaps you did see—perhaps the chords did evoke that in your mind—but for some reason you no longer remember."

GWELLYN COULD SEE that Jakob had been right about the trip downward being more painful for him than the climb up. He saw the strain growing almost hourly in the older man's face.

"Maybe we should have a waited a little longer," Gwellyn said, "in case the singers returned."

"Not on my account," Jakob replied. "I'm just as happy to get this march over with—waiting a few more days would have helped me in no way, and we have no reason to think the singers will return."

Gwellyn insisted that they stop and rest often anyway. In one spot, they flushed out a few plump voles to complement the tubers. The ibex meat was gone. "My grandmother would have vomited to see me eating this stuff, but the Scriptures say we have to keep up our strength," Jakob said.

"You're becoming more religious by the minute, Jakob. You never used to care about following your Kashruth laws."

"It's the singing . . . ," Jakob replied. "I still hear some of it."

They finally reached the place where they had dismounted on their journey upward.

"Well, I see no sign of the horses," Gwellyn said after a brief foray. "No surprise."

Jakob had dropped his body down next to a tree. His back and neck were against its bark. His face looked tired, so tired, and grateful for the tree's support.

"How will we be able to recall them, without Mitxeleta?" Gwellyn asked softly.

Jakob just sighed.

"Surely she knew that we on our own might not be able to find the horses—she knew that when she disappeared with the singers," Gwellyn said.

"Perhaps she knew that there were more important things to attend to; perhaps she knew we would be provided for otherwise," Jakob replied.

"You won't be able to make the distance down by foot," Gwellyn said, with tears suddenly welling up into his voice. "It's far too long to walk."

"I know," Jakob said.

"I can't just leave you here," Gwellyn said. "The tubers will be gone in a few days—it will take me far longer than that to return with horses from the village."

"I can dig up more tubers."

Gwellyn looked at his best friend, his father in many ways now, too, and was unable to speak.

"We have only two choices," Jakob said, marshaling his bit of strength. "If I go with you down the hill, we have the same lack-of-food problem, and we have no certainty when our paths will intersect with anyone else's—we came across no one on our journey up here. If I stay here, I can rest, rekindle some of my energy, and look for food here, in a limited area. There are streams all over, and the dew is thick in the morning, so water will be in good supply for me. And, of course, you'll be able to move far more quickly on foot without me."

"There's no harm in our waiting here at least a few days," Gwellyn said. "Perhaps Mitxeleta will come down after us, perhaps those horses will sense our presence and return. At the very least, I can hunt around here and provide some supplies of food for you."

OF THE THREE possibilities, only the last came to pass—Gwellyn was successful in his hunting, and two ibex were cooked. Jakob insisted that Gwellyn take a least a quarter of the meat along with him. "If you don't survive the trip back, then I have no chance up here, either, so it's in my selfish interest that you take some of the meat, please," Jakob said. And then he was sorry that he had, for Gwellyn again vowed he would never leave.

But four days and an additional ibex later, Gwellyn did, for Jakob's logic was inexorable.

Gwellyn walked down the path, sick to his stomach with sadness—sick of logic, sick of the singers, sick of this world.

He walked and walked. Sometimes he remembered to stop and eat and hunt; sometimes he did not. The air was warm and moist, but the nights were cold, and he found himself shivering even during the day. . . .

His feet felt so heavy, he could hardly command them to move. But the very earth seemed on his side, and he staggered downward and downward, and his legs seemed to work of their own accord. . . .

Somewhere along the way he began feeling hot, too hot, yet he was shivering more, too. Sweat soaked his clothes. He dreamed of illness, plague, when he slept. Paschos spoke of plague in Constantinople. He dreamed of it when he was awake, too. . . . He was coughing. . . .

He heard the singing again and began to understand more. He understood that the singers had but one song—that all of their songs were the same, that each piece of the song contained all the other songs, as an egg contains all the other chickens and eggs and chickens to be born from it over the aeons. . . .

So he had heard their full song, their only song, that night—there were no other songs to sing. That's what Mitxeleta had been trying to tell him. Maybe that's why the singers had left. . . .

And he saw his father smiling, or maybe it was Jakob. And he saw Daralyn and Lilee and that woman with the fiery eyes he had slept with in this strange land, and he yearned to be with all of them, all at once, once again. . . .

And he thought again about chickens and eggs and wondered if he had produced any children with any of the women he had loved or made love to. . . . He thought he had. . . . He hoped he had. . . . Because he wanted at least something of his to survive. . . .

And he thought again about the plague. That was the key—that's what the singers and Jakob and his father and everyone had been trying to tell him. It somehow infected not living beings, but life itself, and changed it. Maybe it *was* life now—was that what the singers were trying to say? Life to whom? To the singers? No, they didn't have much life now—who knew how many of them were even still alive? . . . .

Who knows how much longer I'll *be alive?* Gwellyn thought, in his fever and coughing and shivering. . . .

And one morning, when he was sure he was either dying or already dead, he awoke. . . . drooling on a fragrant moss beneath a tree. . . .

And he dreamed he was Alexander, dying in his prime of the same illness. . . . after he'd conquered the world, but before he'd had the chance to tell the world what he'd really learned. "Don't be angry with me," he pleaded with his mentor, Aristotle, the student of Plato, the student of Socrates, who hated writing. . . . And Socrates said to his great-grandstudent, Alexander/Gwellyn, "The books in the great city that bears your name will burn. . . ." And Gwellyn replied, "I cannot hear you. You are no longer alive. I could read words by you, if only you had written them."

And he dreamed that Paschos approached him on a fine black horse. And he dreamed that Paschos fed him butterflies, whose wings spelled words, and Paschos wrapped his shivering body in Phoenician silk. . . .

And eventually he realized that he had not been dreaming about Paschos. . . .

"THE FIRES HAVE burned out," Paschos told him, days later, maybe weeks. "None of the forests were destroyed, just the caves. The Vascones say, 'The lamps knew when their work was complete. No more, no less.' Ibrim has gone, too."

Gwellyn propped himself up on his elbows, the first morning he had strength enough to do that since his return. "We must set out for Jakob," he said.

"We'll talk about that later," Paschos replied.

"We'll talk about that now." Gwellyn managed to sit up, shaking.

Paschos looked away. "I sent men back up there, as soon as we returned to this village. They found nothing."

"Then we'll go and look again! How far up the path did they go?"

"To the place that a horse can go no farther," Paschos replied. "Then they continued on foot to the cave of the singers."

"How could you know where that is?" Gwellyn asked. "Only Mitxeleta—" And then he remembered something—something that he had thought of in his dreams or perhaps had realized during the singing. "Euskaldunak, Vascones—Euska, Vasco, Paschos—you have some deeper connection to these people, don't you?"

Paschos nodded slowly. "Vascones have been part of my family since Justinian the First—his armies reclaimed part of the southern part of this continent, by the Gates of Hercules, for the Empire, for a while. There was much mixture of people then—there still is in Constantinople."

"How much of this did you know when you first joined our party?" Gwellyn asked, and thought again of Jakob, and vowed again to go look for him.

"Not much, not much at all," Paschos replied. "I had an interest in the singers—lots of philosophers do, quietly, for such interests do not help their professional reputations. Jakob knew of it, though, and likely that is why he invited me to come along. But I knew nothing of a Vascones connection—I learned that only after we arrived here. My prior knowledge of the language helped. . . . I knew *Mitxeleta* meant 'butterfly.' I talked to people who knew her. Eventually I pieced enough together to head out in the right direction. . . ."

They set out again five days later, at Gwellyn's unbending insistence, to look for Jakob. They brought along extra men and extra horses. Gwellyn regretted Ibrim was not among them. He had left weeks earlier for points south.

They found nothing. Just the remains of small cooking fires in the place from which the horses could no longer proceed—Jakob's last fires, Gwellyn thought, and cried within—and nothing at all outside the cave that Paschos and Gwellyn reached again on foot.

They entered the cave and looked around. With Mitxeleta gone, there had been no one left in the village able—or willing, Paschos said he couldn't tell—to prepare the living lamps. So they made do with ugly lamps that burned fat and gave off a pungent smell. It didn't matter. There were no pictures on the walls or the ceiling anywhere in the cavern. "The moving pictures were in the cave within the cave within the cave within the cave," Gwellyn said, "when we saw them below."

Paschos nodded, but they could find no entrances to other caves within this huge hollow. At one point, in a far corner, there might have once been a portal to something else, but it looked like it had been covered long ago with boulders that no ten men, let alone two, could move.

"Can you tell if these were placed here in olden times or old moldy rocks were placed here recently?" Gwellyn asked.

"Impossible to know with certainty," Paschos said. "But

those fungi between the boulders look like they have been growing here a very long time."

"And how can we know that we're not looking at some sort of very quick-growing fungus?"

Paschos smiled in the light of the acrid fat lamp. "I see you've progressed far in the path of the creative Aristotelian zoologist. You're right—there is no way of knowing absolutely that a rapidly growing fungus is not at work here. But even if it was, we still have the problem of how to move these immense rocks. I doubt, knowing the superstition of the villagers below, that we could find anything close to the necessary number of men to accompany us this far."

Gwellyn had to agree—the fact that the villagers who had accompanied them on the horse trail had refused to go beyond where the horses could not continue had not been lost on him.

"And in all likelihood, these rocks have indeed been here many years," Paschos made the decisive argument. "Most of the time, the first, obvious interpretation of evidence is more or less the correct one—not everything in life is underhanded."

They proceeded back downward.

"If Jakob died somewhere here, then we should be able to find his body," Gwellyn said. "It's not right that he should just be left lying in the woods someplace."

"If he died, his soul will not be left lying there," Paschos replied softly. "But perhaps he did not die—perhaps some people from farther up the mountain came down to the place with the horses and found Jakob and he went back up the mountain with them. I know there are no footprints beyond, but if you want to start thinking about fast-growing fungus, you can also think about fast-growing grass, or grass and soil somehow resilient to lasting footprints. . . . The possibilities are almost endless. . . . We are free to speculate on the side of hope. . . ."

It's a nice speculation; I wish I could believe it, Gwellyn thought.

They rejoined the men and the horses below—Paschos had been right that they could be relied upon. . . .

"Tell me again why Ibrim left?" Gwellyn asked as they rode back into the village. He had been too concerned about Jakob to focus much on Ibrim, until now.

"He did his job here," Paschos replied. "We who love knowledge will always owe a debt to him—he took a human life on behalf of knowledge, the life of one of his brethren, a life that would have brought much grief to this area as well as robbed the future of some of its most precious wisdom. Most of us would never have had the courage to do that—I don't think I have. True, his murder of Aziz set the Vascones to burning the wondrous caves right around here. But there must be others. This village is just one among many Vascone settlements here. And I cannot believe that the caves, if they come from a time in which the singers were many, or close after, are limited just to this area—there must be others, to the north, to the south. . . ."

"But how would we know where to find them?"

"You and I might never know," Paschos said. "But at least Ibrim saved *those* caves, wherever they might be, for the future—he represents the compassionate, wise side of Islam. He felt it was wise to go back to his people now, to urge them not to proceed much farther along this coast. He was very moved by that night in the cave. . . ."

"Will Islam conquer Byzantium now?" Gwellyn asked.

"Perhaps, someday," Paschos replied. "But in the long run, it will not matter—both traditions will continue. The world has gone beyond one culture totally destroying another, I think."

"Not the way it was for the singers, though. . . ."

"I envy your day with the singers and Jakob and Mitxeleta," Paschos said. "I hope you can tell me everything you know about it."

"I will," Gwellyn said. "I will try. But there is much I learned that cannot be communicated with words—much that I am only realizing I now know as I live each minute. There are important lessons there—crucial lessons, life-and-death lessons, for all human beings. Once I thought I would write those down and leave those for my people. Now I'm not sure I know how—"

"Tell me anyway," Paschos said.

GWELLYN MADE HIS way south five months later, to board a ship that would return him to the southern continent.

"He was always on the edge of being a lost soul," Paschos said to the one of the villagers he had befriended and confided in. "Ibrim comes from a great new tradition, I come from a great old tradition, Jakob came from a great ancient tradition—but Gwellyn came from almost no tradition at all, none that we know of. I hope he finds some peace."

"Where is he going?" the villager asked.

"He is trying to return to an island," Paschos said, "where the monkeys are nearly human and the winds are soft and the nights as sheer as silk in the moonlight. . . ."

He is returning to his Lilee, Paschos thought, *and I hope he makes it.*

Paschos did not tell Gwellyn the one thing that might have kept him near the land of the Vascones. It was not about Jakob, for Paschos knew as much or as little about Jakob's whereabouts now, if he was alive, as did Gwellyn.

What Paschos did not tell Gwellyn was that he had fathered a child with the woman he spent that one night with shortly after his arrival in Cantabria.

Paschos did not tell Gwellyn because he understood that although Gwellyn had made love to that woman, he did not love her. Paschos had seen Gwellyn's face when he looked at Lilee, and although Paschos did not partake of that species of love himself, he recognized it clearly enough when it was staring him in the faces of others. Gwellyn had travelled so far, so long, consuming most of his young adulthood in his quest for the singers, that he deserved this chance for happiness. The Epicureans were right—happiness was good in its own right.

Paschos himself would see to the child—he had always

yearned to be a father, even if he had no taste for the way in which fathers usually came to be. . . .

He would take care of Gwellyn's child. He had spoken at length to the woman. He would marry her; he might even do his husbandly duty from time to time. He would live his life here and help her raise her child in the Hebrew religion that she professed. In that way, he would also repay the debt he owed to Jakob, for inviting him to join in this expedition in the first place. . . .

And as for the singers, well, they could rest in peace.

At least, that's what Paschos of Constantinople, the Aristotelian zoologist, hoped. . . .

PART THREE

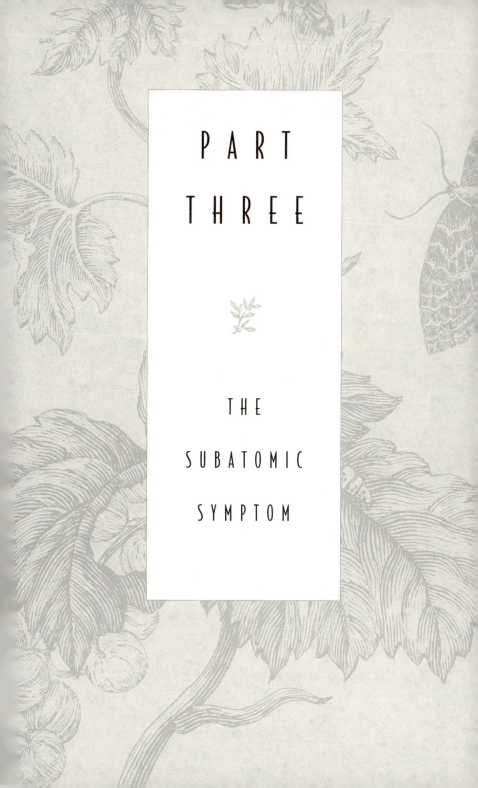

THE

SUBATOMIC

SYMPTOM

SEVEN

"Take a look at this, Phil."

Dave Spencer, the medical examiner I usually worked with, had called me downtown to his examining room.

"What, they have a sale at the Museum of Natural History and you picked this one up for the office?" The corpse looked like it had come out of one of those dioramas of Neanderthals I had been seeing at the museum since I was a kid.

Dave chuckled. "The guy died—maximum—not more than forty-eight hours ago. But the bone structure assessments that just came back confirm what he looks like; those definitely are Neanderthal specifications."

I looked more closely at the remains. Still had some charred shreds of unidentifiable clothing. The last Neanderthal I'd seen in the flesh, as it were, was on some cable special on the Learning Channel a few months ago. There wasn't much of a face left on this one, but otherwise he could have been the cable guy's brother for all I could tell.

"He seems pretty far gone for someone alive two days ago. You sure he wasn't frozen somewhere before the last Ice Age, thawed out in the last two days, and that's thrown off your estimate?"

"Well, take a look at this," Dave said. "It's not the height of fashion, but I doubt it goes back before the last Ice Age." He pulled out a tray from a side cabinet. On it was . . . a blue silk hankie, with hues ranging from turquoise to violet. I examined it as best I could without touching.

"Looks like something my aunt once gave me for graduation," I said. "A Sears special."

"Exactly," Dave replied.

"And what? You find this on the guy?"

Dave nodded.

"Well," I said. "Someone must have put it on the fossil—as a joke."

"Yeah," Dave said. "Except he's not in any way fossilized. Apparently mummified—like those bog people they keep digging up—but not fossilized. And that wouldn't explain why his general description—height, bone structure—matches that of an NYU janitor who disappeared last week."

"What, the janitor was a Neanderthal?"

Dave shrugged. "They say he looked like one."

"How old was he?" I asked.

"In his sixties, though no one knows for sure," Dave said. "He was a refugee from someplace or other in Central Europe. Usually cleaned up in the basement of the library, reading everything he could get his hands on when he wasn't working. Highly intelligent, according to the librarians. Been around for years."

I looked carefully again at the corpse. "So you're thinking one of our modern Cro-Magnon species murdered this bibliophile with Neanderthal genes?"

Dave shook his head. "We haven't gotten the DNA analyses back. And there are no really reliable DNA profiles yet for Neanderthals. But yeah, maybe, about the murder angle. Though so far it looks like he just died of old age—natural causes."

"Seems I've heard that refrain before."

"Tell me about it," Dave agreed. "And then we also have the problem of the carbon dating."

I looked back up at the ME.

"First test I ordered when I was called in on this," he said.

"And?"

"And the gentleman before you is about thirty thousand

years old," Dave replied, "give or take the usual slim range for error."

I whistled. "Jeez. I've pulled an all-nighter, too, at the library. But thirty thousand years is definitely pushing it."

RUTH DELANY WAS the New York University librarian I got to interview. She eyed my papers, my face, my photo ID, my face. "You're NYPD Forensics, Dr. D'Amato?"

I nodded.

"My uncle was on the job for years," she said. "Never made it beyond beat cop. Lots of prejudice against African-Americans on the force back then."

"True." I sighed. "But you know, beat cop isn't the worst—at least you get out in the world. Certainly the best part of the job, as far as I'm concerned."

She looked at my face again. "And you've been out there on television, too. Haven't I seen you on that cable show?"

"Yep," I said. "Every last Sunday of the month, 10:30–11 on—"

"That's it." She appeared to relax a little. "What can I tell you about Stefan Antonescu?"

"Well, how about telling me everything you know—for starters," I replied.

"OK." She smiled, then mused, "I'll be working here twelve years this November, and Stefan—Mr. Antonescu—was here when I started. Harmless sort, did a good job, really loved his work—or at least loved being in a library. I never saw him on a break without a book or magazine in his hands."

"A vanishing breed," I said. "Most people who haunt libraries these days do it through the Internet."

"Not Stefan," Delany said. "He was strictly a book and magazine man. Said he liked the feel of paper in his hands. I think I feel that way, too, sometimes."

"Don't we all," I said. "Was Mr. Antonescu some kind of student—you know, working part-time, taking a course every semester or two?" A dozen or more years, though, was a long time even for an older part-time student to be working his way through college. On the other hand, I could tell already that time frames were going to be oddly attenuated in this case—though on yet a third hand, it wasn't even really a case yet, just some corpse appearing and a similar guy disappearing in the same place, both with Neanderthal characteristics, and the corpse dating back thirty thousand years. Which smelled like hoax, or something pretty damned bizarre, even if this wasn't a case. I rubbed my hands together. More than two hands and strange coincidences seemed to be my specialty. . . .

"Well, Stefan wasn't really a student," Delany said. "He may have sat in on a course somewhere along the line, but the library was his only real passion. I think he regarded this place as his home. He'd come here to read even on days he was off work."

"Really. . . . Is that common?"

"You'd be surprised," Delany said. "Lots of lonely people in this world, Doctor. If one or two of them find some comfort in centering their lives around our books, our magazines, well"— she shrugged—"it's OK with us. I think just about every library has people like that. Sometimes they're maintenance staff; sometimes they just hang out."

"Are there any other janitors around here like Stefan Antonescu?" I asked.

"No, Stefan is the only one on the staff with that kind of love for reading. Everyone was always so shocked at first to find that out about him. You know, I think it was those features—those heavy set features. People always assume that people who look like that are, you know . . ."

"Stupid?"

"Well, yes," Delany said. "It's so unfair to judge people's intelligence by their looks."

"Yeah," I agreed. "Especially people who look like Neanderthals. I knew a guy in college who looked like that—everyone thought he was on the wrestling team, but his love was numbers.

He was a whiz in my calculus class. The truth is we don't even how intelligent the Neanderthals themselves actually were. Maybe they were *more* intelligent than our ancestors—after all, their cranial capacity was larger."

"Stefan was a *human being*," Delany said, "just like you and me. And anyway, I thought Neanderthals *were* our ancestors."

"Well, it's more complicated than that. But getting back to Stefan—anything special he liked to read?"

She nodded. "Silk. That was his thing."

"Really. As in—what?—satin sheets, expensive ties, handkerchiefs . . ."

"As in everything," she said. "His consuming interest was silk. Just last month I noticed him reading some physical anthropology tome about silk culture in China in prehistoric times. It was outside my area of interest, frankly."

"You wouldn't know how prehistoric?" I asked. For some reason, the number 30,000 popped into my head.

Delany considered. "No, I didn't pay that much attention, and the book came right off the open shelves upstairs, so we have no record of which book it was." She shook her head, frowned. "You folks sure it was him—that the body was Stefan's? He was such a nice man, so . . . gentle."

"We don't have much on medical file for Mr. Antonescu, so we can't be 100 percent sure. But unofficially, yeah, it's certainly a possibility we're looking at." The truth was that we had *nothing* on file for Stefan Antonescu—and NYU's employment records were no help. The man had existed, apparently—that was a fact. But other than his height, weight, hair, and eye color—the contents of the photo ID the university kept in their records office— nothing was on file about him. Amazing how often employment records were like that, when you dug below the surface.

Delany of course had no idea about the DNA dating of the corpse—she'd have politely escorted me out of her office and called Bellevue if I'd told her it was thirty millennia old and I was even remotely considering the possibility that it could be Antonescu. It had been found in a corner of the men's room early in the morning by some temp on the maintenance staff, one Hassan Saleen, who barely spoke a word of English but knew enough to call 911. Our people had gotten the body out of the library before anyone else had seen it. And Hassan, however much he might have been shaken by finding a dead caveman in the corner, simply hadn't the language to talk about it.

"One other thing." I showed her a picture of the blue hankie. "Does that look familiar?"

"Yes." Her eyes dilated. "Stefan always wears one like that in his pocket. I used to kid him about it: 'You're a janitor, but your hankies are better than most professors'.' And he's smile and say, 'Today's janitor is tomorrow's archaeologist—we both make our living with garbage.' "

I smiled. "Sounds like he had a head on his shoulders. Anything more you can tell me about him? Names of professors, students, who might have known him?"

She passed a piece of paper over to me. "I thought you might want that, so I put this together for you. Eight names on this list— five students, three profs. But they probably know even less about Stefan Antonescu than I do," she said.

I thanked her, gave her my obligatory card and reminder to call if she thought of anything else, and left.

It was pushing past four-thirty, and Jenna would be back from England already from her bi-yearly conference at the London School of Economics, so I called in to the office that I'd be heading straight home. So far the only thing that seemed to connect in this case was that even before Antonescu died—if by some insane set of circumstances he was indeed the prehistoric corpse— he didn't seem to have much of a life. He seemed a man not only out of time but out of place.

The most likely explanation was that they were probably two different people after all, either with no connection or, who knows, maybe Antonescu had been involved in some sort of relic-smuggling operation that had gone sour and had dropped his handkerchief on one of the mummies. Lots of stuff going on like that in the post-Communist world. And powder from ground-up mummies had been used for thousands of years to make aphrodisiacs, some odd part of my brain remembered. But so far no prehistoric graves from anywhere had been reported robbed; no museums had reported any specimens missing. . . . And Dave's preliminary findings said that the corpse had been alive just a few days ago. . . . Well, we all needed to look into this more carefully. . . .

Jenna's bags were right inside the door. "Honey?" I called out softly, and walked into the bedroom. She was sleeping. She needed the rest—it was nearly eleven already, British time. I started walking out quietly—

"Hey, you. Don't I get a welcome-home kiss?"

I turned around and smiled. Jenna was propped up on one arm. I walked quickly back to the bed, knelt down, and gave her a long, slow kiss. . . .

"Mmmmm . . . ," she said. "So how was your day today?"

"Good." I brushed her lips with my finger. "A wild case cropped up yesterday; I'll tell you about it over dinner—if you're hungry."

"I'm ravenous. I've been yearning for calamari all day."

"San Martino's?"

"Perfect," Jenna said, and slid out of bed. All she had on were light blue panties. I watched her walk out of the room and wondered whether we should be ruled by our stomachs or . . .

"I'm just gonna jump in the shower for a second," she said.

The curtains swished closed and water began pouring.

I sat down in my favorite plump chair and picked up a newspaper—yesterday's *Times,* of London.

I stopped at the small headline on page 5: "Neanderthal Mummy Pops Up at LSE."

WHY WAS I not surprised that the mummy found under a table three evenings ago in the cafeteria of the London School of Economics apparently looked the same as mine? You get a sixth sense in this business—my "sick" sense.

I tracked down Mallory at Scotland Yard by phone early the next morning.

"Hmmm . . . ," Mallory said, when I'd explained the reason for my call. His full name was Michael G. B. Mallory, and he always sounded like a mixture of Michael Caine, in his Harry Palmer role, and Michael Rennie, in that 1950s science fiction movie.

"So," I prodded. "Anything more you can tell me about your Neanderthal? Could he possibly have the same, ah, possible vintage as mine?"

Long pause.

"Michael?"

"Yes." Mallory cleared his throat and coughed. "I'd imagine he very well could."

"Is that British for 'he does'?"

"Philip." Mallory cleared his throat again. "I was instructed to keep this under wraps. It's sheer damned coincidence that some reporter at the *Times* picked it up and your friend Jenna brought home that paper."

"And your people are conducting an investigation into this? And that's why you can't talk about it?"

"Right," Mallory replied.

"And you think I'm just going to take that for an answer and forget we ever had this conversation?" I asked. "We've known each other for how long now—ten years on and off? You ever know me just to take no for an answer?"

Mallory sighed. "Max Soros was a porter at the LSE. Worked there for the past twenty-nine years. Prior to that he worked in the kitchen at Wright's—"

"The hole-in-the-wall coffee shop right outside the LSE?"

"Right," Mallory said. "It's neither a hole-in-the-wall nor a coffee shop—it's a restaurant—but Max worked there. For many years, apparently. And prior to that, we think he was a fixture at the British Museum. We have a description of a Max Soros reading, right near the desk used by Karl Marx, in 1907—"

"Just a second. Exactly how old was this character?"

"As you said. Our carbon dating fixed the corpse at about thirty thousand years."

"No," I said. "I meant how far back have you traced Max as a . . . living person?"

"At this point, back to the nineteenth century," Mallory replied.

"Jeez," I said.

"Precisely," Mallory replied.

"You have records for no other person named Max Soros? Sounds like a reasonably common Central European name."

"Hungarian," Mallory said. "The name's Hungarian. The only other Max Soros that Inland Revenue has on file is thirty-two and he's gone visiting relations in Budapest right now. That's far too young to be our missing person, let alone the mummy."

"Jeez," I repeated, "nineteenth-century. . . . Well, I can certainly see why you'd want to keep the public out of this—your guy's even stranger than mine."

"I'm glad you understand," Mallory said. "And there's one thing more."

"Yes?"

"Max Soros isn't the only one. Another heavy-browed gent turned up dead in Toronto last week. So your man in New York City makes the third."

"Goddamn glut of Neanderthal mummies," I muttered.

"Quite," Mallory agreed.

"And all seem naturally mummified—like the people in the peat—rather than treated with chemicals like the ancient Egyptians?"

"Right," Mallory again agreed.

"And you weren't going to tell me about this? Knowing that I had information about a third incidence?"

Mallory's voice lightened. "I never said I wouldn't tell you. I was merely explaining to you why someone in my position would be reticent to blurt out this story. You jumped to conclusions. That's a key difference between you Yanks and us."

"Quite," I said. "So now that we've got that out of the way, I assume you'll tell me everything you know about your corpse and the guy in Toronto, in return for my continued full cooperation in the case of Stefan Antonescu."

I BIT INTO an *ebi* sushi and savored the flavor. Sweeter than candy, cold rush of protein . . . I'd once been strictly a Neapolitano man, thought if I'd wanted raw fish and seaweed I could stretch out with my mouth open on a beach somewhere, but now I ate sushi, sashimi—*chirashi* was my favorite—every chance I got.

"Assuming the corpses and the missing aren't different sets of people, only two possible kinds of explanations I can think of," I said to Jenna, who was working on a crisp piece of *akagai*—red clam, raw. "One, these guys time-traveled from thirty thousand years ago to our present or to the past hundred or so years. Two, they somehow managed to actually stay alive for thirty thousand years. I suppose the second has the obvious explanation of why they would turn up dead—I mean, jeez, talk about dying of old age . . ."

Jenna's green eyes smiled. I still found them enchanting. I especially liked seeing her like this, at this table, our table, at the Taste of Tokyo in the Village, where we'd first munched sushi and gotten to know each other more than three years ago. "Are we sure they're real—you know, not just some clever concoction of old and new bones, like a Piltdown scam?" Jenna asked.

"No, Dave would've spotted that right away," I replied. "He's sure the body is all one person, thirty thousand years old, died just last week. And Toronto says the same about theirs."

"And you don't go for scams as the likely explanation anyway—you like your entropy more exotic," Jenna said, smiling now with her lips as well.

I smiled back. "Scams are usually the more likely. But right, the exotic evils are more alluring . . ."

"But you don't like time travel, either," Jenna said.

I sucked in another shrimp, this one not as sweet. "Let's just say I've never seen an actual example of it—I'm not even sure I believe it's possible."

"Of course, time travel wouldn't be consistent with a thirty-thousand-year half-life decay," Jenna said. "I mean, the usual expectation is someone steps into a time machine or portal and emerges on the other side having not actually aged a minute."

"Well, the point is, there *is* no usual expectation in time travel because we have no actual cases of it," I said. "For all we know, half-life decay does take place in the time traveller, but at an instantaneous pace. Anyway, that's why I don't want to get into time travel on this thing—no point trying to solve a puzzle by bringing in an impossibly more complicated one."

"How about cryogenics? That wouldn't freeze the half-life clock, would it?"

"Hard to say," I replied. "The clock starts ticking when the organism dies and stops accumulating carbon 14—that's when the decay begins. Could be that some kind of quick flash-freezing short of death would stop the carbon intake, or maybe not."

Jenna nodded. "All right, so that leaves accidental cryogenics as still a possibility here—the gentlemen were frozen alive thirty thousand years ago, then thawed out, accidentally or not, and revived a hundred or so years ago, and now their age suddenly caught up with them. And there's also just the straight octogenarian explanation. The goal of some alchemy was immortality—the Chinese kind, not the European variety, which was just trying to make a quick buck, gold from lead."

"But as far as we know the Chinese failed," I said. "And that kind of immortality wouldn't account for the carbon 14 dating, unless the alchemy somehow also caused the isotope to decay. I don't know..." I put a dab of Japanese mustard on the tip of my tongue and applied it to the roof of my mouth. It was supposed to clear not only the palate but the mind. "The most likely explanation is someone screwed up the tests somewhere."

TESA STEWART WAS a professor of anthropology at New York University—a sixty-year-old lady, sharp as a whip, who knew more about Neanderthals than anyone else I knew on a first-name basis in this town. The fact that she had taught at NYU for two decades and might have known Stefan Antonescu or something about him had also figured in my decision to bring her into this case—the profs and students on Ruth Delany's list had been no help at all. But Tesa and Antonescu had proved to be a dead end, too. She had no idea who he was, not even a recollection of seeing him in Bobst Library.

"You don't mind walking in the mist, do you?" she asked. A light April rain had come on as we ambled around Washington Square Park.

"Not at all," I replied. "I actually love the rain—to me it's more tangible, more real, than sunshine."

"I never knew that about you, Phil," she said, and wrapped her arm around mine. "I like a man who likes the rain."

I patted her hand. "I wonder how Neanderthals liked the rain."

She smiled. "Well, seeing as how the DNA profiles in all three corpses seem pretty much in the *Homo sapiens sapiens* range—not much different from yours and mine—I guess they had as much likelihood of liking the rain as you or I or anyone else these days."

"You think that, despite what they look like, the corpses aren't Neanderthal?"

"Well, that's one reasonable conclusion from the data suite," Tesa said. "Another is that is the corpses are indeed Neanderthal, but Neanderthal DNA turns out to be the same as ours—that would be a revolutionary finding indeed. A third possibility—frustrating, but always a threat in these situations—is that the current state of our DNA analysis just isn't up to tagging whatever it is in the genes that makes a Neanderthal a Neanderthal. In any case, preliminary profiles of the nucleotides you gave me from the three corpses differ from average *Homo sapiens sapiens* DNA in a range of six to nine positions. Paabo's Neanderthal DNA differs from ours in twenty-seven positions; human populations themselves usually vary in seven positions."

I frowned. "And of course Paabo's data is itself not completely accepted."

"Exactly," Tesa said. "He took extraordinary precautions to make sure his Neanderthal DNA wasn't contaminated by ours—that's what usually messes up the data in these studies—but even so . . . His mitochondrial strand came from a bone at least thirty thousand years old, found in Germany in 1856. All kinds of time for all kinds of contamination—human and otherwise—before and after the bone was discovered."

"Interesting, though, that our corpses chime in at thirty thousand years, too." I shook my head. "Dave Spencer told me today that the carbon dating was the only thing keeping him from closing this case—and it's now been corroborated in retests in two separate labs. Without that thirty-thousand-year reading, we just have a guy who looks like a mummified Neanderthal, with genes the same as ours, dying of apparently natural causes. Lots of strange-looking people in this city—on this planet. Hell, I'm sure *I* look strange to some people."

"Well, you could let your hair grow a little longer." Tesa squeezed my shoulder. "Nice shirt, though. Silk?"

"Nah, just polyester washed so often it feels like silk."

Tesa chuckled. "I was going over the Canadian profiles this morning. They found a few moth sequences among the *Homo sapiens sapiens* DNA in their corpse."

"Moth?"

"Yes," Tesa said. "*Bombyx mori*. Its larva is the most widely raised silkworm around the world. Easy to see how the contamination could've occurred. Lab guy was making love to his wife in her satin pajamas last night, didn't wash his hands, or he helped tie his son's silk tie for assembly this morning, who knows? Like I said, contamination is the main culprit in this business. But hey,

I don't have to tell *you* that—you run into it all the time with your forensic analyses, right?"

"My guy had an interest in silk," I said.

"Stefan Antonescu?"

"Yeah—"

"Mom! Enjoying the Spring weather I see!" A woman with curly red hair, in her late twenties, joined us. She was a more vibrant version of Tesa, which was saying a lot.

"Debbie, oh God, I forgot completely about our lunch today!" Tesa exclaimed.

"It's OK," Debbie said, and smiled at both of us. "You look familiar . . . ," she said to me.

"Oh, I'm forgetting my manners, too," Tesa said. "Dr. Phil D'Amato, Forensics, NYPD, this is Debbie Tucker, my daughter. She may have seen you on your cable show, and you may have seen some of her science reporting in the *New York Times*."

"Yes, I have," I said and extended my hand. "You had a good piece on the Amish—"

My new cell phone rang in my jacket pocket. "Excuse me." I turned away and pulled out the phone.

"Phil, old man, sorry to ring you up like this on the cellular phone. Damned expensive, I know." It was Michael Mallory.

"That's OK," I said. "What's up?" A stray raindrop bounced off the phone into my mouth.

"Well, I just rang off Gerry's assistant in Toronto. Bad news, I'm afraid—Gerry died of a heart attack this afternoon. I know you don't like coincidences—"

"No, I don't," I said. Gerry Moses was my counterpart in Toronto.

"He was doing some investigating down near your neck of the woods," Mallory continued, "in Chautauqua, south of Buffalo—"

Debbie touched my arm. "How about the three of us go to lunch, after you finish on the phone, OK? Mom tells me you're working on a *fascinating* case!" She half-whispered and mouthed the words in exaggerated motions, so as not to interfere with my phone conversation. Why anyone would think that would *not* interfere I couldn't say—

"The important thing now is to try to stay on track," Mallory was saying. "Gerry's assistant is looking into this—let's see what he comes up with. He seems like a good man: H. -T. Lum—"

Debbie was still gesturing. She gave me another smile.

I was barely able to return it. I could see already that the deaths in this case were getting less prehistoric.

EIGHT

I looked at the Neanderthal who looked back at me, across seventy-five thousand years, at the Museum of Natural History. What could the brain that once inhabited that skull have been thinking when it was alive? Could it ever have imagined that, sometime in the future, some distant relation—maybe a descendant, maybe just a cousin far removed on a parallel line—would be staring at it, wondering what it was wondering?

"Phil! Sorry I'm late."

I smiled at Debbie. "No problem—I was in good company."

She took in the crowd—men, women, children. Not a single one a *Homo sapiens sapiens*. Not a single one on our side of the glass.

Debbie looked at my two bags, packed to go with me on my flight to London. "Can I help with these?"

"No," I said, and picked them up. "Let's get the taxi."

We flagged a cab on Central Park West.

"OK," she said after we'd settled in on the springy backseat and I told the driver I was going to Kennedy. "Is it OK if I record you?" she asked.

"Sure," I said.

"What can you tell me, then, in the way of background about these events? You didn't say much at lunch with Mom last week."

"Well, not much that you don't already know, I'm afraid. Corpses were found in New York, Toronto, and London. There's no apparent danger to the public—we've found no evidence of disease or foul play. But it's still a mystery to us as to how the corpses got here . . . and who they were."

"But that's always a question with ancient remains, isn't it?"

"Yes, but usually you can tell something from the surrounding environment about who the people were—if they're found buried in a copper mine in Peru, it's a good chance they were Inca, that sort of thing," I replied.

"And nothing around the corpses you found—nothing on them—can give you and your colleagues a clue as to who they were? What about their clothing?"

"Clothing was one of the first things we looked at," I said. "And it's glaringly neutral—no distinctive pollen, just shreds of fabric, possibly silk, and—"

"Some sort of ceremonial clothing?"

I shrugged. "Impossible to do more than speculate at this point. Maybe it was part of a burial ceremony—Neanderthals interred their dead."

"True," Debbie mused. "Does the silk suggest some ancient Chinese connection?"

"Possibly," I said. "Neanderthals have been found in Central Asia, not too far from China down the Silk Road. But of course we have no evidence that knowledge of silk making goes back that far, though it does go back a long way."

"OK," Debbie said. "Let's get back to the question of how the corpses got to London, New York, and Toronto. Is there any evidence they were hijacked out of a museum somewhere?"

"None as yet," I replied. "It's not the easiest thing in the world to smuggle mummies into major cities. And we've checked extensively with all the museums and universities that have any Neanderthal remains—none were reported missing."

"Perhaps they were uncovered recently, at some original sacred site?"

"Well, maybe, but then what? Some benefactor distributed them to three cities without telling anyone?"

"You have a best guess about this that I could quote you on?"

"Honestly, I don't have one," I said. "That's one of the reasons I agreed to talk to you. Perhaps one of your readers will be able to give us a push in the right direction."

"All right. Let's talk about another aspect of this. Do you see any possible connection between the death of Gerry Moses in Toronto and this case?"

I looked at Debbie. "No, not really. Not yet."

"Are you concerned that perhaps your life, and those of your colleagues, might be at risk here?"

"In my line of work you're always concerned."

Our cab went into the Midtown Tunnel. . . .

MALLORY SHUT OFF the telly in his office with a flourish via the remote. "Damn BBC. I told you they were trouble." He nursed his scotch and scowled.

"No harm done," I said, sipping my warm lager and lime. "You agreed beforehand—we have to do something to shake this case loose a little. I talk to the *New York Times;* you get interviewed for the evening news."

Mallory sighed. "What's galling is the fuzziness surrounding each of the victims—for all we know, the mummies and the missing porters are not the same people."

"Death is less certain than taxes—we both know that, despite what they say," I said.

Mallory gave me a crooked smile. "I think our best bet for getting to the bottom of all this is with H.-T. Lum, his being Chinese and all. Assuming, of course, that your silk hankie is significant."

"It doesn't carbon-date at thirty thousand years; that tells us something. But the secret of silk's been out of China for a long time, so I'm not sure how especially helpful H.-T.'ll be with that." I swallowed more lager.

"Damned strange business," Mallory said. "The whole thing's probably a bloody hoax, is what it is."

"I don't think it's a hoax," I said. "You know, we're all chronocentric—most modern civilizations are. We think, we assume, as an unexamined given, that we're the most advanced expression of humanity that's ever been on this planet."

"The reverse of how they looked at things in the Middle Ages, and in ancient times, isn't it?" Mallory said. "In those days they thought they were the degenerate phase of a golden cat's meow."

"Yeah," I replied. "And I'm not saying they were more right than we are, either. I'm saying we always misunderstand the past. Just as the future is likely to misunderstand us. What would future archaeologists make of our most advanced technologies, if they lacked the context to understand them?"

"Hell." Mallory polished off his scotch, winced a little, refilled his shot glass from the bottle on his desk. "They'd probably look at that telly over there, and not having any record of the bleeding BBC or anything like it, no videotapes or recordings of what was on it, would come to the conclusion that those screens were some sort of mirrors we all looked into in our vanity, wouldn't they? And they'd be right in a way, too, wouldn't they?"

I nodded. Mallory was one of those people who got more allegoric the more he drank. "And we likely stare with the same uncomprehending eyes at the relics of the past that are all around us. Genes are an incredibly complex information system—obviously. Who knows, maybe some greater intelligence lurks behind them—maybe they're markers of someone else's plans. . . ."

"Genes and the organic technologies they propel," Mallory said. He drank down his new glass of scotch, poured himself another, drank that down, too, looked me straight in the eye. "You mean like those Amish farmers you tangled with last year?"

"What?"

"When Gerry Moses died, we instituted an immediate investigation of the principal investigators in this case. We're very good at that, you know. It's how we won the Second World War, in

spite of our own intelligence agencies being riddled with trai-
tors.''

I started to object that American know-how had something
to do with winning, too, but decided to keep quiet and see just
what he knew about those events I'd discussed with no one but
Jenna.

"It's not as if your discoveries in Pennsylvania were top secret
anyway," Mallory continued. "There are snippets all over the scientific literature."

"I don't see the connection," I said.

"Biology. Hints of ancient biological *savoir-faire*—you don't
think the Neanderthals tie into that in some way?"

He was doing what? Testing me? Well, I guess I deserved it—
still, I was accustomed to being the driver, not the pedal to be
stepped on, in an investigation. . . . "Not that I can see, so far.
The Amish business involved massive allergens. No trace of anything like that in the Neanderthal corpses—Dave Spencer is convinced our man in New York died of strictly natural causes."

"Allergens aren't natural?"

"Not in the way they were introduced in Pennsylvania," I
replied.

"Fair enough, but Gerry Moses died of so-called natural
causes, too," Mallory said.

"Not so-called," I countered. "He had a long history of high
blood pressure and was overweight." I brushed my hand against
my own bit of paunch and frowned. Less veal, more sushi, that
was the ticket.

Mallory nodded, fingered his empty shot glass. "OK, but you
still should have told me about Pennsylvania, you shit. Coppers
don't like surprises—you know that." He smiled.

"I THINK THE Harris Tweed suits you, Sir. It's durable—and it's
never out of style."

"Hmm . . ." I eyed myself in the mirror—I had decided to
treat myself to a jacket and slacks with Savile Row tailoring before

catching my flight back to New York at Heathrow, something I'd been meaning to do every time I'd been in London but never quite had the time. After four nonstop days of meeting with Mallory and his people, inspecting the scene at the LSE, doing some research in the British Museum, and still no closer to a solution, I figured I owed myself this much. I buttoned and unbuttoned the jacket, looked at myself from side and full profiles. I am one of those guys who usually cuts a better image in my imagination than the mirror.

"You don't think it's too, ah, professorial?" I asked.

"No, I do not, Sir. There are many varieties of Harris Tweed—many subtleties. The one you have on has no elbow patches—it's not particularly academic at all. And may I ask what your profession is, Sir?"

"Science," I said.

"Of course. And may I say that I think the jacket you have on now suits that line of work *very* well."

I couldn't help grinning. Why did I have the feeling that this fellow who looked and spoke just like Hudson, the butler from *Upstairs, Downstairs,* would have said the same thing if I'd told him I hauled fertilizer around for a living—

"And may I take your measurements for the trousers now, Sir?"

"Sure," I said. The trousers were a shade of gray you could find only in England.

"And will this be all, Sir?"

"Yeah, I think so, thanks," I said.

"Well, then, might I recommend that you take two of these ties instead of the one? We do have a half-price sale on the second; they're made of silk, so they won't go out of style."

"Ah, I'm not sure I have any more room in my luggage. . . ." Great excuse, I realized—who wouldn't have room for an extra tie in his luggage?

"Well, then, why not do what I always do in such circumstances, Sir. Just wear the tie home with you." He put the tie in my hand—it was a beautiful off-gray color, with a thin thread of blue running through. He gestured to the mirror.

I put the tie on—double-Windsor knot, the only kind I knew how to make—and smiled. It did look great—maybe it would bring me slightly better service from the stewardesses in the steerage section of the plane, which was all the cost-conscious NYPD was ever willing to pay for. "OK. You talked me into it."

"Very good, Sir!"

I could easily get used to such affirmation.

"I'll have this ready for you in forty-five minutes, Sir—that should leave you more than enough time to catch your plane at Heathrow," Hudson said.

"YOUR ATTENTION, PLEASE. Would passenger Joseph Beiler please pick up the courtesy phone. . . . Passenger Joseph Beiler, please . . ."

The placelessness of airports . . . the food, the people, the announcements, the shops that seemed practically the same wherever the airport was . . . something about airports was a summary of life and therefore not really like life at all.

And I was feeling more and more at home in them. . . .

"Ta!" the woman behind the counter thanked me as I proffered a pound coin and waited for my change. The tea—as always in England—smelled delicious. I brushed my lips against the liquid—still too hot to even sip—and walked the cup carefully over to the row of phones that said they would welcome my credit card. They told the truth, and I put a call in to Jenna.

"Hello," she answered.

"Well, I finally broke down and bought that new suit I've been threatening you about," I said. "It should look great, if it doesn't crush too much in the luggage—"

"Good—I'm glad you called," she interrupted.

"Everything OK?" I asked, realizing that her voice sounded a bit stressed.

"Yeah. I just got off the phone with Dave and was trying to figure out how to get in touch with you—"

"What's going on?" I asked.

"Well, I suppose it's good news. Dave called to check what time you'll be arriving—he wants you to call him as soon as you get back; he didn't want to tell me anything more at first."

"But knowing you, you had no trouble wheedling it out of him," I said, smiling. "So tell me the news."

"Stefan Antonescu walked into Bobst Library about three hours ago."

"What?"

"That's right," Jenna continued. "That librarian you interviewed tried to get in touch with you, and they put her through to Dave. Antonescu says he was down with a nasty case of the flu and was recuperating over at a friend's house."

"Jeez," I said.

"Yeah," Jenna agreed. "And Dave, as you might expect, was making noises about turning this whole thing over to the Museum of Natural History—says you and he and the Department have more pressing crimes to work on than some mummy that hasn't even been reported missing."

"Damn, the typical syndrome," I said. "Something bizarre turns up, and as soon as you start to examine it, it melts away like ice cream off the stick. Dave is sure this new guy is really Stefan Antonescu?"

"No," Jenna said. "There's no DNA or even fingerprints on file for the original Stefan."

"And of course the new Stefan's DNA won't look anything like the mummy's," I said. "Well, Antonescu showing up doesn't explain Gerry Moses. And what about the other mummies?"

"Dave said he was going to check," Jenna replied. "I thought you were writing Gerry off as unrelated natural causes."

"I go back and forth," I said. "Jeez!" A man who made New York derelicts look like royalty almost bumped into me—

"I don't blame you for being upset, sweetheart; it's aggravating—," Jenna said.

"No, it's not that," I replied. Now the man was starting to veer into me again. He had dark, deep-set eyes and a thick, filthy beard. I extended my arm, spilling my tea. "Take it easy, buddy," I said, trying to keep him at arm's length.

"Everything OK?" Jenna's voice said through the earpiece, now a few inches away.

"Yeah . . . ," I tried to say back to her. But the derelict suddenly swiveled and shoved me against the phone bank with a powerful hand. I managed to push part of his shoulder away from me, but his other hand had something very sharp that ripped through my jacket—

Another voice shouted, and two, maybe more, people fell on top of me and the derelict, knocking us all to the ground. . . .

I rolled over and looked up to see a bobby getting to his feet and no sign of the derelict.

"Good thing I happened by, Sir," the bobby said. "That bloke with the knife looked like he was ready to cut your heart out. I got a quick glimpse of it—looked like some sort of glass, transparent to our metal detectors. You and he have a row about something?"

"No." I shook my head and stood up. "Never laid eyes on him before. Where'd he go?"

"He won't get too far; don't you worry," the bobby said. "I'll call in his description to airport security. I also have his wallet, must've fallen out of his pocket in the scuffle. Pretty thick billfold for someone who looked like—Hold on, are you all right? Looks like you're bleeding a little."

I followed his gaze down to my shirt, which was indeed sporting a slow mushroom of blood in the stomach area. I patted it. "Just a surface cut, nothing serious," I said. "By the way, I'm with the NYPD." And my legs folded like soggy cardboard. . . .

"We'll have help for you here in a few seconds, Sir; don't you worry," I heard the bobby say.

And at the edge of my fading vision I could see the phone I'd been talking to Jenna on, hanging now like a useless broken arm at the end of its coiled wire . . .

And damn, the blood was going to leave a stain on my new silk tie. . . .

NINE

"You daydreaming, Doctor?" Sheila Jameson, my nurse, finished taping up the new bandage. "It looks quite good for a wound just two days old."

"Thank you," I said. I was trying not to think about my stomach. It made me wince to even think about not thinking about it.

"That hurt?" she asked.

"No."

"It will; don't worry," she said, and smiled. "You still have some drugs in your system, so you're feeling a bit better than you should. But you're on the road to recovery."

Jenna and Mallory walked in. Jenna ran a cool hand over my bandage, kissed me, and frowned. Nurse Jameson left, closing the door behind her.

"She says it's healing OK," I said, and squeezed Jenna's hand. "Shouldn't have happened in the first place—my reflexes are usually sharper."

"There's no self-protection from that kind of attack," Mallory said. "Happens all too often in London these days—we're becoming more like New York City every day."

"Hey, the crime rate in New York has been down for a while now," I said, managing a smile.

"You can't think what happened to Phil is coincidence," Jenna said. This was the first time she and Mallory had been in my hospital room at the same time. She was not smiling at all.

"I don't know what to think," Mallory said. "Antonescu turns up alive in New York. Phil, the New York man in this investigation, turns up slashed at Heathrow. Coincidence? Maybe. Maybe not. If someone, whoever it is who is behind this, wanted to shut down the New York part of the escapade, that one-two punch would be a good way of doing it. Damn good thing that knife wasn't a few inches higher."

"But killing Phil, if that's what they wanted to do, only calls attention to this," Jenna said.

"Yes, but it's the ancient calculus of assassination, love," Mallory replied. "If the death of someone has a net result of less adverse knowledge afoot, even with the publicity the death brings, then you kill that person. Assuming the folks who do the calculus have no moral qualms about murder."

"I'm enjoying this conversation immensely," I said sourly. "What do you know about the guy—you said the ID in the billfold was Joey Beiler—who apparently lacked that qualm, at least regarding me? His grunts sounded Cockney, with maybe a German or Swiss undertone."

"Lots of nuances for a grunt," Mallory said. "And an odd combination. Germans are usually closer to royalty than Cockney hereabouts." He said this with a faint air of disdain, directed to the "royalty" part of the comment.

"What made you think it was Swiss?" Jenna asked.

"I don't know. . . ."

"The Amish have Swiss-German roots," she said.

"Amish?" Mallory asked. "You think they have a connection to this?"

"Well, Chautauqua has an Amish community," she replied. "My aunt used to go there every summer. That's where Gerry Moses died."

Mallory took it in. "Righto. In any case, we're still checking after Joey Beiler. Nothing on that name anywhere as yet."

"Great," I said.

Mallory exhaled slowly. "Well. I'll go ring up my man to see

if our car is ready for you. This time we're taking no chances—
you'll be under our protection until your plane takes off.''

I WAS BACK at my desk three days later. My knifing had convinced
the Department to keep the case open a "little longer"—hey,
whatever it took. First order of business was seeing Stefan Antonescu. I could see as soon as he walked in that he would be a
reluctant participant in our conversation.

"Thanks for coming by, Mr. Antonescu. Please have a seat.
Make yourself comfortable. Can I get you something to drink?"

He certainly looked a lot younger than the mummy, though
I couldn't say the same about his jacket, which hung like a slice
of withered shiny green corned beef off his stocky body. Likely
some old gabardine—certainly not silk. But there was that dandy
blue silk hankie all right, sticking right out of his pocket just like
Ruth Delany had said.

"Thank you. Do you have tea?"

"Of course we do, Mr. Antonescu. Would you like it hot or
with ice?" His voice was amazingly sweet, almost musical, with a
soft, unplaceable accent. Didn't jibe at all with his heavy-browed
face. But I understood exactly what Delany had meant about his
being gentle. He seemed more than that—almost childlike, big
but fragile. A fragile Neanderthal who liked tea. Not your average
diorama Neanderthal by any means.

"Hot, please."

"Milk? Sugar?" I poured the water over the bag in a cup.

"Neither, thank you. And please, let it brew for about five
minutes."

"Of course," I said. "OK, now that we—"

" Incidentally, your thanks for my coming over here are misplaced. I hadn't much choice in the matter—two of your police-
men conveyed your invitation. I could hardly have refused."

"You aren't under arrest, Mr. Antonescu. You could have refused. But I'm glad you're here."

"And here I am. What's on your mind, Dr. D'Amato?"

It wasn't five minutes yet, but I brought the tea over to him anyway. "I've left the tea bag in. You can keep it in longer if you like."

Antonescu nodded. He coaxed the tea bag in and out of the water like he was making love to it.

"You know about the mummy that turned up in the men's room where you work?" I asked.

He nodded again. "Lots of people work at the Bobst Library. Lots of people use the bathroom."

"I'm interested in your views on that mummy."

"My views?"

"That's right."

For the first time, Antonescu smiled. Almost laughed. "What do you want me to say? Mrs. Delany told me you think the mummy is Neanderthal. I obviously look like a Neanderthal—I've lived with that all of my life. You thought the mummy was me. I find this whole thing ridiculous."

"Well, you're not alone in that, but there are still some things about this that we need to investigate." I rubbed my stomach, which still itched over the wound. "Looks just like my mother's cesarean," Jenna had said. "Let's try another subject," I continued. "I understand you have an interest in silk."

"That's right," Antonescu replied. Something flickered in his eyes, just a bit too fast for me to fathom. "*Ssu*—what the world now calls silk—is one of China's greatest gifts to humankind."

"Hardly a gift at first," I said. "Raw silk was exported. But export of silkworm eggs was punishable by death for most of China's history."

"That didn't prevent some monks from smuggling the eggs out of China in a hollow cane, in the time of Justinian and your Eastern Roman Empire," he retorted. "Not that I blame you—the recipe is always more valuable than the cake."

"That so?" This man spoke as if I were in the employ of the Empire rather than the City.

"Yes," he said. "Cakes, even when made of stone, crumble. Recipes can endure forever."

"And is the DNA of the silkworm part of the recipe?"

Antonescu sipped his tea for the first time. "It's good," he said.

"My friend brought back some bottled water from England," I said. "Works every time."

He looked at me appraisingly. "So you understand that the key to good tea is not only the tea but also the quality of the water—the flesh in which the recipe finds its life. That is commendable." He nodded. "Few people comprehend that."

"I've known that for some time," I said. "It's why the tea in Teaneck tastes like dishwater."

He frowned, presumably in low esteem of New Jersey tea.

"Let's get back to flesh and recipes," I said.

"Yes, flesh," Antonescu obliged. "You know, unexpected mummies and their desiccated flesh are not unique to New York. You found a corpse here; more than a hundred Caucasian mummies have been found in the past few decades in the Tarim Basin in Xinjiang Province. I'm sure one or two people associated with that project met their deaths since then, too. I haven't read about anyone conducting an investigation about that."

"You mean the Tocharian mummies? Long noses and deep-set eyes, light hair, thin lips, and their language was some sort of Indo-European?" I'd cut out and saved the front-page article that had appeared about them in the *New York Times* science section. Indo-European gene-pools were one of my fascinations.

Antonescu nodded, sipped more tea.

"But the Tocharians got to northwest China by a well-trod route—the Silk Road," I said. "That was in what? Six or seven hundred A.D.? Not long after Justinian or the Persians had broken the Chinese monopoly on silkworms."

Antonescu nodded again. "That's the date of the Tocharian manuscripts that were found there. The oldest Caucasian mummies go as far back as four thousand years. Maybe earlier."

He was right about that. "OK, and we know how they got there. That overland route was well established. What road brought us the mummy we discovered in the NYU library?"

"Perhaps the road of frost—the killing frost—the road not taken."

I looked at him. Was this janitor who looked like a Neanderthal and dressed like he had raided a discount store on 14th Street quoting Shakespeare and Robert Frost to me? His erudition was astonishing.

"The mummy had a handkerchief just like yours," I said.

"Really? You know what they say: clothes make the man."

"You're a real font of wisdom, Mr. Antonescu."

He smiled. "An advantage of working in a library."

"Hard to believe someone with your intelligence would be satisfied working as a janitor, even with its reading privileges," I said.

"One could well say the same about you, Dr. D'Amato— conversing with possible criminals is not likely what Comenius had in mind when he talked about participating in the Great Dialogue."

The phone rang. Some great dialogue from Dave on another case—one that I couldn't bring myself to care too much about.

Antonescu stood up. "Can I go now?"

I asked Dave to hold on. "Yes," I told Antonescu. "And thanks again for coming by. I'll be in touch again if I need anything more."

"I'M BEGINNING TO feel like the wound is closing, healing up, before we've had a chance to come close to understanding what caused it," I said to Jenna. I wasn't talking just about the scab on my stomach.

She ran her hand over it, her ear on my breast. "You want what?" she murmured. "Another corpse or two? Another knife attack? That's the trouble with forensic science—it collects evidence at the price of human life."

I sighed. "You're right. I know. It's just that usually one person dies here, another there, a third one in somewhat different but related circumstances, and I can begin to see a common denominator, a pattern. With these mummies, everything's stopped cold. I got a message through to John Lapp on his farm—he got back to me that he has no idea what's going on. No one other than Antonescu has turned up alive. No one else has died; no one else has been injured. I'm glad about that, of course—"

"Me, too," she said, and moved her mouth close to my lips, sucking in my lower lip, grazing it with her teeth, extending her body full and naked and warm over mine. . . .

Later, I gently stroked the small of her back as she lay soft and sleeping at my side. Maybe I ought to let the whole case slide, get back to the grungy, mundane business of murderers and their victims that I was paid to investigate in New York. The world seemed so peaceful, at rest, tonight. So soft. . . . like silk. . . .

Dammit, there was too much silk in this case to be just coincidence. Lum had finally sent down a report with Gerry Moses's DNA profile, and that had the *Bombyx mori* signature. The traces of Antonescu's DNA we'd managed to recover from his teacup—pretty much right-down-the-middle *Homo sapiens sapiens* DNA, varying from the average in just eight positions—also came with a few sequences of *Bombyx mori* DNA. I guess that was no surprise, in view of his blue hankie. But still. . . . there was silk in too many places here—places where it may have belonged, places where it didn't. And I didn't care what John Lapp said—silk is produced by caterpillars, they're insects just like beetles and fireflies—Mallory had the right idea about the Amish. There had to be some connection. Dave had laughed me off the phone when I'd mentioned it, but what did he know about bug-tech?

I recalled what I'd once read in an old philosophy of science book years ago, maybe by John Dewey. You need to do more than merely observe the universe, wait for evidence, to really understand it. You need to perturb it—disturb it—cause some sort of significant ripple, and then gauge its effects. You had to shake it loose to comprehend it. Fire a particle into an atom to fathom its structure. . . .

I had an idea firing a few of my own.

TEN

May wasn't the month I would have chosen to go back to Pennsylvania. Even the first part of June was too early, ahead of the cherries, strawberries, corn that would dress up this area, make my mouth water just to look at it.

But this was not a trip of choice—or pleasure.

I pulled in my little Buick against the sidewalk next to the General Sutter Inn in Lititz. After a lifetime of parallel parking in New York City, this was child's play. I doubted that much of what lay ahead would be.

I looked around the restaurant—simple wooden tables with plain tablecloths and a single milk white flower in a Tynant blue water bottle on each. One of the tables had something more.

"John?" I walked over and extended my hand.

He took it in an iron squeeze. "Did you have a comfortable trip? Please, sit down."

"Thank you."

He looked just as he had last year—Abraham Lincoln beard, suspenders holding up sacklike pants, but something more in his eyes, his demeanor. Amish, plus something else.

Lapp smiled. His teeth looked yellow, uneven—yet healthy. He drank what looked like lemonade, from a glass that looked like it was made out of quartz. "Lemonade tastes better in glasses, wouldn't you agree? It's the container that counts. Your science makes too much of the inside, I think. The vessel, the carrier, is sometimes more important."

"Oh?" In addition to everything else, Lapp was an Amish McLuhan. The medium is the message. . . .

"What are genes—what can they do?—without vessels to actually move them about in this world of ours?" Lapp said. "We, my people, devote our attention to the vessels and let the genes take care of themselves."

"What about genetic diseases?" I asked.

"Genes only kill when someone tampers with them," Lapp replied.

"So you're saying what, that what we know as genetic diseases were the result of someone tampering with genes? When exactly do you think this happened?"

"History didn't begin with what your historians think was the beginning," Lapp replied.

A cat with long silken hair brushed against my leg and purred. I extended an index finger, and the cat met it with it's nose. I smiled. "I guess I remind her of someone."

"Him," Lapp said.

"Him," I echoed. "Interesting eyes." I stared into orbs that looked up into mine and almost made me dizzy. "They look sort of canine. What kind of cat is he?"

"Watchcat," Lapp replied. "We call them watchcats."

"How long have you had them?"

"A very long time," Lapp said. "Your biology books say the cat and dog lines first diverged many millions of years ago."

"Who is Stefan Antonescu?" I asked. "That name means nothing to you?"

Lapp slowly shook his head no. "Never heard of him—as I told you when I answered your message."

I shook my head, too. There was no point playing police interrogator with this man, trying to get something out of him by rattling him with an unexpected question.

"Allow me to at least give you a little temporary gift, to see you through these difficulties," Lapp said. "Although in truth, it seems Hyram has already chosen *you*."

He looked down at the cat, who now was snuggling the whole length of his body against my leg. . . .

A waiter who looked to be Amish but probably was Mennonite, since he was working in a restaurant, finally appeared. "Nothing for me," I said, and rubbed my unsettled stomach. Then . . . "Wait a minute? Amos? I hardly recognized you with your beard grown in!"

Amos smiled, clapped me on the back. "So I see our medicine worked well for you."

"Yeah," I said. "Though I have to admit I don't feel too great right now." Truth was that I had had a splitting headache the last few miles on the turnpike. In fact, one of the reasons I had come out here is that I hadn't been feeling too well. . . . Now my stomach was really acting up. "Is there a bathroom . . ."

"Sure," Amos said, and pointed to the far side of the room. . . .

I barely made it to the sink.

I splashed cold water on my face, but I couldn't feel it.

Amos and John and Hyram came through the door. . . .

I AWOKE IN a bed with no recollection of how I got there, for the second time in a month.

I heard someone mumbling about "the cure". . . .

I awoke again, later.

There was no nurse in the room, just a cat, with wise brown eyes. "Hyram . . ."

He purred and left.

He came back with Lapp, a few moments later.

I propped myself up, feeling pretty good. "You're going to tell me, 'You had us worried there for a while, it was a close call, but you're all right now,' right?"

Lapp frowned. "No, I don't go to the movies. But I'm glad to see that you're better."

"How long was I out?"

"Three days," Lapp replied.

"What did I have? How did you cure it?"

"The remedy was silk."

"Jenna—"

"We got word through to her," Lapp said. "She knows you're OK."

"Is what I had . . . contagious?"

"It depends. . . ."

I DECIDED TO go straight through to Toronto. Let Jenna think I was still in Pennsylvania—no point in exposing her to this illness any more than she already had been. Better to give her a few more days away from me, in case there was anything still infectious in me. I arranged for packages with Amish medications and explanations to be sent to Jenna and Dave and Mallory. As for Lum—well, I'd bring him these in person. And if I was right, he'd already had a lot more exposure to this than I could possibly give him in my recovered state. . . .

The Toronto airport felt cold—even though it was May, even though the inside would certainly have been heated had it been earlier in the year. Somehow, just being in Canada made me cold. Or maybe it was a lingering symptom of what I'd just been through. . . .

"Business or pleasure?"

"Business," I said, and handed the customs official my passport.

"Oh? What kind of business?" He looked up at me for the first time.

"I'm a research scientist. I'm going over to the University of Toronto for a special seminar." That's the way Lum had insisted on doing it—strictly off-the-record, out of the spotlight, he'd said.

"What's the seminar about?"

"Well . . . it's about the impact of communications media on DNA research."

"You mean like cloning?"

"That's right," I replied.

"Will there be Canadian scientists at this seminar? Are you taking into account the contributions that Canadians have made in this area?"

What was this guy's problem? "I don't know," I said. "I mean, I'm sure Canadians have made important contributions. But I don't know for sure who will be at the seminar."

"Who invited you here?"

"Derrick de Kerckhove, director of the McLuhan Program at the University of Toronto." At least I was safe on that score—de Kerckhove was out of town, Lum had said.

"McLuhan, what does he have to do with DNA?"

"Uh . . . media. McLuhan studied the impact of media. DNA is a medium," I said quickly. "The medium of life."

The customs official looked up at me again, studied my face. "Do you have a letter of invitation?"

"No," I said. "I was just invited to come up here on the phone." I of course had no letter because there was no seminar.

"I see." He proceeded to write copiously on some kind of form.

He finally looked up at me again. "You understand that you're not permitted to accept any employment while in Canada, Dr. D'Amato. We're quite happy with our own doctors and our own health system."

"I'm just going to the seminar."

"Enjoy your stay in Canada."

I hurried out of the airport. I was dying for a cup of tea but was sure that if I tarried I would be hauled off to some Canadian prison somewhere for entering the country on false pretenses. What was the law here? Were you even innocent until proven guilty?

"39a Queen's Park, Crescent East," I told the cabbie. "The McLuhan Coach House at the University of Toronto."

"Very good, Mister." He had some sort of vaguely Asian accent.

I opened my wallet, to make sure I had the address right.

"Don't worry; I take American money."

"That's OK," I said. "I have Canadian currency." Tesa Stewart had given me some before I'd left for Lancaster. She had been in Canada in February. I exhaled slowly—life, as strange as it always seemed to me, had felt a lot more normal in February.

"You come from New York City! I recognize the accent!"

I smiled. "You got it, buddy!"

"New York is a wonderful city! Everyone is equal! Everyone is free!"

"You think so?"

"Oh, yes," the cabbie replied enthusiastically. "I lived there for several years, in New York City. I was equal there, like everyone else. No one looked at me different! Not like here, in Toronto. It's a nice place; don't mistake me. But people look at me—'he's Indonesian!' It's not the same. It's prejudice. Prejudice. In Paris, too. It's a nice city. But people see me there—I'm different. Only in New York City is everyone the same people!"

The cab pulled up to a sidewalk.

I squinted through the dirt-encrusted window. "It says 'Medieval' on the building."

"Don't worry—McLuhan stands behind it. You'll see."

"OK," I said. "Keep the change." I handed the cabbie a twenty-dollar bill, Canadian.

The Coach House was indeed behind the Medieval Studies Building.

I opened its creaky door.

"Hello?" I stuck my head in.

"Hello!" A woman with short dark hair was on her feet and smiled at me. "I recognize you from the fax. He's inside," she said and pointed to another room, "waiting for you. You two will have the place to yourselves. I'm late for a meeting."

"Thank you," I said as the woman left the building.

I walked into the other room.

"Phil!" H.-T. Lum jumped up from a couch. His outstretched hand of greeting protruded from a green silken shirt.

"Sorry we have to meet in such circumstances—but my office at the Centre for Forensic Sciences is no place for this."

I shook his hand and sat down on a dusty couch perpendicular to his.

"I'm sorry," Lum said again and gestured around the room. "I know this is peculiar. But we need to be careful—my colleagues can't know that I'm meeting you. It was a bit of a walk for me—from Grosvenor Street to here—but I've still got my energy. And how was your flight?"

"Fine," I replied. "You're afraid of your colleagues finding out—"

"Wouldn't you be?" Lum asked. "Gerry Moses dead. You practically dead . . . I'm sorry—"

"It's OK," I said. "I mean, not that I nearly died in Lancaster—though I much prefer that to the alternative—but it's OK for us to talk about it. That's what I'm here for—I appreciate your seeing me."

Lum leaned back on the couch and appeared to relax a little. "Even before your illness, I wasn't willing to talk to you or anyone about this on the phone—you never know who may be listening. There are bugs all over—even in my office; I'm sure of it. But here it's safe—no one pays attention to McLuhan anymore. I attended the last of McLuhan's seminars in the 1970s. It's a shame people don't appreciate the great contribution of the man—it's a shame. But at least it's safe here now—we can take advantage of the public's ignorance of McLuhan." Lum offered a quavering smile.

"Makes sense," I said. "And I'm sorry that my illness delayed my visit. So tell me what you had on your mind."

"That Gerry Moses did not die of a heart attack," Lum said.

"I suspected as much."

"Oh, that's what we put on the death certification," Lum said. "You'd be surprised how often the cause of death gets listed as cardiac arrest—because, after all, the heart does eventually stop beating—but the real insult that provokes the heart attack is something else.''

"Tell me about it," I said, seriously as well as sarcastically. "What was the real insult to Gerry Moses?"

"He had a very bad case, worse than the flu," Lum replied. "It came on very suddenly, and nothing had any effect. He tried all the meds—all the antibiotics—and they were no help. So he knew it wasn't bacterial. That's why he went down to Chautauqua."

"He had enough strength to drive? I was barely able to walk when mine hit me."

"Someone drove him," Lum said.

"You?"

Lum nodded.

"And what happened in Chautauqua?" I prodded.

"We went there to seek the Amish cure," Lum said.

"You knew about the silk?"

"Yes," Lum said.

"And it didn't work for Gerry?" Either he got a defective cure or maybe he was suffering from something else. I apparently had been in the best hands in the world when my illness struck.

"We got there too late," Lum said. "Gerry thought his illness was somehow connected to the DNA, some kind of viral substance, some tiny piece of genetic bad news—that's what Sir Peter Medawar called viruses; I took his seminar in London, too, in the 1970s. But this mutant nucleotide, or whatever it was, attached itself to the DNA in many of Gerry's cells, so that the next time they reproduced, that was their last. Gerry thought it turned the clock all the way forward in his cells, to the point that the DNA broke down, didn't survive in its proper form in the next reproduction. . . ."

"Sounds like he died of instant old age." I shuddered.

Lum nodded, tears in his eyes. "He just fell apart. The Amish couldn't help him—they said he was too far gone. There was nothing I could do."

"Did Gerry have any idea where he picked up this virus or whatever it was?" I asked, though I thought I had a pretty good idea.

"Yeah," Lum said hoarsely. "Gerry was sure he was infected by the Neanderthal corpse."

"But weren't you also exposed to the Neanderthal—," I began to ask.

"Yes, of course." Lum nodded. "But some of us have a natural immunity—that was Gerry's theory. . . ."

H. -T. Lum was apparently a survivor, if a frightened one. As was I—at least, apparently, for now. . . .

Natural immunity—the enigma of medicine since the earliest days of germ theory. There seemed to be at least three fates afoot for the Neanderthal flu. One, some people exposed to it—such as Gerry Moses—died horribly. Two, some people—such as Lum—had a natural immunity, whatever exactly that was. And there was a third possible outcome for this illness. There was some kind of silken cure—the Amish cure—that worked on some people exposed to the Neanderthal virus. It had saved my life. But it hadn't worked for Gerry. And although Lapp had given me extra packets of the cure to give to everyone on this case—including Lum—the Amishman had been unable or unwilling to tell me exactly what it was . . . which left me almost as much in the dark as I had been to begin with about just what the damn illness was. . . .

"Gerry thought the virus sheared off the telomere," Lum finally offered. "Without the telomere, the cell can no longer divide."

"And the cure works how," I asked, "by inserting telomerase to safeguard the tips of the DNA strands?"

Lum nodded.

"But how could the Amish possibly have accomplished such insertions?"

"Gerry thought it might be with another virus—"

"Natural gene splicing?"

"I guess you could call it that," Lum said.

I looked at him. "Why the hell didn't you say something about this sooner? Look, we don't know each other very well, so I hope you won't mind my being blunt. You had no way of knowing anyone else had your natural immunity—jeez, we could have all wound up dead, like Gerry."

"I'm sorry," Lum said quietly. "It was just a theory—I can't *confirm* what Gerry died of. I'm new at this job—I have to be careful what I say to colleagues. . . ."

"Sometimes being careful can kill you," I replied.

MY PLANE LANDED in the splashing rain at La Guardia. I hailed a taxi home.

"You goddamn bastard!" Jenna pulled away after we'd kissed. "Why didn't you call me sooner? Let me know what was going on?" She pounded on my chest. "Why the hell do you always have to be the hero, trying out these cures on yourself?"

"I didn't exactly volunteer for it," I replied.

Jenna was not mollified.

"I guess it wouldn't help if I told you I didn't know what we were dealing with—I still don't know, completely—and I didn't want you exposed?" I added.

"Right. It wouldn't help. You still could have told me and trusted me to do the right thing," Jenna said.

I stroked her face with my hand.

She pulled my hand away.

"I knew you would come after me," I tried to explain. "I knew you would do that, whatever I said. You might have traced my call, someway, and found me. I didn't want that. Let's say I was contagious—"

"The virus comes from the corpses—"

"We can't know that for sure," I said. "It's still too soon for definite conclusions." Too soon for some. I hoped not too late for others.

"You're OK?" She suddenly put her arms back around me

and pressed her face against my chest. "You're OK?" she murmured, and kissed me.

"Yeah, I think so." I kissed her head. Her hair smelled good, made my eyes blur.

"The cure didn't work for Gerry Moses," Jenna said.

"I know."

"I took the cure you sent along," she told me.

"Good."

"That damn Lapp! I left a message at the number you have for him, and he never even responded!"

"Lapp's smart to be protective," I said, and ran my lips along her ear. "Being suspicious of outsiders is what saved his culture, their wisdom. Now it may be all we have."

"It saved you," Jenna said, and turned her face up to mine.

I kissed her lips, moved my hands down her face, her shoulders, her dress. When I got to the bottom of the dress, I moved my hands inside and up to her soft cotton panties. I slid them off. . . .

"Your back feels silky," I said to Jenna later as she snuggled against me, my fingers running down her spine, in our favorite very-late-night position.

She shivered. "I'm not even going to ask if that has some significance," she said. "I'm too happy to have you home."

"The Chinese must've understood it," I replied anyway. "They punished the export of the silkworm not because they wanted to keep their monopoly on luxurious fabrics but their monopoly on life—or its preservation. And then the secret was lost, or forgotten, but not by everyone. It's never forgotten by everyone. And the Amish—somehow with their farming, I don't know, they picked it up. Or Lapp's splinter group did."

"Is that what he told you?"

"No, it's what I surmised—based on what happened to me in Pennsylvania and what Lum said. My guess is the Amish have a virus with elements of *Bombyx mori* DNA that can spread through the human system in less than a day, and repair damaged telomeres. They don't *call* it a virus—they've never seen it under an electron microscope because they don't have those things. They just know that it works. They're part of some kind of worldwide *sub rosa* agricultural society out there—like a Masonic organization of farmers. It's very old—part of what I ran into last year. . . . Sweetheart?"

"I was just thinking," Jenna said. "The Neanderthal corpses, how do they fit in?"

"I'm not sure. Perhaps the Neanderthal corpses all had that silk cure and that's why they were able to survive these thirty thousand years. . . ."

"I still can't believe they were that old," Jenna said.

"That's what the carbon-14 says."

"So why'd they die?"

"I don't know," I said. "Something in the Neanderthal DNA, as it reproduced and reproduced all these millennia, eventually reasserted itself, negated the silk cure, so Antonescu—or whoever the guy who died was—died immediately. Or someone, something, deliberately introduced a new genetic agent into the mix, which cancelled the *Bombyx mori*. . . . I don't know . . . viruses preying on viruses preying on viruses . . . editing of editing gone exponential . . ."

"But Antonescu's alive again now. That means he's what? A clone?"

"Dunno." I shrugged. "Either way, the new DNA in the corpses—the DNA that led to their sudden death—infected me and Gerry Moses. So that the DNA in our skin and lots of other cells started reaching the end of its rope—pushed our cells up to their Hayflick limit. No one knows exactly how many divides each kind of human cell has in the body. Some cells, like brain cells, never divide at all after infancy. But human cells grown in test tubes divide about fifty times and then break down. That's what my cells were doing. . . ."

"But now that you have the silk fix, you've got a life span of thirty thousand years. And me, too, right?'' She turned over and gave my neck a playful nip.

"I wouldn't mind a second of it, if it was all with you." I ran my hand down her back one more time and let my fingers come to rest, lightly . . .

ELEVEN

"Take a look at this, Phil."

I was downtown again in Dave Spencer's examining room.
He gestured to a young woman, couldn't have been more
than twenty, lying on the table.

"Take a look at her, Phil. Beautiful, no? So beautiful that her
boyfriend or who knows who wanted to sleep with her, but maybe
she didn't want to, so he put some fizz in her drink, fucked her
senseless when she was already knocked out, had himself a great
time, and guess what? She never wakes up. She's dead. The son
of a bitch Od'd her on the stuff."

I looked at her soft blond hair. She probably had soft blue
eyes, but her lids were closed. She must have been beautiful. She
still was.

"Take a look at her, Phil—a good look. That's what our job
is—take a look at it. We're paid to find out who the hell robbed
this girl of her life or help convict the miscreant when the detectives find him, so maybe this doesn't happen again—at least not
with the same guy."

"They're not mutually exclusive," I objected. "Rape isn't the
only crime—"

"Crime? Where's the crime with your ape-man? You've got a
crime right in front of you—this girl was murdered. Raped, murdered, maybe raped again. Where's the crime in *your* case? You
weren't feeling well? OK, I'm glad you're feeling better. Your

DNA now seems to have a trace of silk worm? OK, I grant you, that's interesting, it's a mystery—but it's not a crime, Phil!"

"I was knifed in London—"

"That's Michael Mallory's problem—his crime, his jurisdiction, his problem. Not yours, not mine. Has no connection to the mummies anyway, am I wrong?"

"And Gerry Moses?"

"He died," Dave said. "It happens. The man died."

"Lum told me he thinks it's more."

"Well, I have trouble understanding much of anything that Lum says these days—he talks in circles," Dave said. "The job's probably too much for him. Not that I can completely blame him—sometimes I feel the same way, like more and more lately when I'm talking to you. I'm telling you this as a friend."

I just shook my head. I could see this wasn't going to get much better.

"Where's Lum's evidence? Where's yours?" Dave pressed his attack. "You think those Neanderthal corpses are spreading some modern plague? Where's the evidence under the microscope?"

"Let's say whatever causes it, whatever it is that reengineers our DNA, is subviral, too small to be seen with a microscope? Let's say we're no more equipped to see this than people were to see bacteria before Leeuwenhoek?"

"OK, fair enough," Dave said. "I'm willing to grant that possibility—I'm a scientist first, just like you. I know my history. But even so . . . we still need evidence, right? The people who died of the plague were the evidence that something was wrong. Where's your evidence? Where are the dead bodies piling up?"

I thought again about the oddities of natural immunity. Clearly there were some things, probably the most important, that we didn't understand yet about all of this.

"Phil, I'm going to be honest with you. You've got to start carrying more of your weight. The Captain . . . some of the brass are beginning to talk. You wanna run off to Pennsylvania, you wanna sneak in and out of Toronto like some goddamn spy on a mission—fine, but do it on your own time. I'm saying this as a friend—when you're on the job, do your job!''

"OK," I said quietly. No point in riling him up any further at this point.

Dave forced a smile. "I don't mean to be lecturing you like this. We go back a long way, you and I. It's just—I don't know. Maybe I'm getting too old for the job myself. Used to be—when I started out, in the late seventies—everybody looked up to us, looked up to me. Hell, it's no pleasure, what we do. But we do it. It's a calling. But now—hell, we sell our testimony to O. J., to the highest bidder. That's what they say about us. That's why we can't lose sight of the important things, like this poor girl here. . . .''

He was shaking—I'd never seen Dave so upset.

"OK," I said again. "I hear you." I'd pick this up with him another day. I squeezed his shoulder and walked out the door.

DAVE WAS BRAIN dead two days later.

The doctors wanted to bury him. "What's the point of prolonging it?" the young MD at the hospital said to me. "Life support's all that's keeping his body going. That's no way to live—not for a man like him."

You didn't know the man—you're not entitled to a goddamned opinion on the subject. Save your textbook ethics pieties for someone else, I felt like saying. But I just thanked the kid for his opinion.

I went to see Rose, Dave's wife of thirty-six years.

"Can I get you a cup of tea, Phil?"

"No, Rose, please, sit. What can I get *you?* Something to drink?"

"No, nothing for me. I'm OK, Phil." She started to cry. "I'm OK, really."

I put my arm around her.

If I could just spend some time with Dave—just sit next to his bed, hold his hand a little, talk to him, on the remote chance

that somehow he could hear me—maybe I would have been able
to take this better. Maybe I'd get some kind of clearer insight into
this nightmare. No, there was no chance that this could be any
better. The neurologists were firm on that. Dave was dead in all
things not serviced by the machines that moved the oxygenated
blood through his physical frame. There was no way I could take
this any better. The best I could hope for was a little more com-
prehension of what was going on.

But Dave's family was adamant: no one other than immediate
family and tending physicians in his room.

I suspected that edict had come from Dave's children, not
Rose. I wanted to respect it, but—

"It was so sudden," she said. "I guess it's better that way.
Walking around till the very end—never sick a day in his life. It's
better that way."

"Oh, yes," I said. "That was Dave—so much vitality."

"He'll be walking with Jesus soon. It's better that way—better
to walk with Jesus than limp on Earth. I'm a Baptist, Phil; did you
know that? You're Roman Catholic, right?"

"Well, actually no. I'm a Marrano Jew—my ancestors pretended to convert, during the Inquisition, because they figured
that was better than being tortured and killed, and they didn't
want to leave their homes. But my people kept the Jewish tradition, secretly, even though they gave up their Jewish names."

Rose nodded. "Yes, I remember now; Dave told me about
that. I've always admired the Jewish people—imagine that, a religion that goes back over five thousand years!"

"Yeah, we go back a long way. Dave and I went back a long
way, too. It was one of the last things he said to me. . . ."

Rose took my hand. "You and Dave were working on a case
together, right? That's why you wanted to come see me. The
house is a mess; I haven't had time—"

"It's OK." I squeezed her hand. "Look, why I don't I come
back in a few days? There's no real urgency. How about I take
you out to lunch now?"

"No, no," Rose said. "You and Dave were working on a case; that comes first. That's the way it always was with Dave. Would you like to look in his den? I'll try not to get in the way. I didn't see anything in Dave's papers about anything recent he was working on with you, but you look around now. If it's for your case, that means it's important."

"You sure?"

Rose nodded, tears in her eyes.

"Thank you." I squeezed her hand again and headed toward the den. They lived in a co-op right down the street from the Dakota, on the Upper West Side, across from Central Park. I'd been here at least a dozen times over the years.

The first thing I noticed on his desk was the package I'd sent him from Pennsylvania—with the silk medication. It had been opened, but the contents hadn't been touched.

I sighed. So I now knew why he was practically dead. Goddamned stubborn man. . . .

What I didn't know was why he had been healthy so long.

I walked from the den into their bedroom—the answer might be there. Rose was still sitting in the living room. I could do this quickly.

I opened up the closet. There must have been two dozen ties hanging on the rack, all of them hopelessly out-of-date. Dave's specialty. I smiled sadly. I ran my hand around each of them. Only two had what I was looking for—not enough to make a difference, unless maybe he'd worn them every day, and these looked like they hadn't been worn in a decade.

I opened several drawers in the dresser until I found one with shirts. Cotton, various blends, not a single one with any possible connection to this case.

I looked around the room at the curtains, bedspread, pillows, anything for inspiration.

Nothing.

I was pretty sure I knew what had felled Dave Spencer.

What the hell had kept him apparently well after the exposure—far more intensive than mine?

What had he been doing, eating moths for breakfast?

I joined Rose in the living room. I insisted that I make her some coffee, she insisted that she make me some tea, so I compromised and made both. Finally, I delicately began to broach the possibility of my visiting Dave. If I could get to see him, even in the state he was in, that might answer some questions—

The intercom rang.

Rose got it. "OK, sure, send him right up." She looked at me and started crying. "It's the boy from the Chinese laundry."

"Yes." She was the first person I'd heard of in years who used a Chinese laundry, but that obviously wasn't why she was crying.

"He's bringing back the sheets," she said, dabbing her eyes. "I sent them out for cleaning—two days before Dave got sick. Beautiful satin sheets, real silk—we got them just this March, daughter Terry's present for our anniversary. Dave said sleeping on them every night made him feel like a king!"

DEBBIE TUCKER HAD an article in the paper the next day—"The Coroner's Contagion." It spoke of the death of Gerry Moses in Toronto, the near-death of Dave Spencer in New York, my illness on a trip to Pennsylvania. It spoke of corpses that looked like Neanderthals. It mentioned a silk cure but nothing of the Amish, because I'd sworn her to secrecy on that. John Lapp wanted it that way—even though I suspected he well knew that sooner or later the world would find out.

Mallory was quoted from London: "I had my DNA thoroughly examined a fortnight ago. My telomeres are all as they should be."

I was quoted from New York: "My superiors have removed me from this case, and I can't comment any further, except to say I intend to keep working on it, on my own time."

The article noted the price of silk skyrocketing on half a dozen commodity exchanges around the world.

I put the paper down and rubbed my eyes.

The phone rang.

It was a friend at the hospital. Dave Spencer had been taken off life support an hour ago. He had just been pronounced dead.

I tried to call the attending physician but could not get through.

I MET TESA Stewart for lunch the next day.

"Jesus Christ, Phil, you're crazier than I am, and that's saying a lot."

"Thanks for the vote of confidence." I refilled her glass with Beaujolais. Not likely it would dramatically improve her opinion of what I was trying to do.

"And you think you'll even get a judge to listen to you?" she asked.

"Not me—but I know some top-notch people in the DA's office—hell, I know the man himself. I've done plenty for them over the years. I got one of them signed on to present my argument in court. And with you as an expert witness—"

Tesa shook her head. "What am I supposed to say that could be of any use in this mess?"

"Just talk about Neanderthal DNA—what you told me when we had our first conversation about this case. That we don't really have much reliable evidence at this point about what Neanderthal DNA really looks like—that so many times when people try to nail it down it gets contaminated with *Homo sapiens sapiens* DNA. Just say what you know—the truth—that's all I need." Jeez, the tritest coaching line in the witness book. But let's face it, the likely reason things become trite is they're true. What I didn't get was why Tesa was being so resistant. It wasn't like her.

"And Spencer's wife is OK with this?"

"She's not happy about it, of course not," I replied. "But she was married to a coroner, for crissakes. She knows the score." I sighed. "No, Rose doesn't like it, but she's not the one who's behind the opposition to my request. It's her kids—and she can't bring herself to oppose *them*. But I can't let that stop me. One of the last things Dave said to me was: 'Do your job, Phil; do your job!' That's what I'm trying to do here. Those kids stopped me from seeing Dave in the hospital—I'm going to do my job now and see Dave out of the grave." I sucked down the rest of my wine.

"How about Moses? You going to exhume him, too?"

"Right," I said sarcastically. "I might as well try to exhume the real Moses himself and get the Canadians to agree to a rush request from me. But we'll get to Gerry eventually. Right now—first things first. We go after Dave."

Tesa helped herself to more wine. "When's the hearing?"

"Some attorney dropped dead unexpectedly, and the judge has an opening on his calendar—Friday afternoon, day after tomorrow, 2:00 P.M."

"Jesus, the burial's tomorrow, isn't it?"

I nodded. "Yeah. In and out."

Tesa sipped her wine for a long time. "All right," she said at last. "But just don't tell me that that lawyer who dropped dead had anything to do with a Neanderthal."

JENNA WAS WITH me, so was Tesa, and two of the brass up from One Police Plaza. Rose Spencer and her family had declined to join us. I couldn't say I blamed them.

"What's keeping him?" Tesa asked nervously.

"He's new on the job," I said. "He'll be out soon." That would be Herby Edelstein, stepping up to Dave's job until a permanent replacement could be found. Or at least as permanent as any job in this life could be. It hadn't been too permanent for Dave—his was the body that Herby was presumably unwrapping, looking at, right now. We were outside those pitted doors, waiting for word, waiting to be invited in.

"You ever see Hitchcock's *Frenzy*?" I asked Jenna, anyone who was listening.

"Sure, I saw it," one of the brass, Jack Dugan, spoke up. "Guy strangles his best friend's girlfriend with his necktie, right?"

"That's it," I said. "And remember that scene, right after he strangles her? The camera gradually pulls out, out of the apartment, down the flight of stairs, out into the street. And as it pulls out, the sounds of the street gradually come in. Finally, the camera is looking at the apartment building where this horrible murder just took place, from across the street, and we see cars and people, the world going about its business, kids running around, and no one has the vaguest idea that right under their very noses this woman was strangled, with her eyes left bulging. . . ."

"Yeah." Dugan nodded. "Great example of Hitchcock using mise-en-scène."

I smiled. Only in New York—a top cop who's a film buff. Well, maybe also in LA. "DNA is like that," I said. "All these combinations and drill and deaths and battles going on under the surface, right before our eyes, only we don't know it. We look at people and see complete individuals—but they're actually communities of underlying DNA, constantly in flux, constantly in battle."

"Yeah," Dugan said. But his eyes were beginning to glaze.

Jenna started to say something—

The pitted door swung open.

"You were right, Phil," Herby said to all of us.

He looked pale.

He ushered us in and directed our attention to the table.

Someone was talking, but I couldn't hear anything.

All of my perception was taken up with one thing: Dave Spencer stretched out on that table.

I walked over to take a closer look.

Maybe it wasn't Dave?

No, this was Dave. No doubt about it.

Except in three days of life support he had begun to develop features that were distinctly Neanderthal. They were clear as day, embalmed now in death.

TWELVE

"It's worse than you think, Phil."

I swallowed the scrambled egg I had in my mouth and looked at Tesa, who had just joined me for breakfast at Le Bistro in the Village, some forty-five minutes later than our appointment. "I doubt it." I beckoned her to sit, and reached for the tea.

"I'm sorry I'm late; I—"

"It's OK," I said. "Believe me. I'm late for everything. I'm sorry I started without you, but I was starving."

She sat down. She looked terrible.

"Tea, whole wheat toast and jam, and one poached egg," she told the waitress, who must have been a college student. I had trouble keeping my eyes off her stone-washed jeans.

"Juice?"

"Yes," Tesa said. "A small glass of orange juice, please."

"And I'll have a refill in my large glass, please," I added.

"Sure," the waitress said. Probably an NYU student.

I looked at Tesa. "So tell me."

"Dave's remains are carbon-dating at thirty thousand years now."

"What?"

"That's what the first series of tests show," Tesa replied. "You want to bet that they won't be confirmed?"

I shook my head, in disbelief as well as no. "So this means, what? That the other corpses are recent deaths as well? I suspected that there might be some connection between this telomere illness, whatever it is, and looking like a Neanderthal—that's why I had Dave's body exhumed. Something about the way the family didn't want anyone to see Dave when he was in the hospital got me thinking about that. . . . But how the hell could a virus, or whatever causes the illness, also throw off the carbon-14 dating like that?"

Tesa wiped her mouth with a napkin, even though she hadn't eaten anything as yet. "You tell me."

"Carbon-14 dating measures the amount of radioactive carbon that remains in an organic compound after death," I thought out loud. "The living organism incorporates carbon-14, it stops doing that when it dies, we know how long it takes for the carbon-14 isotope to decay into carbon-12, we do the math, and bingo, we have an estimate as to how long ago the organism stopped incorporating carbon-14—how long ago it died."

"So far, so good," Tesa said. "But how could a virus possibly interfere with that?"

"I don't know," I replied. "What do viruses do? They rearrange molecular material. . . ."

Tesa nodded. "Yah, but then what? Taking over the machinery of cells, messing with their molecules, is a far cry from leaching neutrons from a carbon-14 nucleus. To do that, the virus would have to pierce the atom's subatomic structure—an order of magnitude at least two levels lower. Totally unheard of."

The food arrived.

Tesa poked at hers, as if it were carbon. "The way you break into the nucleus of an atom," she continued, "is you aim a high-energy particle at the nucleus in a suitable high-tech chamber." She teased the white of her poached egg with her fork. "And even that doesn't cause the kind of rapid decay of the carbon-14 isotope we're considering here."

I drank my orange juice and smacked my lips. As frightening as some things were, I found the attempt to understand them among the most exhilarating feelings in this world. "Is there nothing other than high-energy particles that ever molests, undermines, an atomic nucleus?"

"What are you driving at?" Tesa asked.

"I'm not sure. What are we overlooking? On the one hand, perhaps the same thing that got into Dave Spencer's cells and killed him, and hijacked his DNA enough to half turn him into a Neanderthal before he died—let's call that a virus for now— perhaps that same thing was also able to penetrate the atoms in his body and change their subatomic composition, reduce the carbon-14. On the other hand, we run up against the wall that nothing short of bombardment by high-energy particles can breach the nuclei of atoms. Are we completely sure about that? Is there anything in the literature about alterations of atomic nuclei *outside* of particle accelerators?"

"Well . . . ," Tesa began. She looked down at her plate, then stabbed the center of the poached egg with her fork. The yolk leaked a pool of yellow onto her plate. "There's cold fusion, of course. But cold fusion is itself controversial. . . ."

"Go on," I prodded.

"You probably know more about it than I do," Tesa said. "Didn't Debbie have an article about it a few months ago?" Her face strained in recollection. "Lots of experiments are still going on, on the side streets of science. The whole claim of cold fusion is that the nuclei can be breached by some chemical means— outside the particle chamber. In hot fusion, the action takes place in a near-vacuum, because there's so much empty space, so much distance, ordinarily, between the nuclei of one and another atom. But in cold fusion, it's thought that a lattice is created between two atoms, which allows them to get much closer, so that neutrons and energy can be exchanged."

"Lattice?"

"Yeah," Tesa replied, eyes closed as if she were reading Debbie's article on the insides of her eyelids. She looked haggard— looked her age. "Palladium gets loaded with deuterium, or tritium," she continued, "and one theory is that a pair of equilibrium sites come into being, through which energy and particles are passed."

"Jeez," I said. "So maybe we're talking about some kind of virus packing the equivalent of palladium for carbon-14, so that it sets up those equilibrium sites when it gets close enough to the carbon-14. . . . Hmmm . . . palladium is to tritium as x is to carbon-14—"

"Well, yes, tritium and carbon-14 are both radioactive isotopes—"

"Exactly—"

"But that's still quite a stretch," Tesa said, opening her eyes, tired, bloodshot, looking at me. "And how would you account for the Neanderthal features? That's at least something I'm supposed to be an expert in."

"That's the easy part," I replied. "The virus gets into Dave's DNA; it edits the DNA; the amended DNA does its thing— instructs proteins how to grow—and that growth turns out to look like a Neanderthal . . . not enough to save Dave's life—hell, it likely wiped out his brain—but enough to make him *look* like a Neanderthal before he died."

"Fast work, even for a virus," Tesa said.

"Not necessarily," I said. "If we're right, the virus or whatever it is infected Dave months ago. Same time it infected me. Except he was lucky enough to get the silk every night, until . . ." I sighed. "I sent the cure to Dave, and he didn't take it. I gave it to Herby Edelstein, just to be sure. You took yours, didn't you?"

"Yes, yes."

"OK," I said, not entirely reassured. "Dave's collapse must have been just the final stage—the prelude to the metamorphosis, the culmination of months of *sub rosa* viral editing."

"One hell of an edit," Tesa said. "Almost suggests that we already have some explicit Neanderthal DNA in our genome. . . ."

"Why not? You yourself told me how close our two genomes seem to be," I said.

She concentrated. "I can't see how any virus, or whatever we call it, could possibly *edit* our DNA into something it wasn't, to create a new species on the spot, even over a few months. A more likely explanation—if any of this is what is actually happening—might be that we are in effect Neanderthals. That our baseline DNA is Neanderthal. But that somewhere along the line, in evolution, some kind of blocking agent arose that suppressed the Neanderthal genes. Switched them off. And now this virus somehow shuts off the suppression agent? I suppose it's possible. . . ."

"I could buy that. I'm not wedded to the editing."

"So what does that say about all of the world's Neanderthal specimens—the ones uncovered in the fossil beds in Europe, the Middle East, Asia? Some were never alive as Neanderthals? Their carbon dating is all off? Some unknown number—who knows, maybe all—are just are a bunch of poor shmucks, and women, who died in the past 150 years and happened to be infected by this strange carbon-altering virus we're hypothesizing?"

"I think the word you're looking for is *shlimazel*—a hapless soul—not *shmuck*," I said.

"What?"

"Have you or anyone ever seen a Neanderthal alive?"

"You want to throw out a century and a half of paleoanthropology?"

"If that what it takes," I replied.

Tesa took a perfunctory sip of her tea.

I looked at my watch. "I'm fifteen minutes late," I said. "But this has been very useful."

She smiled weakly.

"Tesa, what's wrong?" This definitely wasn't like her. "You used to be even more excited by these things than I am."

"Work isn't everything, Phil. I guess I'm concerned about Debbie."

"What's the matter with Debbie? Does she need the cure?" As far as I knew, she hadn't had any direct contact with any neo-Neanderthal.

"No, it's not that," Tesa replied. "It's her taste in men. As in: she has none. And she's involved with some guy now.... I don't know; I just don't like him."

"Tell me about him," I asked.

"Nothing I can put my finger on," she said. "He talks like he's lived in the Bronx or Brooklyn—I never can keep those two accents straight—all his life. He works on Wall Street. I don't know—he just gives me the creeps."

I took her hand, squeezed it. "Well, as long as he doesn't look like a Neanderthal," I said.

But the joke was becoming worn, for both of us.

ACTUALLY, I DID know someone who looked like a Neanderthal— and so did Tesa.

After kissing her good-bye on the cheek and telling her to please get some rest, I walked over to see him again at the Bobst Library.

"Phil D'Amato!"

"Mrs. Delany, how are you?" I smiled. I didn't expect to see her out here in front of the earth red library.

"I'm fine, and I bet you're not here to see me but Stefan Antonescu."

"Well, yes, I am. But it's good to see you, too." For a second I had a feeling I was going to hear that Stefan Antonescu wasn't in today. Could he have forgotten our appointment—

She smiled. "Stefan's downstairs, on the lower level, right where he always is on his days off—probably reading *To the Ends of the Earth!*"

"*To the Ends of the Earth?*"

"Oh, yes," Delany said. "A wonderful book about the Silk Road, the Spice Route, all the ancient highways and byways."

I nodded.

"I heard about the medical examiner, Dave Spencer," she said, and leaned closer. "It's a terrible thing, losing a colleague like that."

"Yes, it is—"

"But I guess things are at least beginning to get back to normal now for you, and thank goodness Stefan was OK. I guess things all fall into place, sooner or later."

"Yeah, that's the plan." But as much as I thought I was beginning to comprehend, I was sure it was going to be later.

"Well, I'd better get this book to the professor who requested it." She leaned over even closer. "Those Humanities professors are the worst—they think we've got nothing better to do than to wait on them hand and foot, and immediately! Now a science professor or an engineer, they understand that sometimes it can take a while to locate a book in our stacks. They understand the meaning of time. . . ."

I nodded sympathetically. "Librarians never made house calls in my day!"

"Isn't that the truth!" Mrs. Delany came back for a last confidential communication. "They say he'll be Dean next year, and I figure it doesn't hurt to have friends in high places. And the sun is beautiful today. . . ."

As indeed it was. I followed it into the library's huge atrium, where its rays came down like quicksilver strands of silk from the skylight. Silk . . . everywhere I looked now, I saw silk. When I wasn't seeing the result of viruses turning corpses into prehistoric Neanderthals. . . .

I showed the guard the temporary pass Ruth Delany had been good enough to send along to me several months ago, and walked down the stairs to find Stefan Antonescu.

I FOUND HIM at one of the reader desks, poring over *To the Ends of the Earth*, just as Ruth Delany had said.

"Stefan? Sorry I'm late." I had called him on the phone the day before, told him some of what I knew—or thought I knew—about the silk cure, and set up this meeting.

He looked up at me, thick-boned face with keen gray-green eyes. "Dr. D'Amato. No need to apologize." He caressed the book. "It was time well spent."

I marveled again at the gentleness, the sheer musicality, of his tone—not only the voice, which seemed to sing as much as speak, but his demeanor. I still could not tell if this quality was enhanced because of its contrast with the face and torso or would be as pronounced in any physical frame.

"I was wondering if I might entice you into a little conversation with some tea," I said. "And since you're not really at work here today—"

"Yes," Stefan said. "The Library is very kind to me in that way—there's always a seat for me here, whether I'm working or not."

I nodded. "Ruth Delany seems like a very compassionate woman."

"The best," Stefan said.

"So, shall we decamp to that new tea place on Waverly?" I asked.

"It's not as good as some, but I had some pretty nice Monk's Blend there last week," Stefan replied.

"Good; let's go then," I said. "I'd like us to be working together rather than against each other on this, Stefan."

"I'm beginning to find some of this of interest," he replied.

WE WALKED ALONG the east side of Washington Square Park. I decided to take advantage of Stefan's apparent lack of hostility today and lay out some of my cards. I told him about our virus theory—how whatever it was that had crushed telomeres and killed Dave Spencer had also worked on his DNA to turn him into a Neanderthal whose DNA dated back thirty thousand years.

"Ah, I see," Stefan said. "So I become the anomaly again, because I look like a Neanderthal and I'm still alive."

"Yes," I replied. "But there's no insult intended. I'm just interested in who you really are—I'm not looking to hurt you."

"Thank you. So what would like to know about me?"

"How old are you?"

"Well, you already know I'm not thirty thousand years old," Stefan said.

"How would I know that?"

"I assume you recovered a cell or two from my lips from the last cup of tea you gave me," he said.

I smiled. "Yes, and that did date as contemporary. But what can be triggered can also be reversed. If a cold-fusion virus can breach atomic nuclei and lower the ratio of radioactive material so it dates as much older than it really is, a similar virus could raise it so it dates much younger. If an unknown agent shears off telomeres and causes people to drop dead in their prime, it's not that big a leap to look for another related agent that keeps telomeres intact and confers longevity."

Stefan gestured to a vacant park bench. "Shall we stay outside for a while? It's a lovely day."

I sat down gingerly—a habit I'd no doubt acquired after too many years of splinters in my backside from the rotting green-painted wood of New York's inimitable park benches. This one seemed smooth and new, though.

"I assure you I'm no immortal," Stefan said. "There's more to immortality than your telomeres, in any case."

"You're amazingly well-read," I said. And I was sure I'd said that to him before.

"Thank you."

"And, of course, if you were thirty thousand years old, that would be more than enough time for your comprehensive reading. And you'd still be telling me the truth—technically—about your not being immortal."

Stefan laughed—soft rain, pinging against a new window. "You're way off," he said. "By a factor of a hundred."

I BECAME AWARE of a flute playing—a boy with sallow skin and sunken eyes had settled in against the next bench, actually on the ground right in front of it, with his back up against the edge of the wood. Or maybe he'd been there all along—he certainly looked no more strange than many of the other park inhabitants. But it was suddenly difficult to take my eyes and ears off him.

"Don't look so dazed," Stefan said. "You were suggesting I was thirty thousand years old. Surely a mere three hundred isn't that shocking."

"It's still an astonishing admission," I marveled. "What more can you tell me?"

"You've already guessed a part of it," Stefan said. I was born in Magyar territory—what we now call Hungary—some three hundred years ago. I came by my Neanderthal features honestly— naturally—there must have been some interbreeding between Neanderthal and Cro-Magnon, whatever the current theories say. There are actually lots of people walking around with at least some of my features. I'm just a more extreme case."

"Go on," I said.

"There were alchemists from the Far East moving through my city when I was boy. They were always more concerned with sexuality, immortality—the *tan*—than we in the West. There was a fire in a tavern one night. I happened by at the right time—I ran in and pulled out a burning man. I don't know what could have possessed me to do that. But I did, and he recovered, and he was grateful. And he told me about silk. . . ."

"It conveys immortality—longevity?"

"No," Stefan said. "It's not as simple as that. It only has that effect—*longevity* is a good word—on people who already look like me. True Neanderthal telomeres react as bit differently to *Bombyx mori* DNA than the telomeres of *Homo sapiens sapiens.*"

"But silk saved my life."

"Yes, it saved your life," Stefan said. "It counteracted the virus, if that's what you want to call it, that killed your friend. But you will not be immortal—you will not even live any longer than your natural life span. For you, the silk treatment repaired the damage to your telomeres that the virus was beginning to cause and that is all. Think about it—silk is almost as common as dirt in our world. If contact with it in any way extended people's lives, everyone would have already known about it for a very long time."

"All right," I agreed. "This is beginning to make a little sense. But why the knife attack on me? I don't believe in coincidences like that."

"Maybe it was a coincidence," Stefan said. "If it wasn't and someone wants you dead because of your involvement in these recent events, you'll likely be hearing from that person again."

THIRTEEN

"Fax coming in for you, honey."

"Be there in a second. Who's it from?"

"Hold on," Jenna said. "Looks like it's from England—44 country code—yeah, it's from Michael."

"Good; he said he'd be sending something along. Nice to see we're not the only ones working on a Sunday," I said.

Jenna took a scissor to the shiny thermal paper.

"I know; I know. We need to get a new one," I said. "Mallory told me his people were looking at some bizarre possible mention of a Neanderthal curse in Tocharian manuscripts. Is that it?"

Jenna nodded. "Yeah, it's a translation of a part of a Tocharian manuscript, with a copy of the original attached for comparison. Looks like this one was written on some kind of paper."

"Chinese paper," I said "Some of those manuscripts were bilingual, with words known in Sanskrit, so translations have been available for years. The manuscripts date from the seventh and eighth centuries A.D.—commercial documents, permits for caravans, lots of religious stuff, and a few medical and magical texts. Mallory told me the Brits had been working up some new translations and someone spotted a possible connection to our case."

"Hmm. . . ." Jenna pored over the translation. "This does seem to be a piece of a medical text—or maybe magical; I guess there wasn't that much difference between the two back then." She pointed to a page.

I've come to understand that we are the brutes, it said, *and the singers are angels—*

"Did the Tocharians believe in angels?" Jenna asked. "You've got to be careful with translations not to impose your own concepts."

"Well, sure, they could have believed in angels," I replied. "All they would have needed for that was some kind of Christian or Jewish contact, and there must've been plenty of that on the Silk Road."

"OK," Jenna said, and we looked again at the translation.

Our ancestors must have been jealous of the singers, for they killed most of them. Not because they were ugly, but because their minds were beautiful, and more knowing than ours. Their intelligence must have frightened our forebears, far more than their faces. Our forebears bred precautions, but the blood of the singers had its revenge, in the illness it has bestowed upon us and the children like a curse.

Mallory had underlined most of that last phrase at the bottom of the page—*illness it has bestowed upon us and the children like a curse.*

"Anything more?" I asked.

"No, I don't think so," Jenna replied. "Mallory says the word *cure* appears a few pages below *curse* in the manuscript, but the rest of the original has been corrupted."

"You gotta love that British usage: *corrupted,*" I said. "Let's see the original."

There was something magical indeed about seeing the graceful Indo-European script of the Tocharians, courtesy of a photocopy in London and a trip across the Atlantic via fax. But the manuscript did appear to be burned or charred at the end—whether by deliberate flame or natural oxidation, who could say. And the word that apparently was *cure* floated alone in a sea of smudge on the fax. . . .

"So can we assume that these 'singers'—these ugly brutes—are at least our Neanderthals?" I asked.

Jenna held her hands up in an I-don't-know gesture.

"I think it's time to get Mallory—and Lum up in Canada—on the phone," I said.

———

I SET UP a three-way conference call the next day—London, Toronto, New York City. Expensive as bloody hell, as Mallory would say. But like the vagrant who sneaks in to see the expensive doctor in the old joke also says, "Hey, Doc, when it comes to my health, money's no object."

How much was the health of our whole species worth?

The city would get the bill, a month from now, in any case. The Department had quietly reopened the investigation, with me in charge, in the wake of Dave's metamorphosis.

H.-T. Lum was explaining. He had just been about to call us, or fax us, or send a letter to us, with his own important news. . . . "People heard about what happened to Dave Spencer—word travels quickly up here," Lum said. "My guess is some tourist, maybe someone working for a museum in the States, bribed someone here and stole the body. A Neanderthal corpse in good condition could fetch a fortune!"

"So you're saying Gerry Moses turned ape-man on us, too?" Mallory asked.

"Why not?" Lum replied. "I don't know for a fact that he did. But it happened to Dave Spencer."

"But you don't have Gerry's body," I said.

"No. As I said, it's missing," Lum replied.

"Jesus H. Christ," Mallory said. "And you've known this for how long? Two days? And you hadn't thought to pick up a bloody phone and let us know? Good thing Phil thought to initiate this call."

"No need to be so angry!" Lum retorted, aggravated. "It was the weekend—some of us don't work seven days a week. And I have misgivings about the phone anyway. You never know who's listening in!"

"Yet you're talking on the phone right now," Mallory said.

"Yes, and maybe therefore I'm not saying everything I know!"

"All right," I said. "Let's each of us take it easy. Let's

go over the current status of each of our corpses, so we're all on the same wavelength." I still preferred *wavelength* to *page*—a more dynamic metaphor. "H.-T., I assume your original Neanderthal mummy is still in evidence?"

"Yes," Lum said.

"And the man you thought might be him—"

"Sidney Eigen—"

"Yeah, Sidney Eigen. He's still missing?"

"Yes," Lum said.

"Same on this side," Mallory provided. "Our mummy is still at home, and there's no sign of Max Soros. Your Stefan Antonescu is the only one of the three who has come back to life—sorry, reappeared; we never knew with a certainty he was a corpse. We still can't say for sure with either Eigen or Soros. But your Stefan is clearly the odd man out on this, Phil. Either a cock-up in the New York theater, if there's some sort of master plan behind all of this, or, I don't know . . . but Antonescu is in some way a key. Has he been any more forthcoming, Phil?"

"No, not really." Well, here I was lying on the phone a little after all. I still didn't feel completely comfortable about Lum, and I had to do what I could to protect Stefan. He indeed was a crucial player.

"You know, it seems to me that there may be two master plans—or at least phenomena—at work here," I continued. "One is this virus, or whatever is, that not only kills some people but also turns them into Neanderthals and produces a false thirty-thousand-year carbon dating. About the only thing we know about that with any kind of confidence is that silk seems to be some sort of a cure, an antidote, a preventative, something along those lines."

"That's what your Amish friends gave you?" Mallory asked.

"Yes."

"The missus and I been sleeping in satin here, too, just to be on the safe side," Mallory said. "And we took the cure you sent along."

"And the second phenomenon?" Lum prompted. "The other factor to which you referred?"

"Well, we don't know if the two are related," I said. "But there's clearly some sort of knifist afoot. Gerry and Dave presumably died of the virus; I got sick from it but received the Amish cure in time. But that doesn't account for the guy who gave me a little engraving on my belly—duty free—in Heathrow Airport."

"You're still harping on that, Phil? It's hardly a phenomenon—London, alas, has its share of vicious criminals roaming the streets and, no doubt, airports, too," Mallory said.

"True, but I've just been in contact with my Amish friends. I'd sent them a sketch I'd had worked up here of the guy who knifed me in Heathrow—it was the least I could do after they'd saved my life. I wanted them to be prepared. And you know what? Seems that same vicious criminal jumped on a plane and reached our side of the pond. He tried to knife one of my friends in Pennsylvania over coffee this morning."

"You're back in Pennsylvania, Phil?" Mallory asked.

"Actually, no—my friend called me."

"So your friend was OK?" Lum asked. "He was just wounded, like you, not killed?"

"Yeah, he's OK," I said. "But from all accounts our man from Heathrow *tried* to kill him. Fortunately, my friend was wearing a special shirt—safety weave, they call it—which wraps around the blade, blunts it, slows its motion, so it's not much worse than a thumb jabbed into the stomach."

"So we come back to those unique Amish you have over there," Mallory said. "Knife-proof vests, telephones—"

"Well, there's a lot of misunderstanding of the Amish," I said. "Some of them don't mind phones, as long as they're not inside their homes."

Mallory laughed dryly. "What's the bleedin' world coming to, eh? Amish use phones; the Centre for Forensic Sciences in Toronto refrains from using them—"

"Not the whole Center," Lum protested. "I just find it advisable sometimes not to—"

"To each his own," I said. "Anyway, the important thing is that my friends in Lancaster County have this bastard's picture now, they know what he looks like, so they'll see him coming if he should visit their area again."

"I take it, then, that you've ruled out the possibility that your friends in Pennsylvania are lying," Mallory observed.

"WHY ARE YOU so sure one of them's lying?" Jenna asked, over the first sushi dinner we'd treated ourselves to in a long time. It was just yellowtail for me tonight—three rolls with vinegared rice and scallion. Yeah, I know there's some ecological reason not to eat it—the fishermen kill other innocent species in the nets that they use to catch the yellowtail. Or maybe it was OK now. I, frankly, didn't give a rat's ass tonight. I figured I was doing enough for ecology already, running after this Neanderthal thing that seemed to be biting us all in the gluteus.

I poured some green tea for Jenna and me. She was more adventurous—and environmentally sound—than I was this evening. She had just been brought a big plate of *chirashi*.

"OK, let's look at each of them," I said. "Let's start with H.-T. Lum. First, he seems weak, frightened, barely competent. Right away I'm suspicious: weak, incompetent people rarely rise to his position."

"Well, he didn't exactly attain the job the usual way," Jenna said. "Maybe he was good as second in command, but he's weak as top dog."

"Nah, I don't believe it," I said. "I mean, I think that's possible, of course. But usually seconds-in-command get even that far because they have something on the ball. Look at Herby Edelstein—some of the brass have been mumbling already that he's better than Dave. Look at Theodore Roosevelt—at Anwar Sadat."

"OK," Jenna conceded. "I agree from what you've said that Lum lays it on a little thick. And he's likely more competent than he lets on. Let's grant that he's a very peculiar man. But maybe that's just his way of dealing with crises—feign a certain amount of fear, even lack of competence, as a way of keeping everyone off-balance, to gain yourself a little space and time. Not everyone works the same as you, you know—plunging straight ahead." She smiled.

"I'll take that as a compliment, thanks."

"But what else do we have against him, other than his attitude?"

I sniffed the hot green tea—I needed all of its fragrance I could get to clear my head.

"We never seem to get anything from him," I said. "And when we do, it's always in a weird way. I don't care how the hell he feels about phones. Who in his right mind would find Gerry Moses's body missing and wait two days to tell us about it? That's an eternity in a case like this. Mallory was furious, and I don't blame him."

"But Mallory's been up-front with you about everything—as far as you know—almost since the day all of this began," Jenna pointed out. "Yet you're doubting him, too. He sent us the fax with the Tocharian translation."

"How do we know the translation is accurate?" I asked. "How do we know Mallory didn't doctor it to tell us what he wants us to think?"

"No problem," Jenna said. "I have a friend in Linguistics at Columbia—Bonnie Mitcham—who can translate that. Mallory also faxed us the original."

"How do we know that's the original?"

"Well, you can question everything and drive yourself crazy," Jenna said. "I know you like to do this, but where does it really get you? It's a game—like solipsism. We've talked about this before. If I want to believe the world is my dream, if I want to doubt that any stimulus, any evidence, offered to the contrary is real, well, then, no one could ever logically talk me out of my view."

"I have faith that *you're* real, angel."

She mouthed a kiss to me. "Anyway, we could probably get another copy of the Tocharian original from someone other than Mallory. . . . You know, everyone running around here, suspecting that the other one is lying, is just what someone who is really behind this would want—to sit back and watch you tear yourselves to pieces."

"Yeah, if the virus doesn't get us first."

"Are you making progress on that—"

"Progress? I can't even demonstrate to anyone's satisfaction that there *is* a virus! Herby's people have run every test known to humanity on poor Dave. There's nothing there—other than the fact that he looks like a Neanderthal and somehow put on thirty thousand years overnight."

"So it's something that's been unknown to humanity—or at least, its existence has been unknown, maybe not its effects, like you always say about viruses themselves before the nineteenth century or even bacteria before Leeuwenhoek."

"And that's precisely the problem," I told her. "Let's say I somehow suspected that bacteria, not rats, not filth, not bad humors, were the ultimate cause of the Plague in the year 1400. Without a microscope to pinpoint *Pasteurella pestis,* how could I ever prove it? I'd have as much as three-quarters of the population dead in some locales as evidence—far more by a factor of God knows how many than our newly minted Neanderthals—but no way of investigating what I saw as its truest cause. Even after Leeuwenhoek, it took the human species a hundred and fifty more years to come up with a Pasteur."

"But if your hypotheses about bacteria and what they were like were to some extent accurate, you might be able to draw reasonable expectations that you could test about their impact even if you could never see them per se," Jenna said. "You might hypothesize that, as living organisms, they would die in boiling water, or flames, and treat the site of plague victims that way, and get results. . . ."

I refilled Jenna's cup with tea and realized the pot was just about empty. I looked up for our waiter—usually waiters and wait-resses have an uncanny knack of knowing just when to intrude on a sensitive conversation and throw it off-track, if not when a teapot or a pitcher of sangria required replenishing. But no one who could help was in sight.

I did see a couple at a table halfway across the room, who seemed to be looking in my direction, pointing to a menu on their table, then looking at me again and whispering in exagger-ated motions to each other.

Jenna turned to see what I was looking at. "Looks like a news-paper," she said.

"Yeah," I agreed. "I thought I was on their menu at first. I guess I was talking a little loudly."

Our waiter finally appeared. Jenna started telling him we needed more tea—

"I'm off to the men's room," I said.

I of course went by way of my audience's table. The man stood up and offered his hand as I walked slowly by. "Dr. D'Amato? Sorry for staring at you before."

I took the hand and shook it. "Hey, I'm flattered," I said. "Assuming the stare was out of admiration." I smiled and gave his hand another pump.

The woman reddened and turned embarrassed eyes down to the paper.

"Yes, well," the man said, "have you seen tomorrow's *Times*? Has a very flattering picture of you, but, well . . ."

He gave me the paper—tomorrow's edition indeed, available in town the night before—open to the middle of the local section. There was a beaming picture of me, in my favorite vest and tie. In fact, the very vest I was wearing this evening. And the article . . .

Its headline read: "New York Forensics on Neanderthal Wild-Goose Chase."

The subheadlines read: "Experts Deride Three Months of Work as 'Pseudoscience'—Commissioner's Office to Investigate."

And it got worse from there.

By this time, Jenna had joined us.

"Unbelievable," she said. "Why would Debbie write something like that?"

I COULD STILL feel the yellowtail swimming around in my stomach in Jack Dugan's office at nine o'clock the next morning, somewhere under the tea and toast I'd dumped in there about an hour earlier.

"Not to worry overly," Jack said. "Believe me, the Commissioner's far more pissed off at the *Times* than he is at you—he doesn't like finding out from *them* that he's launching an investigation."

Somehow I was still worried—not that it mattered; I was going to continue with my work on this whatever the hell the Department said.

"I told him just this morning," Herby Edelstein, who was also in the office, piped in. The "him" was the Commissioner. "I saw Dave's body; anyone could see there was something strange going on there. I told him I was behind you 100 percent on getting to the bottom of this. It's just this virus thing—you know, we've got to keep a lid on that until we're sure. We don't want the public panicking."

"Right," Dugan said. "Like that idiotic Dustin Hoffman movie with the monkey."

"*Outbreak,*" I said. "That was the name of the movie. Except in that movie the public's panic was justified. . . . Look, I don't know how Debbie got her information." But I had a pretty good idea. I'd tried to call both Debbie Tucker and her mother, last night and this morning, but had no luck with either. Debbie's obvious source was her mother, but I didn't want to focus attention on Tesa until I had a better sense of what was going on.

"Well, we're on that," Dugan said. "We've got some detectives over to Debbie Tucker's apartment even as we speak. But the point is: her information about your theories and goings-about was accurate. So she got it from someone who knows."

"Yeah," I said, "unlike those bozo 'experts' from NYU she interviewed about my Amish work. 'They abjure technology—recognize it for the crippling detriment it is to humanity—and would never be involved in the kinds of schemes Dr. D'Amato imagines them to be.' "

Dugan smiled. "Well, they're profs from the Communications Department, right? Wha'd you expect?"

I returned the smile, barely. "And what about her information about the Department's investigation of my investigation—you know, the one the Commissioner was so furious to find out about in the paper? Was her information reliable about that, too?" In other words, just because the Commissioner didn't know about it didn't mean it wasn't going on.

Herby cleared his throat. "Phil, I'm sure Dave explained to you the, ah, resistance some of the folks at One Police Plaza have to your theories. I'd be lying to you if I told you there was no one in the upper echelons out gunning for you—"

The phone rang.

Dugan picked it up. "Yeah? . . . Jesus. . . . Yeah, all right. . . . Jesus—he's right here. . . . All right. Jesus. I'll get him over there."

He hung up and looked at Herby. "Your presence is requested at Debbie Tucker's apartment."

"What, there's a body there?" Herby asked.

"Yeah, two of them—Debbie's presumably and some older woman's. One cut up pretty nicely. The other, we don't know the cause of death yet—"

I was halfway out the door—

"You can come, too." Dugan called after me. "In fact, I think I'll tag along and make it three's a crowd. . . ."

They joined me at the elevator. Dugan straightened his uniform in the reflection of the smooth brass door.

"We'll get the son of a bitch who did this, don't you worry, Phil," Dugan said. "They said the apartment's crawling with prints."

FOURTEEN

"No sign of rape in either case," Patricia Chu, Herby's chief assistant, formerly Dave's, informed us.

Debbie was stretched out spread-eagle on her bed, a red scarf her only garb, knotted tightly around her neck. It just had to be silk—someone was trying to send a message. *Bombyx mori, memento mori* . . .

"As you can see, no marks anywhere on the front of the body, and nothing I could see on preliminary on the back," Patricia said. "Best guess at this point is strangulation. We'll know more after the full examination."

"Better take a closer look at that, too." I pointed to some red fibers in the hair just above Debbie's pudenda. Red silk on red hair—color coordinated for death tied up in some way to some Neanderthal phenomenon.

"Yeah, I noticed that," Patricia said.

"How long do you figure she's been dead?" I asked.

"I'd say about eight to ten hours. This happened in the middle of the night," Patricia replied.

Herby was busy with the other body, stabbed to death in the foyer and dragged into the bathroom.

Tesa's clothes all seemed to be on, except for the four or five parts of her blouse that had been rent open with the knife. No signs of silk that I could see.

"I only met her once—that day at Dave's exhumation," Herby said. "She seemed like a fine lady."

"She was," I said.

"Someone must've been pretty angry at her," Herby said.

"She must've come in on the strangulation," Dugan, who had joined us, added. "Or right after."

"The other one was strangled?" Herby asked.

"Looks that way," Dugan replied.

"We'll know more after the full autopsy," Herby said.

"Speaking of timing, what were you doing in the middle of the night last night?" Dugan asked me.

"Sound asleep, right next to Jenna," I replied.

"And since she was presumably sound asleep, too, that's not much of an alibi," Dugan said.

"Since when the hell do I *need* an alibi—"

My OFFICE FELT like a dungeon.

I'd managed to pick up some folders—when I hoped no one was looking—that apparently had slid between Debbie's desk and her printer table. I had no idea how much of her work she did on-line, how much through old-fashioned notes and clippings, but it certainly could not hurt to see what I could find here.

My first glances had revealed nothing too interesting—nothing at all, in fact, on her article about me in today's *Times*. I'd assumed that her murder had something to do with that article, but now I began to suspect Debbie had not written it. So she was murdered why? To cover up the fact that someone had somehow planted that article under her name?

I rubbed my eyes and flipped through the manila folders again. She'd managed an article at least once every two weeks, and there were scribbled notes for most of the recent ones. That lent some kind of credence to my thought that she had not written the article about me. Or maybe her murderer stole her notes.

The most current folder had material about her human genome article in the paper last week. The usual suspects were quoted from MIT, Rockefeller University, and—jeez, I hadn't noticed that highlighted section on the back of one of the sheets the first time I had leafed through them. And the phone number that was scribbled alongside it. . . .

"I DON'T CARE how much you don't trust the phone," I said, trying to keep my raised voice as civil as possible. "I don't have time to fly up and see you now. I swear to God, if you don't talk to me, I'll call up the *New York Times* myself, right after we get off the phone, and see to it that your name is plastered all over the front page tomorrow!" Of course, I didn't have that kind of clout, but Lum couldn't know that for sure.

"It's just speculation at this point," he said.

"Good; speculate then," I told him.

Lum sighed. "The genome people think they've identified some sequences in the human code that look a lot like *Bombycidae.*"

"*Bombyx mori?*"

"Not exactly," Lum replied. "A different moth. But the same family."

"So someone contaminated the human DNA with silk? Where did these studies originate? MIT, Caltech, England?"

"That's the problem," Lum said. "The silk sequences seem present in all human samples thus far examined."

"But how—"

"The presence in itself is not surprising," Lum said. "There are lots of specific sequences in humans that seem taken from other species—we've known about near-identities in the *Lachesin* gene in grasshoppers and fruit flies and similar genes in cows and humans for years now. All DNA life on Earth is, after all, related."

"Sure, but—"

"What struck me about this one is that I had just been going over a Neanderthal profile and it seems to lack that *Bombycidae* sequence."

"So the differences between us and Neanderthals is we have a silk sequence already in our genes?"

"Maybe," Lum said. "There are lots of genes, as you know,

that apparently amount to nothing—have no discernible effect on the phenotype as far as we can tell. Free riders, genes that served some purpose in the distant past and now serve none—who knows. The real question, I think, is how was this *Bombycidae* sequence introduced into our genome? Did it arise naturally?"

I thought of John Lapp and Amos Stoltzfus and the artificial selection they claimed their people had been practicing for centuries, maybe longer. . . .

"You and Debbie talked about all of this?" I asked.

"Tesa Stewart, too," Lum said. "We had some mutual friends in the field. A great loss to science!" His voice cracked with emotion.

"I know," I said softly.

"I talked to Tesa and Debbie on the phone," Lum continued. "I trusted them. I guess I don't mind talking to you. But let's be smart about this. Let me send you a letter with a public phone number that you can call. We can do it by appointment—that's how I did it with Tesa and Debbie."

Yeah, and a lot of good it did them, I thought.

I RECLINED IN my chair and closed my eyes after I got off the phone with Lum.

Could *Bombycidae* sequences in our genome—or sequences that resembled *Bombycidae*—have made us fully human? Could they account for our differences from Neanderthals, our language, our culture, our technology where presumably they had so little? Hard to believe. Certainly moths had no Beatles, no Mozart, no Picasso. But insects, in their way, were masters of communication, and technology, too. The societies of bees and ants, the communication among their members, the hives and nests they constructed had been the stuff of sociobiology for decades now. And the very *Lachesin* gene that Lum had mentioned, if I remembered my *Science* readings correctly, helped govern the growth of neuronal cells. . . .

But what connection did this have to Tesa and Debbie?

They were killed because they knew something more about this?

Killed by whom?

And what connection did it have to Dave Spencer and Gerry Moses?

Did the virus I was postulating somehow undo the effect of the *Bombycidae* in our genes? Is that why *Bombyx mori* seemed some kind of antidote?

The phone rang.

"Hello."

"Hi, honey." Jenna was returning my call. She'd left before I'd awoken this morning, to see her friend for breakfast up at Columbia. "Bonnie says Mallory's translation of the Tocharian is good, so that's at least a start."

"Fine."

"What's the matter?"

I told her about Tesa and Debbie, about my conversation with Lum, about how I didn't feel very good right now about involving anyone else in this goddamn case.

"Oh, God, we just had dinner with Tesa last week," Jenna said.

"Yeah. It looks like she walked in on the murder. Debbie was killed ritually. Tesa was slashed in a rage. It had something to do with Debbie's last two stories in the *Times,* I'm sure. I just can't tell which one."

"I still can't believe Debbie wrote that story about you."

"I was thinking the same thing," I said.

"So who wrote it?" Jenna asked.

"I don't know," I said. "If someone wanted me off the case but didn't want to come right out and kill me because it would attract too much attention, a good way of doing that would be to somehow get a story in the papers under Debbie's byline that made me look bad and then kill Debbie, which has the double advantage of stopping Debbie from protesting the forgery and casting suspicion on me as her murderer by giving me a motive.

And maybe it also provides the additional service of shutting down Debbie's investigation of the *Bombycidae* in our genes, if she was digging into that."

"You were so angry at her that you killed her? Anyone who knew you would know that was absurd."

"Maybe the killer doesn't know me. . . . Hell, this case has gotten everyone so crazy even Dugan half suspects me."

"Ridiculous," Jenna said. "You were in bed with me all night."

"I know," I replied, and thought again, as I often did, about how good it felt waking up with her next to me every morning. . . . "I'm worried about you," I said gently. "Heathrow was one thing—that was across the Atlantic, and Mallory was right to think that guy with the knife likely had nothing to do with this case. But Debbie and Tesa are another story. Their killer is probably still in town. And Tesa was slashed. Puts what happened at Heathrow in a whole other light—"

"Stop it! You're scaring me!"

"That's the idea," I said. "Look, this could still all be coincidence. Tesa was acting a little strange recently, maybe a boyfriend of Debbie was stalking her, but—"

"I know. You don't believe in coincidence."

"Right. Especially not when there are more plausible explanations. I'm going to go downtown and see if I can talk to Stefan—maybe he can be of help. But you've got to be careful, observant. Let me know right away if you see anything odd, if you sense anything unusual. I'd rather you overreact with a false alarm, then . . . well, you know what I mean. OK?"

Jenna didn't respond.

"You OK?"

"Yeah," she said. "You know, I just remembered, when I left our apartment this morning I stopped into the Yorkville and grabbed a tea to go."

"Yes?"

"Well, there was someone wolfing down a big breakfast at a

table. And I sort of felt like he was staring at me, in an odd way."

"What did he look like?"

"Definitely not Neanderthal." Jenna laughed nervously. "And I mean, he didn't look like anyone I actually knew, but, well . . ."

"He reminded you of someone? All right, listen. I'm sending a patrol car over for you right away. Sit tight, and tell me where you are."

"The library. I'm at a pay phone in the lobby of Butler Library. Bonnie was called in for some sort of consult in the Basque section over here—"

"OK, good. The lobby should be safe. Don't move from there until you see the two uniforms."

"OK," Jenna said. "It's not that he reminded me of someone in particular. But that guy in the restaurant—I don't know, he was wearing normal clothes, but he looked Amish."

"Stefan Antonescu? My name is Amos Stoltzfus." A man under twenty extended his hand to a man who said he was three hundred.

Antonescu regarded the hand but didn't take it. "Do I know you?"

"No," Amos said. "May I sit down?" He sat down as quietly as he could at the Bobst Library table.

"There's no point in my answering," Antonescu replied. "It seems you've sat down already. And this is a public table, so you're entitled to sit here whatever my preference."

"You don't know me," Amos said. "But we both have the same friend, Dr. Phil D'Amato."

Antonescu nodded. "Are you Amish?"

Amos nodded back.

"I thought so," Antonescu said. "You'll be safe here—people will think you're just one of the *Hasidim*."

"*Hasidim?*"

"Yes," Antonescu replied. "Members of an Orthodox Jewish

sect with beards and black clothes. Much like you. Many *Hasidim* are in this part of the city—New York University is really just over the bridge from Brooklyn."

"Phil—Dr. D'Amato—once told me he was Jewish. Marrano?"

"Yes," Antonescu said. "His people were persecuted doing the Spanish Inquisition. Some changed their names, pretended to be Catholic, but they kept their Jewish identity. Persecution's a terrible thing. My people have been persecuted for more than thirty thousand years."

"I know," Amos said softly, his eyes wide. "I'm sorry."

"Don't be sorry," Antonescu told him. "Your specific people are not the ones responsible."

"I know," Amos said. "But . . . I'm still sorry about what happened to your people. My people have known persecution, too. That's why I'm here—I thought we could put together our information. There's danger. My friends know many secrets of nature. That's why we succeed without electricity—nature is stronger."

"You know one of the secrets of silk. You saved Dr. D'Amato's life with it. He told me."

Amos nodded. "But now he's in danger again. All of us are. We may need more than silk."

Antonescu looked around the room. "Shall we go for a walk in the park? It was a lovely July day when I arrived this morning—not too hot."

"OK . . . ," Amos said.

"I'll just return these books to the stacks," Antonescu said.

Amos trembled. "A room with stacks and stacks of books makes me nervous. I prefer voices and people."

"I understand," Antonescu said. "I'll just be a minute."

Amos walked over to Ruth Delany's desk.

"Did you find him?" she asked, and smiled.

"Yes." Amos returned the smile. "Thank you, Missus."

————

A PHONE RANG once on a corner of Washington Square Park.

"You took your sweet time to get back to me," a man said answering the phone, looking out at pigeons and passersby with equal malignance. "You'll never guess who just walked by here not ten minutes ago—that moron Amish waiter I took care of in Pennsylvania last month! I stuck him right proper with my knife! And here he is strolling bright as day into the bleeding library! I can finish the job right now." He felt the hilt of the knife in his belt.

"I see you're back in fine Cockney speech," the voice on the phone said. "Good; I much prefer it to the Brooklynese."

"What about that Amish waiter—"

"No, I think there's been nearly enough killing for one day, don't you?" the voice on the phone asked.

The man with the knife laughed. " 'Nearly enough'?—now what the hell does that mean? Listen, that waiter saw my face— he can identify me—that's why I need to take care of him."

"We'll deal with that problem another way," the voice said. "No need for you to worry."

"OK, so how much longer do you want me to stay here?"

"Not much longer," the voice replied.

A lady with a shopping cart full of groceries approached the phone. She smiled sweetly. "Excuse me. Will you be on the phone much longer? I need to call my grandson."

"Yeah, a lot longer. Use another phone."

"Who's that?" the voice on the phone said.

"I don't know. Some hag—Hey!"

The woman had pulled out a hypodermic needle and with one swift motion plunged it into his arm in the second he turned his back on her and talked into the phone. Into his vein she emptied the contents—an ancient compound virtually indistinguishable in composition and effect from pure heroin, except she didn't have to get it from a dealer. . . .

He slumped to the ground, first happier than he had ever been in his life, then dead.

The woman bent over the body and removed the knife from the belt. She stood up, took hold of the dangling phone receiver, and said a few words.

"Thank you," the voice on the phone said. "And you can tell our recently departed friend that now the killing has definitely reached the saturation point for today. We've progressed from nearly enough to more than enough, I'm sure. Unfortunately, now that the meaning of 'nearly enough' is clear, it's too late for him to understand it."

The woman didn't understand much beyond the first two words, either, but she said, "Yeah" and concluded cheerily, "I'm heading up to catch my train at Penn Station. The air is still too polluted in this city for me to be really comfortable here. . . ."

Antonescu and Stoltzfus passed her on the corner a little while later. They walked by the phone a few minutes after that.

Stoltzfus never noticed the body on the ground. His eyes were on the trees.

Antonescu did but said nothing. He'd seen much like it in this city, this life, this world before.

I GAVE THE cabbie a five-dollar bill and told him to keep the change.

He stuck his head out the window and glared at me. "Hey, thanks, buddy; the fare comes to five-dollars!"

"Sorry." I handed him another five-dollar bill.

Washington Square Park was bursting in every direction—flower ladies from the Phil Ochs song, skateboarders crisscrossing around me at angles that made fractals look simple, a drunk passed out on a bench, another under a phone, babies and toddlers and mothers and grandmas, couples in all combinations. . . . But no sign of Antonescu or anyone Amish, even though Ruth Delany had told me on the cell phone that Stefan and "an Amish boy" had gone out for a walk here just minutes ago. . . .

A doo-wop group was singing "Life Could Be a Dream" by the fountain and attracting quite a crowd. I stopped for a moment to collect my thoughts and a bag of peanuts from a vendor. How could the same world accommodate such joy and such brutality? Because some people took their joy in brutality, that was why. Because for some people, erasing another person, erasing a whole people, was no more than erasing unwanted data from a hard disk. Digital data, DNA, just another code, another recipe discarded. . . .

I looked at a stream of butterflies on the far side of the fountain. Flutterbys to the sky. I followed their path back down to the hand that was releasing them. A small crowd had gathered around the person setting the butterflies free. The monarchs glittered, gold and black, in the sunlight. And then the emigration was over. The crowd began to unravel. The man with the hand turned toward me.

Amos!

I rushed over to him—

"Phil! I was just sending a message home," he said, "and then I was going to get in touch with you."

"Where's Stefan? Is he OK?"

"Stefan Antonescu? Yes, he's fine. He went back to the library about ten minutes ago. We had a very good conversation."

I looked through the park toward Bobst Library, red sandstone through green trees.

"What's the matter, Phil? You look like you don't believe me! We can go see Stefan right now—"

"No, I believe you." I told Amos about the murders, about Jenna thinking she saw someone who was possibly him at the Yorkville Restaurant.

"Yes, that was me," Amos said. "I guess seeing Jenna threw me off—I didn't know if she would be heading back home; I didn't know how much of this you had told her, what you wanted her to know. I remembered your not wanting us to tell her too much when we were giving you the cure. So I figured I'd see Stefan first and contact you later. . . ."

"How did you know what she looked like?"

"You showed me her picture, remember?"

I nodded. I had.

A silken cat approached us and sidled up to Amos.

"Hyram," I said. I hadn't seen him since I'd left Pennsylvania—

"He alerted us early this morning that something was wrong here," Amos said. "That's why I came to the city now. He's been keeping an eye on you and your friends—your guardian angel—since you got back to New York City. I'm sorry that I upset Jenna. . . ."

"It's OK," I said. Jenna was safe and sound in our apartment now, with officers stationed outside just in case. "So what did you learn from Stefan?"

"His people were smarter than all of us, you know."

"How so?"

"I mean the original Neanderthals," Amos said. "They had bigger brains, more room to store wisdom about nature."

"Brains don't necessarily work that way—connections count more than raw storage capacity."

"More room for connections, then," Amos allowed. "And our ancestors—your ancestors and my ancestors—we killed them. Our peoples killed them. Because we envied their wisdom. That may be what these murders are all about."

"Stefan told you that?"

"Not exactly that," Amos replied. "He didn't know about the murders. I didn't know until you just told me. Our watchcats tell us with their eyes when there is trouble—they don't actually speak to us." He smiled, I guess at the absurdity of a cat relating specific descriptions. Cats travelling hundreds of miles to communicate turmoil with their eyes—that was old hat to these people.

"What connection could these murders have to the Neanderthals?" I asked.

"I believe the people who first wiped out the Neanderthals are the same people who plagued us with their Mendel bombs, who killed Laurie's father. They are a prehistoric people. They are responsible for the Neanderthal corpses in your cities, I'm sure of it, though I don't understand why they did that. But they kill people—with illness if possible, with weapons if they must—who get in their way. You've already seen some of their handiwork in Pennsylvania." He touched his abdomen. "I felt the cold kiss of one their knives—fortunately I was wearing this safety weave." He stroked his shirt, moss green.

"I'm glad you're OK," I said. "You should have told me about this connection to the Neanderthals sooner."

"It's just a theory—as you would call it," Amos replied. "We probably know less about the Neanderthals than you know—we have no access to their remains around the world. All we're going on are our old stories, passed down from father to son, uncle to nephew, oldest to youngest brother."

I sighed.

"I wish I had more butterflies," Amos said. "I should tell John Lapp about the murders. He should be alerted about the danger. He doesn't use a phone—like I do. He knows to look at the sky."

"You were using those butterflies to send back a message to John Lapp?"

"Yes. They're very dependable."

"Those butterflies can fly from here to Pennsylvania?"

"Oh, yes," Amos said. "Monarch butterflies fly every year from here to Mexico, with pinpoint accuracy. These were bred to fly right to the butterfly bush in the back of John Lapp's garden."

"You came here how—by train?—with a cage of butterflies?"

"No, by bus. It's OK for our group to ride by bus, as long as we don't drive it. I could've brought some butterflies along in a bunch of envelopes—they travel just fine that way, as long as you don't sit on them. But I figured I'd need a lot of butterflies for this, so my friend brought them down to me from Union Square—I saw him on my way down here. He runs an Amish bakery stand there."

"Yeah, I think I've had his bread. It's delicious," I said.

"Don't worry about letting John know about the murders—I'll call someone in Lancaster, and he'll figure out a way of getting John the message."

"OK, thanks."

"Butterflies," I said, and looked at the sky. "Even if you'd saved a few, how in the world would they be able to carry a message that two people were murdered?" If cats couldn't talk, how the hell could butterflies?

"It's all in the way they land—which butterflies set down first and where on the bush. I have to let them go in just the right order—it took me years to learn. We can spell out all sorts of things that way. It's a pattern—a code—each pattern of landings stands for a different letter. It takes a lot of butterflies, but ours are bred to land and take off and land again as many times as needed to spell out the message. We call it moth code—we had it long before Morse had his. It's ancient. Maybe he got his idea from us."

And what code was causing all of this to happen?

PART

FOUR

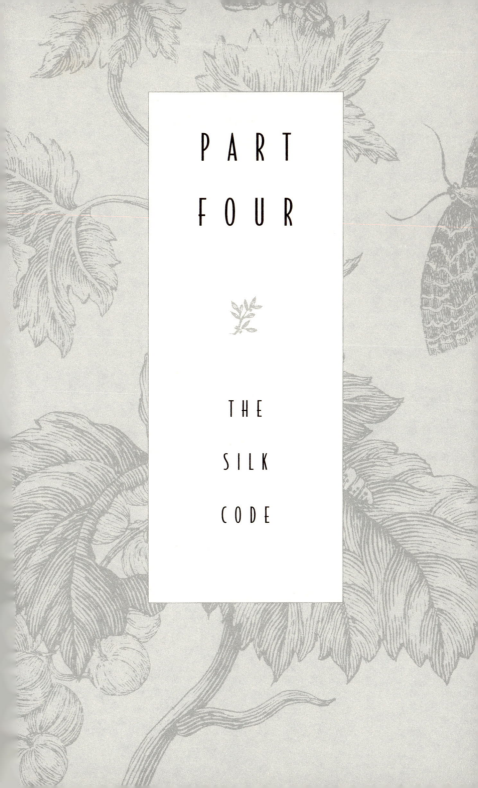

THE

SILK

CODE

FIFTEEN

"Nothing but a few dead moths and two past-due bills in the mailbox." I closed the flimsy front of the box in my lobby. Would that the DNA codes we were trying to crack had been as readily revealing of their contents.

"Is that your idea of a joke?" Mallory asked. He was over here for a "consultation" with me, the wheels of UK funding having finally ground around and come up with the "requisite bob," as he put it, that he had requested from his superiors months ago for this trip. I was working at home today.

"I wish it was," I replied, "but we get lots of moths in these kinds of brownstones in the summer." I looked at my watch. "It's 12:50. Let's go over to the Yorkville for some lunch."

We walked to the restaurant. Mallory handed me a sheaf a papers, after we'd seen ourselves to a table. "First, here's the report I was telling you about." You could always tell a British report or a letter from an American—even before you looked at the words. British paper was about a quarter-inch slimmer and three-quarters of an inch longer. Sometimes I found the difference pleasing, sometimes irritating. Today—

"So you'll see the summating data beginning on page 20," Mallory said. "Our boys found some real differences in Dave Spencer's DNA."

They had indeed. The DNA from the three original corpses had been spliced, diced, measured, tested, inserted, all with the same result—it was stable, predictable, hadn't done anything unusual since its initial recovery from the corpses months ago. Same for Stefan Antonescu. But now Dave Spencer's DNA, or whatever the hell it had become, suddenly seemed to be a work in progress. Inserted into rat cells, it went off in all directions—a Fourth of July of bizarre combinations, none of which were survivable. So far. . . .

"They call it hypermutability," Mallory continued. "There's a similar effect known in some *E. coli* genes."

"Yeah, I know about the *E. coli*," I said. "Our rat cells with Dave's postmortem DNA coincide completely with yours. What I'm wondering is how long Dave's DNA will retain the *Bombycidae* sequences." I had filled Mallory in on Lum's theory.

"I'll tell our lab boys to keep an eye on that," Mallory said. "My superiors have become very interested in this."

More than mine, I thought. "Is that why they finally sent you over here?"

"I don't really give a rat's scrotum about my superiors," Mallory said, "except insofar as they can help me do what needs to get done. You know that. I'm here because I'm concerned about this case—and about you."

I looked at Mallory. "Michael, we have a problem here. A body was found in Washington Square Park the same day as the double murder. His prints match some partials found in Debbie's apartment. He might have been the guy who knifed me at Heathrow—I can't be sure, but he looks familiar. He died of a drug overdose, but no one thinks for a minute that he was a junkie— no needle tracks on his arms, nothing else to indicate he was a user. He was likely killed by whoever it is who is really calling the shots here. Now I didn't tell you this before, because I can't be sure that it isn't you—whoever or whatever it is that is behind this seems to know lots of information about lots of things. So: I don't trust *you*; you don't trust *me*. Where does that leave us?"

"Look at this from my point of view," Mallory replied. "It's not a question of trusting you—actually, I do—but you may be being victimized, under the control of forces you're not even aware of. All the action's taking place here, in your town. Yes, you were knifed in Heathrow, but for all I know you staged that to throw us off—you yourself have said more than once that there's always occasion to doubt *attempted* murders, wounds that are less than fatal; they make great smokescreens for their 'victims.' And after the initial corpses turned up, just about everything else has been happening here, hasn't it? Antonescu reappears, Dave Spencer dies and turns Neanderthal, and those two ladies are murdered. I would be one lousy investigator if I *didn't* suspect you of something more than you're letting on here, wouldn't I?"

"I understand," I said. "Except I *know* what I've really been up to in this case; I don't really know what you've been up to—so, as far as I'm concerned, everything that you just said could be so much more smoke, however logical, to divert my attention from *you*." And of course that very argument, from *Mallory's* point of view, could just be more clever argument by me to throw *him* off. There was no way we could settle this now—every argument, every bit of evidence, could point both ways. Like that scene in *The Bridges of Madison County* I once told Jack Dugan about. Meryl Streep watches Clint Eastwood drive away at the end of the movie, after they'd agreed that parting was the best thing. *If he really loves me*, Streep thinks, *he'll keep on driving; he won't turn around.* And Eastwood does just that. But what if Eastwood keeps driving not because he loves Streep so much, but because he never loved her that much in the first place? In that case, driving away is not that difficult, no act of blistering self-sacrifice for love. But how then can we tell, from just that one act, what's really going on in Eastwood's soul? The one act, Eastwood's driving away, supports two contradicting hypotheses. Just like each facet of this damn case Mallory and I were rehashing. . . .

"Phil, Phil . . . ," Mallory began. I'd taken my eyes off him while I was deep in my thought. Now in the corner of my vision I suddenly saw his hand dip down below the table—

I reached out and grabbed it, pitching a glass of orange juice off the table. It smashed loudly on the stone floor—

"Phil, for crissakes, I was reaching for a handkerchief—take it easy."

I held on tightly to his wrist, allowing him to fish out whatever it was he was taking from his pocket.

It was indeed a handkerchief—silk and embroidered. Not blue.

"I'm sorry. . . ." I shook my head.

"Is it all right with you if I blow my nose now?"

"I'm sorry," I said again, dumbly. "Maybe whoever, whatever, is behind this isn't on the inside. But whoever it is sure seems to know a lot about what we're doing and thinking. Now I *know* it isn't me. So I start looking at you and Lum. And I've gotta like you more for this. Lum doesn't seem to have the energy—I know, I suppose that could be an act, too. Jeez, once you get on this slope—"

"Forget about Lum. It isn't him," Mallory said.

"Well, look, if it isn't you and it isn't me, we have to start thinking about Lum. He could easily have been involved in the Gerry Moses death—"

"Listen to me," Mallory said, his face white with intensity. "It isn't Lum. He died this morning."

Mallory would have to be crazy to bald-facedly lie to me about something like this, but I had to check it out anyway.

"Stay right here," I told him as I stood up. "Please." I had no right to order him to do anything, but he nodded.

I walked to the front of the restaurant and a pay phone attached to the wall—I'd absent-mindedly left my cell phone home. I punched in my credit card and hunted down Lum's number in Toronto, keeping my eyes on Mallory, who was coolly pouring a cup of tea from the pot.

Someone answered the phone—not Lum's usual assistant; what the hell was his name? I identified myself and asked to speak to Lum.

"Just a moment, Doctor."

I was shunted to three different numbers, each of which was voice mail. Mallory was on his next cup of tea.

On the fourth shunt, I got to speak to a live person again and this time explained my reason for calling.

"I'm sorry, Dr. D'Amato; I can't release any information about H.-T. Lum at this time."

I guess that confirmed Mallory's story—why else would this factotum refuse to talk to me?—but I pushed the issue anyway. I told him: lives are at stake, cooperation between our two great countries, lives are at stake, we have a long history of sharing information on things like this, lives are at stake—

"I'm sorry, Dr. D'Amato. We do like to share information, but everything has its limits. We believe in freedom of speech up here, but we don't worship it."

"What in bloody hell does freedom of speech have to do with this—"

The factotum hung up on me.

Great. I was even beginning to talk like Mallory already but obviously lacked his facility for coaxing information from these people. Damn Canadians, damn Brits—neither knew the first thing about freedom of speech and the First Amendment anyway. . . .

I calmed myself and looked at Mallory sipping tea.

I made a decision.

"So you believe me now about H.-T. Lum?" Mallory asked as I rejoined him at the table.

"More or less. The guy on the phone didn't say much. Can't you call him up and *order* him to tell me about Lum? Canadian money still has the Queen's face on it, doesn't it?"

"That's not the way it works, Phil."

I signalled the waiter for another pot of tea. "All right," I said to Mallory. "Here's how I see things: Assuming Lum is dead, that indeed most likely means that he was not the one behind the killings. Logically, that just casts further suspicion on you or me. But if we go that route, if we follow that logic, then there's little sense in even continuing this conversation—we would do better each of us to just place the other under arrest, if we could. So let me propose something else."

"I'm listening," Mallory said.

"If we start from the premise, however unlikely it now seems to each of us about the other, that neither of us is the ultimate miscreant here, we're still left with the fact that people who were involved in this case, or knew a lot about it, are dying in alarming proportions—Gerry Moses, Dave Spencer, Tesa and Debbie, and now Lum. Plus an attempt was made on one of my Amish friends and on me."

"Right," Mallory agreed. "That brings us, again, to why we have reciprocal suspicions."

"Yes. But if we take you and me out of this, just for the sake of argument, what does it tell us about where to look further? The most likely way that someone could know so much about this case and not be seated at this table right now would be if that someone was close enough to at least one of us to pick up that information."

Mallory made a face. "You want, what—I put a tail on Jenna and you do the same for my wife?"

"Not quite—here's what I'm suggesting," I said. "You and I call a truce. We combine our forces and go over all the people associated with each of us. You look at my people; I look at yours. You can stay right here and do it yourself, if you like, or put someone else on it. I'll go over to England again myself. If things point to someone in Canada, we can go up there together."

Mallory brought the cup of tea to his lips.

He eventually extended his hand.

I took it and shook it.

"Of course, if either one of us is the next one to die, that would pretty well clinch it that the survivor is the killer," he said.

SIXTEEN

Mallory assigned a special British agent to the American side of the case—Amanda Leonard, who worked undercover over there at the BBC. I couldn't imagine that happening over here, but maybe I was naive.

Her BBC cover as an investigative reporter did have the advantage of opening some extra doors to her. She looked more than the part with her jet-black hair and violet eyes.

I pushed through the revolving door at Bobst Library. Amanda followed.

"Thank you for seeing me on such short notice," she said, and extended her hand to Stefan Antonescu, after we had made our way to the lower floor, where he was at work.

"You mean, 'Thank you for seeing me on *no* notice,'" he replied. "Mrs. Delany told me only forty-five minutes ago that you were coming down here and wanted to talk to me. Other than leaving this task right in the middle"—he gestured to the refuse bin he was wheeling around, half-filled with paper in various states of crumpledness—"I had no choice but to remain here and entertain your visit. I did insist that Dr. D'Amato join us—I have nothing but distrust for the media."

I smiled as engagingly as I could. "I'll just be the fly on the wall here and stay out of your conversation."

Amanda smiled as engagingly as *she* could—which was engaging indeed, full wattage. "And I thought we Brits were supposed to be the sticklers for exact use of the language. It's good to see there's such concern for it on this side of the Atlantic as well."

"My kind transcends the Atlantic, madam, as you no doubt already know."

"Yes, and that's what I was hoping we might talk at least a little about," Amanda said.

"As long as you do your part and pick up a piece of paper from the floor from time to time as I make my rounds, I have no objection," Antonescu said. "It's possible that the bright light of publicity might be good for my survival, keep away the cowards who lurk in the shadows. Maybe that's the reason I've managed to survive these past few months."

Amanda bent over and picked up an announcement of last week's special events, festooned with footprints. Antonescu took in the view.

"Is it true that you're three hundred years old?" she asked, after lodging the announcement in the bin.

"Should I give you my personal impressions of Louis Napoléon or Frederick the Great? Would that convince you?"

"Did you know those men?" Amanda asked.

"No," Antonescu replied. "I've led an essentially anonymous life until now. But given the slovenly state of history these days and the careful reading I've had time to do on so many subjects, I probably could have fooled you into thinking I did personally know those two."

"Well, thank you for your honesty."

I picked up another piece of paper.

Antonescu bowed slightly. "You see, there is no absolute proof I could provide about my age. Even my genes would likely look not much different from yours. They're self-repairing, to a limited extent—an extent longer than yours—but at any given time when they're in a state of repair they look no different from other human genes. You would have to watch them for decades to begin to see the differences."

"You consider yourselves, Neanderthals, part of the human race? Forgive me; I intended no—"

"I'm not insulted," Antonescu said. "Of course I, Neanderthals, all beings your current science pleases itself to classify as 'Homo,' are part of the human race. Others as well. It's only the most recent member of our 'Homo' clan—*Homo sapiens sapiens,* your Cro-Magnon—that saw fit, still sees fit, to make such distinctions."

"I guess making distinctions—hot versus cold, man versus woman, dark versus light—is basic to human cognition," Amanda replied. "Claude Lévi-Strauss called that the human imposition of bipolar opposites on a continuous reality. We did a BBC special on his theories more than a decade ago—I was just an intern then. Do you know his work?"

I had to give her credit—this woman drew upon deep wells of research. And she was highly intelligent.

"Yes, I was thinking of Lévi-Strauss just last night," Antonescu one-upped her, "as I was dining on sweet-and-sour pork in the Canton Garden. He's right about the human penchant for distinctions—I make them, too. The problem arises in what people *do* about the distinctions."

"What did the Cro-Magnon do about the distinctions they made?" Amanda asked.

"You know the answer," Antonescu replied. "They tried to distinguish us into extinction. But we devised remedies."

I FLEW TO England three days later and sandwiched in a quick trip to Bath by train. It contained some information that I thought might be useful. . . .

Emma Roberts lived at 19 Marlboro Lane, halfway up Sion Hill. I enjoyed the hike—it was a cool day for August in England—and also the way the town looked as I gazed back down at its bright beds of flowers and chalk orange chimneys. Hard to believe that Roman soldiers had once tramped in the mud down there, had sought to cleanse their souls in the ablution of the public pools for which Bath was named. But the Romans were known for their superb plumbing, some of which had remained unequaled until well into the nineteenth century. They weren't much in the way of sailing across the sea, those Romans, but they knew how to move water to people—just as we do these days with information.

Sometimes, though, you had to go physically to the source, or as close as possible.

I knocked on the door.

It opened.

"I'm Phil D'Amato," I said, and extended my hand. "Professor Roberts?"

"Yes. Come in, please." She had light brown frizzy hair and eyes that flared with her smile. I could see the resemblance immediately.

She was actually a Lecturer, not Professor, of Art History at Bath Spa University farther up the hill. But "Lecturer Roberts" sounded awkward to my ears, and besides, her academic post and art history had nothing to do with my reason for being here.

"Would you like a nice cup of tea?" she asked.

"Yes, I'd love one—if it's no bother."

"It isn't; I have a pot all ready," she said, and disappeared into what I assumed was her kitchen.

The room I was seated in was simple but striking—sunlight refracted through a window and a dozen pieces of blue Bristol glass that must have been a century old.

"Here we are." She returned with a whole setup.

"Just a splash of milk for me, please," I said.

She gave me a porcelain cup on a saucer, both of which felt weightless. The cup felt just right to my lips—warm, not hot, not cold—sipping hot tea from a cold cup spoils half the pleasure.

"So," she said, "what can I tell you about Amanda?"

I CAUGHT THE evening train to London.

Amanda Leonard's sister had given me the information I'd

wanted. Actually, from nothing that she'd said, but I had what I'd come for anyway. In my left vest pocket. A sample of Emma's DNA.

I was beginning to feel like a DNA pickpocket already, but that's what this business was coming to.

Before boarding I'd grabbed a gammon-steak sandwich—British for ham of some kind—and a splendid old vase of some indeterminate Victorian sort made of Bristol glass, for Jenna. I'd gotten the idea, of course, at Emma's. . . .

The trees rushed by; the sandwich tasted good. I wouldn't be seeing Emma again—first and last time. Too dangerous for me to be paying anyone too much attention in this mess. I didn't want another homicide.

But I had her DNA. I'd tried to get a swatch of Amanda's when she was in New York, but to no avail. She was off to see John Lapp in Lititz—after my insistent prodding of him through Amos—and I had a plane to catch to England. But at least I had her sister's—the second best way of doing my kind of in-depth "interview," my kind of deep background investigation, of Amanda. It used to be you subpoenaed someone's records or got an order for a wiretap or even hired a hacker to break into the requisite computer when you wanted information that could be crucial to a case. But the information I was looking for didn't require a subpoena or a hacker—it was there for the taking, if you found the right person with the right genes. Times were changing. DNA was the ultimate dossier.

Not that I knew exactly what I was looking for. A touch of *Bombyx mori*, a missing *Bombycidae* sequence, a profile closer to Paabo's Neanderthal on that position scale—I didn't know. Amanda and her sister certainly looked the complete antithesis of Neanderthal. But there was something in Amanda's expression when she was talking to Stefan—something in the way she tilted her head—and the way he looked at her that made me feel like . . . I don't know, like they belonged together.

I'd send the DNA along to some friends at MIT—better to

keep this out of New York and its possible leakage to London—
and see what they came up with. I wondered what Mallory really
knew about her. . . .

I finished the last of my sandwich and settled in for a nap.

I had a call to put in to Amos tonight about Amanda's interview, and then off tomorrow morning to the big meeting with
Mallory and his man heading the Tocharian translation team.

I GOT AMOS in his phone shack—1:00 A.M. my time, 8:00 P.M.
his.

"So how did it go?" I asked.

"She's very beautiful," he replied.

"I know," I said. "Too bad you didn't have a video camera
running on batteries. She didn't spot the little audio cassette recorder?"

"I don't think so," Amos answered.

"OK, good. Let's hear it. And feel free to stop and jump in
with any explanation if the tape is unclear about who is talking."

"OK," Amos said: "Here it is."

I heard a click, and then—

"Thank you for seeing me on such short notice—"

"That's Amanda Leonard talking," Amos said, and stopped the
tape.

"I know," I said. "I probably can recognize her voice and
John's and yours on the tape. Just stop it if something's unclear."

"OK," Amos said. "Should I rewind it and start again?"

"No, not necess—all right, sure, go ahead."

I heard a split-second squeal of rewind.

"OK, here we go again," Amos said.

"Thank you for seeing me on such short notice," Amanda said.

"Please, have a seat," John Lapp replied.

"Thank you," Amanda said.

"Are you hungry?" Lapp inquired.

"Actually, I'm famished," Amanda replied. "I missed breakfast."

"The chicken salad is delicious," Lapp said.

"Sounds lovely. A chicken salad sandwich, please—"

Amos stopped the tape. "That's Amanda talking to me. I came as the waiter to take her order."

"Understood," I said. "Let's continue."

"I've already eaten," Lapp said. "I understand you're gathering information. We usually want nothing to do with reporters."

"I know," Amanda said, "and I greatly appreciate your making an exception for me. Stefan Antonescu spoke very highly of your people—"

Hmmm . . . Not that I recalled, when I was there. . . .

Amanda continued, "Are you and he good friends?"

"I wouldn't know him if he walked right into this restaurant," Lapp said. "Let us just say that our two groups go back a long way."

"And what group precisely are you? Please don't take offense at my asking," Amanda said.

"No offense taken," Lapp said. "But before I give an answer, I would ask you, on your honor, not to tape-record this conversation—not even to take notes. Nothing I tell you can be quoted."

Amos stopped the tape. "John didn't know this was being tape-recorded. Only you know and I know."

"OK, understood," I said. "I appreciate your doing this."

"I feel it was right. Should I continue the tape?"
"Yes, please."

"I understand," Amanda said. "No tape recorder, no need for notes. I have a pretty good memory."

"If you report any of what I tell you in exact detail, I'll deny that our conversation ever took place," Lapp said sternly. "This is what they call . . . plausible deniability? Background briefing in your business?"

"Understood," Amanda said.

"I won't answer any questions about who I am," Lapp said. "That's not what this conversation will be about. I'll talk to you only about the silk cure—that is what Dr. D'Amato pleaded that I talk to you about. He thinks it might save some lives."

"Dr. D'Amato pleaded with you to see me?"

"He thought it was important to the world that some information about this become public now," Lapp said. "And after all, however much we may hold ourselves separate from it, my group lives on this world along with yours and many others. Diseases rarely respect such separations—they roam and ravage the world freely. We're not dealing with your AIDS here, which, horrible as it is, can be protected against by self-restraint and separation."

"Tell me about the illness, then," Amanda said, "and the cure."

Dishes or something clanked on the table.

"I'm arriving with the sandwich," Amos said.
"OK," I said.

"The cure treats an illness caused not by living organisms, but something below them on the tree of life," Lapp said.

"A virus?" Amanda asked.

"I'm not sure I know what a virus is—" Lapp said.

"Well, it's—" Amanda interrupted.

"No, I know what your science says it is," Lapp interrupted back. "I'm saying I don't know if I entirely agree with that—I don't know if your *science* completely agrees with what it says a virus is. It's really a marker for something no one completely understands. We just say, in the teachings that have come down to us, that, well, a building block of life causes this illness—not something living in itself."

"How does it cause the illness?"

"We're not completely sure about that, either. We think it puts the wrong building block into the process—a wrong ingredient in the recipe. Or perhaps it neutralizes an important building block, a building block that restrains."

"And the result?" Amanda asked.

"It causes the building blocks to work too fast . . ."

"Which causes?"

"Which causes the building to collapse," Lapp said. "The bad block does its damage silently, until the unnatural speed reaches a certain level. And then the infected person dies a very sudden death. Had Dr. D'Amato been delayed even a few hours on the road that day . . ."

"How did the cure work?"

"The silkworm is made of different building blocks," Lapp said. "You see, in our view of life, all life is made of different, yet sometimes interchangeable, building blocks. It's all a question of getting the right set of blocks. The Master Builder saw to most of that."

"You mean God?"

Silence.

Then—"Yes," Lapp said.

"What did you mean by 'most of that,' " Amanda asked, " 'saw to *most* of that' "?

"Well, some arrogant members of our species believe they can take it upon themselves to do the Builder's work. You see, we proceed very carefully, respecting the integrity of each block. But when you *cut* the blocks . . ."

Sounds of one hand smacking another. . . .

". . . when you *splice*, try to interfere with the workings *within* the blocks, then the trouble can start," Lapp said.

"Gene splicing," Amanda said.

"Yes," Lapp said.

"But your people respect the blocks, and the silk cure works in that, well, in that way?"

"Yes," Lapp said. "The blocks in the silk stop the bad blocks from having their effect. The unholy speed is slowed, and the building can survive the quake."

"I see," Amanda said. "It works almost like an antibody. . . ."

"No, not really," Lapp replied. "Antibodies lock onto invaders and destroy them. Our healing blocks just block the blocks that cause damage— create a shield around the rest of the living building, around each of its tiniest blocks, so it can function as intended. Nothing is destroyed."

"How exactly is the cure—the healing block— administered? You don't believe in injection, right?"

"Some of us do; my particular group does not— why breach the outer shell of the building, even for a good purpose? No, better to introduce the blocks in a natural way. . . ."

"That being?" Amanda asked.

"Could be from a drink, through the mouth," Lapp said. "Could be from a vapor, inhaled through the nose. Could be from a medical garment upon the skin, with the correcting blocks entering through the pores. Could be even from making love. . . . Our tradition and study have disclosed many ways. Some operate more quickly than others. Some are preventions rather than cures. The people in our group all have taken preventions—not only for this illness, but for many other insults to the body, man-made as well as natural—in homemade candy we consume as children, or as adults if the prevention is new. That's why we can survive as well as you, without your hospital machines and your MDs. . . . Dr. D'Amato of course arrived here far too late for any prevention. He was in grave condition, and needed the cure."

"I know you prefer not to talk about viruses," Amanda said. "But does your cure contain a virus— a retrovirus—that transfers elements from the silkworm DNA into the genome of the human under treatment? Is that how this works?"

"Blocks of different species—what you call DNA sequences—are sometimes interchangeable between species," Lapp replied. "That is all we need to know. *Viruses* is just today's scientific wording for yesterday's evil spirits."

"OK," Amanda said. "And you've known about this illness, and this cure, for how long now? Centuries?"

"More than centuries," Lapp replied. "The special qualities of silk have been known for millennia. Tea has some good properties like this, too. Both were prized in China, and for very good reason. And even before China . . ."

"Tea and silk," Amanda said. "Are their effects cumulative?"

"Sometimes," Lapp said.

"Could you tell me more about the prevention part?" Amanda asked. "What happens if someone takes the silk cure who is not already ill? What impact does that have on the . . . building?"

The phone went dead.

"Amos? Amos? God damn!"

I dialed the London operator and asked her to reconnect me.

Five minutes later an American operator got on the phone. "I'm getting a 'circuits busy,' but I'm sure that's not the case," she said. "They're putting in ISDNs all over the country, and sometimes that interrupts the service—"

"Well, what the hell should I do?"

"Try again in fifteen minutes. It may be OK then."

I reached Amos an hour later—past two in the morning, my time. Good thing Amos was five hours earlier.

"Should I start from the top and play it again?" he asked.

I HURRIED UP to the British Museum on Great Russell Square early the next morning. A Beatles song was playing on the radio out of someone's car—made me feel like I was back in Columbus High School in the Bronx again. " 'You've Got to Hide Your Love Away' on BBC1," the announcer said. "John Lennon wrote it for The Silkie . . ."

Mallory was at the doorway of the appointed room. He ushered me in and introduced me to the man at the table. "Dr. Phil D'Amato, Dr. Pedro Sanches da Silva." Pedro was short, bald, and bearded, with bright lively eyes. He half-rose from his seat and took my hand in a firm grip.

"I'm pleased to meet you, Dr. D'Amato—"

"Call me Phil—"

"I've heard of your exploits among the Amish," Pedro concluded in a perfect and crisp British accent.

"You're British," I said stupidly. "I mean—"

"Yes, quite British," Pedro said. "Although my name obviously bears the stamp of my family's passage up the Iberian way—we were thrown out during the Inquisition."

"You're Jewish?"

"Yes," Pedro replied.

I smiled. "So am I."

"Really? D'Amato?"

"Yep," I said. "Marrano."

"Ah, yes," Pedro responded. "The Spanish name for 'pigs'—the Catholics suspected some of you of not being sincere in your conversion, and that's how they showed it. My hat's off to you—I always thought your approach far more ingenious than just leaving as my ancestors did."

"Thank you—"

"Gentlemen," Mallory interrupted. "Do you think you could forgo the seder until *after* our meeting?"

Pedro laughed. "See? Anti-semitism rears its head everywhere! Michael—Spain, the Amish, the Jewish experience—all of this is relevant to our problem, you see."

"How is Spain relevant?" Mallory asked.

"How is Spain relevant? Why, some of the last of the Neanderthals—under thirty thousand years old—have been found there. Some of the most beautiful Cro-Magnon cave painting—the ceiling of Altamira—is in Spain. And Spain is of course next door to France, which has Chauvet and Lascaux and—"

"OK, I get the picture, pardon the pun." Mallory sat down and bade me to do the same. "And this has some relevance to the Tocharian manuscripts you're translating?"

"You see," Pedro said softly, "we're all connected. We're all of us stories of persecution of one people by another, and what the persecuted did to survive. The Tocharian documents speak of such a conflict, a fearful conflict, between two or more kinds of people. I'm convinced the documents were written to try to warn us—the future—of something. But I can't quite figure out what that is, because the language is so *allegorical,* you see. The writer— I'm pretty sure the documents I'm now trying to translate were produced by the same person—was struggling to explain something. Perhaps it was something he—or she—did not, could not, completely understand. Perhaps the writer just retreated to metaphor to cover up what was not understood—that's a common-enough practice in our current intellectual world. I just can't tell as yet."

"When exactly were these manuscripts—the ones you're translating now—discovered?" I asked. "Not in the last few years?"

"Oh, no," Pedro replied. "Mummies and artifacts have been recently recovered. But these manuscripts have been known since the 1890s. Marc Aurel Stein brought many back to Europe from the Tarim Basin in the early years of the twentieth century. They just have not been translated—properly—until now."

"Why not?" I asked.

"Well, that would just be conjecture on my part," Pedro said.

"My favorite kind of discourse," I said, sincerely.

"Well, you see, the texts that I am working on now were early on labeled as magical texts—because of their references to singers, spells of the flute, et cetera. So not much attention was paid to them. And when they were examined at all, the early translators took them *totally* as metaphor—the battles were contests between good and evil in the *soul,* you see, not out here really in the world."

"But you think differently," I said.

"Well, yes," Pedro replied. "People are dying of strange illness now—the Tocharian manuscripts speak of an illness in the blood."

"Is there any further possible mention in the Tocharian manuscripts of Neanderthals? I know there was a reference to 'brutes' in your translation."

Pedro shook his head. "Nothing as explicit as we might like—there of course are lots of modern people who might be referred to as brutes. But the frequent references to brutes and singers as the same race are intriguing. We think Neanderthals may have had flutes. Conceivably, they sang. And if Bickerton et al. are right that language began in song, well . . ."

"Pretty tenuous connection," I said.

"We have anything better to work on?" Mallory asked.

"No," I admitted. "Who are the contestants in this battle?" I asked Pedro. "The brute singers—let's say they are Neanderthals, for the sake of argument—and who on the other side? Early Cro-Magnons?"

"Presumably," Pedro said.

"So, our Tocharian author is an historian, describing an ancient battle that he—or she—knew about. How? By oral tradition?" I asked.

"No." Pedro shook his head. "I don't think it's quite that, either."

"How then?" I asked.

"Well, I can't be sure, but from what I can tell about the verb tenses in the text—and we're pretty sure about these kinds of tenses—it seems that the author was writing in the current tense."

My face must have creased in doubt.

Mallory's smiled. "And now we get to the denouement," he said with relish.

"Just a second," I said. "You're saying the manuscripts are really thirty thousand years old? That would be news to me, and one hell of a discovery!"

"No," Pedro said. "These manuscripts date from about A.D. 750, give or take the usual couple of years."

"Then—"

"Right," Mallory said. "He's saying that if the singing brutes are indeed Neanderthals and the text is indeed reportage, not fanciful allegory, then what they are describing is some sort of extermination of Neanderthals in A.D. 750."

SEVENTEEN

 I joined Pedro the next day at the restaurant by the Serpentine in Hyde Park. Mallory had a place at our table, too, but he was on the phone.

"It's a tourist trap, I know," I said apologetically, and looked at the roast beef on the menu.

Pedro shrugged. "Sometimes the tourists are right. They visit our Silk Museum in droves—they keep my little town well employed."

My ears perked up. "Silk Museum?"

"Oh, yes," Pedro said. "The Silk Museum in Macclesfield— the little market town, oh, about seventy kilometers out of Manchester. You've heard of it, haven't you?"

"Well, I've heard of Manchester, of course—"

Pedro gave me a smile. "Macclesfield's been a center of silk production since the Napoleonic era—we don't like to call it that here, but that's what it was, of course. People worked like slaves on the Jacquard Looms. The Luddites hated those looms. But the looms did keep the people alive, after all. I've always agreed with Hayek that of course the industrialists were responsible for the proletariat, because those workers wouldn't have been alive at all were it not for the industrialists and the standard of living they created. Karl Marx never considered that! Wouldn't you agree?"

"Well—"

"Precisely! And now of course it's all done differently—silk is manufactured with power looms and such like—and so they've made a Museum in Macclesfield, to commemorate the Jacquard Loom and the prosperity it first brought to our area. Incredible device, that Jacquard Loom. Jacquard of course was not the only person who invented it. Monsieur Falcon came up with the perforated cards, and Jacques de Vaucanson—you know, the inventor of the mechanical duck that digested and evacuated. Pardon me; I shouldn't be talking this way over dinner—"

"No, no, please continue," I urged. "What was that about perforated cards?"

"The cards? Well, you see a code is punched into them—like an early computer—and that code controls the weaving of the silk, you see. I'm sure Charles Babbage—"

Mallory appeared, grave, furious. "Would you excuse us for a moment," he said to Pedro, and beckoned me to join him.

"Yes, of course," Pedro said.

I wanted to talk to Pedro more, but Mallory looked in no mood to be denied. He whispered rapidly in my ear as we walked away from the table. "They tried to kill Amanda—she's all right now, but they tried to kill her! I'm sure of it!"

"What happened?" I put my hand on his shoulder, tried to calm him.

"I don't know exactly. We had a listening device implanted in her skin—even she didn't know it—to pick up all of her conversation."

"You're a real piece of work," I said. "What did you do, have Q slip it into her when she was in the dentist's office?"

"Never mind about that," Mallory half-shouted, half-whispered. "The point is that the device recorded everything that she said, everything that was said to her, but not when she was on the phone—it wasn't strong enough to pick up what was said to her on the phone, wasn't intended for that. But it relayed everything it did pick up to nearby cellular devices, which in turn forwarded it all to the British consulate in New York and then back here—"

"Jeez, the KGB had nothing on you people."

"—and we just got the latest from the relay. She was at the hotel and received a phone call from someone, then left her room—and then, wham, she's out cold for at least fifteen minutes, apparently. I hear her thump on the floor, and no one makes a sound until someone, obviously a security guard, starts saying, 'Are you all right, Miss?' What the hell happened to her?"

I shook my head. I didn't think for a second that she'd just fainted. "Same thing that happened to Lum, Moses . . . but she's alive?"

"Yeah," Mallory said. "She's fine. But I haven't a clue why, or what happened to her. That person who rang her must have tripped it off. . . ."

"Well, it's a step in the right direction that she's OK," I said. "If it was an attempt on her life, then maybe we finally did something right, whatever it was."

Mallory cursed. "This is getting way out of control—way out of control."

"No," I said. "It's been out of control for a long time. If anything, we may be getting closer to what's going on."

"What? Did Pedro tell you something useful about the To-charian manuscripts?"

"Yeah, that," I said, "and maybe also something useful about silk. And if someone tried to kill Amanda, that means that maybe she touched a nerve with one of her interviews. That could narrow down the field considerably."

"You were on hand for the Antonescu interview, but not the Amish," Mallory said. "I've been telling you all along that I didn't feel comfortable about those Anabaptist farmers—"

"I heard the whole Amish interview, too," I said. "Nothing untoward there, either."

"But Amanda told me it was just she and—"

"I know," I said. "I wasn't with her in Pennsylvania. But we have tape recorders, too, you know—"

Mallory just shook his head. "She'll be in my office tomorrow morning for the debriefing. Be there at nine sharp, please."

MALLORY'S SECRETARY SHOWED me in.

Amanda was on the couch, her eyes closed.

A tall, gaunt man in a gray suit was sitting on a chair next to her.

Mallory saw me, held up a finger to his lips, and motioned me to a seat. "Good," he whispered. "You're here. Just about ready to get started. Soames has put her in a light trance—best chance we have of finding out what happened."

Mallory looked at Soames. "Is she ready?"

Soames nodded. He looked intently at Amanda's closed eyes and spoke softly. "Tell us what happened in the hotel room, after you rang off with Michael. Tell us everything you were thinking, everything that happened, and your reaction to it." His tone was gentle but insistent.

Amanda spoke right up. "First things first," she said, talking as much to herself as anyone else. "Even though the BBC is paying for the call, and my room at the Hilton. I wanted to stay at the Plaza for my night over in New York, after the interview in Pennsylvania, but the Plaza was way over budget. Well, better the Hilton than the Holiday Inn—some man groped my hiney in the pool there, the last time I was in the States. Anyway . . . I'll call the Beeb later, after I've had a proper dinner."

"OK," Soames said. "What happened next? Had you already ordered up your dinner?"

Amanda nodded. I could see her eyes moving under her lids, as if she were viewing the story she was relating. "Yes. Room service should be here already. What's keeping them?"

"Please continue," Soames said. "What happened next?"

"Knock, knock, knock on the door! I look at my face in the mirror. 'Room service,' a man's voice says. A nice deep voice. I look through the peephole. Not as attractive as the voice, but not bad."

"Does he look at all familiar? Like anyone you have ever seen before?"

Amanda shook her head.

"You sure?" Soames prodded.

"I never saw him before," Amanda said.

"Very good, then," Soames said, and looked meaningfully at Mallory. "And what happened next?"

"I open the door. 'Thank you for bringing the dinner up here on such short notice.' The man enters with the tray and sets it up between the end of my queen-size bed and the dresser.

"Sometimes I daydream about what would happen in a situation like this if I answered the door totally starkers—totally nude. I worked on an hilarious BBC documentary a few years back about how hotel people are trained. A man entering a room with a woman inside is supposed to look only at her eyes—'remember, the eyes only, the eyes only'—the training makes a point of emphasizing that any glance at the body of a female occupant, whether clothed or not, was strictly verboten. . . ."

"I see." Soames betrayed the slightest smile. "Please say what happened next."

"The man is smiling at me, looking at my entire body. *You fail the course.* I thank him and put a dollar bill into his hand. He nods, says, 'Thank you,' and leaves without looking at the bill. Well, he gets points for that."

"OK," Soames said. "And did you eat your dinner?"

Amanda frowned. "Not all of it. The steak is medium rare. It looks pretty good. I'm cutting it—but damn, the phone is ringing. Why can't they leave me alone for a few minutes? I put a piece in my mouth anyway—I'm too hungry not to. I'm answering the phone with my mouth full. Too bad!"

"OK, tell us about the conversation now. As exactly as you can."

"I say, 'Yes? . . . Well, hullo! Of course I do! Right now? . . . OK, sure, just give me a few minutes. . . . Sure, the coffee shop would be fine.' "

"Whom are you talking to, Amanda? This is very important."

Amanda furrowed her brow; then her whole face scrunched up, in an exaggerated pantomime of thinking.

Then she shook her head slowly. "I don't know," she said in a very small voice. "I can't remember."

Mallory leaned over and whispered to me, "Whatever it was that happened to her seems to have knocked out this part of her memory—the doctors think that maybe it was the trauma of the experience."

"Selective amnesia," Soames agreed. "It's not uncommon with this sort of thing—the victim blots out the proximate trigger of the offending event. Less painful that way. Sometimes a persistent hypnotherapist can retrieve it, often not."

Mallory sighed. "All right," he said. "Have her continue."

Soames nodded, and so instructed Amanda.

"I gobbled down about half the steak," she said. "I'm very keen for this meeting, but there's no point having it serenaded by my growling stomach. Mmmm . . . that's good. I should slip out of my blue jeans into something a tad more elegant. Maybe I should call Michael again and tell him about this meeting? No. Time for that later. I've kept this appointment waiting long enough."

Mallory cursed quietly.

"OK, Amanda," Soames said. "Now please tell me, exactly, everything that happened, everything you saw."

"I'm in the elevator," Amanda continued, "down to the first floor. It's a long corridor to the coffee shop. There's gray carpet all around. I'm walking as fast as I can—ouch! Something bit me in the back of my thigh. It hurts. I feel sick. I'm very tired. If I could just lay down on the floor . . . Ah, that feels good, so good. . . . But the carpet hurts my face. . . . I'm scared; please help me, someone! But I can't remember how to talk. I'm scared. . . ." Her face was a sea of fidgets and flinches.

Soames leaned over to Mallory. "I should bring her out of this now."

"Just a bit more," Mallory insisted.

Soames hesitated, then nodded. "Ok," he said soothingly to Amanda. "Don't worry; you're OK. You're perfectly fine, really. Can you tell us what happened next?"

Amanda nodded slowly. "Someone's turning me over. He's pressing his head against my chest. He stinks of whiskey! 'Thank God! She's still breathing,' he says. 'Last thing the hotel needs is some high-priced hooker keeling over and dying in the corridor like this.' There's another man standing there, too. 'Call EMS,' he says. I'm so frightened. . . ." Amanda started whimpering.

"All right, take her out of it," Mallory said, his jaw twitching in anger and frustration.

"I have a pretty good idea what happened," I said. "Amanda was very lucky."

"You sleep now," Soames said to Amanda. "Sleep deeply, and peacefully. You need your rest. Everything's OK. When you wake up, in a little while, you'll feel very good. . . ."

Amanda's lips parted, her face regained its beauty, and her body relaxed into full unconsciousness on the couch. . . .

Mallory motioned Soames and me to follow him into an adjoining room.

"Right," Mallory said to me when we all were seated. "So tell us what you think happened."

I told them about Amanda's interview with Lapp and how it had gotten around to "preventions"—the Amish equivalent of inoculations against illnesses and "insults" to the body.

"Lapp gave her a 'silk phosphate,' before she left Lancaster," I explained. " 'Tastiest way I know of getting some of those blocking agents into your body,' he said. Amanda said it was a sweet, milky seltzer—"

"You reckon that caused her to pass out in the hotel corridor, hours later?" Mallory asked.

"Just the opposite," I said. "I think that someone got some poison into her body with a needle, whatever—that 'bite' that she said she felt on the back of her leg—and the Amish phosphate saved her life. Its compounds blocked the poison—the way Lapp was explaining it—and rendered it harmless."

"I'm a great believer in homeopathic remedies," Soames offered, "but I don't believe I've ever encountered anything quite like that."

"I'm still not clear why you're so sure the Amish drink was the remedy and not the problem," Mallory said.

"Because I know these people," I said. "John Lapp and Amos Stoltzfus. They saved my life. At least twice. They gave me an antidote once, for an allergen that had killed my friend, and I was fine. And two months ago they gave me their 'cure' for the cold-fusion virus that killed Dave Spencer."

"Perhaps they were setting you up just to believe them now," Mallory said.

"No," I said. "They're fighting the same thing we are—some kind of ancient Amish-like group that has some connection to the Neanderthals. I'm sure of it."

"But you have no idea who that group is," Mallory said.

I stood up and walked to the door. "I have an appointment with someone for lunch in Manchester who may be able to provide some help. Then I have a plane to catch. In the meantime, ask Amanda about the silk phosphate when she wakes up—she'll at least be able to bear me out on that part. Run a screen on her blood, too; do a new DNA scan for her—maybe it'll pick up some trace of the poison."

"I'LL HAVE THE veal parmigiana, it's very good here," Mary Radcliff said to the waiter. She turned to me and wrinkled her nose mischievously. "I *love* Italian food!"

"Me, too," I said. "And I'll have the shrimp scampi," I said to the waiter. We were in Manny's in Bolton, near Manchester. Mary had asked to eat there after graciously accepting my last-minute invitation yesterday to lunch and conversation. She was seventy-eight, associated with the Silk Museum in nearby Macclesfield, and reputed to know all there was to know about the Jacquard Machine. Well, others likely knew as much, maybe more, but Mary was the only one available today.

"So tell me about the Jacquard," I said, pouring her some red wine from the carafe we had ordered.

"Oh, it's a wonderful machine," Mary declared. "A real miracle of of human ingenuity."

"How do the cards work—how do they control the weaving?"

"Oh, the cards are mounted on the cylinder, which controls the griff that lifts the hooks. And this lifts the warp threads. . . ."

"Warp threads?"

"Yes, warp, like full speed ahead!" Mary chuckled. "But, seriously, the warp is one of the *longitudinal* threads—"

"OK." I smiled. "So tell me more about how the cards work in your star-drive silk machine." I refilled her glass.

"Where were we?" Mary said. "Yes, the cards in the Jacquard. Well, the face of the cylinder has perforations opposite each needle, so when the cylinder and the needles press close together the needles enter the perforations. But when a card is placed between the cylinder and the needles and the card has only *some* perforations, the unperforated parts of the card will prevent the needles from entering the cylinder's perforations at those places. Those needles get pushed back on their springs, so when the griff ascends, the hooks for those needles are not lifted, so they don't touch the warp threads. . . . It's all quite beautiful, really, a mechanical ballet."

"Yes, and you describe it beautifully, Mary. Tell me, how are the cards perforated in the first place?"

"The design is painted at first—the design of which parts of the card should be perforated—and then a special machine punches out the sets of cards. The number of cards needed for any pattern equals the number of weft threads—the number of *horizontal* threads in the weave."

"Amazing," I said. "It's a computer before computers—the design is a code for weaving. And all of this was done in the early 1700s?"

"Well, Falcon did *some* of it back in 1728—he operated his machine with perforated cards. But that machine was much more cumbersome than the Jacquard—another worker was required to physically pull the cords after the card's selections were made. The Jacquard does that automatically. That's the beauty of it."

"Could such devices go back even earlier—perhaps to the ancient world? Heron of Alexandria and of course Archimedes invented some pretty sophisticated things. . . ."

"Well, it's of course *possible*," Mary said. "Since no electricity was required—it's all mechanics—certainly it was within reach, in principle, of the ancients. But, of course, so much was destroyed in those fires in Alexandria . . . Who can say—"

The waiter appeared with our food. I turned around to take the plates for Mary and me and spilled a drop of wine on my tie—story of my life. I patted it dry.

"Happens to me all the time," Mary said, smiling. "Good conversation, good eating, and neatness do not go well together! The tie suits you well, by the way—as does your suit. Very nice, very . . . academic!"

"Thanks," I said. "I bought the outfit last time I was in England, on Savile Row."

"Well, you can't go wrong with a Harris Tweed, you know—keeps you warm in winter, lets you breathe in summer. Perfect for a professor!"

I laughed. "I do teach a course once every few years. . . ."

"You're not a professor? Oh, sorry, of course, you told me. My short-term memory isn't what it used to be, I'm afraid. You're a forensic detective!"

"Right, but that's OK—I like to think there's at least a modicum of scholarship sometimes involved in my work."

Mary smiled and dug into her veal.

I fingered my tie. "Mary, are Jacquard Looms still used? Could you tell if this tie and this suit were made on Jacquard machines?"

She looked up. "Oh, no. Today's looms are all power models.

They operate on the same general principles of the Jacquard, mind you, but they project the . . . the code, as you put it, in different ways."

"Hmmm. . . ." Something occurred to me. "Do you suppose someone knowledgeable in all of this—like you—might be able to take apart a tie, or any woven cloth, and from that weave deduce the exact perforations on the cards that wove that cloth, that pattern, into being?"

"You mean, like reverse engineering?" Mary asked. "My grandson spent some time in Japan—just came home last month. And he was telling me that's how they got the jump on the West over there after the Second World War! They take a piece of our technology, take it apart so they see how it works, then build something that does the same thing, but better, and without violating our copyrights—"

"Our patents—"

"Yes, our patents. But, yes, I suppose it might be possible to deduce the card pattern from the weave—but wouldn't it be easier just to consult the patterns in the cards and see what matches up best to the weave?"

"Yeah," I said. "But I was thinking about maybe ancient kinds of weaves in which the cards, if they even existed as cards in the first place, were no longer available. So all we had we were the weaves, the results of the code, to work with. . . ."

"Oh, I see what you're saying," Mary said, and finished the last of her veal. "That would be like DNA, in a way, wouldn't it? There was a *marvelous* program on the BBC just last month about the human genome project. And they made the point that we have the *results* of the human genetic code all around us—in what we all look like, how we behave, and so forth—but we don't fully know the code as yet at all . . ."

EVIDENCE . . . INFORMATION . . . MESSAGES . . . these were the stock-in-trade of my forensic profession. Or, at least, finding them in unlikely places . . . being spoken to by faces that didn't look like faces were supposed to look. . . .

Some people called the homicide detective a speaker for the dead. But my profession was actually a little different: I was a *listener* for the dead . . . a listener for the message that the dead might have communicated, a scout for the sign that the unprepared eye might well miss. . . .

Messages came in different forms. There were the Tocharian manuscripts—messages deliberately left for someone, if not us—for why else would any human being, any intelligent entity, ever choose to write, if not to leave a message for someone else?

The DNA in everyone, all life, of course also contains messages—code in the form of formulae for constructing a living organism, to live and behave this way or that. Of course, those messages were presumably unintended—though, jeez, I'd had my share of run-ins with nasty messages in the nucleotides that were quite explicit. But who knows what messages the breeders of prehistoric times intended their plants and animals to convey? Of course, who could even know with assurance the degree to which there *was* deliberate breeding in prehistory—how far back, and by whom? With mutable life as its only marker, the record is by definition unstable. . . .

So Tocharian manuscripts, DNA itself, all perhaps had relevance to what had been going on—all perhaps had some message or messages relevant to a viruslike thing that caused death, mangled carbon dating, made some of its victims look like Neanderthals . . . an insane illness that seemed to violate the laws of physics as well as biology—an illness that silk seemed in some way to shield against, even cure.

And there was Lum's theory about the *Bombycidae* sequences in all of us—which seemed in line, at least somewhat, with John Lapp's talk about building blocks and blocking agents. Let's say, as a working hypothesis, that Neanderthal DNA lacked the *Bombycidae*—it's appearance in the human genome coincides with, maybe even causes, the rise of Cro-Magnon. The Neanderthals, nearly exterminated by the Cro-Magnon, fight back with some kind of illness that undermines the *Bombycidae* and turns its victims back into Neanderthals. Cro-Magnons—*Homo sapiens sapiens*—come to prize silk, derived from the *Bombyx mori* relative of the *Bombycidae*, because its application either guards against the illness or restores some aspects of the *Bombycidae*. . . .

Still a lot of conjecture and very little evidence. A clear, unambiguous Neanderthal genome would be the best way to test it—but we had none. And there were still lots of questions. Why did the virus not only turn its victims into Neanderthals but also kill them? How widespread was it?

The only way we could make progress on this was to proceed step by small step. . . .

I explained most of this to Mallory the next day and suggested the next little object of our scrutiny.

"You think the answer lies in a bleeding blue handkerchief?" he exclaimed.

"I'm not saying the complete answer is there, no. I'm saying we need to look at it more carefully. We overlooked an important source of possible information here. The very weave in that handkerchief could contain a piece of this puzzle—silk was woven for two centuries with computer punch cards, for crissakes! It's all information—DNA, writing, weave patterns, any of those could contain a message for us."

"Silk's not the only fabric that's woven," Mallory countered. "Why not examine every cotton hankie that someone mopped his brow with?"

"Because silk's the thing that's been rubbing against this case from the very beginning," I replied. "The blue hankie we found on the first corpse in New York was silk. Antonescu has an obsession with silk—as well he should, since it seems to cure the damn Neanderthal-death virus, or whatever it is. The Amish put great stock in it, too—"

"Our mummy at the LSE and the corpse in Toronto had no silk hankies," Mallory said.

"Makes my hunch even stronger," I insisted. "I'm beginning to think London and Toronto were red herrings—designed to throw us off, by whoever or whatever is behind this. New York's had most of the action since the beginning; you've been saying so yourself—"

"Two people were killed in Toronto, and they still haven't found Gerry's body."

"True," I said. "But even so. No corpse has come back to life in Toronto or London. No real live Neanderthal who says his birthday cake has three hundred candles has appeared anyplace other than New York. And we're also the city with the silk hankie on the corpse."

"OK." Mallory put his hands up. "Have the hankie examined. Do you even know how to decode it, if it does contain a message you can retrieve from the pattern?"

"No," I admitted. "But I'm working on it. Mrs. Marple's willing to help out, and she seems to have written the book on silk weaving and Jacquard Looms—"

"Mrs. Marple?"

I smiled. "Yeah, Mary Radcliff. She's a sweetheart—"

"OK," Mallory said again. "Have fun—me, I'll stick with Pedro and the Tocharians, if it's OK with you, and see what else I can debrief from Amanda when she's up to it."

I GOT THE call from Herby in my hotel room the next afternoon—morning, his time.

"What the hell do you mean, it's missing?" I demanded.

"Happens sometimes; you know that," Herby replied. "The way the case had been going, that hankie wasn't a high-priority item. You know how it is. Nobody said anything about it for months. With Dave gone, I shifted around a few of the workers—these kinds of things happen. Someone likely walked off with it, is all—maybe one of Dave's guys wanted a souvenir."

"Bullshit."

"Take it easy, Phil. I'm checking into it—we may come up

with it. We have names and addresses of everyone who had access to that evidence room."

"You shouldn't have let it disappear in the first place," I said. "Goddamnit, things are finally beginning to come together a little now, and you lose the fucking hankie!"

"Just a second, Phil. I don't blame you for being upset, but please don't make unwarranted assumptions here. When was the last time *you* saw the hankie?"

"I'm not sure."

"Exactly. So, for all we know, it might well have gone walking on Dave Spencer's watch."

"Dave was more careful than that," I said.

"I'll pretend you didn't say that," Herby replied, though the edge in his voice showed that he wasn't too good at pretending. "So, what else did you come up with in England other than this handkerchief idea?"

"The handkerchief is pretty much it," I said. "We're making a little progress on the Tocharian manuscripts."

"I see," Herby said. "I think it's probably getting to that time when you should be heading home now."

"That's not your decision."

"That so? Check with Dugan. He'll tell you he told me to tell you, if you and I happened to talk before you and he, that he wants you back here—now. In fact, he asked me to help with the arrangements. You know Jack; he shies away from confrontation. So let's see . . . we can book you a flight on a plane tomorrow— no, wait; there's some special deal if you stay over the weekend. All right—how does Monday sound?"

I CALLED JENNA right after I hung up on Herby.

"Jerk," she said. "OK, I'll call you right back."

She called me back twenty minutes later.

"He's missing," she said.

"What?"

"Ruth Delany isn't at work, either. The best I could get from some other librarian there is that Delany is on vacation, and this one doesn't know where Antonescu is. She's going to check."

"Goddamnit," I said. "Whoever's behind this always seems to know what we're doing. The silk hankie's missing; Antonescu's the logical person to consult; now he's goddamn missing, too!" I punched the pillow on my bed. "Better call Jack Dugan on this and report Antonescu missing. You have his number?"

"Yeah," Jenna said. "What about Herby?"

"The hell with Herby. Just call Jack—I'm going over to see Mallory."

"OK," Jenna said. "Oh—I forgot to tell you with all the commotion. The MIT people called with a preliminary on Amanda's sister's DNA. You were right that there's something there—she's 22 on the Paabo scale."

I BARGED INTO Mallory's office.

He was on the phone. He looked up at me. "Righto," he said into the phone. "I'll ring you up later. You get some sleep." I could just tell by the tone of his voice and the way he looked at me that he had been talking to Amanda.

"That was Amanda," he told me. "She confirms that John Lapp gave her the silk phosphate, and her feeling is there was nothing wrong with it. No word yet from tox screen—"

"I don't give a shit about the phosphate now," I said. "There are two other things we need to talk about."

Mallory looked somewhat stunned.

"One, the hankie's missing, and so is Stefan Antonescu. You have anything to say about that?" I barked at him.

"Jesus, again?" Mallory yelped, now looking incredulous. "We're goddamn back at the bloody beginning!"

"Right." He was convincing, I'd say that for him. "You ever give any thought to a career in acting? You do shocked surprise very well."

"You think *I* had something to do with this?"

"No one other than you and Jenna knew about my interest in the hankie. Did *you* tell anyone?"

"No one," Mallory insisted. "Except, of course, Amanda. . . ."

I smiled, without pleasure. "Ah, sweet Amanda. That's the second thing I wanted to mention to you. Did you know that her DNA differs from ours—*Homo sapiens sapiens*—in twenty-two positions? Humans differ among themselves on an average of seven positions, and humans from Neanderthals on twenty-seven."

Mallory looked at me. "What in bleeding hell did your NYPD do? Take a snatch of her skin from her crotch in that damned hotel in New York?"

"No, we don't operate like that."

Mallory muttered a string of vivid Cockney curses.

"Thank you," I said. "I'm complimented. But the point still is: did you know that about Amanda? . . . Of course you did; I can see it in your face. . . ."

Mallory said nothing.

"How did she hide it?" I asked. "She is beautiful, no doubt about it. Her sister's nice, too—I actually got the DNA from her." No need to keep that facet of this a secret.

"Plastic surgery can do miracles," Mallory finally said. "She and her sister come from a lot of money—our plastic surgeons are quite talented."

"But the bone structure—"

"Proves that not all Neanderthals have that bone structure, I guess. Or perhaps her mixture of genes gave her the more petite structure. I suspect if you examine her genes more thoroughly you may even find some of that *Bombycidae* you're so keen about— she certainly has loads of silk in her flat. Hell, for all I know, she looked lovely to begin with and the plastic surgery was just to alter her nose. All I know is that she told me she'd had it, about ten years ago."

"Dammit, Michael—how the hell can I believe *anything* you say now?"

"Because I'm telling you the truth, Phil. Like you said in that conversation we had in the Yorkville, there's no way I can prove it to you, but I'm telling you the truth. I care about Amanda. I'll even admit that I know a bit more here and there than what I've let on. But when it comes to the murders, to what happened to Amanda in New York, to Antonescu missing—you've got to believe me, I'm as much in the dark about this as you."

I shook my head and turned away.

"In fact, I've been thinking this through," Mallory continued, "and I firmly believe you may be closer to getting at what's going on here than anyone. I may have been wrong about London and Toronto. I don't care how much your fine mayor has cleaned up your city; it's still a goddamn shithole. The answer lies there."

EIGHTEEN

Jenna looked at our grocery bag as the clerk squeezed in two bottles of Valpolicello.

"Too heavy for you," she said to me. "Could you put the wine in a separate bag please?" she asked the clerk.

I started to object but knew better. I took the bag with the steak, salad, crusty bread, and two half-gallons of Tropicana and let Jenna carry the wine. I looked at her face and realized how much I was looking forward to seeing it in the candlelight flickering off the red wine tonight.

I opened the door of the store to big, warm raindrops—the kind you find in New York only in August, maybe the beginning of September. "Should we make a run for it or wait?"

Jenna smiled. "I've never known you to wait for anything."

We ran for it, and I wondered the same thing I always did when I was carrying something heavy: was it less strain on the body to move fast and get the heavy carrying over with quickly, or walk slowly, which required less energy per step but took longer? I'd never been able to figure that one out and so always just moved as quickly as possible. Jenna kept up, hugging her paper bag, chin just peeking over the top, as we scurried across the street against a changing light.

"My neck itches," she said as we turned onto 85th Street.

"It's probably the wet edge of the paper bag against your skin."

"No, it's something else. I always get this feeling when I think that someone's following me."

I turned around and peered into the rain, which had gotten heavier.

Jenna clutched her bag tightly and increased her speed. She pulled ahead of me, then turned around quickly and nearly bumped into an elderly man struggling along with a cane. I swerved out of the way of two small dogs yapping on chains. . . .

Then—what was that, across the street? It looked like someone familiar. But on more careful, watery scrutiny it was just a tin garbage can at a peculiar angle in the rain. . . .

Our brownstone was up ahead. "We're almost there!" I called out as cheerily as I could.

"Good!" Jenna called back.

We rushed up the outside stairs. Jenna groped for her keys. "I'm sorry for overreacting—," she started to say.

A hand touched my shoulder—

I whirled around—

Jenna screamed and dropped the wine.

"Dr. D'Amato? I'm sorry if I frightened you—"

"That's OK," I said. It was Mrs. Devlin, the busybody from the ground floor. Every apartment house in the city had one.

"Someone was here looking for you before," she said. "Did he find you?"

"No. Did he have a uniform?"

"No, I don't think so."

"Did he look like a caveman?"

Mrs. Devlin gave me a look. "What is that supposed to mean?"

"Well, I'm just trying to figure out who—"

"I'm surprised at you, Dr. D'Amato. Someone of your intelligence and education should know that looks don't count. People are all the same. Black and white, men and women, young and old, I don't see any differences. We're all of us God's children. . . ."

During the lecture my eyes wandered off to find Jenna. She was at the bottom of the stairs, putting the bleeding paper bag with the broken wine bottles into the trash. The rain had stopped, and the sun was out. "I'll go back and replace these," she half-said and signalled to me, smiling that everything was all right now—

"No, I will—"

"Dr. D'Amato! Are you listening to *anything* I've been saying? That's the trouble with everyone these days—no one *listens* anymore. All people do is talk, talk, talk. . . ."

For an instant I contemplated throwing her down the stairs and running after Jenna. Or maybe asking Mrs. Devlin to hold my bag as I went after Jenna. No, I'd enjoy throwing the talk-machine down the stairs more. . . . But Jenna was already out of sight, so I decided to spend a few more minutes questioning Devlin.

"Did the man have any facial hair that you can recall. Beard? Mustache? . . ."

DEVLIN COULDN'T HAVE been more unhelpful if she'd tried. The more I pushed her for details, the more she receded, until she offered that she wasn't even sure whether the man who was looking for me had come by today or the day before. The heat was up after the rain and our salad was in danger of wilting, so I ended the useless conversation and dashed upstairs.

Three messages were waiting for me on the answering machine, all in response to calls I had made in the morning.

"Phil, glad you're home," the first message said. "We have to talk about some things. Stop breaking Herby Edelstein's balls on that handkerchief thing—you can't push people so hard. That's not the way we work—you know that. Things take a hike from the property room once in a while—that's just the way it is." I pressed fast-forward and turned Dugan's voice into a screech.

"This is Maria Heske from the Bobst Library at New York University returning Dr. Phil D'Amato's call," the second message told me officiously. "Ruth Delany is out of the office today but will be available to receive your call after nine o'clock tomorrow morning.''

Thank you.

The third message was from Jenna's friend Bonnie—the one she'd consulted here about the Tocharian . . .

"Bonnie Mitcham calling at 2:15, returning Phil's call. Actually, I was thinking of calling you anyway. Phil, I was wondering how your meeting went with Pedro Sanches in London? I sent him some e-mail yesterday about a thought I had about how we might interpret the manuscripts. Sort of a reversal of what—well, no need for me to go into that now; that's not why I wanted to call you. Pedro—Dr. Sanches—usually responds to my e-mail promptly the very next morning, and, well, I haven't heard from him yet today, and I know it's only the afternoon, but, well, I guess I'm jittery about all of this and just wanted to make sure everything was OK. . . .''

One of those jittery days for everyone, it seemed. I listened to Bonnie's message again, then picked up my phone and pressed *69 for call return. Great, she had it blocked and hadn't left her number in the message. All right, let's see. . . .

I rifled through the papers on Jenna's desk. She always kept her most important phone numbers scribbled on papers on her desk. . . . She should be home any minute, in case I couldn't find it, but . . .

Ah, here it was. . . .

Bonnie's number rang and rang. No answering machine.

I put the phone down and thought. I picked it up and dialed Mallory at his office. No answer—of course not; it was past ten in the evening there already.

I got out my old-fashioned Rolodex and called him at his home.

No answer there, either. Didn't the kids have school tomorrow? Nah, I guess not; it was August. . . .

I thought a bit more and put in a call to Amanda's home number. She'd left it, amazingly, on the card she'd given to

Amos—in case he or Lapp thought of anything else they'd like to share. . . .

Her phone began that British chirping ring. . . .

"Mmmm, I'll let the machine take that," Amanda said. "See how much I missed you? That could be an important lead on the phone, but I'd rather stay right as I am with you." She put her head on Mallory's chest. "I missed your heartbeat." She kissed his breast and sighed contentedly.

"We're becoming too attached," Mallory replied, and ran his hand down her back. "We'll just have to do something about that, now won't we."

"Oh, yes? And what might that be?" She extended her legs so her toes were just on top of his in the bed.

"Dunno," Mallory said. "I guess see more of each other."

"But you're a married man."

"I know," Mallory said, and pulled away. "OK, enough of this, then. Let's talk about the case."

"Mmmm, don't." She pulled him back and snuggled. "I'm sorry for raising that dreadful issue. I promise I won't mention it anymore, this evening."

"Right, that's all right," Mallory said. "We need to talk about the damned case anyway."

"See what a good lay will do for a journalist?" Amanda said. "My colleagues at the Beeb say they have to talk to you until they're blue in the face to get the *slightest* information from you, and even then they're never sure you're telling the truth."

"It's not just that you're a good lay, you know." He draped his hand over the back of her thigh. "Working for New Scotland Yard yourself may have something to do with it."

"Mmmm. . . ." She put her mouth against his, stretched out more fully on top of him, and was glad to feel how aroused he had become again. . . .

"Oh, all right," Mallory said. "We can talk about the case later. . . ."

AMANDA DROPPED ICE cubes in a glass. "What'll it be, love?"

Mallory was sitting up, leaning back against the big mahogany headboard on Amanda's bed, hands clasped around the back of his neck. "Just ginger ale for me. I decided to go on the wagon, at least until this ugly business is over."

"That bad, eh? When did you decide to do that?"

"Just now," Mallory replied. "Looking at you, thinking about what happened to you in New York. I don't like feeling so out of control."

"We don't really know what happened to me in New York. I just woke up on the floor down there, remember? Even under Soames and his trance, I hadn't a clue of recall about who brought me down there."

"Exactly," Mallory said. "That's the problem—we don't know enough."

"I'll tell you one thing," Amanda spoke up with a sudden surge of anger. "Don't ever stick another bug under my skin when I'm sleeping—not if you want to see me again."

"OK." Mallory had told her how he'd rubbed some powerful local anaesthetic on her shoulder while she was asleep, the night before her trip to the States, and inserted the tiny bug. No point lying about that now—they needed to get everything out in the open. "I did it in part to protect you."

"Didn't work very well, then, did it?"

"No, apparently not. Look, I'm sorry—"

"It's OK." Amanda came back with his ginger ale and a Perrier for her. "I forgive you." She kissed him.

"So let's talk about the States," Mallory said.

"You heard the tapes that you got off the bug—you know, I *promised* those people that I wasn't taping them."

"I said I was sorry."

Amanda snorted. "Well there's not much more I can think of than what's already in those interviews. None of those people seem like murderers, that's for sure. The Neanderthal man was a real gentleman; the Amish man's got a bit of a stick up there for sure, but he's sincere, too—"

"So the Neanderthal seemed like a real gent to you, did he?"

"Yes, he did," Amanda said. "Why—"

"And you would be in a good spot to know that, wouldn't you?"

"Yes. I mean, what exactly are you—"

"One might even say you have the right genetic endowment for that?"

Amanda said nothing.

"You see my problem, then."

"How did you find that out?" Amanda finally asked.

"From Phil fucking D'Amato," Mallory answered, pronouncing the last name so that it sounded the way he'd imagine *tomato* being pronounced in Brooklyn would. "I covered as best I could—pretended I already knew. Managed to stammer something out about your plastic surgery. Just who the hell are you? You work for us; you work for the BBC—who else do you work for?"

"You think what? I'm part of some secret society of people with Neanderthal genes plotting to take over the world?"

"You tell me," Mallory replied.

"I'd wager there are millions of people on this Earth today who have some genes like mine," Amanda said quietly. "Some of them have formed groups, certainly. Some are indeed very old. Just like there are very old ongoing groups of *Homo sapiens sapiens*. For God's sake, Christianity is two thousand years old. Judaism is even older."

"Indeed," Mallory said. "And does your group have a Bible?"

"No, of course not," Amanda said. "You're not listening. It's not formal like that. We don't take our marching orders from some central authority."

"No? How then does the 'we' that you keep mentioning keep in touch?"

"Mostly memes in the music," Amanda said. "Melodic

phrases, catchy pieces of lyrics. They may be composed by *Homo sapiens sapiens,* but others—we—use them for our own purposes. It's, I don't know, I guess a whole subterranean communication system. It's been going on for millennia, in folk songs and the like, but radio and rock 'n' roll did a lot to help us. You know how it works? There's a musical riff from a Beatles song or an old rhythm and blues song, and it shows up on lots of new songs, and each time we hear that riff it conveys something to us. Sometimes it evokes a specific past experience—I've heard older people say that when they hear an early Beatles song they immediately think of the death of JFK. I think all *Homo sapiens* respond in that way. But for us, it's also something deeper. If Plato was right that we have innate knowledge, even recollections of things that happened before we were born—genetically conveyed knowledge, we might now call that, or maybe a Jungian innate archetype—then for my kind certain types of music actually trigger certain kinds of genetic memories, certain kinds of knowledge. I guess you have that, too, when a minor chord makes you sad or restless and a major chord makes you feel happy or complete. With us, that general feeling is just more precise, more specific, in terms of telling us things. Does that make sense? I don't know—I don't fully comprehend it myself."

"Tell me about our mummy, Max Soros," Mallory urged.

"Soros was alive after the LSE mummy was discovered," Amanda said. "He and our mummy were two different people— like Stefan and the mummy in New York."

"So where is Soros now?"

"Dead," Amanda replied. "Likely at the hands of the same person or persons unknown who lured me down to that lobby in New York."

Mallory touched her face with his fingertips, tentatively at first. Then he pulled her close to him, kissed her head, until she stopped shuddering.

NINETEEN

 I awoke with a start and looked at my watch. Goddamnit, I close my eyes for a moment and here it is an hour later. "Honey? Jenna?"

No answer.

She definitely should have been home by now.

I rubbed my eyes. I was bone tired—still on British time. No response yet from Mallory or Amanda on the message I'd left about Pedro on her machine—who knew if Mallory even had received it? Well, I'd have to leave England to its own devices a little longer. Jenna was my first priority.

I'd trace her steps to the liquor store. I'd throttle that busybody on the ground floor's neck until she told me who the hell had come looking for me this morning. . . .

I grabbed my wallet and keys, yanked open the door—

"Jesus Christ!" Jenna screamed. "You almost gave me a heart attack—what are you doing opening the door so suddenly like that?"

I put my arms around her and held her. . . .

She kissed my ear. "I miss this when you're away."

"Me, too." I felt something crunchy, glassy, under my feet.

Jenna looked down. "Two bottles of red wine. Hopeless case for us today. I went over to Maurino's on Second Avenue; he closed early for some unknown reason—so I had to trudge all the way over to Lexington and 86th. And then I ran into that guy from the bookstore on the way back—he wants you to talk at that panel they're doing on strange detectives."

"It's OK," I said. "I mean, I'm sorry I made you drop the wine." I knelt down and carefully picked up the oozing bag. "Hey, it looks like one of the bottles may have survived my panic attack."

"Good," Jenna said. "I also bought coffee ice cream and morello cherries, so it wouldn't have been a total loss in any event." She held up in her hand a small bag that I hadn't noticed at first.

"Impossible for anything to be a total loss where you're involved."

THE PHONE RANG the next morning—it hurt like hell.

Jenna got it. ". . . Oh, I'm fine. Thanks. . . . Sure, hold on a minute; he may be in the shower."

She came over with the portable phone, on hold. "Jack Dugan. Should I tell him you'll call him back? I've got breakfast for you in the kitchen. No point in my asking him to give me a message for you—he never does."

"Nah, I'll talk to him now," I said, and rubbed my stomach. It felt like an elephant herd had been trampling over it all night. Damn jet lag—took me days sometimes to get over it, even on this side of the Atlantic. I'd once heard of some head of some huge corporation who insisted that all his employees operate on his time, wherever in the world he went. Nice perk if you could get it. . . .

"Jack." I sounded as crisp as I could. "How are you doing?"

"Fine, Phil," he said back, even more crisply. "I've got something to brighten your day. And I hope you learn something from this: you've got to lay back more, let events take their course. You can't always force everything onto your schedule."

Good ol' lay-back Jack, featuring a little pseudo-California philosophy with a New York accent. . . .

"Yep, you're right," I said. "So what have you got for me?"

"Well, I just got off the phone with Herby—you really should call and apologize to him. That blue hankie turned up after all.

The box had been misplaced, just as I'd guessed, by one of Dave Spencer's people whom Herby had let go. I'm not saying it was deliberate. But like I say, these things happen. So now, if you call up Herby and apologize for questioning his professionalism, I'm sure he'd be happy to give you the hankie if you went down to his office. We're all on the same side here—fighting the bad guys. Let's not fight amongst ourselves, Phil!"

"You're right, Jack—that's good advice. I'll take it—and thank you!"

I clicked off the phone and handed it back to Jenna.

"Good advice?"

"Fuck the advice—Herby found the hankie," I said.

"Great! What are you going to do with it?"

"I'll send it over to Mary Radcliff and see if she can really reverse-engineer it into a set of punch cards. Then we'll send the cards over to my people at MIT and see if they can wring any language, any message, out of the code in the cards."

"But how can we be sure that this hankie is even the original Dave found on the corpse?" Jenna asked. "I mean, if it was missing at all, then doesn't that contaminate the chain of evidence?"

I smiled. "Yeah, it does—but this isn't a court of law. We're not looking at the handkerchief for evidence in that sense. We're just trying to see if it might be able to tell us something. But here's what I'll do, anyway—I'll buy two other blue handkerchiefs that look as much as possible like the original and send all three over to Mary. I of course won't tell her which is which. If she gets the same punch cards out of all three, then that means the handkerchiefs are meaningless. But if she gets something different from the Neanderthal hankie—well then, that'll at least be *something*."

Jenna considered. "That wouldn't protect against a false message, though—say if someone had deliberately replaced the original hankie."

"No, it wouldn't," I agreed. "The only way we can check on that score is to see what kinds of messages we get from the other sources—like the Tocharians."

I WAS AT Bonnie's office two hours later. My news was bad. "Pedro Sanches is dead."

"Oh, no!" Bonnie cried.

"Look, I'm not going to lie to you," I said. "I think we're in some sort of race here, some kind of contest, with whatever or whoever it is who is doing this. And part of the race seems to be their killing, or trying to kill, anyone who seems to be getting too close to understanding what's going on. Now no one other than Jenna, Mallory in England, maybe one or two of his associates, and I know that you've been working on these Tocharian manuscripts—sort of secondhand, from what first we and then Pedro sent directly over to you—right?"

Bonnie nodded. I could see she was frightened, and I felt terrible about it.

"I can't guarantee that no one else knows—that they're not on to you already—but I can guarantee that I won't tell another soul and won't even discuss this with you ever again, won't come to see you again, if you decide you want to end this right now. And frankly, I wouldn't blame you in the slightest. But I also need to tell you that we could really use your help now—you're the only one we can turn to now at this late stage about those manuscripts—if you're willing to take the risk."

Bonnie nodded again. "I understand," she said.

I looked around her tiny office at Columbia. Assistant professors, someone once had told me, rated one step better than bathrooms when it came to office space. . . .

"This is the most exciting thing I've ever worked on," she said. "I've always had a dual specialty—early Indo-European Celtic, and Basque. I've been trying to find some similarity— actually, any similarity—for years."

"With no success?" I knew something about Basque and how it seemed to have no connection whatsoever to any Indo-European language.

"No, none," Bonnie said. "Every lead I tracked down—

archaeo-linguists are like detectives in that way—every similarity I could find always turned out to be a result of contamination from a more recent source. You know, the Romans occupied some Basque territory, so Latin crept in—"

"Yeah," I said. "But you see some connection now between Basque and the Tocharian?"

"No, not linguistically—but reference-wise."

"I don't get it," I said.

"Well, the language or the manuscripts is thoroughly Tocharian—an early Indo-European language, just like what we'd expect. And, of course, they were found in the Tarim Basin. But there seem to be some references in them to places on the extreme west coast, right against the sea, with mountains to the back, and some of the names look like they might be Basque."

"Hmmm . . . this was in the magical part of the texts?"

"Yes," Bonnie replied. "Those are the ones we're trying to get new translations for. The monastery stuff and commercial ledgers are all cut-and-dried. Poor Pedro. . . ." She caught herself in a sob.

"It's OK," I said. "I feel like crying about it, too."

"You're a nice man," she responded. "I can see why Jenna and you—"

"Thanks," I said.

"I want to keep working on this."

"I know. I'm glad. Just . . . please, please be careful." *As if being careful would do any good!* my conscience screamed at me.

"OK," Bonnie said, and smiled.

"One other thing—you mentioned something about a 're-versal' on the phone machine yesterday. But I didn't quite understand it. . . ."

"Yes," Bonnie said. "I sent some e-mail to Pedro about that. There is some ambiguity in the Tocharian wording that could be coincidence or maybe not. All languages have it—you know, *victim* and *victor* mean the opposite, but if you didn't fully understand English and had a sample of our writing that was partially obliterated, you might get the wrong message—and think that the victim in an account was really the victor. . . . See what I'm saying?"

"Yeah, sort of," I replied. "Don't they have the same Latin root?"

"Well, it's tricky," Bonnie said. "*Victim* comes from *vincio,* to bind, and *victor* comes from *vinco,* to conquer or vanquish. With just that one "i" difference in the words there could be an overlap—maybe both were the same in some very early Latin. But my point is they went on to mean two opposite things—the conquered and the conqueror—in English, and someone who didn't know English with precision, let alone Latin, could render a not unreasonable, but completely wrong, interpretation of either *victim* or *victor.* Or, for that matter, *conquered* or *conqueror.* It's a very common phenomenon in language—that's the problem. Here, let me hunt down the Tocharian—"

"No, not now. Let's just concentrate on getting the best possible complete translation of all the relevant manuscripts in the fastest possible time. We can consider specific problem areas and alternate interpretations when we get that far."

"OK."

"Good," I said. "What did Pedro think of your reversal theory, though?"

She sobbed again. "I just got my e-mail returned with that automatic advisory that they had tried to deliver it for two days and were giving up."

I WAS BACK in my office the next day. It felt good to be at my desk again. Not that anything was solved, but it felt good anyway. I sometimes thought I could use more days like this—just coming into my office, tracking down leads, like any normal forensic detective. Except I was so accustomed to abnormality, I'd probably die of boredom.

Which was it better to die of: (a) boredom; (b) weirdo Neanderthal virus; (c) knife, like Tesa Stewart; or (d) homicidally induced asthma, like Pedro Sanches? Mallory had said the poor guy didn't show so much as a single asthmatic reaction on any hospital record anywhere in the UK for as long as they had been keeping records like that over there, and with their nationalized health insurance they'd been keeping those kinds or records very carefully and for a very long time. No way Pedro hadn't been murdered.

Answer: (e) none of the above—better not to die at all, goddamnit.

I had round-the-clock protection on Jenna and Bonnie—not that it made me comfortable about them, but it was better than nothing. And Mallory had a plan to throw them off the track of what Mary Radcliff was trying to do. "Them"—I didn't think any one of us was the least bit safe from "them."

"This is for you, Phil." Megan, a bright young face who had just started in the Department, gave me a DHL package.

"Thanks." It was a videotape from Mallory.

I toyed with the idea of watching it in the office but decided to take it home. "I'll be back in a few hours," I said to Megan.

A patrol car was right outside our brownstone, keeping an eye on Jenna, just where it was supposed to be. Good.

I put the tape in the machine and sat down with Jenna to watch it.

"Next on the BBC at 10: 'A Special Report': 'The Silken Secret'—and an interview with Mrs. Mary Radcliff, of the Silk Museum in Macclesfield."

"Good evening," Amanda said. She brushed back her hair and looked sensuously, seriously, into the camera. She was standing in front of the Silk Museum, with Mary Radcliff at her side. "Silk has long held a special fascination for man—and woman," Amanda continued. "Here at the Silk Museum at the Heritage Center in Macclesfield, the splendid Jacquard Looms of bygone days still glint beguilingly in the moonlight."

The scene dissolved to an aerial shot of a glass ceiling and then moved in slowly through the glass to rows of Jacquard Looms within, closer and closer, until a single Jacquard Loom filled the screen.

"Those looms worked on punched paper cards—nearly two centuries before cards like that were employed by our first computers," Amanda's voice went on. "They produced so much of beauty. Tonight we consider a new mystery: might those same cards have served an additional purpose—conveying messages in their punchings from Victorian and earlier times?

"We are joined tonight by Mrs. Mary Radcliff, one of the leading historians and experts at the Museum. Mrs. Radcliff will be our guide as we plumb the silken secrets."

Mysterious music played in the background.

I chuckled. "Bring on Robert Stack."

"Shhh . . . ," Jenna said.

Amanda and Mary Radcliff were back on the screen. "Mrs. Radcliff," Amanda said, "is it really possible that silk garments could hold hidden messages? Isn't this just like the Paul-is-dead brouhaha of the 1960s? Play a recording backwards or at a different speed, and you suddenly hear 'turn me on, dead man,' or such like?"

"There's of course always the danger that what we see in our artifacts is of our making, rather than the people who created the work," Mary said. "But that does not mean that there cannot be a hidden message in a recording, or a word in silk—both are, after all, the result of human creation. And humans send messages, do they not?"

The music faded. . . .

"Of course we do," Amanda said. "But tell me then, how exactly might a message be embedded in a silk weave?"

Mary held up a blue silk handkerchief. "If this handkerchief was made on a loom which used punch cards, then we might be able, in principle, to reconstruct the punch cards by examination of the handkerchief." Mary put down the hankie and held up a bunch of punch cards.

"OK," Amanda said. "I'm with you so far. But how would we get from the punch cards to a secret message?"

"Ah, that's the interesting part," Mary said. "Scientists at MIT supply a different letter for each set of punches. They do this again and again, each time changing the letters assigned to the punches. And they feed this all into a computer, which puts the letters together for each group of assignments and sees if any add up to words or sentences."

"Fascinating," Amanda said. "But how can you know that each of the punch configurations represents a letter or series of letters? Maybe they each represent an entire word."

"Yes, that's possible," Mary said. "I'd imagine the scientists at MIT checked for that, too."

"So you have already forwarded these cards to the people at MIT, and they have already done their work?"

"Yes, we forwarded the cards. The people at MIT are checking the punch configurations right now."

"And you were therefore able to retrieve a series of punch cards from that handkerchief?" Amanda asked.

"Oh, yes," Mary said. "That part was easier than we expected."

"Could you tell anything about the message just by looking at the punch cards?" Amanda asked.

"No, not really," Mary said. "They are essentially meaningless until the letter substitutions are made."

"And what do you expect the MIT people might find there?"

"I really couldn't say," Mary said. "The New York City Police Department forwarded that silk handkerchief to us to see if we could reconstruct the cards. We did that. The handkerchief, as you know, was apparently found on a corpse of a Neanderthal—"

"Did Neanderthals have looms?"

"Well, I suppose that's possible," Mary said. "But we won't know until we hear from the scientists at MIT. It's out of our hands now. . . ."

"Mary was fabulous!" Jenna said, as the credits ran over a closing shot of the Museum. "She puts you to shame when it comes to dissembling."

"Thanks." I smiled. "There are few liars as effective as little old ladies."

"So how far along is she actually with the cards?"

"She's not even sure, yet, that the Neanderthal hankie was created by a loom—certainly not a Jacquard, classic or current. But the Museum is tied into a whole worldwide network of silk specialists—they have silk museums in China, Japan, other places. Mary's plan at present is to check with each of the museums, any place she can find that has any access to a card-punching silk loom, and see if the weave in the handkerchief correlates with any of those. Probably just running after rainbows. But at least her story that the project's now in MIT's hands should draw our killer away from her.''

"I'm sure the MIT people are thrilled," Jenna said.

"Well, we didn't give any names," I said. "And I checked with my contacts there, and they said they had no problem with Mary mentioning MIT's name in this broadcast. Truthfully, I don't think they believe that there's anything more than coincidence to all the deaths. But the killer really isn't a threat to MIT anyway. What's he going to do—murder everyone in the university? And, in the meantime, it buys Mary some time."

"When does this show air?" Jenna asked.

"Tomorrow night, London time," I replied.

"Let's hope the killer's still in England and watches the BBC," Jenna said.

A BRITISH AIRLINES plane landed twenty minutes later at JFK.

A man waited on line fifteen minutes after that, for Customs.

"That's very pretty, Mommy," a little girl said to her mother, and pointed to an iridescent blue-green handkerchief sticking out of the man's pocket.

"Here, would you like it?" The man pulled the handkerchief out of his pocket. "I have many more like it—my company makes them—and this one is new and fresh. I haven't used it."

The little girl smiled shyly, then slowly nodded.

"No, I don't think—," the mother began.

"Please, Mommy?" the little girl pleaded.

"Really, I assure you, it's not expensive, and I haven't used it at all, see?"

"Please, Mommy?"

"Well, OK . . . ," the mother relented. "But let me hold it for you until we get home." She took the hankie from the man and thanked him. That would give her time to talk her daughter out of wanting it before they got home. A chocolate ice-cream cone with sprinkles should finish the job. . . .

They went to separate customs lines; the man passed through with no problem.

The dispatcher hailed a cab for him in the rain.

"Washington Square Park in Greenwich Village," the man instructed the cabbie. "How long has the weather been like this?"

I CALLED RUTH Delany the next morning.

"Phil—I know you were trying to get in touch with me. My sister's family came over, the weather's been gorgeous this past week—except for that downpour yesterday—and I couldn't resist taking some time off with them. August is a slow time in the library anyway."

"Absolutely," I said. "You had the right idea. I was really just wondering about Stefan. . . ."

"Oh, I thought you knew—I told him he should call you so you wouldn't worry. . . ."

"Ah, I guess he forgot—or maybe he missed me because I was out of the country myself for the past few weeks . . . in England."

"Beautiful country."

"Yes, it is," I said. "Anyway, about Stefan . . ."

"Oh, yes. He told me he had an urge to see the country— the heat and humidity were getting him down. He's not a young man, you know."

Yeah, I knew. "And this was when—week before last?"

"No, I think the week before that—three weeks ago," Ruth said. "He's been banking vacation time for years now, and truthfully, a memo came around earlier this month that said folks had to use some of their banked time by the end of the year or else they'd lose it. I *hate* when they do that, don't you?"

"Yes, I do," I said truthfully.

"So he said he was going to take a month off—just see the country, by Greyhound. He said they were having a sale—for seventy-nine dollars you could take a bus anywhere in the country and get off as many times as you liked."

"Wouldn't mind a little trip like that myself," I said.

"Ain't it the truth? So I wished him a good time, but I told him to call you—and that nice Amish boy who's come around here a few times, too.''

"Amos Stoltzfus?"

"That's right," Ruth said.

"And what did Stefan say when you said he should call Amos?"

"He laughed in that way of his and said didn't I know that Amish don't use phones? And then he said he was fresh out of stray cats and butterflies. But I didn't pay that any attention— Stefan always says things I don't understand."

"Like that old joke about what happens when you cross a mafioso with a semiotician—he makes you an offer you can't understand."

"Oh, Doctor!" Ruth said, and chuckled heartily.

"I wish Stefan had called me," I said.

"You think some harm's come to him? You were wrong last time, thank the Lord, remember?"

"Yeah."

"Wait—I tell you what. Stefan left me the key to his apartment—he has some snake plants there. They can go a long time without water, but I promised him I would come over and give them a drink if the heat really got brutal. It can do that sometimes, you know. August is a tricky month—"

"Jeez, you have the key! I mean, sorry for the profanity—"

"Oh, that's OK, Dr. D'Amato. I've heard far worse than that in my day—"

"I mean, last time we talked about Stefan, you didn't even have an address for him. He gave me an address later on Patchin Place—is that the one he gave you the key for?"

"Yes, it is—right off Sixth Avenue, about a five-minute walk from here."

"I'll be right down."

TWENTY

I talked Ruth Delany into accompanying me to Stefan's apartment. Without her, I might have needed a search warrant, and that meant contacting Jack Dugan, and I wasn't in the mood for more advice. . . .

I just prayed I wasn't getting her into anything that could result in her harm. But if Stefan was a victim in this and the killers were completists, she was likely already in their sights. . . .

"Pretty exclusive, this Patchin Place," I said. "I'm surprised Stefan could afford it, on a janitor's salary."

"I think it's a friend's place," she told me, "someone letting him stay over."

"Ah, that would explain it. How long he has he been staying here?"

"I don't know," Ruth replied. "I can't recall his saying." She put the key in the wrought-iron gate in front of the street—really more of a classic mew, a little alleyway with flowerpots dappling every entrance and windowsill. "This should work here," she said. It did.

We walked quickly to the third set of stairs, all of which were on the right. An Irish terrier pulled a man with bushy white hair out of the door and down the stairs. He smiled at us as the terrier pulled him out of Patchin Place entirely. . . .

I hustled up the stairs, with Ruth in tow.

"OK, here it is."

Stefan's apartment was on the second floor. I rapped sharply on the door. And then again.

I looked at Ruth.

"I guess no one's home," she said. "Feels a mite hot and dry today, wouldn't you agree, Dr. D'Amato? I'd say the snake plants could definitely use a bit of watering."

I knew I liked this woman, from the moment I first saw her—not your typical by-the-book librarian by any means.

The apartment didn't seem exceptional at first glance—a couch and a chair in some earthen fabric that looked well sat in, a nice wooden hutch, probably oak, with art nouveau carving. Lots of stuff like that in the Village. There seemed to be a bathroom off to one side, a kitchen on the other. No bedroom—likely the couch was a convertible. I looked more closely and saw that it was. . . .

And a bright sunny windowsill indeed had not only snake plants but also a few pots of spider plants hanging from the ceiling. Ruth walked over and touched the soils of the botanical menagerie. "They're dry, all right," she said. "These plants make an honest woman out of me!"

I began a closer inspection of the apartment. No prescription medication in the medicine chest—nothing at all with a name or an expiration date. Just some bars of soap and about a dozen bottles of cologne, most of them nearly full. I opened one—English Leather—and sniffed carefully to verify the contents. Ah, sweet memories of splashing too much on my face as I hurried to pick up Denise Yablon that last weekend in high school. . . . It was English Leather, no doubt about that.

I went into the kitchen. The refrigerator had lots of gallon bottles of Poland Spring and that was it. Again, nothing with an expiration date—nothing I could use to figure out when a human being had last been here. Except—how long had Poland Spring been available like this? What, ten, twenty, thirty years? Did me no good at all. I was beginning to see a pattern here, and I didn't like it.

"Dr. D'Amato, look at this!" Ruth called to me from the living room.

She had what looked like an old 78-rpm vinyl in her hand—
they'd stopped making those kinds of records, what, in the 1940s?
The label was worn. The printing on it was barely legible. . . .

"Looks like Cyrillic," Ruth said. "Stefan's from Roma-
nia. . . ."

"He told me Hungary," I said. "But Antonescu's certainly a
Romanian name, and there must have been Romanians in Hungarian territory over the years—the two countries are right next
to each other." For that matter, the Hungarian language was a
relative of Finnish, if I remembered correctly—a non-Indo-
European language like Basque. Talk about tangled webs. . . . "I
think the Romanian alphabet is Latin, though, not Cyrillic," I
added.

"It's all so confusing," Ruth said. "I wonder what this record
sounds like."

"Would be great if there were an old Victrola around here
somewhere—where'd you find the record?"

She pointed to behind the hutch. "I saw it peeking out," she
said. "It's very dusty back there."

"Yeah, Antonescu, or whoever lived here then, probably let
it slip away when packing. Who knows how long ago that even
was."

"No sign that Stefan's ever been here at all," Ruth declared.

"My feeling exactly," I said.

"What does that mean? Why would he lie to me about this
and go through all the trouble of giving me his key and *urging*
me to come here? Makes no sense."

Welcome to almost everything else I'd encountered since I'd
first seen the corpse that Dave Spencer thought was Stefan Antonescu. . . .

"Could be he's not lying," I said. "Maybe someone got here
first. . . ."

"Who?"

"I don't know. Maybe whoever's responsible for the murders.
Someone who doesn't like Neanderthals—someone who doesn't

like us—maybe both. I'll interview the neighbors here and see what—"

The phone in my pocket rang.

Had to be Jenna.

It was.

"OK, I'll call you right back." I threw her a kiss, pressed "End" on the phone, and then realized that Ruth was smiling at me.

"We might as well go—I don't think we'll find much else here," I said, and grabbed a glass from the kitchen with my gloved hand. Possibly it had a fingerprint or recoverable DNA.

Ruth had the 78 record. "Should I take it back to the library? We may have a record player squirreled away in some room there that can play this."

"Sure," I said. "Here's my private cell-phone number. Call me right away if you hear anything interesting. And I'll call you if I find out anything more about Stefan."

I WAVED GOOD-BYE to Ruth and called Jenna right back on the phone. "First thing is, you're OK? Nothing strange going on outside the apartment?"

"I'm fine," Jenna said. "There's a cute guy in a uniform right outside my door, another patrolman right outside on the street—what more could I ask for?"

"Thanks, that makes me feel much better now," I quipped, glad to have any excuse to cut the tension even a little. "So tell me about Bonnie's new translation."

"She said you should call her about it later—she was up with it all night and needed a nap. But she gave me what she had."

"OK," I said.

"It has to do with singers and killers and some sort of warning about children—assuming we take it literally," Jenna began. "Remember the segment that Pedro translated—it ended with *illness it has bestowed upon us and the children like a curse?* Well, first of all, Bonnie says Pedro was able to do some more work on the oxidized part and recover a few more words that Bonnie translated as—"

"Why don't you read the whole thing to me—with the original and then the additional wording?"

"OK," Jenna said. "The original was: *Our ancestors must have been jealous of the singers, for they killed most of them. Not because they were ugly, but because their minds were beautiful, and more knowing than ours. Their intelligence must have frightened our forebears, far more than their faces. Our forebears bred precautions, but the blood of the singers had its revenge, in the illness it has bestowed upon us and the children like a curse.* That's where the initial translation ended. But now Bonnie says there is no period after *curse*—Pedro just put that in there because it looked as if the sentence was finished. And there are additional words in the manuscript after *curse*, and the part with *the children* was apparently initially translated out of place, so . . . Here, let me read the relevant part as Bonnie now has it: *but the blood of the singers had its revenge, in the illness it has bestowed upon us like a curse and the children it has set to walk among us like men.*"

"Hmm. . . . So in this new translation, the children are not the target but the vehicle of the revenge . . . victims to victors. . . . But what does *walk among us like men* mean?"

"I don't know," Jenna said. "Bonnie also has an alternate translation for the last phrase—more metaphoric—*in the illness it has bestowed upon us like a curse and the caterpillars it has set to fly among us like butterflies . . .*"

"Hmmm . . . ," I said.

"I know," Jenna said. "Silk worms again. . . ."

"Except this time the moths seem to be bad guys. . . . Or maybe the bad guys make use of them too. But how could the same word mean either 'children' or 'caterpillars'?" I asked.

"Bonnie says it's a question of context. The word apparently does mean 'caterpillars,' but when taken as part of the overall passage it seems to be an allusion to children. The problem is there aren't enough unambiguous words in the documents to be sure."

"How come Pedro made the mistake with the placement of 'children' in that sentence in the first place?" I asked.

"Those kinds of transpositions happen in translations all the time—think about word orders in Latin," Jenna said. "It's really hard when you have so little of the language to work with. The better word order became clear to Bonnie only after Pedro translated the rest of the sentence—*it has set to walk among us like men.* I suppose a curse could 'walk among us like men,' too, but 'children' works much better there, even though we still can't tell exactly what it means."

"Has Bonnie figured out anything more about a specific author for this yet? Any indication of age, gender—name?" *And species?*

"She can't tell completely yet," Jenna replied. "The most she's been able to glean, so far, is that the writer had lived a long life—by whatever the contemporary Tocharian standards were, of course—and makes references here and there, in otherwise untranslated parts of the manuscripts, to having travelled far and wide in the world. We can't even be sure it's all the same writer—though I asked Bonnie about that and she says if she had to bet she'd say it was."

"So here are these manuscripts waiting thirteen hundred years in the Tarim Basin, maybe with answers to some of our questions, and we finally have them in our hands now, but we still can't fathom what they're trying to tell us—or even who is trying to tell us," I said.

"Like everything else we seem to be dealing with here—right in front of us, but we still can't see exactly what we're looking at," Jenna said. "But Bonnie's still working on it. She's good. She'll get more."

"All right. If you speak to her before I do, tell her to keep in close touch with you, and I will, too. And be careful—you know the drill. Don't go out anywhere without an escort—better, don't go out at all—and stay away from windows. . . ."

"Yeah, yeah, I'll be careful. I love you."

"I love you, too," I said, and beeped off the phone.

The man with the bushy white hair opened the gate—I'd been standing right inside it.

I described Stefan to him and asked if he recalled the last time he'd seen him.

Never, he said. He couldn't remember ever seeing anyone around here who looked like Stefan.

"But there was an Amish boy here just this morning," he added, "and he asked me the same question."

A MAN IN uniform proceeded along 85th Street slowly, deliberately, but not to attract undue attention. He reached the brownstone—good; there were no cops stationed outside it.

He walked up the stairs, smiled at a bleached-blond lady walking down, and entered the vestibule.

Three possible apartments.

He rang the buzzer on the first, and most preferable.

No answer.

He rang it again, got the same result.

He tried the second buzzer.

That got no answer also.

A woman holding a white cat opened the inside door—the one he was trying to get into—and gazed balefully at him. *No special delivery for you today, lady, don't worry.*

He was tempted to go inside but thought better of it. The woman passed by and out into the street. The cat's hisses lingered in the vestibule like a bad smell.

He rang the third bell. If that didn't get an answer, he'd have to go back to the park or maybe a coffee shop, wait an hour or two, and try again. This building was his only option. . . .

"Hello?" a female voice, crackly with static, inquired.

"Yes, Express Mail, for . . . Michele Politico," he said, moving closer to read the blurry lettering below the buzzer.

"Polito," she corrected him. "OK, come on up."

The door buzzed. He pushed it open and climbed the stairs to the third floor.

He knocked on her door. He flashed the Express Mail envelope at the peephole.

"OK, just a minute." Michele opened the door a moment later. She had glistening long black hair, but it didn't matter.

She went down, sprayed full in the face, gasping, coughing, dead of an asthmatic reaction seven minutes later. By then he had picked up her oxygen-depleted body and nestled it comfortably on a couch in front of a television.

Deaths from asthma were really on the upswing these days. Maybe some researcher would draw a connection between them and watching television.

He walked carefully to the window and looked across at the brownstone with Phil D'Amato's apartment.

It wasn't the cleanest angle, but this was the best he could do.

Their window was open. Lucky break for him. A fine, beautiful August day—much less humid than usual, pollution in the city down—why use air-conditioning? *Good ecological thinking, Dr. D'Amato.*

He could have used a bullet to penetrate a closed window, if necessary, but that would announce this as murder. This way was better. His insect-dart was biodegradable. The break in the skin would be so small that it likely would go unnoticed. Healthy folks died of aneurysms all the time. People close to the investigation, people like Phil D'Amato who didn't believe in coincidences, of course would know. But knowledge and proof were two different things, and with any luck D'Amato wouldn't be around to suspect coincidences or anything else. The silk cure wouldn't help him this time. . . .

The silk cure . . . he had to laugh. As if one antidote could work for everything. That BBC woman had just been very lucky—preventatives usually don't take that quickly. But he had lots of toys in his pocket. Asthma, aneurysm . . . the time was long since past for catalysts that metamorphosed the body and confounded carbon datings.

The time had passed for that, as it was passing now for him. ...No time left anymore for testing the prowess of his antagonists, for sowing confusion, for calling forth the snakes in them to consume their own tails...just time for cleaning up the details. ...

The wisdom of millennia said the best way of erasing knowledge was elimination of the living vessels that carried it.

He looked at the open window. He'd get the first person who appeared there—if not Phil, then Jenna—and then he'd get Phil when he discovered Jenna's body. . . .

And if no one appeared there, he'd figure out a way to get them out of the apartment.

MY PHONE RANG. I was just finishing my third worthless interview on Patchin Place.

I thanked the man—he had said he was a "media critic"—and took the call.

"Hi, honey," Jenna said. "I've got Amanda Leonard on hold on the other line. Should I make it a three-way conference call?"

"Good idea. Easier for you to jot down any important information than for me in the street."

"OK, hold on," Jenna said.

"Hullo?" another voice said a moment later.

"Hi, Amanda. We saw you on tape last night—you were great."

"Thank you—is that you, Phil?"

"Yep. Jenna's on the line, too."

"Great. Well, we've heard back from Mary Radcliff at the Silk Museum, who heard from MIT," Amanda said. "The code in the silk hankie turned out to be a snap to crack!"

"Excellent! Tell me the whole story."

I heard some kind of rusty scraping. "I'm just raising the blinds a little," Jenna said. "The sun's gone behind a cloud. . . ."

"... Mary tried to derive punch cards for all three handker-chiefs," Amanda was saying.

"Right," I said.

"And only one was the product of a Jacquard Loom, or some-thing like it. The two others were much more modern in creation, and nothing about their weave could be reduced to a code. Mary says their code is Marks and Spencers—or maybe JC Penney would be better." She laughed.

"Sears," Jenna supplied.

"Ah, yes," Amanda said. "But you of course knew that—the two Taiwanese hankies, if that's what they are, were controls."

"Exactly," I said. "We had to do that because—"

"No need to explain. We understand—and approve—com-pletely. Now, the third hankie, that's where the story is. Mary says it's definitely early to middle Victorian—nothing prehistoric, of course; they didn't have Jacquard Looms then, as far as we know. But 1850 looks to be its time, and that fits perfectly with Jacquard use, certainly here and on the Continent. And Mary back-worked a set of cards for them and faxed their image to MIT. They didn't need the actual cards, of course, just their pattern—"

"Right," I said again.

"And the code proved very easy to crack. And they got one clear word out of it—"

"Yes?"

"*Mitxeleta*," Amanda said.

"What was that?" I asked.

"*Mitxeleta*," Amanda repeated. "The MIT people did a mas-sive search in all on-line dictionaries. *Mitxeleta* is Basque for 'but-terfly'...."

A DEFTLY AIMED winged living dart flew silently through an open window.

A teakettle whistled.

Jenna jerked, involuntarily, toward the kitchen.

And the insect-dart sailed clean through an inch of baggy

fabric around her thigh, never touching skin. It lodged in an area rug close to a far wall, taking its woolen composition as an environment suitable for its complete biodegrading, which it promptly did.

A finger would find a hole in the slacks later that week. It would be blamed on a moth. . . .

"HOLD ON A second; teapot's whistling," Jenna said.

"I could use a cup myself," Amanda remarked.

"Me, too," I said.

"I wish I could send each of you a cup through the phone," Jenna said.

"Oh, one other thing," Amanda said.

"Yes?" I asked.

"One of the fellows at MIT is working on some sort of digital music project—you know, the kind that reads computer code and turns it into music?"

"Right," I said. "A digital synthesizer. All kinds of stuff like that going on at MIT these days."

"Yeah," Amanda replied. "And this fellow ran the hankie code through the synthesizer just to see how it would play—he does that with all the code he gets his hands on, almost a hobby with him. And he said the 'Mitxeleta' code produced the most *beautiful* flute music he had ever heard—"

The call-waiting beeped on my phone. I asked Amanda and Jenna to hold on a second and took the other call.

It was Ruth Delany. "We found a record player here," she said.

"Anything unusual on the record?"

"Well, I'm not sure. . . . There's a very enchanting flute—"

"I'll be right over," I said.

THE MUSIC ON the 78 recording was the strangest concoction of sounds I'd ever heard. Flutes, klezmer, moaning, chanting, pleading in languages I couldn't understand . . . it made Stravinsky and

Cage and rap all seem like the sweetest symphony in comparison
. . . and yet it was captivatingly melodic, too. . . .

"See what I mean? It's like Stefan's record is trying to tell us
something," Ruth said.

"Yeah, but what?" I did have the feeling that if I could just
let myself go, let myself be totally swept up in the music, it would
indeed tell me something, something so crucially, fundamentally
important that it couldn't be expressed in just words. . . .

But I couldn't let myself go like that. I didn't know how.
Maybe with time. . . . I kept listening. . . . I saw images of silk, the
sounds of silk, images of the music of the flute, not the flute . . .
sweet flying synesthesia . . .

I wondered what Stefan had made of this. . . . I wondered
what Amanda might hear . . . Amos—

I heard a sound that was wrong for this . . . that didn't belong
. . . clashing—

"Dr. D'Amato? Phil!" Ruth was talking to me. She'd pulled
the needle off the speedy old record—

"Yeah."

"I think your little phone's ringing again," she said. "You
sure get lots of action on that!"

"Ah, yes, thanks." I took the call.

"Phil? I'm sorry to call on this number—"

"That's OK, Bonnie. Just hold on a minute." I put her on
hold.

"That recording is really something," I said to Ruth. "Had
me practically mesmerized."

"Me, too, the first few times," Ruth agreed. "I think I'm
learning how to deal with it."

"Good," I said. "Look, I've got to take this call now. But that
recording may have something important for us—a message—I
don't know. Is there some way you could make a copy of it? A
digital recording or even a cassette? It's too fragile for me to just
lug around right now—those 78s fall apart if you even look at
them the wrong way."

Ruth nodded. "No problem, Doctor. I'll have one of our computer people take a look at it—we have all kinds of fancy new equipment upstairs."

"Great. Thank you. Did you tell anyone that you had it?"

"No," Ruth said. "I had an inkling where this old record player might be, and I went right to it."

"All right, good; don't tell anyone about this then." I squeezed her shoulder and hustled out into the corridor to talk to Bonnie.

"SORRY TO YOU keep hanging on," I said to Bonnie.

"No problem. I'm sorry I called you on this number, but you weren't in your office, and Jenna said I should call you right away if I couldn't reach her—"

"Where is she? I was just talking to her." Actually, that had been almost an hour ago. The music had been that captivating.

"I don't know—"

"All right—hold on again, just another second."

I dashed up the stairs and out into the street.

I hailed a cab. "Eighty-fifth and York," I told the driver.

I took Bonnie off hold.

"What's going on?" she asked.

"I'm just heading home," I said. "I don't like not knowing where Jenna is."

"She's OK, isn't she?"

"Sure, I'm sure she is—she probably just ran out of milk or something and one of the officers gave her an escort to the grocer. But look—you make sure you stay inside or, if you have to leave for any reason, please call me first."

"OK, I will—"

"Good." I took the phone away from my ear and put my thumb on the End key—

"Phil—"

"Yes?"

"The reason I called—"

"Right, yes," I said. "You've done some work on the translation?"

"Yes, I have. . . ."

And she read to me the latest part she had translated—material beyond what Jenna had read to me. . . .

"You sure of that?"

"Yes—"

"OK. You've done a wonderful job. Just stay in your apartment now. It's the safest place for you." I ended the phone call and went for my ID.

"There's a hundred in it for you if you break every speed limit and get me to 85th Street as fast as fucking possible," I told the driver. "Plus, consider this a police emergency."

JENNA WAS STANDING in front of our brownstone, with two nervous cops—and Amos Stoltzfus.

Worst place she could be.

Amos was arguing with the cops, and it looked like Jenna was trying to mediate. . . .

Kids were playing stickball in the street—no way my cab could get through quickly.

"OK, here is fine," I told the cabbie, and peeled off six new twenties for him. He deserved it.

"Jenna!" I called, and started running toward her. But she was too far away to hear.

"Jenna!" I kept calling and running. . . .

"Please, let's go upstairs!" Amos was shouting at Jenna, too.

"Keep back, son," one of the officers said loudly, pushing Amos back.

"Leave us alone!" Amos shouted. "You don't understand! I have medicine for her—"

"Phil!" Jenna shouted, and waved at me. Thank God!

One of the officers turned and glared at me. The other put an arm on his shoulder. "He's OK. That's Dr. D'Amato."

I reached them, out of breath.

"I was just telling Mr. MD over here," the officer who knew me said, and gestured to Amos, "that there was no way in hell we're going to let him inject Jenna or anyone with his shit and maybe she winds up dropping dead or coming down with AIDS—"

Amos protested, "It's not an injection—"

"He's right," I said to the officer about Amos, "and also, that we shouldn't be down here in the open like this—"

The officer collapsed.

"What—" the second officer began.

I pinned Jenna to the car and covered her body with mine.

The second officer had his gun directed at Amos.

"Look there!" Amos pointed to a man dressed in a mail carrier's uniform across the street. "He killed your partner! He's getting away!"

The officer turned for a second, gun still in hand—

"I'm OK; I'm OK," Jenna said.

"He's not," Amos said, and gestured to the fallen officer.

I felt his neck; he was dead.

"Call for backup," I told the other cop, who was torn between the running man and his brother officer on the ground. "He won't get very far on foot."

"How do you know he doesn't have a car stashed around the corner?" the officer asked.

"Stefan Antonescu doesn't have a license—one of the first things I checked in this goddamned case. My guess is he doesn't drive."

"Stefan?" Jenna asked.

I shook my head yes, as did Amos.

"OK." I made some instant decisions. Jenna was safest with me—whatever the risks, they were preferable to leaving her back here, either alone or with Amos or the officer. "Let's go after him. All of us. But don't fire unless he turns around to face us," I told the officer, "and if you take him down, just make sure you don't kill him. We'll never get to the bottom of this if we kill him."

WE CAUGHT UP with Stefan by the East River. He had climbed up on the railing.

"Just watch for the dart blower," Amos said. "As long as he doesn't have that in his mouth, he can't hurt anyone."

I nodded to the officer—Richard McCall was his name—and he nodded back.

"But drop him if he makes the slightest move to his mouth," I said, and McCall nodded again. His revolver was drawn and pointed.

I walked a few steps toward Stefan.

He just looked at me.

"Just as it ever was," he said. "You hunt the animal to the edge of the cliff and push him over."

"We're not trying to kill you," I told him.

Stefan sneered.

"You run pretty fast for a three-hundred year old," I said.

"That's because, depending on the scale, I'm closer to thirty," he replied.

"What does that mean?" . . . *and the children it has sent to walk among us like men.*

"It means your scientists discover our bones from the past and think the longest we lived was thirty, forty years when in fact, we live ten times that amount of life in that time. . . ."

"All the more reason to come with me now," I said. "No one wants to kill you, believe me. You've got so much to teach us— you have most of your life ahead of you."

He smiled. "You still fail to understand—my kind doesn't live much longer than thirty of your years, maybe thirty-five, forty at most. I'm at the *end* of my life—short and brutish, as some poet once said, by your standards—long and delicate, by mine. . . ."

"And you spent so much of that time reading about silk in the library?" But it made sense, Stefan being thirty years old. We had found no records of him—and none for the corpses in London and Toronto—because we were looking for men we thought were much older.

"Our brain capacity and our capacity to learn quickly far exceed yours," Stefan said. "I learned ten lifetimes of knowledge in that time, and not just about silk. But silk is relevant—we're the caterpillar, the mother of your flimsy, flittering lives."

"So why kill us, Stefan?"

He smiled again, his lips quivering, oddly beautiful in the sun that bounced off the water. "You can ask that?" He lost his smile in the light. "You can ask that when you have been killing us for thirty thousand years? We gave you music; we gave you magic—we gave you your much-vaunted looks and what passes among your kind for cognition. Lum, at least, understood that. Who do you suppose was responsible for the *Bombycidae* in your genome that suppresses Neanderthal characteristics? *We* were. It was there all along in us, like genes from all sorts of insects, and we brought it forth, increased its prevalence so that it made an impact on the phenotype, over millennia of careful breeding. An experiment that went horribly wrong for us—an attempt to increase our longevity, our capacity to communicate—that instead brought into being you, our murderers. Eventually we came upon a cure—*our* cure, a cure for the disease that Cro-Magnons posed to Neanderthals. You might call it a retrovirus today—transmission of genetic material from the environment back into the genome. We found a way to infect you with something that undoes the *Bombycidae*, that brings back the Neanderthal within all of you."

"That infection of yours also kills its recipients," I said.

"Only if they are over thirty five or forty," Stefan said. "Remember, we do not live as long as you in actual years. A reconstituted Neanderthal over fifty dies almost the instant the reconversion is complete."

I thought of Dave Spencer dying, of my surviving, after we had both been exposed to the virus. Dave had been in his early sixties, had had a good twenty-five years on me. And I thought of the additional piece of the Tocharian manuscript that Bonnie had read to me in the taxi. The writer was a singer or thought he had become one. A very old man—Yacob—who had sung with the singers and then joined them. How had he survived? He had managed to join them "without transformation," Bonnie had read from the manuscript—which must have meant that he had remained *Homo sapiens sapiens*, because either he had not been infected or he had been a given a more powerful dose of *Bombyx mori* antidote, or perhaps he had some natural immunity. But Yacob had realized that some of the singers were bent on taking revenge. And he had come to realize the scope of it—"our entire human family is in peril," the manuscript said. Of course we were if the difference between us and Neanderthals was *Bombycidae* in our genes and a virus or whatever was afoot that could block out the *Bombycidae*. . . . How much protection could even all the silk in the world provide from that? How long would the protection last with more and more of the virus at large? It presumably had been a rarity until now. . . . We had the murderer now, but the death he had caused could be a drop in a bottomless bucket. . . .

I looked into Stefan's dark eyes. "Those first three corpses—in New York, Toronto, and London—they were the first round in your plan to infect all of humanity? What made you start that now?"

"My kind didn't start it," Antonescu said. "Just like we didn't start the killing thirty millennia ago. Your kind did—both times! Gerry Moses had been hunting us down for years. He thought he could make a name for himself by exposing us—he thought he could get everyone's attention by presenting newfound Neanderthal mummies to the world. He knew some things about the virus, what it could do. . . . So he took three patients on life support from a Toronto hospital—patients for whom the families had indicated that they wanted cremation, so no one would be the wiser when he talked some doctor into pronouncing them dead, all for the sake of your science. And he gave them the virus and treated them with homeopathic compounds after they died a few months later so they appeared to be naturally mummified, and he had one planted in Toronto, one in London, one in New York. He was a clever man. He timed it to coincide with a meeting we were having in Budapest, while we were away. He figured you and Michael Mallory would get the investigation rolling and then he would come up with the answer, be the hero. But the virus got him, too—he underestimated its power, realized too late how tea enhances the silk, how other stimulants reduce it. He lacked your Amish friends and their understanding, feeble as it was, but accurate, of the silk cure. . . ."

He looked at Amos.

"How come *you* drink tea and stay so close to silk?" I asked.

"The virus hurts us, too," Stefan replied. "It not only turns your kind into us, but it kills our kind as well. My ancestors realized this too late—their secret weapon cut both ways. It nearly completed the job that your kind started thirty thousand years ago. Silk against the skin, amplified by tea in the belly, is our best defense against it. . . ."

I heard police sirens. The backup. . . .

I had to keep Stefan talking about this. "I promise you that—"

"That what? If I come in to your custody I won't be harmed? Just like *Homo sapiens sapiens* has been promising us since they first walked so proud and erect on this Earth? You'd better worry about your own kind—what will happen to all of you if that virus ever makes love to another and jumps from a contact sport to a plague. You'll wish my little darts had felled all of you when that happens—"

"Stefan—"

"—but even if I believed you, that I wouldn't be harmed, you think I want to live in what you would have in store for me? A living fossil, to be examined? You want me to live so much? Tell you what: I'll put this reed to my mouth and blow its poison bee at you, and then I'll surrender. Your life for mine, Dr. Phil

D'Amato. Are you willing to make that trade for your people? Do you care *that* much for my knowledge?''

"Please, don't do that," I said. "Please keep your hands where we can see them. We can talk about this—"

"I didn't think so. I didn't think you really cared that much about your species to make the sacrifice. Good-bye, Dr. D'Amato. I won't say good-bye, my friend. Because you aren't my friend; your kind never can be, never truly—"

And he swiveled around and leaped from the railing.

"Call in the divers!" I shouted to the officers behind me.

I rushed up to the railing, just in time to see Stefan's body swallowed by the blue-black waters below.

"Get the divers!" I shouted again. But I knew that bodies were rarely recovered once those currents got ahold of them and swept them out into the ocean. Give me your tired, your hungry, your dead. . . .

Jenna was at my side, her arm around my waist.

"There are others like him," Amos said. "It's hard to hate them, isn't it, despite all the harm they have done. Now you see what we are up against—my people have been fighting them for years. I didn't think Stefan was one of them—he was so gentle. He fooled me. They hold a grudge against the world itself. . . .''

That made me think of Bonnie—likely there was no one else like Stefan out stalking today, but it still made sense to keep her protected, or as protected as anyone could be from reeds with poison bees that killed you on the spot.

I put my hand in my pocket, reaching for the phone, but I got glass instead—glass crushed into lots of little pieces, mixed with some of my blood now.

I took out my bleeding fingers.

"You OK, honey?" Jenna asked.

"Yeah. I was hoping to recover maybe a fingerprint or some DNA from this glass," I said. "Came from Stefan's apartment. I must have smashed it in the commotion—it's far too contaminated for any decent DNA samples now. . . .''

I took off my jacket and shook the pocket over the East River.

A cloud of glass shards went down slowly, glittering in the sunlight, tinkling in the breeze like a distant flute. . . .

And a rash of russet butterflies rose up to greet us and proceeded to the sky.

CODA

The sun shone on the Serpentine.

"Phil. Good of you to join me." Mallory shook my hand, then gestured to the lake. "She's at her best in September, like England herself, wouldn't you agree? The tourists are back home, all except the true believers. Shall we take advantage and stroll the shore?"

I nodded. "More than one good reason to be out of the office."

Mallory grunted in agreement. "They're yanking me out of the investigation now, just as you predicted. I'm not supposed to be working on this anymore, effective the day before yesterday."

"You outlasted me by at least two months."

"We do things with more deliberation here," Mallory said ruefully. "Precious little to work on, anyway. Dave Spencer's DNA disintegrated into its component compounds—just a broken jumble of molecules now. The rat cells weren't viable in the long run, either. Dead ends, all."

"Same with our samples," I said. "The Antonescu gene hypermutated itself out of existence. Not surprising it had such a short shelf life—it wasn't intended for rodents."

"Barrel of murders gets your name on a nonexistent gene," Mallory said. "I guess there's a logic in that."

I shrugged. "The glory's even more fleeting than the gene. With the gag orders they slapped on us, I doubt that anyone other than a handful of people will even recognize Antonescu's name a year from now. His work was so shadowy, our theories so bizarre, that he never really came across as more than an oddity in the public's awareness."

"He preferred to do most of his dirty work through others."

"Exactly," I said. "Joey Beiler killed Tesa and Debbie. He

apparently wasn't Neanderthal. I don't know what his problem was. But he was a master of accents—he sounded Cockney to me, Brooklyn to Tesa, and he must have been charming when he wanted to. He gained Debbie's confidence and spent lots of time in her apartment. Logging on to someone's computer account is easy in circumstances like that. He used it to send that bogus story to the *New York Times* about my department cracking down on my investigation—except there was enough stupidity in the Department that the story wasn't completely bogus—and then he killed Debbie and Tesa to cover his tracks. And then Antonescu must have had him killed in turn. No loose ends—just like the self-destructing DNA.''

"You said Beiler—if he's the guy your people found in the park—died of some kind of drug overdose. Hard to imagine he would just stand still long enough for someone like Antonescu to creep up and slide a needle into him.''

"No doubt Antonescu had lots of people working for him," I said. "And most, like Joey Beiler, probably didn't look the least bit Neanderthal. . . .''

Mallory's face tightened.

"I wasn't implying that Amanda was working for Antonescu," I began. "Hell, he was the one who likely tried to kill her—his forte was darts—''

"I know," Mallory said. "I mean, I know you weren't suggesting that Amanda was one of them—one of the demented Neanderthals. It's clear from poor Pedro's Tocharian translations that Neanderthals came—come—in many moral dimensions, just as we do. Many physical dimensions, too.''

I thought about Pedro. "Lum and Pedro were also Antonescu casualties, either direct hits or otherwise.''

Mallory nodded, absently. He was still thinking of Amanda. "She can be of help to us," he said.

"I know," I said.

"How are we going to fight this, Phil?'' he asked. "The virus in the labs is dead, but it's still out here in the world. We can't rely on our superiors, or the super-agencies. They'll bungle it, like they do most everything else."

"Ever been to Lancaster in the Fall? Amos tells me the caffeinated apples are delicious—a special hybrid that goes back millennia . . ."